D1520747

What Lies in the Sea

A JOSH BAKER AND EDDIE DEBORD ROAD TRIP
ADVENTURE

1st Edition, May 2017

**Book Cover Design by J. Caroline Ro—Graphic Design
and Illustration**

**Book Cover Copyright 2017 Graphic Design and
Illustration**

Cover photo development by Gilberto Salazar

Fotoxpose

Content Edited by Kathy Russ

For Debbie and Dan — high school sweethearts…

ACKNOWLEDGMENTS

Who doesn't love a trip to the beach? Those family road adventures we used to take as kids, crammed in the car with pillows, books and Dramamine—many of us winding our way south and east to our favorite spots along the coast. That first time jumping into the ocean, that first vacation dinner at "Captain *something or others*", and sleeping in hotel beds—for better or for worse. By the time the vacation was over, our exhausted parents swore they would never do it again but after about a week back home, we all were thinking about the next one, including our parents! Dad couldn't find it in himself to vacuum that white sand out of the car.

The months rolled by and occasionally we would play with those seashells from the last trip or chase our little sister with the alligator head we purchased at the state line souvenir stand. Before we knew it we were back on the road, heading south and east again. Those trips become precious memories that we grow up and share with our children and then try to relive as we, too, pack our vehicles and head south and east—on a Road Trip!

So here's to the beach! That soothing, relaxing, rejuvenating, restoring, reenergizing, peaceful place where we go to chill-out, dig our toes into the sand and reset our life's goals—and here's to a little adventure, to go along with it!

I hope you enjoy…*What Lies in the Sea.*

Follow Steve on Facebook at : Steve Kittner Books

Twitter: @SteveKittner

Instagram: Steve Kittner

What LIES in the SEA

STEVE KITTNER

PROLOGUE

On the morning of July 24th 1715, two Spanish treasure fleets joined together as one and departed with the tide from Havana Harbor en route to Spain. These two fleets were comprised of eleven Spanish ships and one French vessel. General Juan Esteban de Ubilla commanded five ships of the armada, and General Don Antonio Echeverz commanded six. The French vessel commanded themselves and was what they called a tag-a-long tobacco ship. The armada was to deliver the wealth of kings to a war-poor Spain under the rule of King Phillip V. They also had onboard an elaborate queen's dowry for the king's new wife-to-be, said to be sixty-two chests in all.

As the ships passed through the Florida Straits and then made their turn northward up the coast of a sparsely populated Florida peninsula, veteran sailors began to notice the waves were running long as the winds began to build on a clear horizon. Behind the azure skies and fresh breezes a massive hurricane spun slowly across the Atlantic and grew stronger with every hour. The treasure fleet was directly in its path.

On July 30th, as day turned into night, the storm drew upon them with all its fury. Ships were tossed and dismasted—blown directly west onto the reefs along the coastline, sending man, woman and child into the thrashing jowls of an unforgiving storm.

Along with the tremendous loss of life was the tremendous loss of treasure. On board these ships was a combined cargo worth 14,000,000 pesos in Peruvian gold, silver and emeralds. The armada also carried Chinese porcelain, tanned hides, tobacco, jewelry and Brazilian wood—all lost to the bottom of the shallow waters off what is now called Florida's Treasure Coast.

Both commanders perished, along with half of their passengers and crew, over a thousand in all, after having their vessels thrown to the reefs by the massive storm. Only the French vessel survived, having made its way across the Atlantic on a different course in much deeper waters further east. The Spanish ships had no chance to tack into deeper waters given the course they had chosen.

Once word got back to King Phillip V, a salvage effort was immediately ordered and, by the completion of it, it was said that every peso of manifested gold and silver was recovered. Keeping in mind that there was twice as much actual cargo onboard than was manifested, this still left a lot of gold, silver, emeralds, rubies and finished jewelry lying on the bottom of the ocean. Soon after, as the tides ran in and out, sand began to cover what was left of the decks and holds of the ships, privateers would swoop in and recover a few stacks of coins here and there, but without modern diving equipment, their efforts were also limited to how long they could hold their breath. Treasure trapped within the deep holds of the ships was simply inaccessible.

With the exception of the occasional coin finding its way to the shoreline and into the hand of a lucky beachcomber, the ocean claimed the balance of the cargo and kept it for herself…for three hundred years.

"…and though we may put in to port, the sea is always home…"

Long John Silver

CHAPTER ONE

December 3rd, 1973

Vero Beach, Florida, 6:55 p.m.

The captain tried to conceal his nervousness as he stood alongside his 1956 Cherokee trawler. The evening breeze was cool and steady—directly from the north and a little early for the season. He checked his watch and then glanced down the wooden walkway of the working marina. The graying lumber of the old docks creaked and groaned as the tide washed in and out on that cool evening. Twilight was upon him, and his freight delivery was due any minute. The deck hand was busy coiling lines and preparing for the planned cargo. The captain had given him instructions to expect a large box of seafood.

Headlights from a van swept across the adjacent parking lot just as the pay phone rang on the pole by the gate. The docks were nearly empty, as the fishermen had all returned from the sea and gone home for the day. It rang three times before he decided to answer. He lifted the receiver.

"Hel...hello?"

"Did they drop my cargo yet?" the voice asked calmly.

Captain Chuck Henderson nervously wet his lips and looked toward the near-empty parking lot. "There's a van. It...it looks like they just arrived."

"What does the van look like?"

"Umm...white van, *Fresh Seafood* sign."

"OK. That's my guys." The man paused for a moment. "Don't be nervous Chuck. It's an easy job. You'll never make better money."

Captain Henderson nodded— still holding the receiver as he watched the white van back into position.

"Yeah...I know."

"Now my guys will give you the final instructions and money up front as agreed. OK Chuck?"

Henderson took a deep breath and quickly exhaled. He needed the money and was ready to get *this* job over with. "Yep...that sounds good. I'll get it done for you."

After hanging up the receiver, Chuck felt only a little better. The man had reminded him of the money that was involved. Ten thousand dollars for a little milk run up the coast.

The men parked the white van in the freight loading area of the docks and exited the vehicle. Two hours ago, the place was buzzing with fishermen processing and boxing their catch. Trucks had been there waiting and all of that delicious, fresh seafood was now on the way to local restaurants, seaside and inland.

The driver was a tall, stout-looking man and his partner was not much smaller. Both men were Italian. The larger man had a very distinctive lazy right eye. It was the smaller of the two who approached Chuck.

"Our man call you?"

Chuck looked at him and then to the other man. "He did. He said you would have the money."

The deckhand looked up from his duties at the two deliverymen who drove the van. He knew something wasn't normal. These men who drove the van were no more seafood vendors than he was *Gilligan!*

The man grinned and reached inside his jacket. "Of course we have the money, Chuck. Here you go."

The man handed him a plain white envelope. Chuck Henderson opened it and fanned the bills. Without pulling the money out he could see it was short. His eyes drifted downward and then lifted to the two men.

"The deal was ten thousand up front," Chuck said, shaking his head. He could feel the agreement falling apart.

The driver grinned. "And you know our man is good for it. You get half now and half when you return—when the job is complete. It's very standard in this business."

Chuck swallowed hard. "That wasn't the deal."

The driver walked towards him with his palms wide. "He said he would give you money up front...he didn't say he would give you *all* the money up front. It's the way the big guy does business, ya know? Hey…I'm putting five grand in your hands right now. What are ya gonna do? Are you going to walk away from that? And listen, you do this job right for the man—you are in like Flynn. You'll pull in a lot of cash if you are good with the big guy, you know what I'm sayin'?"

"I know what you're sayin."

"Listen, Chuck—ten grand is nothing to our boss. He ain't gonna stiff you on that. Believe me… this is well worth the money! Truth is, you should have negotiated for more but, hey, it's your boat. It's your deal."

Chuck Henderson looked at the man and then back to the envelope.

"OK. OK, let's get loaded and get outta here!"

The man moved in closer to the captain. His demeanor became a little more serious and his lazy eye drooped even more.

"Chuck… you know what to do, right? This one can never be found. We just want it to disappear. Drop it on the other side of the reef; up the coast somewhere the sharks can have it. Somewhere quiet. We don't even *want* to know where!"

Henderson looked at the man curiously. "Why me?" Chuck asked. "Why did your man come to me?"

Lazy Eye grinned at him, "Because you are the most desperate. You need the money. And because *they* know our boats. FDLE will not be looking for an old bucket of bolts like this."

The Cherokee was a 46-footer that he had purchased two years ago. It had been a shrimp boat for most of its life but Captain Chuck had stripped all the outriggers and all but one winch off its decks and made it into an uncluttered live-aboard work boat. He had plenty of space to customize it for his needs. The pilothouse and the below-decks were comfortable and functional. Fresh paint coated the entire vessel and he had done many, many repairs himself. It was hardly a bucket of bolts, but it was far from new.

Aboard *Maria*, Captain Henderson had accommodated everything from dive parties to birthday parties. From boxes of fresh seafood to weddings on the aft deck. His idea when he purchased the trawler was to live off of the tourists. They came south with money and an eagerness to spend it. It had worked out well for a while but as the oil embargo hit in October of that year, gas prices instantly went up, tourism dropped, and so did his business. People were in shock and simply afraid to travel. Burdened with expensive slip fees, business taxes, fuel prices and insurance costs, Chuck also had a boat to pay for. Immediately, he had to do whatever he could to make his payments. With all his costs, it was all he could do to break even—even on a good month. It was true, he was desperate and with any luck, the Florida Department of Law Enforcement would *not* be looking for his boat.

"I need to go," Chuck said, nervously looking towards the parking lot.

The "deliverymen" nodded in agreement and walked back over to the rear of the van. They opened the rear doors and slid the bottom-reinforced cardboard box out to get a good hold of it from either side. It wasn't the dimensions that Chuck had expected. He had expected a box long and thin and this container was only about three feet long and two feet high. They had packed the "shipment" to look like a seafood container. On its exterior, it was labeled *Fresh Fish*.

The men sat the box down on a flat furniture mover and rolled it along the dock to the *Maria*.

The deck hand's name was Butch Dawson. Butch did not leave the boat, but when the two men positioned the box on the edge of the walkway, he looked at Henderson. Having not been told exactly what the cargo was, he reluctantly assisted the two men in sliding the box to the aft deck area. Dawson was not stupid. He knew what this run to the reef was all about. For his own safety, it was best that he didn't know more and, most likely Henderson didn't tell him, for that reason.

The "fresh fish" was ready for delivery.

Henderson and Dawson stood on the boat. The "deliverymen" paused on the walkway—their job being done for the moment.

"Straight out and straight back. We'll be here when you return with the balance of the money," the smaller man said.

Chuck Henderson gave him a casual salute—more of a good riddance than a goodbye. None of them were there to make friends. He then proceeded to his pilothouse, turned the battery switch on and pushed the start button. The old diesel rumbled to life as black smoke momentarily rolled from the exhaust behind the boat. He let her warm up for about two minutes before checking the gauges and giving the command to Dawson to let go of the fore and aft lines. Dawson did so and the captain engaged the transmission and idled *Maria* out of her slip. Dawson coiled the lines neatly on the deck as they chugged north, up the Intracoastal Waterway.

After they cleared the last buoy leaving the channel at Sebastian Inlet, Captain Henderson gave her a little more throttle. *Maria's* design was classic. The bow rose high and then her lines swept low past the pilothouse towards the aft deck, rising slightly once again at the transom. She looked like a working-man's boat. Rugged and strong, yet sleek and beautiful. *Maria* could do any job her captain asked of her.

About a quarter of a mile beyond the outer buoy, Henderson buried the throttles to the bulkhead and, just like a diesel, the power came gradually but with tons of torque. In just a few seconds, *Maria* was up on plane and heading north.

CHAPTER TWO

Darkness was now upon them. Dawson had moved to the foredeck and was looking ahead, not knowing exactly where they were going. He had worked for Henderson for about five months and they had a good working relationship. They had also grown to be good friends. They would laugh and cut-up while working, and sometimes have a good dinner afterward. Chuck liked Butch Dawson and could not find a better worker anywhere. Butch did everything that was asked of him and showed great initiative.

He watched Butch from the pilothouse as he stood there at the bow with both hands on the rails looking forward into the night. The last thing Henderson wanted to do was to get Dawson in trouble. He didn't deserve it.

As he pulled a cigarette from the package in his shirt pocket, Dawson glanced back at the shoreline and then up to the pilothouse. Henderson gave him thumbs up and Dawson nodded gently. Dawson pulled a Zippo from his pants pocket and fired up his smoke. One long hard draw and he leaned forward on the rails once more, exhaling into the breeze. This was not what he wanted to be doing. This job had just crossed the proverbial line of ethics and morals within him. Even though Henderson had not yet explained what they were doing, Dawson knew. This had to be a drug hit, maybe even a major player in the south Florida drug market. Possibly a turf war infringement. It could also have been a major debt that had gone unpaid. It was dirty, that was certain. Most mob hits would just be left lying on the street but this one was different—it was bigger. Possibly a high profile individual who needed to disappear without a trace. Whatever this was, Dawson wanted it to be the last one that he was involved with. He needed something else.

Butch Dawson had moved south a few months earlier after a run of bad luck. He had lost his job in the steel mills of Indiana and it didn't take long for the stress level of unemployment to divide his marriage. Not wanting to shovel snow another day in his life, he elected for the warm climate and the white sand beaches of Florida. He didn't care what he had to do down there to make a living as long as he wasn't shoveling snow and sucking up the dust and smoke of a steel mill. He had worked long enough to be vested in a small retirement but at thirty-three years old, had quite a few more years to go before he could draw on it. Chuck had said he would be happy selling hotdogs on the beach for a few years. He sold his house, divided the money with his ex and hit the road.

Upon arriving in Florida in the spring of 1973, he observed spring break and wished the he was 15 years younger. He did just what he had thought of doing. Every day he took a cooler full of hot dogs to the beach, stuck a small sign in the ground and sold them to the college kids. This was fun and lucrative for a while but when the frenzy of spring break was over, business slowed to a crawl. Summer vacationers were next and that was the family crowd. Mom and dad were not as excited to buy hotdogs from a cooler on the beach. Butch needed to find something different so he did. He hung out on the docks watching the fishing crews go in and out daily and soon met up with Captain Chuck Henderson. He watched Henderson work his boat singlehanded like a pro but soon got up his nerve to approach him and ask if he needed a helper—a mate. He had caught Chuck at a vulnerable time as he was manhandling six "E-containers" of seafood onto his aft deck to be delivered across the Gulfstream to Freeport, Bahamas.

They talked for a while and soon worked out a deal for employment. Dawson had never worked on a boat before but he was an eager learner and had a strong work ethic born in the mills of the north.

A few months had passed and here he was—making a run to the reef to dump a body. No—he wanted something different and maybe even Henderson did too.

In the pilothouse, the captain made a course change to point them north. He tied off his wheel with a crude autopilot and walked down to the bow where Dawson stood. Butch flicked his cigarette butt into the ocean and exhaled, letting the wind carry his smoke over his shoulder and back towards the shore.

"This time of year, the night sky starts getting real clear down here," Henderson said, looking upward.

"It's a fresh night," Dawson said, and then he smirked. "Friends up north are in snow already."

Henderson grinned and nodded, still looking towards the sky. He listened for a moment to the soothing, rhythmic waves coming off of the bow and then he said, "Ya know—this run is something that I wouldn't normally accept, but…I'm between a rock and a hard place, Butch."

Dawson stood with two elbows on the rail and nodded.

"I mean, I can't go one month late on my bills or I am

sunk…so to speak. I never make enough in one month to make two months' worth of payments. Never! Do you understand what I'm saying?" he pleaded.

Dawson nodded. "I get it."

Henderson now looked out to sea.

Dawson offered, "Chuck, I got to be honest with you—I got a little money from selling my house. I would almost rather loan you some than to get into this type of work. I'm…I'm not cut out for it. I'm incredibly paranoid and this scares me to death.

Henderson shook his head, "I would be too afraid of not being able to repay you."

"It could be like an investment for me. You could pay a little at a time with some interest, if it makes you feel better."

"But what if I couldn't? What if this oil embargo takes me right out of business? Gas price will be double. Tourism will be cut in half and I am done! Out of business!"

Dawson turned back towards the sea. Henderson was right. It was risky and Dawson couldn't afford to lose that much money either.

A north wind made the seas choppy and the bow floated up and down as they worked their way north to an area where the coastline was darker and less inhabited. Captain Henderson didn't even have a destination in mind yet. Just whenever it looked and felt right. One thing was for sure—it would be far north of the fishing grounds of his buddies at the dock at Vero Beach.

After a moment, Henderson said, "One time…one time Butch, and that's all. This will give me four months' salary in one night. A little cushion and time to think and plan." He looked at Dawson.

"And then, you hang with me and we will work out a plan to be successful at this—and get you to retirement."

Still looking forward, Butch Dawson grinned and nodded. "OK…one time is good." He jerked his thumb towards the aft deck, "What happened to that guy is done. That wasn't our fault and we didn't do it. The way I look at it we are just giving him a burial at sea."

"We're just funeral directors tonight, Butch!" Henderson laughed and slapped him on the back of his shoulder, happy to lighten the mood.

Both men enjoyed a laugh and then put their minds to the job at hand. They had to dim the already sparse lights and site around them 360 degrees to make sure they were not being followed or monitored. The trawler chugged on.

Chuck Henderson had run the boat up the coastline for about two and a half hours and Cape Canaveral was now barely visible to their immediate north. He sighed and figured this was far enough away from Vero and was as good of a spot as any. Just a month earlier, this area had been quite active with security as NASA had launched *Skylab 4*, the last of the workshop missions. Now all was quiet and, the best that they could tell, no one was around them for miles. Henderson now steered his vessel toward the shore as he watched his depth sounder. He was looking for the area just before the reef. Butch Dawson now stood on the aft deck near the "shipment" with his hands on his hips looking out at the water and waiting.

Captain Henderson slowed more and was now only about two thousand feet off shore. The gruesome truth was: he needed the box to drop right by the reef among the nighttime feeding activity of the blacktips, hammerheads and bull sharks. He did not want this box to be rolling around out to sea and get snagged by the trawling net of a fisherman. Even the depth of the Gulfstream wasn't good. The body could end up on the shores of Ireland and "the man" had said he didn't want it washing up *anywhere*. Immediate consumption was the goal so the closer to the reef, the better.

He continued to crawl along into shallower water as he made his way towards the shore…and then there it was! The reef. Eighteen hundred feet offshore. He immediately took the boat out of gear and Butch Dawson felt it slow as the engine went to idle. He looked over at the pilothouse just as Henderson stepped from it.

"This is it," Henderson said. "It's just after nine o'clock, shore lights are minimal, no boats around us and all we have to do is dump it and go."

"Let's get it done," Dawson said, walking over to the side to unlock a section of safety-rail to push the box overboard.

As he did so, Henderson plugged in a Q-beam light to an extension cord. "I want to see it hit bottom."

Butch nodded.

With the side rail now open, the two men squatted behind the box and used their legs to push it towards the opening in the rail.

Taking one more look all around them, Henderson said, "OK, let's go—push!"

And with that, the container of "fresh fish" slid off the deck and splashed into the waters off of what would one day be called Florida's Space Coast.

The drop was a bull's-eye, landing right by the reef where the water depth jumped up to about eight feet.

"Grab the Q-beam," Henderson said, as he watched the turbulence of the splash subside.

Butch Dawson retrieved the spotlight, turned it on and shined it into the water. Bubbles were coming from the box and, as it hit bottom, it stirred up the sand somewhat. After about a minute, they could see the box resting on the sea floor. Small fish had come back to investigate what had dropped into their habitat and soon after, the reef sharks came too! It seems that sharks really *can* smell the blood because within minutes, there were more and more of them. They were very interested in what was inside the E container and soon began ripping it apart. Both Henderson and Dawson grimaced at what they witnessed.

After tearing through the cardboard, the sharks, which then numbered around twelve, pulled the unmistakable shape of a human body from it and in a flash were gone!

Henderson and Dawson stood horrified. Neither had ever seen anything like it in their lives. The good news was, the sharks took the body further out to sea and not towards the shoreline. It would most definitely be a total consumption, with nothing left to wash up on shore. That was Henderson's biggest concern with this assignment.

The two men continued to look downward as the sand settled from all of the commotion of the buffet and then looked at each other, both happy it was over.

"Well…let's go home and get paid!" Henderson said.

Butch Dawson was still holding the spotlight and as he started to get up, the beam flashed across the reef. Something caught his eye as he stood. Pieces of the cardboard box were floating around in the water and the sand was still settling but something didn't look right. Something was out of place and didn't belong on the reef. He held the light on one spot and Henderson saw him starring into the water.

"You waiting for more sharks?" Henderson asked, as he repositioned the safety rail.

Dawson didn't respond for a moment—still waiting for the sand to settle.

"No—what is that?"

Henderson positioned himself on the other side of Dawson to better see what he was looking at.

"Where?"

"Right there. That dark… thing. And then look, about four feet there is another one. Same shape.

As the sand settled, the two men could see there was even a third.

"What the…?" Henderson asked, as he looked closer.

Even to Dawson's untrained sea eyes, he could tell it was unusual. But for the knowledgeable Captain Chuck Henderson, he knew that it was out of the ordinary and possibly even extraordinary.

"Let me see that light," Henderson said, taking it from Dawson.

The sand had now settled and the debris from the cardboard box had, too. Henderson focused the light to a tight pattern and aimed it at the closest dark object and then the next and the next.

"Butch…do you know what that is?" he asked.

Dawson repositioned himself to get an even better look. "Am I seeing what I think I'm seeing?"

"The ribs of a ship! Very heavy wooden ribs like they don't build anymore." Chuck said, still looking down into the water.

"You think they're old?"

Chuck's mind danced through his knowledge of the coast and its shipwrecks—searching for an answer. "Could be," he replied.

A couple of sharks darted back into the area to see if there was anything left to scavenge. Apparently they were not invited to the main party. Henderson shined the light from one rib to the other, shaking his head in disbelief. Before them were what was left of three ribs lying flat on the bottom. Each rib was symmetrical to the others in shape and distance from one another. As he studied them it became more obvious that these were very old. They were too heavy to be from a modern ship—even from the past century. The captain had been around the coast and boats all his life and had a pretty good knowledge of the eras of ship architecture. He was not an expert, but he did know the basics. This ship was from a time long past.

The two men continued to examine the ribs, both in disbelief. Henderson looked over his shoulder at the coast to make sure there was no new activity. They had been there now for about three minutes and he didn't want to be there much longer, but he had an idea.

"Turn the light off for a minute," he told Dawson.

The captain walked to his pilothouse and, after a brief moment, selected a nautical chart from his rack. He unrolled it as Dawson stepped in, curious as to what Henderson was doing. Henderson reached up and pulled the chain on the light to turn it on. As he made a note of their position he searched the chart with his finger until he found their general location.

"Here. Right about here is where we are." He looked up and down the reef on the chart. "Look…down here about a mile it shows a wreck. That's the closest one." He shook his head in excited disbelief. "Butch, this wreck may be undiscovered!"

Dawson didn't know much about nautical charts but he had confidence that his captain did. He looked at Henderson and then back to the chart. "So…what would that mean?"

Henderson leaned on one elbow at the high console of his old trawler. He put his chin in his hand and looked off in thought as he grinned.

"Tropical Storm Chris," Henderson said.

Dawson didn't respond but waited for Henderson to elaborate.

"Tropical Storm Chris ripped straight up the coastline last year. That's why it has not yet been discovered. Chris churned up the sand something terrible. The fishermen at the dock had a hard time adjusting after that. I remember."

Dawson nodded. "And you think that storm uncovered this?"

"Yes, it's possible!" Chuck shook his head slowly once again. "It has to be a very old boat hull, or what is left of one."

Dawson starred at Henderson as the captain looked back to the chart. The boat rocked gently in the swells.

Captain Henderson then tapped the wooden console with his index finger. He wanted to see something before they had to go. "Butch, grab the gaff hook off the bow and bring it astern."

Butch Dawson did as told and met Henderson at the back of the boat. Henderson scanned the coastline once more. He noticed a small boat between the reef and the shore. This made him a little uncomfortable but he needed one more minute. He took the long pole with the hook on the end from Dawson.

"Hold the light on the ribs."

Butch Dawson did as told once again, locating the old, heavily built wooden ribs lying just off of the reef. Chuck Henderson put the hook in the water and positioned it between two of the ribs. He then began to rake the sand around, pulling as much of it away to make a hole between the two sturdy beams. In doing so he stirred the sand and had to wait a moment to be able to see. As the sand settled he saw nothing. Moving to the next section of ribs, he did the same thing, stirring the sand even more as he intensified his search. As the sand was settling, he looked towards the shore once more. Nothing had changed and the small boat looked like local partiers as he heard some whoops and hollers.

Both men stared at the area where the light beam was focused and as the sand settled to where they could see, both men's eyes widened. Something glimmered below them. It was the right color and the right size. Simultaneously, Henderson and Dawson's eyes came up to meet each other. Their hearts raced at the possibility. Henderson started ripping at the buttons on his shirt. He then kicked off his shoes, tore off his watch and dropped his wallet on the deck.

"Hold the light right on it!" Henderson said, as Dawson watched his captain slip off the deck and into the water.

Dawson was still in disbelief as he observed Henderson descend to the reef—forgetting all about the shark activity just minutes before. *Was he crazy!* Dawson watched as Henderson fanned his hand across the bottom, again stirring it up and making the bottom a fuzzy cloud of sand. Henderson was down for about a minute and then, only after running out of air, returned to the top. When his face broke the surface, he was already smiling. He climbed aboard and rested while kneeling on the deck. Dawson waited as Henderson caught his breath. Henderson looked up at Dawson, smiling even bigger now. He opened his hand and dropped its contents on the deck. Three Spanish Escudos and an eighteen-inch length of gold chain!

"My goodness!" Dawson exclaimed as he picked one up to examine. "You've got to be kidding! And there's more?" He asked, looking at the captain.

Henderson nodded, smiling. "There *has* to be more. There has to be *a lot* more!"

Butch Dawson shook his head in disbelief as many thoughts raced through his mind. "Well," he paused, "I guess you may not need my loan!" He laughed.

Henderson shook his head quickly and laughed, "Maybe not!"

Both men were ecstatic—giddy! Luck had come their way and in the strangest of fashion. Through an absolute stroke of lottery-style odds, they had just bulls-eyed a possible centuries-old shipwreck. This stretch of Florida coastline was called the Treasure Coast, and for good reason. It was littered with the remains of discovered and undiscovered treasure fleets from the past. Ships that had found themselves caught in Atlantic hurricanes, and were blown straight west into the reefs.

At this point, Henderson had no idea what ship this could have been. That would take research. But for now, it was decided they had to mark their position and get out of there. The last thing that they wanted was to be observed at that location, for a couple of reasons!

Dawson repositioned the section of rail on the side of the trawler. Henderson collected the gold, put it into his pocket and went back to the pilothouse. He then noted their position, not in his logbook, but on a piece of paper and then put that in his pocket with the gold. He gave Dawson a copy of the coordinates, and then flipped him one of the gold coins. Dawson smiled and put it in his pants pocket.

"Just in case…we *both* need a copy, and that's your tip for tonight."

"Gotcha," Butch nodded, still smiling.

Henderson re-fired *Maria's* diesel engine and then throttled her up to move away from the reef slowly and without causing any interest to anyone on shore. On the trip back to Vero Beach, the two men talked excitedly about the possibilities. It was decided that they would need to return in about a week. They didn't want to be seen with the same boat in the same position, two nights in a row. That would be an easy red-flag to an observer—and they did *not* want curious observers.

After a while, Butch Dawson went below to a small cabin that was set up just for him. It had a cot, a locker for his jackets, foul-weather gear, or other clothing, and a small two-drawer dresser. Nicely paneled walls helped to make it comfortable and he even had a narrow window for light. He pulled his green sea-bag from his locker and removed a leather-bound diary from inside it. Butch had bought this simply to keep notes or to journal things he wanted to remember—like personal information or the coordinates to a shipwreck with gold! Taking a pen from the top of the small dresser, he wrote a few lines in his book and then returned it to his sea bag. He also put the coin safely away inside the duffle. Feeling good now about his future and good fortune, he returned to the deck of *Maria*.

Now past midnight, the two lucky men saw the lights of Sebastian Inlet off of the starboard bow. Chuck Henderson made a course change to angle towards the channel. He reduced his speed and soon passed the outer buoy as he made his way towards the Intracoastal Waterway and then south to the docks. They had one more thing to do tonight. That was to collect five thousand dollars from the two "deliverymen" who had promised to be there upon their arrival back at Vero.

As they approached the docks, Henderson could see the white van in the parking lot. It seems they had kept their word and in just a few minutes, Chuck would be a few thousand dollars richer. He would generously share his payment with Butch Dawson and, by golly, things were looking up!

Henderson swung his boat around and expertly backed into his assigned slip. Dawson was ready with the lines and had *Maria* tied off quickly. From the pilothouse, Chuck saw the interior light of the van come on as the two men opened their doors. He felt a sudden nervous flutter in his stomach and couldn't wait for this to be over.

The two "deliverymen" looked around the area and began walking towards the slip. Chuck inhaled deeply through his nostrils and then exhaled. Shutting down the engine, he then stepped from the pilothouse and towards the dock. The two men met him there.

"How did it go, Chuck?" the smaller man asked, somewhat sarcastically.

Chuck, feeling somewhat confident replied, "It went very well. We did our job. Do you have something for me?"

The man looked at his partner and grinned, "I sure do." He nodded once.

Without hesitation, the larger man with the lazy eye pulled a silenced 9mm from his jacket and shot Chuck Henderson three times in the chest at point-blank range. Chuck's eyes widened in disbelief as he flew backwards onto the gray, wooden dock. Two casings dropped into the water and one onto the dock. The smaller man picked it up and placed it in his pocket.

Butch Dawson was coiling the loose ends of the dock-lines and looked up—terrorized by what he witnessed. For a moment, he froze as the two men looked at him and began moving towards the boat. He was next and he knew it! It appeared that this delivery to the reef could have no witnesses. *How could this have gone so bad, so fast?* Dawson thought.

Lazy-eye raised his gun and fired as Butch ran across the deck. He had nowhere to hide and couldn't make the jump from the opposite side of the boat to the next walkway. It was too far. The bullet missed Dawson and buried itself into the hull of another working trawler close by. Dawson had no choice now but to jump into the water and try to hide among the pilings. The two men anticipated his maneuver and repositioned on the other side of the boat towards the next slip. Dawson hit the water and within seconds, bullets were zinging past him. He held his breath as long as he could and then had to surface by one of the larger cement pilings. The men spotted him right away and recommenced firing. He had nowhere to go. There was no good way out of the water and it was just a matter of time until they had the angle on him. He had one trick that he had read in a book and he would try it now.

"Don't shoot! Hold your fire!" he yelled.

The two men *did* stop firing and looked at Butch, somewhat

curious. They lowered their guns. He swam out from behind a piling, treading water and holding one hand up in the air while trying to catch his breath. Waves lapped around him and then feeling a tinge of confidence he said, "There's a treasure! I know where it is!"

They looked at Dawson then the larger one with the lazy-eye shook his head in disgust. "Oldest trick in the book… and you think we haven't heard of it?" He then smiled with malevolence, raised his gun and put two bullets in the chest of the man bobbing in the water. Butch Dawson jerked backwards quickly and then rolled over, face down in the briny waters under the dock.

A few feet away, a fatally bleeding Chuck Henderson had just enough life left to remove a small piece of paper from his pocket and drop it between the boards and into the salty sea. His eyes then closed as the life left his body.

The two men walked back over to where Henderson lay and the larger man kicked him one time, checking for life. When he did, something shiny fell from the dead man's pocket and onto the dock. The smaller of the two men knelt and picked up a sixteenth century Spanish Escudo. He then checked Henderson's pockets and found the other coin and the chain.

Furious with himself, he looked at his partner and shook his head. "Well, well, Frankie… maybe there was a treasure!"

The two goons would keep the gold and the secret of a treasure to themselves.

A small piece of note paper with coordinates written upon it bobbed on the swells, as it floated across the Intracoastal.

CHAPTER THREE

Present Day

Ryder's Restaurant

"All I'm saying is, I'm going too!" Giselle told them. "I need a vacation, you have plenty of room, and I'm going!" she said, shrugging one shoulder, and looking at them as if they had no choice.

Josh and Eddie looked at each other in bewilderment. Sure, she was their good friend—but that was a little pushy! The boys hadn't even considered a third party going along, and the complications— she was a girl! The bathroom issue alone was problematical! But it *did* seem like they had just been leveraged.

Josh Baker, Eddie Debord and Giselle O'Conner sat at a booth at their favorite little diner in the world, discussing a post graduation road trip. For over a year, Josh and Eddie had been planning this trip down to the smallest detail. The boys had a notebook they had used to make their notes and schedules and it was almost time to leave. Their hotel reservations were made, some fun events were pre-planned, and the sunscreen was purchased. They were finally high school graduates. Daytona Beach was their destination and in about twelve hours, they would be on the road!

The means of transportation was Eddies' fully restored and customized Volkswagen Bus. He and his dad had spent the last three years tearing it apart and putting it all back together and they had done an incredible job. The bus was lowered two inches with drop-spindles, stripped of all the original molding, and painted a beautiful two-tone cranberry red and pearl white separated with a hand-painted, gold pinstripe. For the interior, they opted for white vinyl seats piped with a custom red to match the exterior. The steering wheel was a beautiful white leather with three chrome spokes. The stereo was a Pioneer system with old-school Jensen Tri-Axial speakers pushed by a 100-watt stereo amp. Eddie and his father had put a little extra time and money into the engine, providing additional horsepower for pulling the hills of West Virginia. The bus was responsive, restored, and ready to roll!

"Giselle, we only have two beds," Eddie pleaded his case. "You'd have to bring an air mattress or something."

She looked at him as if he were crazy, "I'm not staying with *you* guys! I'm getting my own room. Believe me, I won't be in your way. I just want to lie on the beach and soak up some vitamin D!"

Josh cracked that little sideways grin of his—sort of an ornery smirk. He looked at Eddie and shrugged his shoulders. "Split the gas three ways. It's fine with me," he said.

Eddie nodded, conceding. He thought for a moment and then

looked at Giselle. "We're leaving at 6:00 A.M. Can you be ready?" he asked.

Giselle nodded. "I'll be up and ready before you guys. Can you pick me up? It's on your way—sort of."

Eddie nodded while taking a big bite of his roast beef and Swiss cheese sandwich. "We'll be there at 6:15 then," he said from one side of his mouth.

"Great! Oh, send me your hotel information and I will see what I can book," she said, looking at Josh.

Josh unlocked his phone and in seconds had sent Giselle the needed information for her to make her own reservation. He then told her, "Hopefully, you can get something close to us."

Eddie smirked at Josh as Giselle received her message and began the reservation process. Eddie knew that Josh had always had a thing for Giselle. She was quite pretty, after all. The two had known each other, somewhat, as kids. Their fathers had taken a couple fishing trips together in the past. They were both grown up now and Giselle had flowered into just the type of girl that lit Josh's fire. Auburn hair, green eyes, light-olive skin and a sweet, sweet personality. On top of that she was fun to be around. Adventurous, not as much as the boys but she would take off her shoes and wade through the creek with the best of them! Josh never could tell if any of the adoration was reciprocated. Essential point was, they were friends and he wouldn't mess it up trying to find out. There was also the age difference. Giselle was three years older than Josh. So, her friendship was good enough for him and tomorrow, the trio would head down the road to Daytona Beach, Florida!

"It's going to be so much fun!" Giselle said, dancing in her seat and clapping her hands three times very quickly.

The three friends finished their meals and left Ryders to go home and make final preparations for their trip. Josh and Eddie lived close, so they biked, while Giselle pulled away in her "Silver Bullet"—a well taken care of 2007 Pontiac Grand Prix.

Eddie Debord was about two inches taller than his good buddy Josh Baker. Eddie wore his dark brown hair short all around. He figured low-maintenance was best when it came to hair care and put the extra time into keeping lean and fit. Eddie liked his blue jeans and a cool t-shirt most of the time. Josh, on the other hand, wore his sandy-blonde hair to his collar, opted for khaki shorts almost daily in the summer, as well as a t-shirt. Josh was equally as handsome, as well as fit as his buddy, Ed. They had been best friends and neighbors since kindergarten and had been on many fun, and rewarding adventures together.

Giselle was their friend and sometimes, co-adventurer. She liked hanging out with the boys as well and didn't mind getting her hands dirty when necessary, so to speak. She was resourceful and nice to be around.

By 6:00 AM the next morning Josh and Eddie had packed the van with their luggage, a cooler with drinks and a bag of road snacks. Both boys were wide awake and excited beyond expectation. This was the first time they had ever taken an out-of-state road trip together without parents. The preparation had gone back as far as a year and a half ago when they first conceived the idea. The first obstacle was convincing their parents it was a good idea. That took a few months just for that! Then they had to complete the VW Bus project, which Josh helped with, plan a route, find a hotel, and then plan activities.

On the top of their list was a basic dive course. Adventurous as they were at exploring the riverbanks and hills of their beautiful home state of West Virginia, they now wanted to get underwater. Their good friend Brad Radcliffe, who was in school at Marine Mechanics Institute in Orlando, had taken the basic SCUBA course and told them it was a "must-do." The tranquility of being underwater for periods of time longer than one could hold one's breath was something they needed to experience.

So now they were ready. Everything was in the van and it was time to go. Being close neighbors, all four parents stood in the Debords' driveway, coffees in hand, as they hugged their children goodbye.

Mr. Debord spoke as he patted the roof of the bus. "I have all the confidence in the world in this project, Eddie. Just keep an eye on your cylinder head temperature gauge down through the Deep South this time of year. And keep checking your oil."

"I will," Eddie responded. "It's going to do great, I know."

"Me too, buddy." He hugged his son, which initiated a lot more hugs.

The boys took their seats and Eddie fired up the engine. He let it run for a minute as he checked all of his gauges. Putting it in gear, he and Josh waved to the nervous parents as they pulled out of the driveway.

"They're going to be fine, right?" asked Mrs. Baker.

JoAnne Debord looked at her and smirked. "What could our two boys get in to?"

The two ladies laughed as Mr. Baker and Mr. Debord watched with envy as their two young men drove away.

After picking up Giselle and topping off with gas, Eddie made the right-hand turn off of Highway 119 in Big Chimney that would put them on Interstate 79 to Charleston. The route they had planned would take them through Charlotte, Columbia, past Savannah and Jacksonville and right into Daytona Beach off of I-95. The driving time was about eleven hours plus stops. They were figuring about fourteen hours, give or take, and would take turns driving and napping. Eddie didn't want to push the little engine too hard but instead, run it steady and warm. Sixty-five to seventy miles per hour was fine with them. Hey—they were on vacation!

About three and a half hours into the trip, they were rolling out of the big hills and tunnels of West Virginia and Virginia on I-77. The land was getting flatter and the bus seemed to appreciate it. The little four-cylinder had worked hard but flawlessly across the steep grades in the hills of their homeland. Eddie could almost hear the engine sigh with relief as they now cruised along at about half-throttle and seventy mph. They were now in North Carolina and passing signs for exits to Mooresville, Lake Norman, and Cornelius—NASCAR country!

Eddie and his dad had designed this bus with passenger comfort in mind. The driver's area was what Eddie called "the cockpit." Within easy reach he had everything he needed for this vehicle to be used as a vacation machine. A beautiful custom-made oak center console sat between the front bucket seats. It had four drink holders and slots for a travel atlas or magazines of beautiful destinations they would visit. On the custom dash, they had installed oil pressure and temperature gauges as well as cylinder head temperature gauges, a fuel gauge, and a new speedometer— all white-faced, illuminated, VDO brand. He had a phone mount on top of the dash and a power-panel which would accept four USB cables for charging. This VW was pure pleasure to drive down the road.

Giselle checked her watch. 9:55 AM. "We're doing pretty good, right?"

Josh looked back at her. "Right on schedule." He smiled.

Giselle had just awakened from a nap and still had her sleepy eyes but Josh thought she still looked pretty cute. She looked out the window as they crossed a bridge that spanned a section of Lake Norman. Jet skiers and pleasure boats of all kind buzzed and sailed the waters and Josh couldn't help but think of how much money it must cost to live at *that* playground!

As the day went on they made their stops for gas and bathroom breaks and of course a lunch break at Cracker Barrel in Columbia, South Carolina. They had each put a five-dollar bill on the console for the first person to spot a "Boiled Peanut" sign. A southern delicacy! Josh had won that contest and had promptly collected his winnings. The three friends were having fun, playing music, making plans, teasing one another and looking forward to a great two-week getaway. The bus hummed on, running like a Singer sewing machine. Life was good!

They were cruising along I-26 eastbound, south of Columbia but just before it intersects I-95. Eddie was back in the driver seat after being relieved for a while by Josh. He had just pulled a small grade when at the crest of the hill, the bus engine went to idle and he had no power—no accelerator at all, and the pedal lay flat on the floorboard.

"Oh no!" Eddie said, looking in his mirror and then his gauges.

"What happed?" Josh asked, looking at Eddie and then the gas pedal that Eddie was futilely trying to manipulate.

"I think…I think we broke the accelerator cable," he said, still processing the problem. "I got no pedal."

Josh looked ahead, being Eddie's second set of eyes. "Bottom of the hill is an exit, Ed. Stay in the right lane and we will merge off."

Giselle grabbed her phone and zoomed the *Maps* to the exit. "Yeah, stay right and there is a gas station as soon as you leave the exit ramp and merge on to highway 601," she confirmed.

Eddie turned on his emergency flashers and coasted down the hill at about forty miles per hour. Cars zoomed past him in the left lane as he was watching behind him as much as in front. "It's always something, ya know?" he grumbled.

As they approached the exit, they could see the light at the intersection was red and there was one car there that made a right turn on red. The intersection was clear and now it was all about timing. Eddie braked only slightly as the bus leaned into the turn at the bottom and then he got the green light. Perfect!

Eddie coasted the bus into the parking lot of a "Gas 4 Less" and brought it to a halt in a parking spot by the building. The parking spot was shaded by a tree and under the tree was a picnic table. He stopped abruptly as he noticed a boy about his own age rise up from a nap on the table to see what had so quietly but quickly approach him. The boy lifted the bill of his hat and then replaced it over his eyes and laid his head back down on an old green duffle bag.

"So now what?" Giselle asked.

"Now we fix it," Eddie replied.

Josh looked at Eddie. "We have to get a cable somewhere. I wonder if there is a parts store close."

"Well let's take a look first," Eddie said. "Let's make sure we need a cable. That one is only a year old and I can't believe it broke."

"I'm going to go get an iced coffee," Giselle said. "I'll ask about a parts store inside."

The trio all got out of the van and as Giselle went inside the Gas 4 Less store, the boys went to the back of the bus and opened the engine compartment lid. Eddie reached inside and grabbed hold of the dual-carburetor linkage that the accelerator cable hooks to. The linkage moved freely as it should but on further inspection, Eddie didn't see the cable that was supposed to be connected to it. Josh saw what he was looking at and reached his hand back into the small compartment to see if he could find the missing cable. At that moment, the boys both felt a presence behind them—a shadow had blocked their light. They looked over their shoulder to see the young man that was just napping on the picnic table.

The guy had to be just about the same age, maybe slightly older, with sandy blonde hair, near the color of Josh's but this boy's hair was at least two days away from its last shower. Maybe three. Josh and Eddie looked at each other and then back to the boy who had invited himself over to help diagnose the engine problem.

The boy gestured toward the front of Eddie's bus, "Why don't one of you go up front and make sure the cable is pushed as far as it will go. I'll go underneath to make sure it's fed through the tube and one of you can pull it back into the linkage."

Again Josh and Eddie exchanged glances. Eddie looked back at the fellow and asked, "You a Volkswagen guy?"

He shrugged one shoulder. "I grew up fixing everything that broke," he said.

He looked like that kind of a kid. Real handy to have around when in a pinch.

Josh and Eddie removed their arms from the engine area and turned towards the boy. Josh asked, "How did you know it was the cable we were looking for?"

The boy grinned, squinted one eye to block the sun and replied, "Well, you came coasting in here silent as a cat with your flashers on. Engine was idling but I never once heard it rev. It's the small things that get overlooked on a restoration, ya know?" He said, looking at the newly restored van. "The locking screw on the cable linkage, for instance. My guess is the cable is not broken. It just slipped out because the lock screw wasn't tight."

Eddie looked at him in disbelief. Eddie knew every nut and bolt on this machine. He had stripped and scraped and polished every square inch of it and what aggravated him a little was this guy was probably right!

Eddie nodded slightly and then walked towards the front of the bus. He leaned into the driver's area, reached down and pushed the throttle cable that was hooked to the gas pedal, as far as it would go towards the back of the bus.

The blonde haired kid crawled underneath and saw the cable hanging down. He grinned to himself for being right and then fed the cable back up into the proper tube that would feed it to Josh, who had his hand at just the right spot behind the carburetor linkage.

The boy said, "You should feel it."

"I got it!" Josh said.

Eddie brought a small tool box to the rear of the bus. In less than a minute they had the cable reconnected to the linkage and the bus was ready to roll once again. Giselle walked from the store to the back of the VW where the boys were.

Josh looked at her and then back to the engine. "It's fixed. Small problem," he said.

"Sweet," she replied. "You guys are good."

Eddie offered his hand to the boy. "My name's Eddie Debord. This is my friend Josh Baker and our friend Giselle O'Conner."

The dirty-haired kid offered a handshake to all three and then said, "My name's Nick—Nick Dawson."

"Appreciate your help, Nick. You from close by?" Eddie asked.

"No, no, no." he said, shaking his head and looking towards the ground. He kicked a small pebble around. "From Indiana. Up around Gary," he replied.

"Ah, OK," Eddie said. "You traveling? Heading somewhere?" Eddie looked over at the duffle bag on the picnic table.

Giselle looked on, getting a curious vibe from this kid. She took a drink of her iced coffee.

"I'm uh…Yeah I'm heading south."

Information from Nick seemed a little painful to extract. He was going somewhere. He had a story it seemed, but he wasn't ready to talk about it so quickly.

Josh reached into the back of Eddie's bus and took a rag to wipe his hands. He then said, "We are too. Going to Daytona for a couple weeks."

Nick Dawson's eyes opened a little wider. "Really? I'm going to Vero Beach! Well, for starters anyway."

Giselle looked at him and then looked around the parking lot for a vehicle to match. "You driving?" She quizzed him.

Nick shook his head. "Backpacking. Just hitching my way along."

Now Josh's eyes opened wider. "You're backpacking all the way to Vero Beach?"

"Well, yeah—but when I say backpacking, I don't mean walking, ya know. I left home yesterday morning. Caught a ride out of Gary with a trucker going into Charlotte. Spent the night sleeping in a chair at the truck stop. Caught another ride with a tanker driver this morning who dropped me here. Figuring out what to do from here." He shrugged.

Nick Dawson had captured their attention. Of course, Josh and Eddie were blown away. They loved his adventurous spirit and were now very curious to hear the rest of the story.

"What's in Vero Beach for you?" Josh asked. "You got family there?"

Nick Dawson smiled ever so slightly. He squinted one eye and looked at the trio, his head leaning slightly to one side. "Nope, no family down there. Not too much family anywhere really. Florida is just one of those places that I have always wanted to go to and spend some time, ya know? I've been planning this trip for a long time and…well, I don't have it all figured out yet but just getting to Vero is my first goal."

Josh nodded. "Yeah, I know what you mean. We've planned this trip for a year and a half! Can't wait to get to Daytona."

Nick Dawson snickered and looked around at his present environment and then looked back at the trio of friends. "I've been planning this since I was eight years old!"

"Really?" Eddie responded, amazed.

Nick nodded, looking at them.

Giselle finished drinking a little more, raised her eyebrows and said, "So this is a dream trip for you! How old *are* you?"

Nick Dawson looked at each one of them one by one— assessing them at face value to be a trustworthy group of friends. They seemed genuinely interested in his story and he had not yet even begun to tell them the good part.

"Do you guys have a few minutes?" He gestured towards the picnic table. "The gas station chicken is some of the best I have ever eaten. Maybe you'd like to get lunch?"

Eddie shook his head. "We're good on food but hungry for a good story if you've got one."

Josh added, smiling, "Yeah, I could stand to shake off this road buzz a little. Let's chill a few minutes."

Nick grinned as Eddie stepped around to grab an energy drink from the cooler. The four kids sat down at the table under the shade tree. Giselle sighed, not particularly as excited as her two friends not to be logging miles.

Nick glanced at Giselle as he removed his old green duffle bag from the tabletop and plopped it on the ground. "I'm sorry…I didn't answer your question. I'm twenty-one years old. Just turned."

Giselle responded with a head nod while finishing her drink. Josh decided to go get the cooler and offer drinks all around.

The heat of that sweltering June day was at its peak. At about 1:30 in the afternoon even the mosquitoes were in hiding. There was a gentle breeze that blew through the shade of the oak tree they sat under and that provided a bit of relief. It was beginning to smell like vacation—the wonderfully refreshing scents of the South. A mixture of magnolias and a still far away ocean breeze coming together somewhere above them and swirling down to tease their senses. It smelled, not better, but different than West Virginia. And they were ready for something different for a while. They were ready for this nice relaxing vacation.

Eddie popped the top on his drink, took a big gulp and then nodded towards Nick Dawson. "So you were saying—eight years old?"

"Eight years old. It was the first time that I ever heard the story about my grandpa, and also saw the proof of it." He was slowly reeling Josh and Eddie in with his intriguing bits of information.

"Proof of what?" Giselle asked.

Nick stared back at her and then looked at the two boys. They were never going to believe him, but he would lay it on them anyway.

"Treasure—sunken treasure."

He now had their full attention!

With the three friends wide eyed and mouths agape, he then began his story.

So much for the nice relaxing vacation.

CHAPTER FOUR

"I'll rewind a few years. Back in the early 70s, my grandpa was a steel worker up in Indiana and I'm not sure of all the particulars but he got caught up in a big layoff at the mill. All the mills were starting to lay off employees—they just eliminated jobs with no hope of getting them back. The US was getting its steel from other countries cheaper, I guess. Anyway, he and my grandma split after a few months of arguing about money and he came south to Florida. My dad was born *after* my grandpa left Indiana. Grandpa didn't even know he had a son."

"You're kidding!" Josh exclaimed. "Your grandma didn't tell him she was pregnant?"

Nick shook his head. "She didn't. She didn't want him to stay with her just for a child."

"Well, that's a pretty good reason to work things out," Giselle offered.

"I guess that's how bad things were between them." He shrugged again. "But anyway, so you have my grandpa and grandma divorced, my dad was born a few months later after grandpa moved to Florida. And then there's my dad: Dad grew up in Gary and met my mom there. Long story short, I grew up in a busted marriage and lived with my mom. I don't remember much about my dad. He took off when I was really little—about four years old. From what I have been told, he never had much ambition to do anything or be anyone special. He met my mom at a Denny's where she waited tables and I guess it was one of those instant attraction things. They married quickly and a few months later, I was born. So for whatever reason *they* split and he left town and hasn't been heard from since."

"Dang! Sorry about *that*." Josh said, shaking his head. *This kid has had a tough life!* he thought.

Nick swished his hand with nonchalance. "You don't miss something you never had."

Nick Dawson thought for a moment. "So that's my crazy history, now let me get to the good part. The reason I'm on my way to Florida."

Josh encouraged, "Yeah, you said something about a sunken treasure. We have some treasure stories to share also!" Josh, Eddie and Giselle shared a laugh as Nick shrugged *OK*.

My grandfather, his name was Butch—Butch Dawson, he went to Florida. It was something he always wanted to do anyway and he had the opportunity then to do it so he did. He ended up at Vero Beach which was a nice quiet little place back in the 70s. It suited him just fine." Nick shrugged.

Eddie looked at Nick, "How do you know all of this? Did he keep in touch with your grandma?"

"Yeah. He would write her from time to time and tell her she should come down and warm her bones. But she never did—

until…until he died. Then she had to go collect his belongings and take care of a funeral. I think she really didn't want to see grandpa again and she didn't want him to know they had a son…ya know, my dad."

"Hmm," Eddie responded, somewhat disapprovingly.

Nick continued, "So, Grandpa Butch went to work for a trawler captain named Chuck Henderson. He worked for him for a few months and my grandma received a few letters from him during that time. I don't know if she ever wrote him back but I *have* seen the letters and it seemed like he was enjoying himself! He liked his job and he liked the climate and everything was going well for him until—well, until grandma received a call one morning from the Indian River County Sheriff's Department saying he had been found floating by the docks, shot to death."

"Shot?!" Eddie exclaimed.

Nick nodded. "Two holes in his chest. Captain Henderson was shot also and was found lying on the dock by his boat. Both men dead."

Josh's eyes widened. "Wow…what could have happened?"

Nick shrugged one shoulder. "No one knows for sure. It was never solved and it is an open case to this day. There is only speculation and theories."

"What is the speculation?" Giselle asked. "What do they think happened?"

Nick smirked. "Well, in Florida, when there is a boat and a late-night murder involved, the Florida Department of Law Enforcement's first inclination is drugs. A drug run gone bad."

Josh tilted his head and asked Nick, "What do you think of

that? What does your family think of that?"

Nick winced. "My grandmother always said it was preposterous…that's the word she used, preposterous. She said grandpa would not have ever gotten involved with running drugs. She said he was far too ethical to ever do that. And that comes from a woman who had divorced him…and didn't want him back!" Nick pondered a moment, looking away. "And grandma had a good reason for knowing it wasn't drugs," he said.

"Really? What was that?" Eddie asked.

Nick exchanged glances with the trio and then reached for his old, green duffle. Opening it up, he pulled out an old leather-bound book. "I have this. This was grandpa's journal or diary after he moved to Florida. He wrote in it at least once a week and sometimes two or three times a week. He would write about his day of selling hotdogs on the beach to spring-breakers and then after he went to work for Henderson, he started writing like a sailor! Using nautical terms."

Josh grinned and said, "You mean like *Aarrghh…!*"

Nick laughed. "No…not like a pirate, but like a *sailor*."

The mood lightened a little and everyone repositioned slightly as Nick continued. "He really seemed to be enjoying himself doing what he was doing right up until his last day alive. Even grandma agreed with that."

Eddie looked across the table at Nick. "So what is in that book that brings you to Florida?"

Nick nodded. He grinned and then once again exchanged glances with them as he opened the book to the last entry that was ever made.

"These sentences right here are taking me to Florida."

The four young adults moved in close to read what was written so many years ago. In the breeze under the shade tree, Nick read aloud:

December 3rd, 1973 – 11:55 PM   Aboard "Maria"

On a run tonight that was my last of its kind. Never again!

Fortune has changed as we have discovered the hull of a boat…a very, very old boat and between its ribs we found our future, and quite possibly the means of not ever having to do tonight's work ever again in our lives…or any other work if we choose! My good friend, Captain Henderson and I will return in a few days to see what lies in the sea for us. Tropical Storm Chris, driven by God above, has given us a gift.

I will log its coordinates:

28 degrees 26' 10.57 N, 80 degrees 33'21.41" W

Now back to Vero docks to collect for this vile venture of tonight. And tomorrow, a new life.

BD

Nick Dawson, grandson of Butch, looked up at an astounded audience.

Josh said slowly, "That is very interesting!"

Eddie followed, "That's *more* than interesting…I mean, you have the coordinates! You know exactly where it is?"

Giselle added, "Have you researched it? Do you know what ship it could possibly be?"

Nick nodded, "I have waited my whole life to be twenty-one years old. To be completely legal for anything I may need to do when I go down there. I have maps and books and have researched this for years. I have a theory of what ship it is and the manifest of what is onboard."

"Why has no one in your family gone after this before?" Josh asked, unbelievingly.

Nick shrugged, "I am the lone grandson. My father had no interest in this or anything else, so…grandma said it was my ticket—my future."

"That's just amazing," Eddie said, looking back at the page.

"There's more," Nick added.

He reached into the green bag and pulled out a small wooden box. The box was ornately carved, maybe Asian, and looked like a miniature treasure chest but was much newer than its contents. The trio looked on as Nick opened the box. From it, he pulled a solid gold 16th century Spanish *Escudo.* Once again their eyes opened wide in disbelief—not just at what they were looking at, but what it validated. Nick was telling them the truth. He had tangible proof of his grandfather's claim.

Giselle was the first to reach for it and Nick gave it to her to inspect for herself. The piece was heavy and she couldn't believe she was holding something so cool in her hand.

"My goodness!" was all she could say as she stared at it, flipping it around in her palm to inspect closely. She then passed it to Josh and he passed it to Eddie.

These kids were no strangers to seeing old gold. A few years back, they were the discoverers of their own little prize in their home state of West Virginia. But they *were* fascinated with this coin. It was the closest thing to pirate gold that they had ever seen and who's not fascinated with pirate gold?

Eddie rolled the coin around in his hand. He was in awe of this beautiful artifact and suddenly a thousand questions entered his mind. He asked, "And it's certain that this coin came from the area of these coordinates?"

"As certain as we can be. Grandma said when she went down to collect his belongings and found it in his sea-bag, it still had a little sand on it." He paused. "That right there tells me it was fresh from the ocean."

Josh nodded in agreement.

"Probably, and even *more* credibility," Eddie agreed.

"My grandpa wrapped it in a paper towel and put it away in his sea bag that night. This coin, along with the coordinates to the rest of it, is the best inheritance a poor boy could ever wish for—along with the adventure that goes along with it of course!"

Giselle laughed and said, "Yeah, now you're talking their language," as she pointed a thumb at Josh and Eddie.

Josh shook his head, still in disbelief but in a state of extreme envy of this kid, Nick. "What does your mom think of you putting your thumb in the wind and heading to Florida to chase this adventure?"

Nick chuckled, "Well…she's a mom. She would rather see me focus on finding a good job somewhere."

"Understandable," Giselle said.

"It is…but here's the thing." Nick Dawson looked at the three friends with an expression of self-acceptance. "I have a very average high school education. It was never in the cards for me to go to college. First of all, I'm not a school kid. I just don't like it. Second, I fix things—I work with my hands and I know that those jobs are scaled hourly and, if you are good, you can make a few bucks above minimum wage and that's it. So I figured I have plenty of time to do that and the best thing that I can do to try to have more for myself, is to go see if this gift from my grandpa is real."

Eddie nodded. "Well I don't blame you for that! Hey, at the very least, he left you a Spanish coin!"

"That's it—and this bag!" Nick slapped the old sea bag.

"That was his?" Josh asked.

"That makes it even better." Eddie followed, "It's very cool you brought his bag along!"

Nick nodded and looked down at the ground. He then lifted his eyes to the shade tree as another light breeze flowed past them. He broke off a small twig from the tree and began stripping its bark as the kids looked around at the day that was slipping away. Nick thought for a moment longer and then looked up at them as his hair covered one eye. "Well—so what do you guys think? Are you in?"

Josh and Eddie's faces showed surprise as the energy drink stopped short of Josh's mouth. He then lowered the can and cocked his head like a chicken. "In for what?" Josh asked.

"Well, I need a lift to Florida and I could also use a couple of hands at working all the legal stuff that needs done to do a search and salvage plan. I only have a basic knowledge of where to start and what to do and you guys seem like you would make good partners. So what's it gonna be? Are you in?"

"You're saying that you want us to help you recover this gold from this old ship?" Eddie questioned, just to be sure. He and Josh were both smiling with excited anticipation. Giselle was shaking her head but quite possibly somewhat intrigued herself.

Nick nodded, also smiling. "The state of Florida takes twenty-five percent right off the top. There may be other fees also. After that, I take half of what's left—you guys split the other half however you want."

Josh and Eddie glanced at each other and then quickly stuck their hands out to shake with Nick. "Deal!" they said simultaneously. They looked at Giselle.

"OK, deal, but I still want some time in the sun!" she said, putting her hand out too.

"You'll get it!" Josh promised, confidently looking into her green eyes.

The excitement level intensified slightly as there was some back slapping and talk of plans for the search and salvage. They loaded Nick's bag and the boys' cooler into the bus as Giselle took the very back seat, Nick took the middle seat and Josh and Eddie assumed their positions up front.

With still plenty of room for all and a repaired throttle cable, Eddie fired up the engine once again, and put his VW in gear as the new team of four pointed themselves southbound for Florida on a hot summer day.

Yeah, so much for a relaxing vacation. Hello adventure!

CHAPTER FIVE

As the bus rolled along I-95 south, the four kids made conversation, getting to know each other a little better. Nick listened in amazement to a long story the trio had to tell him about a pile of gold they had the good fortune of locating and also, about an old crashed airplane they had found that had guarded a secret from the 1950s. Nick was fascinated with their tales and also by the fate that had brought him together with these guys and Giselle. Those two stories alone had gotten them all the way to Brunswick, Georgia! They were starting to cross tidal rivers and inlets that flowed a short distance to the ocean to their east. The kids knew the big water was just out of sight and they were getting the fever. Four land-locked young people heading to the beach!

Shaking his head, Nick said, "It has to be divine intervention that I ran into you guys! That throttle cable was never meant to make it all the way to Florida!" They laughed together.

"I mean, look at how much experience you guys have at treasure hunting!" he finished.

Giselle leaned forward, adding, "And hopefully treasure

finding!"

Eddie took one hand off the wheel and turned his palm upward in wonder. "I have no idea how these things find us, but it's starting to become a trend, I think." He grinned.

Josh quickly shrugged and smiled. "That's fine with me!"

They rolled on—conversing and swapping stories of youth as they logged mile after mile. The VW bus was performing flawlessly and even though the heat of the day was now reaching 89 degrees, its air-cooled engine temperatures were right on the money.

As they topped a small grade Eddie made the announcement: "Here we are!"

They all looked forward out the windshield to see the sign that said "Saint Mary's River", and just on the other side of the bridge another sign read: *Welcome to Florida...The Sunshine State!*

There were *woo hoos* and *yee haws* all around! They had made it!

Giselle was still leaning forward with her forearms lying flat on the backrest in front of her. "We have to stop at the welcome center and get some orange juice!"

Josh looked back at her as Eddie glanced into his rearview mirror.

"Tourist!" Josh said jokingly.

"Yeah!" she responded enthusiastically. Josh noticed the excitement in her eyes and her fun, bright smile.

Eddie rolled the bus down the off-ramp and into a parking spot at the Florida Welcome Center. It was a "must stop" for vacationers who came from all points north. As they stepped from the van, the hot Florida sun hit them like a wall. The humidity was stifling and a breeze was nearly non-existent. The Center was beautifully landscaped Florida style. Tall palm trees hung overhead and sea oats as well as many varieties of tropical flowers were planted around the bases of the trees. It was truly welcoming…except for the intense humidity.

"Wow!" Eddie exclaimed. "It feels twice as hot as our last stop.

As they walked towards the building, Josh pointed his thumb back over his shoulder towards the bus. "Maybe we should get a bag of ice for the air conditioner."

"What?" Nick laughed.

Eddie grinned. "It's a hillbilly air conditioner we fabricated."

Nick tried to suppress a smile as he waited for the rest of the story.

Eddie continued as they walked. "We took a cooler and cut a circular hole in the lid of it and mounted a fan. You take a bag of ice and dump it in the cooler onto a wire rack that we installed about halfway down into the cooler."

Nick nodded. "And the fan pulls the cooled air from the cooler out into the van. But where does the air go *into* the cooler. There has to be an inlet as well as an outlet for circulation."

Eddie went on. "Right. We cut two two-inch holes below the rack and inserted short pieces of PVC pipe that sticks out the end of the cooler. So the air is sucked into the cooler below the ice, it flows through the ice where it's cooled and then is blown back out of the cooler and into the bus."

Nick nodded, smiling, "Slick! That's a good idea!"

"The air coming out of the cooler is usually about twenty-two degrees cooler than the air going in. It takes a while to cool the whole van but it eventually does, and on an afternoon like this, it might be a good idea," Eddie finished.

"I think it will be mandatory," Giselle said, wrinkling her nose as Josh opened the Welcome Center door for her.

The kids entered the coolness of the facility and after taking their bathroom breaks, they met back at the gift shop. It was full of the very typical items that people loved to take home from Florida: saltwater taffy, small preserved alligator heads and every sort of knick-knack you can think of made of cedar. They also had fudge, which caught Josh's attention, and Eddie opted for a large cup of boiled peanuts, which he had been thinking about since South Carolina! Giselle got her free sample of Florida orange juice and Nick got nothing.

It occurred to Josh at that time that maybe Nick had no money, or was very low. Josh stepped close to him and said confidentially, "Hey is there something you want? I can get it."

Nick looked at him somewhat startled but appreciatively, "No, no, man. I'm OK. I got some cash. I'm good." Nick was good with saying it aloud. "I'm not broke. I'm just not *wasting* money. Never know how long I will have to be down here."

Josh nodded. "Ok, alright. Just making sure."

"Thanks, Josh."

The four decided to step out back to a shaded area where they had tables with umbrellas shaped and colored to look like half-oranges. The area wasn't crowded—just a family of four enjoying some ice cream, a middle-aged lady reading a paperback, apparently waiting for her husband, and a short, dark-skinned man dressed in tan work pants and a green long-sleeved cotton work shirt. The man was on his phone, speaking frantically in Spanish.

With the change in his pocket, Nick had decided to go ahead and get a drink from the machine in the breezeway of the Welcome Center and they all sat at the table to take a short break from the road and to enjoy their purchases. Giselle had gotten three samples of orange juice before the lady finally cut her off.

Nick took a cool drink and then asked, "So what's the first stop? I'm with you guys!"

Eddie nodded and said, "Well I would say that we go to Daytona and we can get checked in to our rooms. Then we get a good dinner and crash for the night. In the meantime, we can make a list of what we should do tomorrow to get started. Do you have a reservation somewhere, Nick?"

Nick was shaking his head before Eddie finished his sentence. "No…I'm just winging it."

Eddie continued, "Well, we can go to our hotel and get settled and go from there."

The Spanish guy had concluded his call and was shaking his Styrofoam cup around, rattling the ice. The scar over his right eye was a prominent feature he couldn't hide. So was his scrunched and weathered face. It was evident he wasn't happy with whoever was on the other end of the line. The caller had told him he had no more work for him and had no money to pay him for what he had done. The man shook his head in disgust.

Josh held up one finger as he swallowed a bite of his fudge. "We have to investigate what needs to be done to treasure hunt in Florida…legally. If we find something, we sure want to be able to keep it."

Without moving his head, the man's eyes shifted from his phone directly to Josh.

Giselle spoke up. "We can do that today. We can have all that planned. I'll pull out my laptop and we can search all that information as we roll down the road."

The man's dark eyes shifted to Giselle.

The three boys all looked at her. Their eyes were asking *how?*

"I'll show you a trick using a cell phone to create a wifi hotspot. Then I can log on to it using my laptop. Nick turned both palms up. "Awesome! We can get started right away. The first thing we need to know is, where do we go to get the permits to search and salvage a wreck?"

The man's eyes shifted to Nick and a wry grin tugged at the corner of his mouth.

Nick continued as he reached into his pants pocket and lowered his voice. "And with any luck, maybe we will find a very large pile of these." He smiled as he held the prized gift from his grandfather.

The man's dark eyes widened when he saw what Nick held in his hand. He had seen a Spanish *Escudo* before and if he had heard these young people correctly, there may be a pile of them somewhere. Maybe *his* luck just changed.

They all nodded with enthusiasm. Then Eddie said, "Well, let's get back on the road. Daytona is calling!"

The four friends finished their food and drinks, and then walked from the patio area back through the breezeway and out to the bus. Josh paid for a bag of ice and walked quickly to get it in the cooler before losing any of it to the Florida heat. Nick looked on with creative admiration as Josh prepped the "air conditioner" that now sat between the two front seats.

Eddie said, "We can slide this to the center of the van to give everyone some cool air."

Once the AC was up and running, Josh walked over to the trash can by the sidewalk and threw away the plastic bag. A scrunched-faced, dark-skinned Latin man stepped past Josh and opened the door to his very long, very old car. He fired it up and Josh fanned away the puff of blue smoke from its exhaust.

Josh joined his friends in the bus and Eddie, once again, fired up the little engine and pulled away.

Through the windshield of 1974 Chrysler New Yorker, the same dark-skinned man with a scar over his right eye watched them leave. Seconds later *he* pulled away, following a beautifully restored Volkswagen bus as a cloud of blue smoke trailed him.

As the day went on, the four cruised on past Jacksonville and St. Augustine. Now deep into palm tree country, there were smiles all around the bus. They were now starting to see signs for places like Palm Coast and Flagler Beach. Vacation fever was taking over as just the names of these tropical towns excited them! Daytona was just down the road and the thrill level couldn't have been higher. Josh had even gone to the back of the bus to pull his swimsuit out of his suitcase. He wanted to get in the water at the earliest possible second!

Giselle was in the back seat reading a travel magazine she had picked up at the Welcome Center. Something occurred to her and she sat up straight and looked at Nick, who sat on the bench seat in front of her. "Nick, I was wondering, did they ever find the guy who killed your grandfather?"

Nick looked back at her and shook his head. "No...that crime was never solved. They told my grandma it was the cleanest job they had ever seen. Not a trace of evidence was left behind. No shell casings, no witnesses, nobody heard a gunshot, nobody saw a vehicle. Nothing."

"That's too bad," Giselle responded.

Nick looked off, recalling the story. "Yeah, and what was a little unusual, my grandma always told us, was the investigators were not all that cooperative with her. She had to really pry to get information. They didn't offer much, not even consolation. She said they just kept telling her *when they knew something, they would call!*"

Eddie was looking from his rearview mirror. "I think those guys can be a little cold. They see a lot, ya know."

"I know, but from what grandma told us, they went beyond cold to the point of being rude."

Josh had turned around in his seat, "Do you think there was a cover-up?"

"I don't know," Nick said, shrugging. "Nothing about his murder makes sense. He hadn't been in town long enough to make an enemy who would kill him. He didn't owe anybody any money..."

Giselle cut him off. "How do you know that?"

"Because he had thirty-two thousand dollars in his bank account. He wouldn't have borrowed any money from some shady dude when he had that much money in the bank."

Eddie nodded. "True."

Giselle went on, "What happened to that money?"

"Grandma was able to recover it. It took a while but the courts awarded it to her because it came from the sale of their house when they divorced. Two years later she used it to buy back that old house. She said it was her home and she missed living there, and that's where she raised my dad."

Josh wobbled his head. "Well that's kinda cool."

"Yeah, she was happy with that decision." Nick thought for a moment. "But anyway, the only reason for anyone to kill him was because they had found the wreck. My grandpa and the captain were the only ones who would have known the location and the killer wanted the coordinates. But who would have known about that? They had just gotten back to the dock that night!"

Giselle was shaking her head. "Yeah, nothing about that makes good sense. It *had* to be something else. I mean…I hate to suggest it but is there a chance your grandpa was into anything besides hauling fish?"

Nick was not offended by the suggestion. He shrugged and replied, "Well…I mean, it was the 70s! I won't be so naive to say that my grandpa wouldn't have done something like that. But grandma never believed he could have—run drugs or whatever. She always said he was too paranoid. He never wanted to be in trouble. He didn't even like being late on bills. It made him nervous."

"It just seems so random, but I guess a person can simply be in the wrong place at the wrong time," Eddie commented. Maybe it was the captain they wanted to kill and they had to kill your grandpa Butch in order to have no witnesses."

Giselle nodded. "That's very likely."

Nick shrugged slightly, looking out the window, trying his best to spot an alligator in a pond. "I guess we will never know. It's been many years so it's in the cold case files now." He paused. "Just another murder in Florida."

The bus hummed along—taking them closer and to their destination for the day. The little home-made air conditioner was impressively helping to beat the Florida heat. It wasn't ice-cold like a modern cooling system but it did make it quite comfortable inside the vehicle. Nobody was complaining and the beach was drawing closer as the evening fell upon them.

Eddie looked into his rearview mirror, wondering about something that Nick had mentioned way back in Columbia. "Hey Nick, you said you have done a lot of research on the wreck. What do you know about it?"

Nick smiled. It was time to tell a fun story and if they were not excited before—they would be now!

CHAPTER SIX

Rolling along southbound on I-95, Nick began. "There is a lot written about this and the details vary a little bit because of different records that were kept back then. Also keep in mind that I am not an expert on the subject by any means." He looked around at everyone, making sure they understood his disclaimer.

Josh shrugged a shoulder. "That's OK."

Nick took a deep breath and put his mind into recall mode. "Well, in the early 1700s, Spain was on the losing end of a war—a very long war that had severely drained their economy. All of Europe had been fighting each other for around twenty-three years. Spain had been fighting The War of Spanish Succession since 1701, and that didn't end until 1713!"

Eddie looked over at Josh and smiled. Josh said, "OK mister non-expert—keep going."

"Well, this is just what I've read. I don't know details of the wars or anything." Nick grinned and then continued. "So anyway, during wartime, it was very dangerous for the Spanish treasure fleets to sail back from the Americas to Spain. Too big of a chance of getting overtaken. Ya gotta understand that Spain was at war with over a half-dozen European powers during those times. France and, I think, Bavaria were their only allies. It got so bad that Spain just tied up its ships in harbors and was waiting for the end of the war. In the meantime, they had been gathering gold, silver and jewels to take back to their country to, once again, build and support their economy. Guys—they had a massive, massive amount of treasure on those ships. And here is the kicker— sometimes the treasure fleets would have two or three times the amount of treasure on them than what was showing on the manifests! Smuggled treasure would be in every sailor's trunk. Even the captain would make his fortune smuggling back non-manifested gold and jewels."

"Wow, so they were cleaning house over here," Josh said.

"Oh yes! And had been for a long time! Central and South America, and Mexico too. Gold, silver, emeralds, you name it. It was all being mined out of the hills of Vera Cruz, Columbia, Peru, Panama. Guys…families in these countries would have gold in their homes like we have wood today!" Nick exaggerated but was getting excited. "It poured out of Central and South America for hundreds of years! There were many, many treasure fleets that ran between those countries and Europe from the 1500s to the 1800s. On those ships, even a cabin boy could get rich. And there were many that sank and took their treasure to the bottom of the sea with them. Some in deep water but most of them went down on the reefs."

Eddie lifted his eyebrows and blew out a puff of air. "Boy, does that get your imagination going for a career choice."

"Treasure hunter? You bet it does!" Josh was thinking the same thing.

"Guys…there is so much still to be found, you wouldn't believe!"

Giselle had been quietly absorbing all of this information. "So do you have an idea of which fleet this was from?" She pulled out her laptop from her backpack.

"I do. I am certain of which fleet, and I have a theory of which ship!"

Josh and Eddie were getting chills. Giselle, the logical one, and brains of the operation, wanted to verify everything. It only took a few moments to log on to her phone's hotspot. In the meantime, Nick continued with his history lesson.

"It is just commonly called the *1715 Spanish Treasure Fleet*," he said.

Giselle did a search. "OK—looks like that was actually *two* fleets made into one big one. The Spanish *Tierra Firma* and the *Nova Espana*."

Nick confirmed, "Right. One left from Vera Cruz, Mexico, and the other from Cartagena, Columbia. They met in Havana, Cuba, to provision for the crossing. There was also a French vessel that went with them."

"So, strength in numbers was the idea," Eddie reasoned.

Nick nodded. "Exactly. But numbers couldn't help them against what they were going to face."

Josh repositioned his shoulder strap and turned slightly to better see and hear Nick. He pulled his belts tight once again.

Nick continued, "So, fully provisioned and packed with treasure, eleven ships sailed from Havana Harbor on July, 24th ,1715. Their route was going to be the same as hundreds who had gone before them—past the Florida Keys, through the Florida Straits, up the east coast of Florida until they sighted Cape Canaveral. There they were to hang a right until they spotted Bermuda and then to the Azores and finally, Spain."

Giselle had found a website and was nearly reading along with Nick. He really *had* done some research through the years. She said, "Wow, Nick. You are right on the money with what I'm looking at here."

He grinned and shook his head. "I'll tell ya, this has been my whole life. You can imagine a young kid—eight or nine years old, being told his grandfather had found a sunken treasure and had left him the map to it!"

Josh's chill level increased. "It's like a pirate story! Man—I can't wait to get started!"

"I hear ya!" Eddie followed. "I am *so* ready!"

Giselle laughed and continued reading from the website. "Go on, Nick. Keep telling the story."

"There is so much to tell. Like I say, I have read so much on this through the years." He thought a moment. "OK, so the treasure fleet rounded the southern tip of Florida and started heading north. It wasn't long before the experienced seamen onboard began to notice that even though the skies were clear for the moment, the sea was running smooth with long, low swells and there was a breeze from the southeast. The air was heavy, full of moisture and the old salts knew what all of that meant. A hurricane! Now, the Spanish ships hugged the coastline, staying just far enough out to utilize the currents of the Gulf Stream. The French vessel sailed in deeper water—out to sea."

"Wonder if they read the weather better than the Spanish?" Giselle said.

Nick turned towards her and shrugged. "For whatever reason they elected to leave the safety of numbers and sail a different course."

"So a hurricane was coming." Josh urged him on, anxious to hear the story.

"A big one. I have read by today's measurements it was a category 5 storm. Could you imagine being on a ship and have something the size of Katrina come at you?"

"No way," Eddie said.

"So they sailed north and in the early morning hours of July 31st, 1715, the storm reached them and started driving them into the reefs. It blew hard! It ripped their sails to shreds, tore down their masts and sent them crashing to the decks and into the ocean and blew passengers and crew alike overboard to their deaths. There was only one Spanish ship that didn't get torn apart—the *Santisima Trinidad*. The *Trinidad* spotted a cove somewhere and beached itself in the sand. The crew and passengers were able to survive the storm and live off of the provisions they had aboard until rescue ships arrived a few weeks later."

"And the others?" Eddie asked.

"Lost. Ripped apart on the reefs. The storm just drove the ships again and again into the hard coral until they were just firewood."

"But the reefs are fairly close to shore, right? They could be seen and salvaged?" Josh asked.

"Yes, and they were! There was a massive salvage operation by the Spanish and they called it a success. They felt that they had recovered all of the wealth that was on the manifests. And so that just leaves…"

"…The undocumented treasure," Giselle finished.

"Exactly." Nick said. "Maybe twice or three times as much as was manifested!"

Josh looked at Nick. "So they found the value of what was on the manifests but not necessarily the exact treasure that was on the manifests."

"Right," Nick replied. "Once they recovered their lost wealth, the Spanish were happy. The King was happy with that, considering. It was good politically for him to say the salvage was a success."

"So there is so much more to find," Eddie said.

Nick smiled and his eyes sparkled. "This treasure has been washing up on the Florida coastline for three hundred years. You will see guys with metal detectors after every outgoing tide. That's what I've read. That's why they call it the Treasure Coast. Oh and also…there are still four ships that haven't been found!"

"Holy smokes!" Eddie exclaimed. "I can't get there soon enough!" He shoved the accelerator down a little more.

Giselle asked from the back, "So which ship do you think is the one your grandfather found?"

Nick nodded. "Here's what I know and it's not much to go on but it's just my gut feeling based on the process of elimination and common sense. These ships started hitting the reefs from Fort Pierce south to Vero Beach. Not necessarily sinking there but sustaining damage from the coral. There was also one ship named *El Senor San Miguel* that was believed to have made it all the way up to Amelia Island before sinking. That is up by the Florida-Georgia line." He paused. "But… there was one ship—one ship that was hugging the coastline after Vero that was last seen by observers heading straight north and very much in peril, towards the Cape Canaveral Peninsula. And that ship was the *Patache Nuestra Senora de la Concepcion.* And it's my belief, guys, that the *Concepcion* is the ship that my grandfather found purely by accident in 1973."

Josh, Eddie and Giselle were simply amazed at this story.

Giselle wondered something. "Nick, if four are still undiscovered, how do you know, or what makes you think this is the *Concepcion?*"

He shook his head. "Research—just a lot of reading. There are records of eyewitness accounts and they say things like …*The Senora del Carmen was last seen near the Nieves close to Sebastian inlet…*" He replied. "So what I did, I took a nautical chart of the coast and tacked it to my bedroom wall…probably eight years ago. When I would read something like that, I would take a small piece of paper with the ship's name on it and pin it to the chart. That way I had a visual—I could see where the witnesses last saw the ship."

"That's very clever," she responded.

"It helped me a lot. And I may have the *Regala* ship, for example, in two or three spots on the chart depending on the eyewitness who was giving the account, but generally it would be close to one location."

Eddie jumped in, "So the eyewitness accounts are fairly geographically reliable? Generally?"

Nick nodded. "I really haven't found any big discrepancies."

Giselle added, "That's pretty amazing for three hundred years ago—that they could give reference points on land that we can still identify today."

Josh looked towards Nick. "Did you find a lot of information on the *Concepcion*?"

"Actually no. Not as much as some of the others. But what I did find said the same thing. They said that the *Concepcion* was badly beaten and blowing north towards Canaveral."

"Right where your grandfather found the ribs and the gold," Josh said.

Nick nodded. "When we get to the hotel, I will show you my map and where the coordinates place the ship. You will be amazed at how close to shore it is. These reefs are just a couple thousand feet offshore."

Eddie looked in the rearview mirror again. "It could be hard to do salvage discreetly. People will be able to see us from the beach"

Nick agreed. "There's a lot of planning to do. I was thinking we need to look like a dive boat and not a salvage vessel."

Josh nodded. "Well, I can tell ya that we don't know the first thing about salvaging a sunken ship but we are eager learners!"

Giselle leaned forward on the seat again. "We are going to have to rent a boat or hire a captain or…how does that work?"

Nick shook his head again. "Like I say…there is a lot to do and a lot to figure out!"

Eddie played the drums on his steering wheel. "Well, we got the team to do it and guess what? We are here! Daytona!" There was a rousing round of cheers and smiles as everyone took a break from conversation and looked out the windows.

Eddie flipped on his right blinker to exit I-95 onto highway 92—West International Speedway Boulevard. He clover-leafed around and merged into the right lane and soon gazed in awe as they passed Daytona International Speedway. The newly rebuilt front grandstand facility was spectacular and went on forever as all four kids took in the beauty of this grand racing facility.

Giselle said, "Put *this* on the list of things to do while down here!"

"Oh yeah!" Josh agreed.

The kids drove on towards the beach.

Eddie looked up into his rearview mirror once again. "Hey Nick?" He paused as Nick looked towards him. Eddie grinned. "Don't ever say you're not an expert on that subject again, OK?"

They all enjoyed a laugh together. It was true. Nick had done his homework.

A few hundred feet behind them a dark-skinned man with a scrunched face and a scar over his right eye pounded his steering wheel in anger. It seems a 1973 Chrysler New Yorker doesn't get as good of gas mileage as a VW bus. Furious—he would have to stop for fuel as he sputtered into a station.

"*Carajo!*" he exclaimed, watching the bus fade out of sight.

A quarter mile ahead, the four kids had no idea how big a break they had just caught—for now.

CHAPTER SEVEN

Cruising south on historic Highway A1A, the bus continued to hum along, the homemade air conditioner continued to keep them comfortable and the sights were making them smile. One after another, there were souvenir shops with everything imaginable for having a good time at the beach. There were places to get temporary tattoos, hair braids and paddleboards. Suntan lotion that promised to multiply the sun by ten times, (as if that were a good thing) sunscreen, sunglasses and sun-brellas! They sell sunshine here in Florida and ironically they also sell you products to protect you *from* it.

After a few minutes Eddie pointed to the left. "There it is! *Vista al Mar Resort.*"

"Nice!" Nick said. "It looks new!"

"About twenty years old but refurbished," Giselle responded. "I checked it out last night. It should be a nice place. Four and a half stars."

Eddie wheeled the bus into the horseshoe-shaped entry. The entryway was lined with palm trees, shrubbery and tropical flowers. There was a large fountain in the center of the horseshoe and the scent of chlorine was the first thing that teased their senses as Eddie rolled his window down while coming to a stop. A valet attendant whose uniform hung on him like it would on a coat rack, approached from the driver's side. Eddie looked at him. This boy looked younger the he and no way was he parking Eddie's pride and joy! "Do you have self-park?" Eddie asked.

Dejected at losing a tip, the boy said "Yeah...the parking building at the end of the resort." The boy pointed towards the south end of the block. "Can I help you with your luggage? I can bring a cart." A last ditch effort at a tip.

"That would be great. Thank you!" Eddie conceded. They could have easily gotten their own luggage but Eddie figured they were on vacation. Why not enjoy it?

Josh walked around the bus and opened the big side door for Nick and Giselle. Nick jumped out with his grandpa's old sea bag. The attendant brought the luggage cart along with a baggage porter for them and hung around waiting for a tip. Eddie handed him five dollars for not much service, and the boy thanked him and went back to his valet position. Nick put his sea bag on the cart and Giselle crawled from the back seat to exit the bus.

Giselle limped her way out and then laughed, in pain, "Oh my gosh, my leg is asleep!" She grimaced. "I was sitting with it under me!" She was still laughing but with obvious discomfort. Her left leg tingled as it tried to regain circulation. Josh was still standing by the door and offered her his hand. Giselle, instead, put her arm around his neck as she hopped from the bus. With the crook of her elbow gripping Josh's neck, he supported her with his arm around her waist as Giselle shook her leg to wake it up. She then turned a bit to face him and put her other hand on his opposite shoulder as she looked down at her leg. She flexed it up and down and tried to get life back into it. This moment took Josh's breath away. There she stood with one arm around his neck and her other hand on his shoulder. His arm was still around her slim waist as he balanced her. He had never been so close to her in all the years he had known her. She felt good—she smelled nice, her beautiful auburn hair touched his face, and she was completely comfortable hanging onto him. This was all very new!

Finally, as the blood found its way back into her leg, she didn't move away from him but instead looked up at his face, patted him on the chest, smiled and said, "Thank you, Josh. I probably would have gone straight to the ground without you." She laughed at the ordeal.

Josh didn't know what to think of it. It felt so good with her so close to him. Something happened right there that he hadn't expected. Something awoke inside him. He looked at her beautiful green eyes as he tried to compose himself and wondered if she felt the same thing. *Probably not*, he thought. He felt her arms relax and come off of him as she held her stare for a moment longer. And for Josh, it all seemed to happen in slow motion as he savored every second of it.

He then came back to earth enough to give her his little Josh Baker smirk. "That's what friends are for." He tried to be nonchalant. Josh had to remind himself that he and Giselle were friends and even though he would have not held Eddie in the same manner, what happened was only a gesture of friendship. But his heart sure had a thing for Giselle—and it always had.

Nick and Eddie walked from the back of the bus with more luggage and placed it on the cart. Josh went back and got his bag as well as Giselle's second bag. Eddie had gotten the first one. Eddie saw them standing close but said nothing.

Eddie said, "Why don't you guys get us checked in and I will go park the bus? Everything is already paid."

Josh was still gathering himself somewhat. "Yep. We'll wait for you in the lobby."

Josh, Giselle and Nick stepped inside the refreshing coolness of the Vista al Mar Resort as the porter wheeled their luggage behind them. The lobby was grand with tile and marble. There were more fountains inside as well as many plants and a waterfall that cascaded off of a tropical hillside which was built to one side. A large, beautiful chandelier hung overhead and there were walls decorated with locally found sea glass. Treasures themselves, found along the coastline, from sunken trade ships of the past six hundred years.

Giselle looked up and all around. "This place is beautiful. I'm so excited! Oh my gosh, two weeks!" She clapped her hands.

Josh nodded, smiling, looking at her. "I wanna see the beach." He raised one eyebrow.

Outside, Eddie started up the bus and switched off the "air conditioner." He couldn't see it for the fountain, but driving by on A1A was a 1973 Chrysler New Yorker with scrunched faced man looking around in all directions. The large fountain, along with all the greenery, blocked the bus from his view as he drove on by.

Once again, luck was on their side.

After getting settled in their rooms, the four young people had made their way down to the pier. On the pier was *Captain Joes*. One of those places where tourists love to eat. The tables were simply epoxy-plywood. Simple stools to sit on and you could write your name on your table or the walls beside you, if you could find a space to do it. There were license plates from every state in the union and from many other countries. It was also decorated with flotsam and jetsam that had washed up on nearby beaches— sections of fishing nets, cork floats, life preservers, and boat oars. The atmosphere was just exactly what tourists wanted—including *these* four tourists.

Sunset was nearly upon them and dinner that evening was from the reef. The group talked about the Treasure Fleet and what their first step would be to gain access to it. After a short while, there were no remains of two grouper sandwiches, a coconut shrimp platter and a mahi-mahi dinner. Josh would make sure this was his first t-shirt purchase before he left. The waitress cleared away the table, leaving only the drinks.

Giselle began, "Well…as you know, I was online while we were driving and I found out there is a company called Family Jewels who owns the rights to the salvage."

"You're kidding?" Eddie laughed!

"Nope. That's what it's called!" Giselle replied, laughing herself.

Josh rocked back in his seat in laughter and Nick shook his head while wiping a tear from the effects of that bombshell.

Nick said, "Only in Florida!" as they all shook off the fun moment.

Giselle, trying to be serious said, "Family Jewels is a family-owned salvage company that purchased the rights in 1996 from another company who had gone out of business or gone bankrupt or something."

"Boy the jokes that come to mind!" Josh said, still trying to suppress laughter.

Giselle reached over and slapped him on the leg. Smiling she said, "Stop it, Baker."

"But seriously guys, I think anybody can still go search and recover treasure but Family Jewels gets a cut, just like the state of Florida and most likely, we have to go through them to begin with. I think our first step is to talk to them and see what percentage their cut is and tell them our story, of course keeping the location and some other details to ourselves."

Josh offered, "And maybe it's not cut and dry. Maybe the rates are negotiable."

Giselle nodded. "That's true. We don't want to jump at the first offer."

Eddie sat up a little taller. "So Nick, what do we have? Where are we going to be looking exactly?"

Nick produced and then unfolded the nautical chart he had told the other three about. This was the chart that had hung on his wall for years as he decorated it with paper notes and pencil markings. Years back, Nick had drawn little pictures of ships and had taped them on the chart where they had been found by previous salvagers. He also had little drawings of the not yet recovered ships in positions where he believed would be the most likely spot for them to be found according to his research. And finally he showed the other three team members the *Concepcion*—the location that his grandfather had given him after finding the ribs and gold, very near present day Cape Canaveral.

Giselle looked at the location of the wreck. She then pulled out her phone and took pictures—some up close for detail and then a couple of the entire chart. She shook her head. "Being that near the Space Center presents its own set of problems. Look how close that is to the restricted area."

"Yeah but I don't know if it's always restricted or only when they are in a launch countdown."

Josh nodded. "Could be dicey. A local boat captain could answer that question."

Nick nodded, "Giselle, do you have an address for Family Jewels?" Josh and Eddie snickered one more time. She looked at them, pretending to warn them not to "go there" again.

"Yeah, they're in Melbourne Beach—not that far south."

With his hands lying on the table, Nick turned his palms up. "I think we should go there in the morning." He looked around for approval which he received with nods.

Giselle held up one finger, "But by noon I want to be on the beach! I want some Florida sun."

Nods again and they had a plan! Tomorrow they would begin their quest to recover gold—a lot of gold which had laid on the ocean floor since the year 1715! Life was good and vacation was just beginning.

The man in the '73 New Yorker had taken A1A all the way past Daytona Beach Shores to where it turns right and heads across the Intracoastal Waterway and back to the mainland. He turned around in the parking lot of the Pirates Island Mini-Golf and drove back north. At this point frustration had set in and he knew with nighttime fast approaching, his chances of spotting the VW bus were slim unless he cruised every parking lot on A1A. He drove along, casually looking around and began to think about finding a cheap place to sleep for the night and resuming his search tomorrow morning. He knew these kids were tourists and would be up and down the strip numerous times during the daytime. Being at the right place at the right time was the key. He would have to be patient.

That same night, after dinner and making plans for the next day, the kids walked from Captain Joes on the pier, back to the Vista al Mar Resort. Josh, Eddie and Nick piled into one room and Giselle had hers to herself. The boys settled in by unpacking their suitcases and hanging all the clothes they would need for the next two weeks. They also utilized the drawers for socks and underwear and then put their suitcases away in the closets. Of course, Giselle had done the same. They were very well organized, settled in and ready for two weeks of adventure balanced with equal amounts of relaxation and fun! Nick had insisted he would be the one to sleep on the floor and wouldn't have it any other way. Some spare blankets and pillows provided him with all the comforts he needed. After sleeping in a chair in a truck stop, this felt like heaven! The boys had also advised Nick that leaving his coin in the room safe would be a good idea. They would take a picture of it to show the good folks at Family Jewels. Nick agreed and would also leave the nautical chart in there as well. Better to be safe.

The man with the scrunched face and scar over his right eye had settled into a cheap motel. His money was running very low, which made his desperation level higher. He had no trouble making money any way that he could. He had tried the honest dollar approach but it seemed the dishonest method paid more per hour. Much more. He fanned the bills in his wallet and figured he had enough to sustain himself for a few more days. His last employer had stiffed him four hundred dollars after he spent two weeks in June cutting weeds along a road by a Florida subdivision. This made him lean a little further to the dishonest dollar approach. Lying in his not-so-fresh motel bed, he looked at the ceiling and made his own plans for tomorrow. A devious smile slowly spread across his face. He had a plan.

CHAPTER EIGHT

Early the next morning, the four sprang out of bed, had a good breakfast at the IHOP across the street from the resort and confirmed their plans for the day. It was going to be a hot one again so Eddie bagged some ice from the hotel for the bus' air conditioner. Melbourne Beach was their destination and permission to salvage was their objective. They would visit the offices of Family Jewels, the company that held the salvage rights to the 1715 Treasure Fleet.

From the resort, they headed south on A1A all the way past Daytona Beach Shores to where A1A turns right and crosses the Intracoastal Waterway by the Pirates Island Mini-Golf and goes back to the mainland. There they hit I-95 south which took them all the way to Melbourne at highway 192. They crossed the Intracoastal once again which put them back on historic A1A at Melbourne Beach.

As they drove along, Giselle, Josh and Nick were doing the spotting while Eddie kept his eyes on the busy tourist traffic all around him. They were looking for 1112 Atlantic Street. As they counted down the numbers on the sides of the buildings and located their destination, the team was expecting something different. Instead of a corporate office building, the address for Family Jewels put them at a place that looked more like a Tiki Bar. Family Jewels sat on the ocean side of Atlantic Street complete with a crushed-shell parking lot. It was a large hut that, once they thought about it, looked very much like a place called Family Jewels should look. The roof was a very thick layer of dried palm leaves that hung far beyond the woven outside walls of the structure. This decorative look probably covered a shingled or metal roof. The wide eaves covered a walkway that went around the entire building. On the roof were two large spheres sitting side-by-side, airbrushed to look like giant pearls. Just below them on faded sign, was painted Family Jewels Salvage Co.

Seeing the obvious insinuation, Giselle shook her head again. "My gosh…it's true—only in Florida!"

Josh, Eddie, Nick and Giselle walked up a ramp to the porch and near the business entrance of the structure. Looking across the front of the building to the other side, they could see the hut sat beside a canal. Josh peeked his head around the corner and observed that the canal led south to a marina. Family Jewels employees could literally pull their boat right up to the back door of their business, step off onto their dock and walk right inside. Pretty nice setup!

Walking past a couple of well painted Adirondack chairs, the four entered the building and hoped for the best. As they entered, the first room they saw was a receiving area set up with white rattan furniture with tropical flower cushions and slightly tacky tropical décor. It seemed they had decorated their offices with items from Alvin's Island Gift Shop. A preserved blowfish hung from the ceiling and there were bowls of seashells sitting here and there along with an alligator head or two on the floor. Josh walked over to get a good look at them. What really caught their attention, and wasn't the least bit tacky, was a glass case up against the side wall. Inside that glass case were some very interesting little treasures. They all stepped over to look at them and observed a long length of gold chain, three gold crosses, a bunch of silver coins and gold coins as well. They were all beautifully displayed on black velour and identified as having been recovered from the site of the *Capitana Nuestra Senora de la Regla*—one of the ships of the Treasure Fleet!

"Good mornin'. I'm Denise…how can I help you?" the lady said with a thick southern accent.

Giselle spoke up. "Good morning, we wanted to speak with someone regarding salvage rights and how to get… legal access to a wreck." She went straight to the point. Giselle wanted to get in the sun by noon!

Denise looked back at her with a blank stare—as if all the gears weren't turning yet this morning. She lifted her eyebrows, "OK, you want to dive one of our sites? Is that what you are saying? We have different packages. A one-day dive right up to a seven-day…"

"No, no," Nick cut her short. "We are talking about a new site—a new find. A new ship from the 1715 Fleet."

When Nick said that, they all heard a rolling chair move away from a desk in the back office. He had gotten someone's attention.

Denise looked to be in her late thirties with about three shades of blond hair, casually dressed in jean cutoffs and a peach-colored top that read *Metacumbe Island* across the front and flip-flops of course. She was well tanned and gave the appearance of being a woman who was handy outside of the office as well as inside.

Denise cocked her head and asked, "You think you have found

something, is that it?"

Nick nodded. "It's possible, yes. And we just wanted to know what the steps were to be able to do some salvage work—some snorkeling or whatever, and find out for sure."

A gentleman stepped from the back office and walked the short hallway towards them. "Hi!" he said as he walked. The man put out his hand towards Nick. "I'm Louis. Louis Cannon. Call me Lou!" He smiled.

Giselle refrained from rolling her eyes but she was beginning to feel as if she were in a Leslie Neilson movie. And the way he said it too—*Loose Cannon.*

"Hi Lou. These are my partners," Nick responded.

Introductions were made and all six stood in the greeting area in a big circle.

Lou spoke up. "I heard you say you think you have a new location, or something?"

Nick nodded enthusiastically. "Yeah, we think so!"

Lou smiled and looked over at Denise who was also smiling, if not slightly smirking. "We uh…we get quite a few people in here every week—divers, mostly amateur divers and snorkelers who float across something and think it's a treasure ship. Ninety-nine percent of the time it's a modern wreck…I'll tell ya that right up front," Lou said shaking his head sympathetically.

Denise chimed in, "What we do is take your information and we both sign what's called a "short contract". It's a little binding agreement between us that says if it turns out to be something good, we will, at that point, sit down and negotiate a full salvage contract with you. It protects us both in the short term *and* for the long term." She shrugged and smiled.

Lou looked back to Nick and then at the others inquisitively. "What is it that you think you have found?"

The four kids looked at each other and then back to Lou.

Nick laid it on him. "The *Concepcion*."

Lou's eyes opened wide and his forehead furrowed as he looked at Nick with both surprise and interest. He paused for a moment then said, "Why don't we all go back to the big office." He smiled as he pointed with his thumb.

Lou Cannon was about six foot two with a long brown ponytail that had many more strands of gray than he cared to acknowledge. Tall and lanky, Lou wore khaki cargo shorts that had to be five years old and a faded black "Diver Down" t-shirt—possibly the same age as his shorts and, just like Denise, flip flops were the work shoes of choice. It was casual day at Family Jewels.

As they stepped into the office, they all looked around at the many pictures and relics that hung on the wall. Photos with the legendary Mel Fisher, discoverer of the world-famous ships *Atocha* and *Santa Margarita.* Relics from hundreds of dives over the years adorned the seemingly fragile walls of the "hut office."

Giselle was completely enthralled with what simply hung on the walls around her. "My goodness…aren't you afraid of theft?" She asked.

Lou sat down behind his desk and shuffled a couple of things around. His wry grin said there was more to this place than meets the eye. He looked at Giselle and shook his head, "Not really." He smiled. "It's a little safer than it seems." Lou reached back and tapped on the wall. "These thatch walls…are actually twelve-inch cinderblock with the cores poured solid with concrete." He grinned. "That grass ceiling…1/8 inch galvanized metal. Windows…bulletproof and heavily wired with alarms and sensors. Same with the doors."

Josh shook his head. "I'll tell ya, it just looks like a hut from the outside. That's incredible!"

Lou pressed a button under his desk and a portion of an interior wall slid back to reveal a large flat-screen monitor that was divided into eight panels of security video feeds. He took a remote from the desk drawer. "Josh, you liked the blowfish?" He pressed a *rewind* button and then *play.* The group laughed as the video showed Josh's face drawing very close to the blowfish, creating a fish-eye effect to his face.

Lou said, "Camera's right in his mouth. Each alligator head has one too, in its glass eye, and let me show you something else." Lou pressed a couple of buttons. The monitor went to full screen and showed four young adults looking down into the glass case in the front room…from the perspective of the gold. The camera was mounted inside a decorative seashell within the case."

Eddie was impressed. "So it's a little more than what it looks like."

Lou laughed. "And there's much more. Fort Knox would like my secrets," he said. Lou held up one finger to make another point, "And it's completely category 5 hurricane proof. Certified and insured." He smiled.

Nick followed, "Well, I suppose when you display what you have here, you better protect it!"

"Absolutely! I can watch these feeds from anywhere in the world, too."

Josh was looking at a photo on the wall. "This is Mel Fisher?

You knew him?"

Lou looked at the picture fondly. "Oh yes. I worked for Mel for twelve years. I was on his boat the day we found *Atocha*." Lou shook his head as he recalled. "It was crazy…utter pandemonium when they found that first gold chain. Everyone was in the water that day. People were free diving…holding their breath, fanning the sand and finding coins and chain and emeralds. Guys were diving with one tank under their arm…it was insane!"

It was obvious this was a very big day in Lou's life and that Mel Fisher was important to him. There were many other pictures with Mel and his son, whom Mel lost to a diving accident.

Josh, Eddie, Giselle and Nick felt at home right away. They knew they were in the right place to begin their search for Nick's grandfather's discovery. The credibility was all around them.

Totally amazed, Josh said, "You have to tell us those stories sometime!"

Lou and Denise laughed. Denise responded, "There are a bunch of them."

Lou clasped his hands. He was ready to hear what they had to say. "OK guys, why don't you all have a seat and tell me what you have. Did you find something swimming or…?" He turned his palms up. Lou had heard a lot of stories from people who wanted to be treasure hunters.

Eddie gestured to Nick—it was his story. Nick cleared his throat as he sat down in front of Lou's desk. The others sat around Nick. Denise had taken a chair and pulled it close to Lou.

"Well…I'll try to make it as short as possible." He smiled.

"In 1973 my grandfather, his name was Butch Dawson…he

moved down here from Indiana and after a few months he was hired as a deck hand on a boat named *Maria*. It was an old trawler that was refurbished…refitted. The captain's name was Chuck Henderson and I guess he was a captain of all trades. He took any job that needed a boat!"

Lou laughed. "I know a lot of those captains."

"I can imagine." Nick smiled. "But it was a December night that, according to a diary from my grandpa, they were to make some kind of delivery that was way out of their comfort zone. He wrote in his diary that this would be the only time he would ever do a job like that again." Nick shrugged, "I have no idea what they did that night but it was while they were *doing* it that things got interesting for them."

Lou wobbled his head to one side. "Well…I don't want to disrespect your grandfather but shady runs like that are usually drug related or something else just as ugly."

"I know," Nick said. "No disrespect taken. I think he was leveraged into it…like he had no choice that night."

"Happens all the time down here. Could be the captain was leveraged too. That also happens," Lou said, nodding. "An offer he couldn't refuse."

Nick continued. "So they did what they did that night and sometime during the operation one of them happened to spot the ribs of a ship. I don't know who, but someone went overboard and moved the sand around and found something very cool, much like what you have in the case out there in the front room."

Josh opened his phone to his pictures file and showed Lou and Denise the coin. Denise gasped and Lou gently took the phone to examine the coin as if he were holding the coin itself in his hand.

He studied it for a second, obviously knowing exactly what it was. His eyes looked up at Nick and then back to the coin. Lou pursed his lips as he contemplated the story.

Lou said, "And your grandfather noted "ribs"… In his diary he specifically said "ribs?"

With that, Nick produced the diary of Butch Dawson. He opened it up to the page of his last entry and read the words to Lou, stopping short of reading the coordinates. Lou made a respectful effort to reach for the diary.

Nick pulled the book towards himself and said, "The only thing I didn't read to you was the location. If we can make an agreement, then I will sign your contract and share the location."

"Of course. I completely agree with you," Lou answered. He looked off in thought for a brief moment, clicking a fingernail as he did, and then said, "Here's the thing—here is the first thing that pops into my mind about this discovery by your grandfather: a three-hundred-year old ship usually has no wood left to find."

"Hmm. OK," Nick responded.

"Usually. However now, there have been exceptions with ships buried in the sands and out of reach of wood-boring animals. But also there were some ships that, in the early 1700s, were treated with a wood preservative. It was a new process invented by a man named Dr. William Crook. And basically, it was what we now call creosote, the same coal tar…oil tar type product that was still used on telephone poles in this last century."

"Interesting," Giselle said, nodding.

"It was invented to preserve the wood and to prevent shipworm and decay in the planking and structure and it really did work. So…with those two possibilities being said, it is possible that your grandfather could have found preserved ribs of an old, old ship."

Nick grinned, feeling good about the credibility being given his grandfather's story. "I have always felt that everything he wrote down was absolutely accurate."

"But let me say this also." Lou held one finger up. "It's not uncommon to find random old coins in these waters . This *is* the Treasure Coast!" He smiled. "Many, many ships have gone down on these reefs and artifacts are constantly being found."

"Right." Nick nodded, and then he shook his head. "I just think that between him and a boat captain, they saw ribs—something symmetrical that made them sure it was an old ship and then diving in and moving sand, they found treasure. For me…it just adds up." Nick was not only convinced, he was convincing.

Lou leaned back in his chair and clasped his hands across his chest. He looked at Denise and then at each one of the young people sitting in front of him. Denise knew what he was thinking. Lou nodded and said, "Yeah…it adds up for me too, Nick. At least enough to go check it out and see."

There were smiles and deep sighs all around the room as if they had all been holding their breath the whole time. Lou smiled and nodded to Denise. Lou then asked, "Where are you keeping the coin? Did you bring it with you?"

Nick nodded, "It's in the hotel room safe…along with the map that I have been studying since I was eight years old."

Lou nodded. "A good safe place."

Denise cheerfully said, "I'll get the contract ready!"

Lou followed up, "Let's do the short contract today and if we find something, then we can do the full one." Lou looked back at

Nick. "The one that gets the government their share," he added.

Eddie scooted forward in his chair. "So when do we get started?"

"Yeah, I'm ready to go!" Josh agreed.

Lou was holding a pen and was now resting his elbows on his desk. He pointed his pen at the boys and Giselle one by one. "You guys are all dive certified, right?"

You could have heard a pin drop.

Suddenly dejected, Nick looked at Lou. "No. I don't think any of us have any dive experience at all," he said, looking around at his friends.

"Is it mandatory?" Josh wondered. "Can you free dive at all?"

Lou scrunched his face. "Well there is not a law that says you can't free dive a wreck. It's done, I guess, but can you imagine how inefficient that is? We are not going out there with a bunch of dime-store snorkels looking for twenty million in gold and jewels, right?"

Nick nodded. "Right. So, what can we do?"

Lou leaned back again, flipping his pen around while he thought. "OK, we have three options: One, we sign the contract and you guys let me and my team do all the salvage work while you guys are on the boat but not in the water. You will have jobs topside, however."

Nick half smiled and shook his head as he looked at his friends, who did the same. "OK, what's the next option?"

Lou grinned, knowing they wanted to get in the water themselves. "The second option is to use our SNUBA gear."

"Giselle said, "SNUBA? What is SNUBA?"

Lou nodded, "SNUBA is hybrid form of diving that is actually pretty cool. It's half SCUBA and half Snorkel. You wear a mask and then have a regulator with a hose that runs all the way to the boat to your air supply. You have the freedom of snorkeling with the underwater time of SCUBA. We are using it more and more. It requires less training than SCUBA and provides more ease of movement and freedom to salvage."

Everyone nodded and Josh said, "That sounds pretty cool."

"What is the third option?" Nick asked.

"Well the third option would be to get your basic certification in SCUBA and in fifteen to twenty feet of water, your basic would be enough. You guys would just have to learn quickly about currents and riptides. I would be down there with you also. There are some hand signals that will have to be learned and you are not just diving…you are diving and working. There is a big difference. Whether you do SCUBA or SNUBA, it's going to be a whole new world for you down there."

Giselle asked, "So there is some training for SNUBA, you said?"

"Well, there are some quick-dollar tourist trap places where you can go and dive the reefs. They only do a quick orientation and then you are in the water looking at fish. But for salvaging…oh yeah, I require it. You guys have to be comfortable in the water to wreck dive and especially to salvage. I mean in that shallow depth, it will be like diving in a deep pool, add in the currents and tides but I require that you have some training before you jump off one of my boats."

"OK," Nick said. He looked around at his friends. I'm thinking this SNUBA deal sounds best."

Josh and Eddie had plans to do a dive course while on their Florida road trip but with the way things had changed, and the fact that time was now a factor, a quick SNUBA course would be sufficient for now and would serve the purpose perfectly.

Eddie nodded to Josh, "Yep...SNUBA it is!"

Lou opened his palms and said, "Perfect! I have a good friend who can get you guys all set up. His name is Ray and he is good. You will learn tidal terms and patterns and about the coastal currents and such. Only thing is, he is up in New Smyrna Beach at Ponce Inlet."

Josh was wringing his hands, ready to go. "That's perfect. We are staying in Daytona Beach. When can we get started?"

"I'll take your numbers and ask him to call you. He's a pretty busy guy this time of year, but I will see what strings I can pull," Lou replied.

"You'll find out how good your friendship really is!" Nick joked, standing up to relax and look at the relics around the room.

"That's right!" Lou laughed.

Denise walked into the big office with a one-page document that took about one minute to look over and sign. Once that was all done, they all shook hands and patted backs and a new alliance was formed. Lou was quite excited. He knew with his good sense and experience if two people, one of whom was a boat captain, had seen the symmetrical pattern of ribs of an old ship and then found gold coins between those ribs, that there was a good chance this could very well be a new and historic discovery.

With the paperwork all signed, Lou then said, "Alright, let's have a look at the coordinates now."

Nick opened the diary and flipped to the page they needed. Lou looked at the numbers and mumbled them to himself before going to a chart rack to retrieve the proper one. Opening it up, he used his fingers and his knowledge of the coastline to quickly locate the waypoint on the nautical chart. He slid his fingers along lines of latitude and longitude and then tapped the chart twice. "Generally…right there!" He said. "Just off the Canaveral Peninsula about eighteen hundred feet offshore."

Nick grinned and nodded. "Yeah, that's right where I figured, too. I've been looking at these numbers since I was eight years old."

Lou looked at Nick and nodded. He knew just how Nick felt. "You are aware that this is your life's mission. This could be life-changing."

"I sure hope so!" Nick said, looking at his friends with an excited smile.

Lou studied the chart for a moment and shook his head once. "Only thing is…it's real close to the Cape and their security zone. During a launch it is called a "keep out zone." I'll have to check with them and see what laws are in place up there."

Nick nodded. "OK. Sounds good."

He had confidence in Lou.

After a little more hand shaking and a couple of treasure stories later, Nick, Josh, Eddie and Giselle were ready to get back up the road to Daytona. Giselle felt that she just may make her twelve o'clock appointment with the beach. The boys would be anxiously awaiting a call from Ray, the dive instructor, and life was good. They felt as if they had gotten a lot accomplished for only being in town about thirteen hours. A quick stop at a gas station for another bag of ice and a full round of cold coffee drinks and they were back on I-95 north.

The man had signed in to the shabby little motel as Paco Villarreal. Paco slept late that morning. He saw no sense in getting up early. He figured those kids would be up and down the strip many times today and all he had to do was wait. That gorgeous little red and white VW bus would be easy to spot. It was just a matter of sitting and watching. He decided to head north on A1A somewhere popular on the strip and do his recon from that point. He had thought about his plan and, once he knew where they were staying, he would begin to implement it. This was not Paco Villarreal's first time at trying to share someone else's wealth. He was quite the veteran and his police record showed it. He had a long string of "breaking and entering" arrests ever since he was fourteen years old. Old habits being hard to break, he was now in his early forties trying to figure things out, financially speaking. Paco was having a very hard time finding his occupation in the world and he wasn't even a good criminal—but he was willing to give it one more try. He just hoped these kids were right—that there was a nice pile of those Spanish *Escudos* waiting to be found.

Paco was right about one thing—it didn't take long to spot the bus. He let it pass him and then pulled in behind, keeping a distance of about two-hundred feet. It didn't matter where they were going this time—Paco had a full tank of gas!

CHAPTER NINE

Setting the parking brake at the self-park lot, Eddie reminded his friends to lock the doors as they exited. Josh opened the sliding side door for the riders in the back. Nick jumped right out and again, Giselle reached for Josh's hand as she stepped out. She smiled a little as she looked at Josh. His stomach fluttered a bit at this obvious flirt and he couldn't help but wonder, *is she messing with me?*

Squinting his eyes in the midday sun, Eddie asked, "Do you guys want to get a bite to eat before the beach or…"

"Not this girl! I'm gettin' in my suit and heading straight to the sand!" Giselle said.

Josh nodded in agreement, "I figured I would get something at the pool bar in about an hour."

It was agreed that it was beach time! From the self-park lot, they could hear the gentle surf and it was calling to all of them. The rhythmic pulse of the waves crashing on the beach was music to their West Virginia ears.

Taking the elevator up to the seventh floor, the four young people went to their rooms and planned to meet in the hallway outside of their neighboring doors. Nick put the diary back into the hotel room safe with the map and coin. The three boys jumped into their swim trunks and then waited five more minutes for Giselle in the hallway.

As she stepped from her room, Eddie asked, shaking his head, "What takes girls so long?"

Giselle smiled, "We have to look good for you guys," she replied. "It's your guys' fault…not ours!" Her eyes flipped from Eddie to Josh.

Giselle was carrying a beach bag full of essentials and wearing a V-neck, transparent white swimsuit cover up. Underneath, it could be seen that she had on a bright yellow two-piece bikini. Flip flops were on her feet and sunglasses sat on top of her head. She was all set.

The boys, on the other hand, had no bag, white towels over their shoulders and any old t-shirt, along with what looked like fairly new swim trunks. Eddie carried a football and Nick was flipping a Frisbee up in the air and catching it. They walked back to the elevators two by two. Josh chose Giselle as a walking partner.

On the ride down to the main floor, a thought occurred to Giselle. "Ya know, I was thinking…there's really no sense in Nick sleeping on the floor when I have an extra bed sitting there doing nothing but acting as a suitcase storage table."

Josh was shocked and looked at Giselle. Maybe his expression didn't hide it. *Was she really implying that Nick could take the extra bed in her room?*

Giselle picked up on the bad choice of phrasing her statement. "I mean, one of you guys may as well use it and let Nick take one of your beds." She looked at Eddie and then Josh.

Nick shrugged. "I tell ya, I didn't sleep bad on the floor last night. It was fine for me. I'm just happy to be under the roof of this nice place. Coming down here with six hundred dollars in my pocket, I was sure I would be staying somewhere much less elegant." Just when he finished his statement, the elevator doors opened to the relaxing sights and comforting sounds of the lobby's waterfalls and extensive greenery.

Eddie looked around as they exited and said, smiling, "We'll figure out sleeping arrangements later. Let's hit the beach!"

The four young tourists now made their way out the back doors past the beautiful pool, the bar, and down the steps to the beach. All four smiled as they got their first daytime view of their back yard for the next two weeks. As they looked around for the best spot, footballs were flying through the air as well as Frisbees. One dad was catching as his daughter wind-milled fastballs to him forty-three feet away, the bright yellow softball popping every time it hit his mitt. They could smell the scents of the beach—the salt air in the slight breeze, the coconut fragrance of the many different brands of suntan lotion and sunscreen, and the empanada stand just to the left. The sun was straight overhead and it was hot!

As they took their spot on the sand, the boys unrolled towels, and Giselle removed her essentials from her bag. She spread a large beach blanket just for her!

"Check, one-two, check, one-two."

The four looked back up towards a neighboring resort. An acoustic guitarist was sound-checking his mic for an afternoon session. *Perfect* they thought! Live music on the beach and the sweet relaxing vibe of vacation. They all knew that this time off was going to be great as worries and obligations began to distance themselves from their minds as only the beach can do. With their mornings work completed, it was truly chill time! Giselle pulled off her cover-up and began to spread on the Hawaiian Tropics while the boys tried not to stare.

Paco's scarred right eye twitched as he watched the four kids walk down the steps to the beach from his stool at the pool bar. He had followed them into the Vista al Mar Resort just a few minutes earlier, and watched as the elevator went to the seventh floor. That much he knew already. He grinned, and now it was time to do some work. He needed some supplies for his plan and he knew he would have a couple of hours minimum while the four *gringos* sunned themselves. He also knew that when the time came, he would need some help. Taking his phone from his pocket, Paco stepped away from the bar and made his way to a walkway that was beautifully lined with palms and sea oats. It meandered its way around to the side of the resort and from the privacy of that area he made a phone call, explained a few things, and then clicked off the phone. Assistance would be on the way soon. Back into the resort he went.

Paco entered from the walkway on the side of the building. Familiarizing himself with the resort, he noted the positions of cameras and the locations of unlocked doors. Some hallways had more cameras than others but, after taking a nice stroll of the lower level, he finally found the hallway he was looking for. This particular hallway was for housekeeping and janitorial services and the double doors that led to it were not locked. Paco entered as if he knew what he was doing and as if he were supposed to be there.

He passed the supply room which had shelves of detergents, cleaners, mops, rags, buckets, squeegees and anything else you could need for cleaning. He would come back to that room if he needed to. He passed lots of closets with utility sinks, more buckets and dust mops and then found the room he was looking for. The laundry room. He peered through the small window in the door and saw front-load washers and dryers doing their thing. He saw no one inside, so he entered to look around and find what he needed. It didn't take him long.

Along a back wall, behind the washing and drying facility, was a rack with many sets of maintenance coveralls hanging up, just as he had hoped. He quickly ran down the row looking for the right size. Once found, he pulled them on and his plan was beginning to take shape. Now, looking absolutely official and properly dressed to be in the area, he could look around and find the other supplies he needed. Not a moment too soon, Paco heard the door open in the front of the room on the other side of the washers and dryers. Putting on his game face, Paco walked towards the exit. Checking one of the machines was a younger Latin girl who smiled at the man with the scar over his right eye. Her nametag read "Isabel."

"Como estas?" She smiled

"Bien." Paco smiled, nodded, and then exited.

Must be another new-hire, she thought.

Passing the first test, Paco now walked back down the hallway towards a door he saw earlier, which was ajar. The door was labeled "Maintenance" and he could see it was just what he was looking for. Paco opened the door and stepped inside. Along the wall to the right were hanging tool belts. He grabbed one and snapped it around his waist. He was ready! He turned to leave and, on a desk beside the door, he saw what would be a perfect addition to his disguise: a name tag. It would complete the uniform and be the icing on the cake to make him look official. His name would be "Teddy." Paco looked at the name, shrugged one shoulder and pinned it to his coveralls. He grabbed an empty garbage bag from a basket and left the room.

Now in the hallway, he stepped towards the original double-doors that he had come through a few minutes earlier. Thinking he had done it with minimal observance, a suit and tie came through the doors and looked at him. Mr. Suit and Tie held up a hand to stop him. Paco came to a halt in front of the manager. The man squinted while looking at him.

He said, "You're new?"

"Ah, yes sir. Brand new."

The manager smiled. "Well, welcome. It's nice to have you!" He continued without further small talk. "I have an issue on floor six that I need taken care of quickly. It's just a problem with the vertical blinds but it's a Business Rewards customer. Can you knock that out for me? Room 626."

Looking at the manager convincingly, Paco said, "Yes sir…I'll get that for you."

"Ahh…thank you so much!" the manger said, and then looked at his name tag. Confusion replaced appreciation on his face. "Teddy? We have another Teddy?"

Paco's stomach knotted. He thought quickly and replied, "Teddy Martinez. Mexico's finest!" He smiled and stuck out his hand, being as jovial as possible.

The manager shook his hand as he looked at "Teddy. Well…it's good to meet you…Teddy."

"Yes sir. Good to meet you too and I will take care of those blinds for you. Right now!" he said as he walked away, patting his tool belt.

The manager stood there for a moment, thinking, and then shook his head and went on his way to put out the next fire, as managers do.

"Teddy" used a back maintenance elevator to go to the sixth floor. He thought it would be a good idea to go to room 626 and fix the blinds so the manager would not get any more calls on the matter and get suspicious of him. It would also be a good test of his disguise. He figured he had a couple hours to kill anyway while the kids sunned themselves.

Once done with room 626, "Teddy" left the room with a very happy Business Rewards customer patting him on the back and stuffing twenty dollars in his pocket. "Teddy" thanked him and proceeded down the hallway, only to run into the hotel concierge.

"Oooh perfect…I'm ssso happy to ssseee you!" the skinny, well-groomed man lisped.

My goodness Paco thought, *this guy sounds like a tire going flat.*

The concierge took a stance and pointed down the hallway. "I have a real piece of work in 655 who doesn't like the way the water isss coming out of one of hisss faucetsss." He rolled his eyes like a teenage girl.

Paco nodded then smirked. "I'll take care of it," he said.

"Ooohhh you're my lifesssaver!" He hugged Paco.

Paco shook his head and walked away. The concierge swished down the hall in the opposite direction. Paco thought, *By the end of the day I should be employee of the month!*

After cleaning out the faucet screen in room 655, Teddy, the new maintenance guy, decided to find a bathroom and get out of his uniform for a while. He needed to become Paco again. He needed to be able to keep an eye on the kids and, when they were ready to come in for the day, he would be ready.

This would be a breeze if I only had a master electronic key, he thought. He would keep his eyes open for opportunities. A key to access any room was the only thing missing from his maintenance disguise and arsenal, and would facilitate the hardest part of his plan—entry into the room. Either way he was going to make it happen. Patience *was* the key for now.

The four tourists were in total relaxation mode. After about forty-five minutes, Giselle had flipped over and was now sunning her backside, sand sticking to her oily skin. Josh, who was lying closest to her, did the same soon after and turned to face her with his sunglasses on. Eddie was still on his back and looked to be sleeping, Nick had found his way to the ocean. At twenty-one years old, it was his first time in warm saltwater and he was enjoying it immensely. The guitarist was working his second set with a James Taylor tune about Carolina and the shifting offshore breeze wafted the scent of empanadas towards their towels.

Josh's phone rang, snapping him out of his euphoria of peace and fantasy. He reached for it over on the corner of Giselle's blanket. Eddie rose up and looked over, embarrassingly wiping a spot of drool from the corner of his mouth. He had been out cold!

"Hello." Josh answered.

"Hi, I was calling for Josh?" the man said.

"Speaking," Josh responded.

"Hey man, this is Ray, the dive instructor. Lou Cannon gave me your contact."

Josh cleared his throat and sat up to talk. "Oh, yeah…hi Ray, how are you?"

"I'm cool, hey listen…Lou said there are four of you, is that right?"

"Yes…four. Three guys and one pretty girl." Josh just let that fly for whatever reason.

Ray laughed and Giselle rose up on her elbows and snickered.

"Well it's always cool to be in the company of a pretty girl, right?"

"For sure," Josh replied, a little embarrassed, as Giselle looked over at him.

"Hey look, I can work you guys in but it's going to be a couple of days, does that jive with your plans?"

Josh shrugged a shoulder. "Yeah…I think that's fine. So that would be Monday?"

"Yeah man…Monday at eight o'clock in the morning. That cool with you guys?"

"That's cool with us, Ray. Thanks for working us in."

"Yeah, it's good that you dudes are cool with Lou…It's my busy season."

"Appreciate it again, Ray. See you Monday."

"That's cool guys. See you then!"

Josh tapped off the phone. "He likes the word *cool*," He said, raising his eyebrows.

"Monday morning?" Eddie asked, getting the gist of the conversation.

"Yeah at eight o'clock." Josh replied.

"Cool," Eddie joked.

"Two days of lying in the sun!" Giselle smiled, and laid her head back down on a rolled up towel. Josh could see his reflection in her sunglasses. He wondered if she was looking back.

On the patio area of the resort next door to the Vista al Mar, a middle aged Italian man with a noticeable lazy eye sat smoking a cigar and listening to a talented guitarist do an impressive acoustic version of Sinatra's *Summer Wind*. In the man's hand was an amber drink that he sipped as he looked out across the sand towards the water. He was a regular at the Playa del Sol Resort Patio. It was a very large multi-tiered wooden deck with lots of tropical plants and décor. There was always beach music, the atmosphere was good, the drinks were never watered down, and management gave Tony and his friends preferential seating and treatment. Though the patio had changed names a few times through the years, he had done a lot of "business" there. The waiter approached him. He had known him for most of that time.

"Let me get you a refill, Tony," The waiter said to the silver-haired man.

Tony grinned, nodded and swished his hand. "Knock yourself out Geno."

Tony also liked to come to the patio just to contemplate

whatever was on his mind at the time. As the waiter walked away, Tony shifted in his chair and the sun glistened off of his necklace. Tony had had it made in the 1970s. Hanging on a heavy gold chain was a beautiful and very mint condition Spanish *Escudo*. Tony had paid nothing for it back in the day. The man he obtained it from had paid dearly.

CHAPTER TEN

Nick walked from the water and returned to the beach towels with an air of relaxation and contentment. Eddie was still on his back but resting up on his elbows, looking around at the sights. He said, "I was just going in—how's the water?"

Nick's first time in the ocean had overwhelmed him. "It's great. It is so much warmer than Lake Michigan! And the fish just swim all around you!"

Eddie nodded, smiling and happy for Nick. "Yeah, well I'm roasting…time to cool off."

"You *look* like you are roasting. Maybe a little sunscreen is a good idea there, white boy," Nick jabbed at Eddie.

Eddie grinned.

"A little sun goes a long way down here," Giselle warned. "Better be careful…you too Baker."

Josh looked over at her. "What are you, my mom?" He grinned.

"Hardly," she replied, smiling.

Eddie sat up and scanned the gentle waves that were lapping the shoreline. "I'm going to hit it for a few minutes and then flip over to get my back."

Nick said, "I'm going up to the room to get my wallet. The smell of those empanadas are killing me. You guys want any?"

Everyone agreed, gave their orders and offered to pay but Nick waved them off, appreciative that the kids would take no money for letting him stay in the room. That really had helped his meager budget. Eddie had, however, asked Nick to bring the sunscreen back down. He was going to take him up on his advice.

Nick walked past the empanada stand towards the short set of stairs that led up to the pool deck. Paco stood at the corner of the pool deck disguised to blend in, wearing sunglasses, a tank top and shorts. He also carried a beach bag with the straps over his shoulder. He had the tourist look.

Nick walked the length of the deck and entered the rear of the opulent resort and proceeded to the elevators. Paco trailed behind him but not too close to be noticed. As soon as the elevator doors closed behind Nick, Paco pressed the button for the next available car, hoping it would arrive quickly. He got his wish. Behind him, he heard a *ding* as the doors opened. Paco darted into the elevator and quickly pressed the number 7 and the *door close* button. A mother running with a beach bag, a cooler, a boogie board and two young children shouted "Wait!" but Paco would not oblige.

At the seventh floor the doors opened and Nick stepped out of the elevator and proceeded down the hallway to his room. A few seconds later a different elevator on the same floor opened and a maintenance man named "Teddy" stepped out in coveralls. Teddy's beach gear was now in his bag. The beach bag was a canvas type that Teddy now had turned inside out to hide the palm tree design. It now passed as a maintenance bag. Nick heard the second elevator behind him but thought nothing of it. Teddy sped up his pace as Nick slowed, looking for his room number. As Nick approached the door to his room, he heard the steps behind him and glanced back to see a resort maintenance man who was most likely on a service call. Nick did a double-take, nodded and so did the man in coveralls.

The Vista al Mar had a unique number keypad system on their doors. Each guest can create their own entry code at the front desk at check-in or they can keep the random computer generated code. The boys had picked their code. Nick entered the four digits and stepped into his room as the maintenance man passed behind him.

At the same time, Teddy knew this was his only opportunity and timing was everything. The young boy he was following glanced back at him but kept walking. The maintenance man grinned at him and nodded. At just the right moment, Teddy slowed his pace, pulled his phone from his pocket. Held it at arms length towards the door and touched the record button. The boy, now focused on the keypad, had no idea he was being video recorded while tapping in his code. Teddy grinned and kept walking.

Nick entered the room and noticed that housekeeping had already done their thing. Beds were made, fresh towels hung on the racks and the ladies had even made "towel-swans" which were centered on each bed. Nick grinned—he had never seen that before.

In the small hallway that led to the bathroom was a double closet and in that closet was the room safe. Nick slid the bi-fold closet door open, leaned in and entered the code to get his wallet. Safe and sound inside was Nick's Spanish *Escudo* and his folded map along with his wallet and some keys from the others. Nick grabbed his wallet, closed the safe door and double-checked to make sure it was locked. He then proceeded out of the room, down the elevator and straight to the empanada stand.

Teddy sat down in the seventh floor stairwell and opened the videos on his dated but functional phone. He tapped the most recent one and it immediately began to playback. Being just four seconds in length, he watched it and then watched it again. It appeared that he was able to capture three of the four numbers. He did not have the last number. *Not a big problem*, he thought, but it would cost him a little more time getting inside the room with a maximum of ten numbers to try. Teddy zoomed his smart phone video as far as it would go and tapped it to play, once again, to capture the entry code. 0-3-2 was what he had and then Nick's body blocked the last number.

As Nick approached the empanada stand on the beach, he looked across the sand and saw the other three. It was then that he remembered the sunscreen that Eddie had requested. "Oh man!" he said to himself, and spun a three-sixty to go back upstairs. It was the least he could do.

Teddy smiled, nodded, closed his phone and proceeded out of the seventh floor stairwell. As he walked down the hallway he watched the door numbers go by until he got back to the boys' room. The corridor was empty and he got started right away.

On the keypad he entered *0-3-2-0*. Nothing

He tried again. *0-3-2-1*. Nothing.

0-3-2-2. Still nothing!

He heard a door close down the corridor. He leaned his head

back and saw an older gentleman walking towards the elevators.

On his fourth try he got it! *0-3-2-3.* The electronic lock clicked and pulled the deadlock back. Teddy grinned—very proud of himself and his foolproof plan. He had pulled it off without a hitch.

He opened the door and slipped inside, closing it behind him. A quick glance around the room indicated to him that these kids were organized and orderly. They did not have clothes lying in disarray and suitcases opened and messy. This told him that the *Escudo* would be put away somewhere safe. Probably *in* the safe. But he would check the drawers first.

Rummaging, he found nothing. He didn't bother to close the drawers—he had to hurry!

Nick approached the elevators and pushed the *up* arrow. With four elevators clustered together, the wait time was minimal. His elevator opened and he stepped in and pushed the button for the seventh floor. He was on his way back upstairs.

Teddy now had two problems—one he knew about and one he didn't just yet. He knew the safe had an electronic lock like the entry door. He didn't know Nick was on his way.

Teddy opened the closet door and examined the lock. A four number system just like the door he just opened. A quick prayer as he crossed his heart, hoping the code would be the same.

0-3-2-3. The lock buzzed and opened. He smiled and even laughed at his accomplishment. "Ah…the lack of wisdom in our youth these days," he said softly to himself. "Same code on both doors."

Teddy's eyes widened as he looked inside. The beautiful *Escudo* was laying right in front of him…and something he hadn't expected—a map! A nautical chart folded and stuffed in the small safe alongside the coin. Teddy stuffed the coin into his pocket immediately and then unfolded the chart. He saw years of notes and markings that Nick had worked so hard on. So much research and so much studying and so much hope and anticipation was now in the hands of a thief! He had done *none* of the work but the *Escudo* and the chart were his! He simply had to follow the dotted line to the X in the sand, so to speak. Now it was time to go! He quickly folded the chart, pulled on his coveralls and turned to leave.

Ding.

The elevator doors opened and Nick stepped out. He walked quickly towards their room to get the sunscreen he had forgotten. Nick had gotten yet another whiff of the empanadas a few minutes earlier and was now quite hungry! Just as he reached out his hand to tap in the number code, the door jerked open from the other side. Nick gasped when he saw the maintenance man in front of him. His tag read "Teddy".

"Teddy's" eyes flew open in surprise and he stuttered for something to say. Jerking his thumb over his shoulder he squeezed past Nick and said, "Your faucet is fixed, Senor!" He didn't wait for a response, but proceeded quickly down the corridor to the stairwell once again.

Nick watched him walk away, quite confused, as they had not ordered maintenance for a faucet leak. He watched him for just a moment and remembered seeing the man just a few minutes ago. He then shook his head and stepped inside. That's when he knew something was wrong. Clothes were pulled out of drawers and the room was a rifled mess! Nick's thoughts immediately flashed to his coin. He ran to the closet. He was stunned! The safe was open and a quick glance told him the coin was gone along with his chart! He knew it was the maintenance guy!

Nick ran from the room and looked down the hall. The stairway door had just slammed closed. Nick took off at a sprint. He reached the stairway in seconds and flung the door open. Taking three steps at a time, he lurched his way down the stairs. He heard the maintenance man shuffling his way down as quickly as possible. Teddy had known the elevator was not an option.

Nick screamed at the man, "Hey!!! Hey!!! Stop!!!" as he continued to take three at a time. He was gaining on the man.

Teddy looked up the stairway to see where the boy was. He was catching up with him! He had to get creative. As he hit the landing to Floor 2, he dashed out of the door and into the hallway. He had to try some evasive maneuvers in the corridors in order to lose the boy. Teddy ran down a short section of hallway and turned right into a long corridor that would take them to Building 2 of the complex. Perfect, if he could get out of sight in time!

Nick heard the door slam on a level below him. As he jumped from the stairs he stopped on the landing that he thought the noise came from. He burst through it and looked left and right down the hallway. He thought he heard something to the left and off he went. He ran a short distance and came to a hallway that turned right. It was a long corridor and at the end of it was a door. Just reaching that door was Teddy the maintenance man!

"Heyyy!!!" Nick yelled, "I want my coin!" Nick once again took off at a sprint towards the man, anger, deep anger, was embedded in his face for the man who would dare steal this family heirloom! It was priceless to Nick just because it had come from his grandfather.

The maintenance man grinned with malevolence and reached for the door. It was locked! He looked over to the right and saw the card reader. There would be no entering Building 2 without a keycard. Teddy knew he was trapped. He turned and faced the boy who was running at him. With his head down and his eyes up he reached for his maintenance bag. Out came his ace in the hole—the Glock. Desperate times call for desperate measures. Teddy lifted the gun and when Nick saw it, he dug his toes into the carpet as hard as he could to stop himself. Fear enveloped him as Teddy, without hesitation, pointed and squeezed!

Nicks efforts at stopping were so good that he blew out the front strap on his flip-flop just as he heard the report of the pistol and simultaneously saw the flash of the gun. Nick went head-over-heels in the hallway and came down with his head hitting the baseboard on the right side of the corridor. He lay there motionless as Teddy the maintenance man complimented himself on such a good shot at a moving target. A bit of blood now oozed from Nick's head as his eyesight slowly faded to black. Teddy put the next bullet into the door lock mechanism and disappeared into Building 2 and then outside.

On the patio area of the resort next door to the Vista al Mar, a middle-aged Italian man with a noticeable lazy eye was certain he heard the unmistakable sound of a gunshot. He spun around in his chair and looked towards the hotel next door.

CHAPTER ELEVEN

It had been about thirty minutes since Nick had left the beach. Josh, Eddie and Giselle didn't give it too much thought until they heard multiple sirens screaming down A1A, stopping in front of their resort. Again, their intuition told them something was wrong. Grabbing their towels and beach bag, they took off at a trot through the sand, up the short set of steps to the pool deck and into the resort. Looking towards the south end of the lobby, they saw the police had "Crime Scene" tape blocking an exit that would put them between the two buildings of the resort. As they observed the scene for a moment, they were surprised to see Nick walking by behind the taped-off area, being escorted by FDLE detectives as well as some uniformed officers and paramedics.

"Wait, there they are now," Nick said to the officials.

Nick had a head bandage and an obvious goose egg near his right temple, but looked otherwise healthy, to the relief of his friends.

Nick's entourage slowed as the officials looked at each other and then the three young people who were approaching the "crime scene" tape to check on their friend. One of the officers keyed his lapel mic and said something the kids could not hear, but just then the officers escorting Nick stopped and let them greet him.

With his palms turned up, Josh asked in disbelief, "Nick…what happened?"

"We got robbed, guys! I caught a maintenance guy coming from our room. He took the coin and the chart! I don't know what else…I haven't been back up there."

Giselle gasped and covered her mouth.

"Your head—what happened?" Eddie asked with concern as he stepped closer to the tape.

"Blew out a flip-flop running for the guy. Hit my head on the wall or something."

The officials glanced at each other, giving the indication that the what-happened-party was over and it was time to take Nick back to the station.

A man who looked to be in charge of the situation stepped towards Josh, Eddie and Giselle and introduced himself as Detective Crossman. He was dressed in casual tan slacks, a blue dress shirt and a camel jacket. His sunglasses sat on top of his head.

He spoke with the baritone voice of a good radio personality. "We are going to ask your friend some questions and then he will be coming back to join you. He refused hospital treatment—said he didn't have insurance and that he felt OK anyway. Paramedics did the preliminary concussion test on him and he does seem to be fine. Later tonight if he gets dizzy or nauseous, or his pupils get large, get him to the hospital, insurance or not."

The three friends nodded.

"Thank you," Giselle responded.

The man continued, "We will most likely have him get together with a forensic artist later on to see if we can come up with a face for this guy. As a matter of fact, why don't you three come with us? We will get your information too, establish the timeline and collect phone numbers. I know you weren't with him at the time but maybe you saw something you haven't realized yet."

"Happy to do it," Eddie said.

The three friends ducked under the yellow tape and walked to where Nick was standing. The entourage then proceeded down the hallway to a predetermined room which they referred to as the crisis center. Josh was pretty sure it was also used for weddings as well as mini-conventions.

Nick looked back at his friends—happy to see them. "Sure could use a Tylenol."

Josh and Eddie snickered as they walked, but at the same time they were pretty bummed at losing the chart and the coin.

After the police, the detectives and the four young treasure hunters entered the crisis center, a door closed behind them and the standard questions were asked. Detectives have a way of asking a person the same question many different ways to make sure that person isn't filling in the gaps of their story with fiction. It's called filtering the facts—and it takes forever. A few hours later the doors opened and the four friends were free to go. Nick was advised that the next morning he needed to make himself available for the sketch artist. It had to be done as quickly as possible while the image was still fresh in his mind. Nick assured the detectives that the image was forever burned into his mind and tomorrow morning after breakfast would be perfect.

In the early evening the reunited foursome sat at a hi-top table out by the pool bar. The sun was still about three hours from going down and the hottest part of the day was behind them. The shadow of the resort provided a great deal of relief from the sweltering summer day and a slight onshore breeze provided freshness for those who sat outside sipping something cold. The crowd was small, as most guests were still somewhere between their afternoon shower and nap, and before dinner or appetizers at the pool bar.

A few feet away from the four kids was a middle-aged slender gentleman sitting on a barstool. He was wearing a Panama hat, pale yellow slacks and a tropical shirt. He was flamboyant and appeared to be quite a storyteller. He was doing the best he could with a cute young bartender who was serving him slushy drinks. In the shallow end of the pool was a mother with her two children who simply didn't want to leave the pool today. At a separate hi-top table sat a gentleman who was drinking something amber in color and thumbing through a program booklet for a local dog track. He was making notes as he picked his greyhounds for that night. The gentleman had olive skin and a noticeable lazy eye. He wore black slacks and a white v-neck pullover shirt. Aside from those folks, the deck was pretty quiet for the time being. Later on would be a different story.

"I've seen him before," Nick struggled, staring towards the ocean. "He was right in my face as he came out of the door and even right at that moment, I knew I had seen him somewhere. It was hard to put it together—knowing that I had seen him but watching him leave our room as a maintenance man. I was just—startled."

A waitress placed a sampler appetizer platter down at their table and refilled their iced teas.

"It's terrible to have lost the chart and especially the coin," Giselle said. "I got pictures of the chart but the coin—that came from your grandpa."

Nick looked up at her with sadness in his eyes and nodded. "Yeah, that had a lot of sentimental value ."

Josh added, "What's worse is the chart is now in someone else's hands. We are not the only ones to know the location of the ship—the *Concepcion*."

Eddie was shaking his head. "The question is *how*? How in the world would someone have found out that we had that chart and coin? We haven't told anyone besides Lou Cannon and his wife, Denise. Who could have found out about it from the time we met at Columbia, South Carolina, to Daytona Beach?"

Josh picked up a conch fritter and dipped it into an orange-colored sauce. "You don't think Lou…"

"No, no, no." Eddie waved off that idea very quickly. "Family Jewels is a little quirky but they are a professional and reputable company. I'm sure Lou is tight lipped," Eddie replied.

Nick was chewing on his thumbnail and staring off at nothing other than the sea. He was still trying to remember where he had seen that face.

Giselle put two coconut shrimp and a very large onion ring on her small plate. "Ya know…speaking of Lou, we should call him. It's my opinion that this search for the *Concepcion* needs to start as soon as possible, even if it has to start without us."

"Without us?" Josh exclaimed. "We have to be there. We have

to be a part of it."

"I know, Baker, I want to be a part of it too, but let me remind you guys that the bad guys aren't going to wait. They don't apply for permits and permission. Robbers are gonna rob, and they are going to get on it fast."

Nick looked over at Giselle. "You're right, Giselle. They will."

And at that moment, Nick's eyes flew open. "Oh my gosh! I remember! The welcome center at the Florida-Georgia line! It's him! It's the guy who was sitting at the next table over from us at the rest area. The scrunched face and the scar over his right eye, and he had lines all over his face. I remember his features seemed prominent—hard to forget. He was… uncommon!"

Josh looked at him seriously. "Are you sure, Nick?"

"Positive! I am absolutely positive! It was the same guy who was right in my face coming out of our hotel room."

Mr. Panama Hat took a break from his stories long enough to give the foursome a look. He seemed to give Nick a little more time—noticing the bandage on his head or possibly overhearing what Nick had just said.

Eddie thought about the scene at the welcome center and what they had discussed at the table and then added, grimacing, "Makes sense and do you remember what you did at the welcome center?"

Nick nodded slightly, realizing his mistake. "I pulled out the coin," he said regrettably.

"At that point, he must have seen it and started paying close attention to our conversation," Josh said. "It's just bad luck."

Giselle swallowed a small bite of shrimp and then said, "He

would have had to have followed us all the way here to the resort! All the way from the Florida line. A little creepy, I gotta tell you."

"Think! Think, think," Nick said, snapping his fingers lightly and staring blankly out to sea again. "Did anyone of us see him walk out to the parking lot? See him get into a car? Anything?"

A light went on in Josh's mind. "I do. I do remember that guy! He got into an old car—a very long car and I remember it smoked when he started it up. He was parked beside the garbage can when I went to throw away the plastic ice bag."

Giselle leaned towards Josh and slapped her hand on his knee and squeezed. "What color? What color was the car, Josh?"

Mr. Panama Hat looked over again.

Josh thought for a moment as Nick stared at him, hoping he could remember.

"Gold. It was that old gold color they used back in the 70s. And long. That car must have been 25 feet long! I remember because it smoked so badly when he started it up that I took a second look. I think I even fanned it away from my face."

Eddie sat up tall and said, "Now we are getting somewhere! Very long 70s era gold car that smokes! Scrunched-face, dark-skinned man behind the wheel."

"With a scar over his right eye," Nick finished. "He looked very Spanish."

"We have to go cruising. We have to look for that car here on the strip somewhere," Josh said.

Giselle shook her head. "He's not going to stay here. He's going to be gone."

"Why?" Eddie asked. "The gold is here. He has the map and he is going to be looking."

Giselle smirked. "I just think you would be more likely to find him down by Cocoa Beach, closer to the ship location. And to stay so near the scene of the crime would be stupid."

"Maybe," Eddie said. "But for tonight, I bet he is still right here close to us. No one ever said that criminals are smart, ya know. Think about it. His room would be paid for the day so he will stay there tonight and possibly move tomorrow. We can find him by then."

Nick suggested, "So we wait until it's dark and go cruising the strip. I'd say we are looking at the small motels—the little cheap joints."

"I'd say you're right," Josh followed up.

Nick added, "We can't forget this guy has a gun—and he will use it."

"We should call Detective Crossman and give him all this new information" Giselle said. "He could have a hundred cops looking for this car."

Nick looked worried about doing that. "Here's the thing with that—I don't want my chart and the gold coin to go into an evidence bag for the next three years while they try this guy in court. Let's try to locate him tonight by ourselves and if we don't have any luck, we can call Crossman in the morning."

Giselle nodded. "You have a good point and that sounds like a plan! But you will also need a plan for when and if you find him— keeping in mind once again that he has a gun and we don't."

Nick shook his head, still flustered this guy had the nerve to take his prize possession. "That *Escudo* was a gift from my grandfather. He found it. He discovered the ship's location, and I want it back!"

It was quiet for a moment.

Then Josh looked over at Eddie and grinned. "We're gonna need Brad!"

Eddie grinned and nodded.

Behind them, the Italian man's eyebrows raised as he lifted a gold coin from the chain around his neck…and wondered.

CHAPTER TWELVE

Paco's motel room would not have passed the sniff test for most people. He sat on the stained comforter of his bed in dim yellow light. He kept the curtains drawn for privacy as he unfolded the chart that had been Nick Dawson's passion for many years. As he looked at the markings and notes, he rolled Nick's Spanish *Escudo* around in his fingers and then flipped it up into the air. The *Concepcion* was marked on the chart offshore from Cocoa Beach very close to the Cape Canaveral Peninsula. The exact coordinates were written beside the little sketch of the ship that Nick had drawn. The corners of Paco's mouth turned up slightly as he flipped the *Escudo* again and grabbed it in mid-air. He held the coin up and grinned at it as if he were holding a small bird.

Shaking his head slightly, he spoke to the coin. "How much easier can this be for me, little Spanish coin?" he asked. "Later I will sell you, and then use the money to rent a boat! Tomorrow by noon I will be in the water looking for your brothers and sisters, and then soon the riches of a king will be mine!" He laughed as his yellowed teeth and rancid breath did nothing to help the lack of guest appeal in his small, smelly room. He heard a knock at the door. His help had arrived.

Mr. Panama Hat slipped off his stool and sauntered over to the four travelers sitting at the hi-top table. He was carrying his slushy red drink with an umbrella sticking out of it and wearing a crooked but friendly smile. When he spoke, his British accent and sociable demeanor made him instantly likable.

"Hello mates," he began. "Name's Nigel Tompkins." He looked across the table at Nick. "Forgive me, I was just sitting over there and I was just curious…are you the young lad who took the fall here this morning?"

Josh and his friends all looked at each other.

Nick replied, "Yes, that was me." He pointed to his bandaged head.

A dreadlocked pool service guy scooped a leaf from the surface near where the two kids were swimming and glanced toward Tompkins and the four friends.

Nigel continued, "Scary time of it, it must have been! I heard the rumors. Gun shots and all, right? In the bridge corridor? Are you OK?"

Josh and his friends wondered how this man knew about the details so soon afterwards but figured there must have been a lot of talk around the resort. Police and paramedics had made no effort to conceal the incident. Everyone had seen the crime scene tape as well as the blocked off hallways.

Nick nodded. "I'm OK. Nothing that won't go away."

"Well, you're fortunate, my friend. I don't know what it was all about but you must be careful down here in vacation land. A lot of people want to take your money, one way or another." Nigel Tompkins cheered with his glass and took a sip.

Giselle tilted her head slightly. "Are you on vacation, Mr. Tompkins?"

"Oh please…call me Nigel." He laughed. "Permanent. Permanent vacation for me. I'm living the life that most only dream of. You see, I did very well on some stocks I picked up back in the early '90s. A little company called Apple. I cashed out a couple years back and moved to the beach! I'm not a rich man but one doesn't have to be rich to retire. One just has to live within the means of his budget! And that's what I do. I'm not a money spender. I don't need much in the way of extras. I live simple and happy and try to make new friends on a daily basis."

It was clear that Nigel Tompkins was enjoying his retirement life. It was also clear that he liked to talk about Nigel Tompkins.

The Rasta pool guy glanced over again and grinned slightly.

"Eddie nodded. "Well, that sounds like a good philosophy to live by."

"It is, mate. We should all do it."

The waitress stopped by their table once again and asked, "Can I get you guys something else?"

Eddie put up his hands. "I think we're good for now, thank you."

Nigel signaled something to the waitress whom he seemed to know—a sign that was clearly only known to the two of them.

He then turned back to the foursome. "Guys I invited myself to your conversation not to be nosey but to maybe help you out some. Do you have an idea who the man was who took a shot at you?"

The four quickly glanced at each other and then Nick spoke up.

"We kind of do. We don't have a name but I was face to face with him so I know what he looks like, and we know what his car looks like as well."

"Is it the man with the squashed face and scar over his eye? Very tanned, probably Latin?"

They were all quite surprised.

Giselle raised her eyebrows. "How did you know?"

Nigel nodded and readjusted his Panama hat. "He was watching you at the beach this morning. I was here for the mimosa brunch." He thumbed back over his shoulder. "Sitting at the bar just enjoying the sights and noticed that man. He was just staring and watched you guys walk by and go spread your blankets on the beach. I thought it was quite odd that he was just standing there watching you. He had a beach bag over his shoulder the whole time but he never went to the beach. He stayed up here the whole time. And then when you came back up, he tailed you. He watched you walk by and followed you up and into the resort. I guess that's when he got his opportunity to do whatever he did to you."

Nick began to put the puzzle together. "So he was out here in plain clothes and then it sounds like he followed me to the elevators…"

Giselle jumped in, "Changed into a maintenance uniform in the elevator and was able to get into the room."

Nigel said, "he must have a maintenance entry code as well as a stolen uniform."

Nick thought about that and then shook his head. "No…no he walked past me when I was opening our door to go in. I'll bet ya' dollars to donuts he saw me enter our code."

"Ah, there ya go," Nigel agreed. "Your attacker had a very well thought out plan."

Josh said, "He followed us from the state line. He overheard a conversation we had at the welcome center about the treasure and Nick's Spanish *Escudo*…"

Nigel's face instantly grew more interested. He paused as Josh realized he had over-spoken.

Nigel looked at Josh intently and then to Nick and the rest. "Treasure? An *Escudo*?"

The four friends paused and looked at each other. Josh's face flushed.

Nigel could sense the awkward moment. He put his palms up and said, "Oh…it's OK. I don't have to know that. I don't have to know the *whys* and *whens*—I just wondered if you were the young man who had the incident. I like a good story, ya know? Got a few myself." He took another sip.

Josh felt bad for spilling those beans and he hoped Nigel was not another threat to their secret. One could easily tell he was a beachcomber, a tiki-hut regular who liked to talk and listen to a good story, as he had said. Florida was full of them, after all!

Nick felt Josh's anguish. He looked at Josh. "It's OK man." Nick then looked back at Nigel Tompkins and, because he had given Nick some valuable information on his assailant, he decided to give him the skinny on what happened.

Nick began, "Long story short here, and I can't give you details but…my grandfather was down here in the early '70s. While working one night on a boat, he found something very interesting just beyond the reef…a Spanish *Escudo*, and possibly the whereabouts of many more. He immediately put it in his sea bag but unfortunately my grandfather didn't make it through the night. For some reason he was shot when he returned to the docks but he left us the coin which was safely tucked in his belongings. He also left us the location in his diary—coordinates where the rest of them are. So now, thanks to my big mouth up at the welcome center, the bad guys have my coin and the chart with the location of the rest of the treasure."

Nigel's mouth hung slightly open for a moment as he processed the short version of Nick's story. With a deer-in-the-headlights look on his face, he began to shake his head ever so slightly. "That's the most incredible story I have heard since I have been in Florida," he said, just above a whisper. "And I have heard a lot of stories." He grinned slyly as if he had just heard the granddaddy of all tall tales.

Giselle shrugged one shoulder slightly. "It's all true. You don't have to believe it if you don't want to but that's what happened and, apparently, why we were robbed."

Eddie followed up, "And what was planned as being a peaceful, adventurous, treasure finding vacation, has suddenly turned into a gun-shooting, thieving, Wild West show by the sea!"

Nigel Tompkins sat up tall on his chair and gazed at each one of the kids, one by one. He nodded slowly and then spoke in a lowered tone which seemed to accentuate his British accent. "You know, if I didn't see the bandage on your head and if I hadn't seen all the commotion, I may *not* believe you. But you guys are serious? You have coordinates to where a pile of those coins lie?"

"Possibly…if they haven't been found in the last forty years," Nick replied.

Nigel adjusted his Panama hat and sighed, shaking his head in disbelief. "You're gonna have to get that chart back—and you're gonna need some help. It's going to be a very dangerous operation and must be well thought out. You're going to need someone who knows the area, who has the street smarts. You say you know his car?"

Josh nodded. "We do. We were going to search the strip for him tonight, figuring his hotel was already paid for today, and he would go ahead and stay there tonight before moving on."

Nigel agreed. "That's logical enough to assume. You are probably right about that. But you guys can't just go storming into the parking lot when you see his car. You will have to locate him, recon the area and then make a plan and then you will have to make a backup plan—finding ways to bail out if all goes wrong. And here is the thing—he knows all four of your faces. He watched you for a long time this morning," Nigel stressed. "You are absolutely going to need a new face to pull this off."

Nick looked straight at Nigel Tompkins. "And that would be you?"

Nigel cocked his head. "I would be willing to help, just for a small percentage…five percent. That's all. But I have an idea. We can out fox the fox." He smiled and leaned back.

Giselle studied Mr. Tompkins for a brief moment. "So you are bringing the fresh face *and* the plan."

"For only five percent," he answered.

"Why so cheap?" Eddie asked.

Tompkins shrugged and then leaned in as if to reveal a big secret. "I told you…I don't need the money…lots of money is not important to me. But this sounds like a grand adventure, and I want to see it unfold. Plus, I don't want to see you kids hurt…or worse."

Nick leaned in. "We have a contract with Family Jewels Salvage Company, but we can cut you five percent of what *we* get.

I don't think Lou would have a problem with that."

"Family Jewels, you say?"

Nick nodded and grinned.

Nigel finished, "Only in Florida, right?"

They all chuckled.

Nick said, "Only in Florida. Do we have a deal? Five percent of our cut?"

Nigel stuck out his hand to Nick. "It's a deal and if it turns out to be too much, I'll even cut it a percentage or two!"

They all smiled.

"Five is more than fair for putting your neck on the line, Mr. Tompkins," Nick finished.

The foursome exchanged phone numbers with Nigel Tompkins as they made their plan to meet that evening. He then bade them good day, walked over to the bar, signed a check and then left. Josh signaled the waitress for their check. The waitress waved him off, gave him thumbs up and pointed to Nigel Tompkins who was just entering the resort to go home, wherever that was. Their bill was paid in full.

A few tables away, an aging Italian man removed an earpiece. He could not believe what he had just overheard with the aid of technology. His mind raced back to the early' 70s when he was just a goon paired up with another, sent out to take the lives of two sailors who had made a run to the reef for their boss at the time. He recalled the deckhand treading water as he plugged him two times in the chest—*Chuck Dawson.* Could this kid possibly be the grandson of the man he shot to death over forty years ago? And could the *Escudo* he wore dangling from the chain around his neck be the twin of the one Nick just lost? And what was that about coordinates to the rest of the treasure? The man he had shot had said *there was a treasure!* Tony rubbed the coin and grinned as he watched the four kids walk into the resort. He pondered the luck of being at the right place at the right time—twice in his life! Buck Naked watched him… watching them.

CHAPTER THIRTEEN

Brad Radcliffe's phone buzzed as he walked to his car in the parking lot of Orlando's Marine Mechanics Institute. Giving his phone a glance, the screen read *Josh Baker*. He laughed as he took the call. "What's going on, tourist?"

"Got any plans for tonight, Brad?"

"Not if you're buying me dinner!"

Josh laughed. "Oh we got something much better than dinner going on. We may need a diversion. Are you ready to listen?"

Brad's expression changed from jovial to curious. He knew when his friends needed his diversion skills; there was something good going on. "Walking to my truck. Go ahead."

Josh gave Brad the Reader's Digest version of what had happened after picking up Nick in South Carolina and what was going on since they rolled into town. As Josh got further and further into the story, Brad's pace got slower and slower until he was at a complete stop—still three rows away from his truck. Josh mentioned Lou Cannon at Family Jewels and finished with the acquaintance of Nigel Tompkins and his offer to be the local knowledge expert and the unknown face.

Brad felt sweat beads forming on his forehead, both from the heat of the day and the intensity of the story. Brad shook his head in disbelief and then continued walking.

"The things that you guys fall into." Brad hit the unlock button for his truck, opened the door and climbed in. "But, yeah—I'm in for sure. I'll get a little more detail from you when I get over there but give me a couple hours. I'm gonna go by the apartment and then I'll head that way."

One side of Brad's mouth curled upward as he started his truck. He knew, once again, that he was in for some fun with his good friends from back home in West Virginia.

Sitting on his bed in the shabby little motel room, Paco Villarreal was looking over Nick's chart and notes when he heard a car pull up near the front door of his room. Expecting company, he stood and peeked from the stained and frayed curtain. He then stepped to the door and let his friend in without him having to knock.

"Buenos Dias, Paco."

Paco shook his head. "Enough with the Spanish, Dennis. You only know six words and you wasted two of them in one sentence."

Dennis grinned as he shut the door. "Paco, you look stressed." He walked over to the nightstand where he saw the chart. He picked it up. "So, show me what you got."

Dennis McKinney was as white as an Eskimo's butt. His pure Irish blood would never let him tan so he was a major investor in sunscreen products. He tried to avoid being out in the sun as much as possible. With little education, the jobs that Dennis could find in Florida were mainly outdoor labor positions, which of course he didn't like, so he had made the choice many years ago, like Paco, to live a life of crime. It seemed to pay better (when not in jail) and he could avoid the dangerous and swelteringly hot rays of the Florida sun. What came with that lifestyle was a rap sheet similar to Paco's and these two were never afraid to try it one more time. They had partnered before.

Paco began to give Dennis the entire story. As he listened, Dennis glanced back and forth between Paco's dark eyes and Nick's chart. He absorbed all the details of Paco's day and began to understand how easy this could be. After a few minutes, Paco was finished. He looked Dennis in the eye and pulled the *Escudo* from his pocket. "Mi amigo…there could be many, many more of these—and we have the exact coordinates."

He took the coin from Paco and rolled the coin around in his hand a couple of times. "So we take this one to the pawn shop, cash it in to fund a boat rental and some breathing apparatus gear and just run out there and start whisking away the sand," Dennis confirmed.

"Easy as that." Paco flashed his greasy smile.

"Paco, I think it's safe to say that those kids will still have the coordinates as well—even though they don't have the chart."

Paco nodded. "That's why we have to move fast. Just down the street is a pawn shop that I have already checked out. It's a twenty-four-hour place and I say we wait 'til later after the daytime and evening crowd goes away. The fewer eyes that see this, the better."

"The fewer eyes that see *us*, the better too. Maybe go around midnight," Dennis agreed."

Dennis placed the chart on the dresser with the coin on top of it. He then reached out and shook hands with his old friend. They both smiled.

Dennis said, "Gracias, amigo!"

Paco shook his head. "That's *four* of your six, gringo!"

At around seven o'clock, Josh, Eddie, Giselle, Nick and Brad were sitting at a round table in their resort's casual dining restaurant. *Café El Bote* served an evening buffet of American and Spanish tapas, or appetizers. As expected, the décor had a nautical theme, but in a clean modern design that one would expect inside the beautiful Vista al Mar Resort. Brad hit it off with Nick immediately as both seemed to have similar backgrounds. Very quickly, they were chatting and laughing like old friends.

Munching enthusiastically on a platter of wings, tequenos, fried yucca, ceviche and fried cheese, the friends discussed their evening plan.

Giselle, who leaned towards being the cautious and level-headed one spoke up. "What we have to work out, and I mean *really* work out to the specifics, is Nigel's plan with Brad's diversion. It has to be carefully coordinated."

"Yeah," Josh agreed. "It cannot go wrong in any way. There is too much at stake."

Everyone nodded in agreement as they ate. They all knew that

Paco had a gun and would not hesitate to use it, but retrieving the chart as well as the gold coin was mandatory.

Nigel Tompkins stepped into the restaurant, spotted the group and walked over to join them. He was dressed as a tacky tourist, which he did most of the time anyway. Khaki shorts, flowered shirt, his Panama hat, slip-on sneakers and a straw carryall bag that screamed *I'm from out of town!* Paco would not give this man a second look as anything but a tourist.

Brad and Nigel were introduced and then they were off and running, making their plan. Within an hour they were confident they had something that would work. Brad would just have to make a trip to the store to get a few things that he needed.

A few tables away, Tony looked on…but mostly, he listened.

Brad was all set. He had made his trip to the specialty store and had purchased the necessary provisions. Nigel looked on as Brad finalized securing his provisions into place.

The British man stepped back, shook his head and couldn't help but laugh as he watched Brad make the final connection of this mother-of-all diversions. Nigel had the seed of the idea hours ago, but Brad had taken it to the next level, to say the least.

As the sun brushed its final moments of light across the tropical horizon of the Sunshine State, Josh, Eddie, Giselle and Nick walked from the Vista Al Mar Resort to Eddie's bus. Nighttime was close and it was time to start the search for the gold 1973 Chrysler New Yorker. Eddie fired up the bus as the others climbed in. He let the little air-cooled engine warm up a bit and then put her in gear and off they went. They would begin their search to the north of their resort, along A1A.

Gisele spoke from the center seat. "Well here is what makes sense to me, guys…In order to save time, I don't think we are going to find this guy at the five-stars. You know what I mean? We can eliminate the big resorts right away or at least save them for later if we are not having any luck. I think we are going to find him at a place that is priced middle-of-the-road or lower."

Nick nodded, still understandably bitter and resentful for what Paco had done to him. "I think that rat is going to be at the seediest little garbage hole in town. It would suit him well."

Eddie agreed, "Nigel was saying we should hit the back streets for the smaller joints. The roads that run parallel to A1A, but off the beach."

"And that could take some time," Nick said.

"Well, we have eight sets of eyes to scan all around. I think our chances are good," Josh said, while his own eyes followed a pretty young girl on the sidewalk.

Giselle leaned forward and playfully whacked the back of Josh's head. "And you need to keep yours facing out the front window looking for a '73 New Yorker!" She gave him that *look*.

Josh, surprised, turned around to give Giselle a glance, wondering what that was all about. Eddie's knowing grin showed he had taken notice, but he drove on, saying nothing.

Eddie pointed down the street. "Let's cruise up and down A1A one time just to see if we get lucky. After that, we can start with the side streets."

Josh's phone rang out to a few bars of Jimmy Buffet's *Desperation Samba*. The caller ID said *Brad*.

"Hey what's up?"

"Me and Nigel are headin' out. We are gonna start south and move toward you."

"OK. Lotta ground to cover, man. This guy is going to be at the smelly places. You guys know that, right?

"Oh yeah. We're not going to waste our time at the Ritz," Brad replied.

Josh laughed. "Phone right away when you see something."

"Will do, man. See ya later at the show!"

Josh laughed again and ended the call. Brad's diversions were not to be missed.

It was twilight time and people were on the streets. While looking intently for the old Chrysler, Eddie and Nick were also enjoying some of the natural beauty within the crowds. Josh, apparently, didn't have the privilege of being such a free looker. He turned around and half-smiled at Giselle, trying to read her mind. She gave him that *look* again.

After a few miles, convinced they had driven far enough north, Eddie U-turned the bus and headed back south on A1A. Going past the pier and then past the Vista al Mar, the team of four were rubber-necking the parking lots trying to spot Paco's New Yorker. After a few more miles, Josh pointed straight ahead and said, "Ah…look."

They had driven so far south, they had met up with Brad and Nigel coming north. Brad saw them as well. Josh put his arm out the window and made a big circle to indicate a turn-around. It was time to start hitting the side streets. Nigel stuck a *thumbs up* out the window. The beautiful little VW Bus made the next right turn and then another. This put them on the first street parallel to A1A, but still on the barrier island.

Nick was looking out the window and commented, "This guy knows where we are staying. He is going to be smart enough not to be too close to our resort. He could be miles north or south of the Vista al Mar."

Eddie nodded. "He found us first and then got his…accommodations. I don't think it's going to be *too* far because remember—he doesn't know that we know what kind of car he has."

Giselle added, "Yeah, I don't think he will even consider that we are coming after him."

Josh nodded. "For sure, he's not afraid of us, anyway. He's the guy with the gun and not afraid to use it. Tonight is the night. Tomorrow he will be gone."

The bus cruised on. Each of these parallel streets would eventually come to a dead end at a parking garage or a fun center or some other obstacle and they would have to make a left or right to find the next street running north and south. They crisscrossed Daytona Beach and Daytona Beach Shores, doing their best to leave no street uncovered on the outer island. Of course, they had considered Paco was staying on the mainland but they knew there were still enough low rent little forty-dollar-a-night joints out there to keep him close. If he was on the mainland, their search was futile. They were banking that he was within five or six miles of their resort on the coast. After an hour, they hadn't covered much ground.

"Man, I'll say one thing…there are enough possibilities!" Nick said. "Get off the beaten path and the "mom and pop" motels are everywhere."

"He could be long gone," Giselle added. "Talk about a needle in a haystack."

Eddie made another left and then a right, putting him on Grandview Avenue and the search went on. With each city block, and each mile, their hopes grew dimmer. Without speaking about it, the feeling could be felt among the four.

Giselle broke the silence as the others continued to stare into the night. "You know Nick, I understand what that coin meant to you. It had to be really tough to have it taken from you like that— but think of it like this…that coin was not the treasure your grandfather left you. The coordinates were the treasure he left you. Think of that coin as a key…or just a sample of what he found for you—and how he unknowingly has provided for you…providing *we* find the *Concepcion* , of course."

Josh nodded. "That's true, ya know. This guy will be caught and if we don't get the coin back tonight, I think it will be recovered eventually even if it does need to spend a little time in the evidence locker. With time, Nick, you will just be able to flip that one onto the pile!"

Eddie added, "And we do have the coordinates. Josh, you are right—it has to be only tonight that we try to find this guy because tomorrow we must get with Ray the dive instructor and Lou Cannon and get started. We can't wait until Monday because Mr. Scrunch-face will have the chart and be in the water tomorrow, I guarantee it."

Nick took a deep breath and released it. "If we happen to get my coin back as well as the chart, we cannot be so naïve as to think this maintenance guy hasn't also made a copy of the coordinates."

Giselle flared her eyebrows, "Could get a little awkward in the water out there."

Eddie added, "So we find him tonight, and then call the police… let *them* move in."

"No!" Nick exclaimed. "I want the chart and I want the coin…if we find him."

Josh turned around. "Yeah, me too. I'm with Nick—I like our plan for tonight if we locate this guy."

"Then let's sit up tall and keep looking!"

The pep talk helped. It helped all of them even though it was intended for Nick. Everyone in the bus sat up a little straighter and looked a little harder…and another hour went by.

The mood in Brad and Nigel's vehicle was pretty much the same. One parking lot after another, they zig-zagged their way south. They would get jacked up for a while (thanks to Nigel's insistence on hitting drive-throughs for coffee) and then lose their enthusiasm as the caffeine wore off.

The miles went by and the hours dragged on but finally, like a bolt of lightning, Brad jumped tall into his driver's seat and pointed across the dash. There, on the corner of Conch Lane at Van Avenue in Daytona Beach Shores, sat a gold Chrysler New Yorker from the seventies. It was parked at the front door of a shabby-looking place called the Honeymooner Motel and Spa. With the first impression, Nigel hoped there were no honeymooners there and saw no evidence of any spa. The entire facility was L-shaped, single story, white with hunter green trim and probably built in the 1950s.

Now, it seemed…the stars had aligned and guano was about to hit the turbine!

CHAPTER FOURTEEN

Paco crushed out a cigar in the dirty ash tray, glanced at the clock and then kicked the bed where Dennis was taking a catnap. It was 11:40 pm and almost time to make their visit to the pawn shop to cash in the coin to finance their salvage plan. Paco's eyes flicked over to the dresser where the coin and the chart lay waiting. He wasn't sure how Dennis could sleep—this was far too exciting. Paco walked over to the window and peeked through the opening of the grungy curtains. Family time was over and the only ones he could see on the streets now were the obvious partiers, an occasional car and a pickup truck with some sort of unusual decoration on the hood and grill. Paco shook his head...*you see it all in Florida*. It was about go-time.

He looked back at Dennis rubbing the sleep from his eyes. "Wake up gringo...It's almost time to go to work."

"That's gotta be it!" Brad exclaimed. "It's the only one we have seen."

Nigel stretched this way and that in the cab of Brad's truck, in order to get a better look at the car. Being in his early sixties, Nigel knew his old car models within a few years.

"I believe that *is* about a '73." he said and then paused for a moment while looking around. "Brad, let me out and I will walk over and get a picture. We can text it to the others to confirm it."

Brad was already nodding before Nigel had finished. It was a great idea.

Nigel stepped out of the truck and threw his beach bag over his shoulder to complete his costume…just in case. He let his eyes roll towards the room in front of the car to make sure he wasn't being watched. When he got at just the right angle he pulled his phone up and snapped a quick shot of the '73. He continued to walk nonchalantly past the vehicle, through the breezeway of the office and out the other side. Brad had run the block and was waiting for him there. Nigel climbed back into the truck and quickly messaged the picture to the others.

Josh's phone beeped to indicate he had received a message. He unlocked his phone and tapped the message icon. His eyes flew open when he saw the picture. "They found it!" he shouted. He quickly sent a message back to Nigel confirming they had found the correct 1973 Chrysler New Yorker. Josh's phone rang soon after. It was Brad.

"That's the one?"

"That's it. Where are you?"

"Honeymooner Motel and Spa—but don't look for a fancy place. This joint has all the charm of a flea bag."

Josh laughed, hurriedly waiting for directions.

"Corner of Van and Conch Lane. It's about 4 miles from the Vista al Mar."

"OK, give us 10 minutes with lights." Josh's stomach did a flip-flop. They were really going to do this. The others in the bus looked equally as queasy.

Dennis rolled from the well-worn queen bed, raked his fingers through his greasy hair and then stepped to the bathroom. After splashing cold water on his face and coming back to life somewhat, he told Paco "I'm going to the car. I have to get my *gear* ready...just in case."

Paco sneered.

"Park somewhere we can keep an eye on the room," Nigel suggested.

"How do you know the room in front of the car is the room he is in?" Brad asked.

"I don't. That's why we need to watch it. I would hate to go to the wrong door."

Brad cruised past the motel and went through the intersection to park in a shadowed area where they could see the door to the room. Josh, Eddie and the others were on the way and now they would simply wait, get everyone into position and light the candle...so to speak.

Brad got comfortable, gave his back a stretch and looked towards the motel. Just at that moment, the room door in front of the '73 New Yorker opened and a lanky and very pale man stepped out. He left the door open and walked across the small parking area to a mid-90s Buick sedan.

Nigel looked on after being elbowed by Brad. He seemed bewildered. "That's not a dark-skinned man with a scrunched face."

They watched the man open the front passenger door of the Buick and ramble around in the front floorboard for a moment. Brad flipped up his center console lid and pulled out a small set of binoculars. The man closed the door to his car as Brad focused on him. Clear as moonshine, he could see the pale man had retrieved a small firearm from his car. The man quickly tucked it into his pants along the beltline. Brad's eyes followed him to the door and then another figure appeared. Shorter, darker skinned and a scrunched face.

"There he is!" Brad said. "We've got the right room. Problem is, now there are two of them as well as two guns.

Nigel's eyes showed a moment of hesitation, but then his sense of adventure returned and he glowed with anticipation. His adrenaline was revving.

It was hardly any time before the VW bus rolled up beside Brad's truck in the shadows of the opposite corner from the Motel.

Eddie rolled down his window and Brad did the same.

"He knows my bus. I'm going to park around back of this place so he doesn't see it," Eddie said.

Brad nodded. "Just make sure you have it pointed outward in case we have to get out of here quickly."

"Yeah. We'll be right back."

Eddie slipped the bus to the back of the building that sat on the opposite corner of the motel. The team of four walked back over to the shadows where Brad had exited the truck and Nigel was getting in character for his part of the plan. His Panama hat was in place, he had the beach bag over his shoulder and his sunglasses hung from his shirt pocket, even though it was nearly midnight.

Satisfied everything was good, Nigel turned to his team and advised, "This is very serious. These guys can take your life and one minute later, eat a sandwich. No remorse whatsoever. I have seen it before."

Eddie wondered *where*.

He continued. "Let me do my part… and do not show yourself, no matter what happens. Brad, once your diversion is underway, get behind the wheel and stay there. If anything goes wrong, do not come out of cover to help me. Do you guys understand?"

"Got it," Josh replied.

Everyone else nodded.

"Once the objects are recovered, we have to go…we have to go hard! Brad, when I run out, you have that truck running and in gear!"

"I'm ready. I'll be one foot on the brake and one on the gas!"

"Like I say, you guys stay out of sight. We don't want him to have any idea it involves you because he knows where you are staying. We can meet up back at the Vista al Mar once we are sure they are not following us."

They all acknowledged Nigel's good advice and agreed they

would stay in the shadows.

Nigel looked at Brad. "We have another problem we weren't planning on."

Brad nodded. "The second vehicle they have."

"Right."

Brad bit his cheek and wobbled his head. "I have a plan. Don't worry." He smiled.

Josh added, "I've seen that look on his face before. I would say he's got you covered, Nigel."

This brought a bit of nervous laughter from the team and they knew it was time to execute.

"OK," said Nigel Tompkins. "Let's do this!"

Paco Villarreal and Dennis McKinney also had a plan. It was midnight and time to go. They would take the Spanish *Escudo* to the pawn shop, get their cash and be ready to go at first light. They would rent a boat with modern navigational aids, rent some basic underwater breathing gear and go to the exact coordinates on Nick's chart to start moving sand. Their budget would not allow them to salvage with suction equipment like Family Jewels did, but if they could get lucky, they just might be able to find a nice little stack of coins that had been lying there for the past three hundred years.

Dennis placed his pistol on the dresser before making one last trip to the restroom. Paco had concealed his in his jeans and was ready to go.

"Waiting for you, gringo," he said.

Just as Dennis exited the bathroom, there was a pounding on the door to their room. The two men's heads snapped around to look at one another.

"You expecting company?" Dennis asked, just above a whisper.

Paco looked towards the door, shaking his head. His hand slowly went for his sidearm.

Nigel did his best Foster Brooks, "Mary!" an inebriated British voice called out. "Maarry! Let me in Mary!"

Dennis waved off the need for the gun and Paco re-tucked it away in his jeans. Paco stepped towards the door. The voice called out again.

"Mary…please let me in, Mar…."

Paco opened the door. A staggering, obviously drunken tourist stood before him, barely able to stand up. The man wore a Panama hat that, if it were any more crooked, would fall off of his head. He sported a Hawaiian shirt that was buttoned crookedly and had a locally purchased beach bag over his right shoulder. Sunglasses were hanging from his pocket which made it obvious that this guy had been at it for quite some time today!

The drunken man slurred, "H..h..hey…you're not M…M…Maarrry!"

Paco sneered and looked back at Dennis. "Hey gringo…I think your father's here."

"Wha'd ya do wi..wi…with Mary?" The drunken man asked and then wiped drool.

Paco looked at him with disgust. "You got the wrong room,

amigo." He went to shut the door and the man put his hand up.

"I…I…I left her here…yesterday. Room si..six…sixty-two."

Paco looked at the door. Room 26. He shook his head and said, "A few doors down my friend," and went to shut the door again.

Brad Radcliffe lit the fuse – quite literally. He had pulled his truck into a parking spot that faced Paco's '73 New Yorker. Paco had his car facing out for quick departure if needed. The two vehicles were grill to grill about fifteen feet apart.

It was at that second that the first rocket launched.

Ffftttt!

The front of Brad's truck now looked like a warplane. He had removed the camo netting that had hidden his plan for the past few hours and now, pointed straight at Paco's car were fireworks of every size and type, all fused together!

The first rocket was small but zipped from Brad's truck, skipped across the hood of Paco's car and hit the motel's exterior wall. Paco couldn't believe what he had just seen and this brought Dennis to the door as well. They both looked at the wall where the bottle rocket had impacted and then over to the truck, its origin.

Paco was caught off guard and didn't know what to say or think.

And then the mayhem started. The next five rockets went off nearly simultaneously. Three more flew across the hood and then two straight into the grill…by design.

Paco's face immediately grew angry. "Hey…what the…!"

The next few rockets were bigger and louder—one across the hood and two into the grill. *Boom…Boom…Boom!* A trickle of antifreeze could now be seen running from under the big sedan.

Paco looked at Brad sitting in the driver's seat and screamed, "What are you doing?! What are you doing to my car?!"

Brad had the driver's window down. "I'm sorry!" he screamed. "It won't start!" Brad pretended to not be able to start his truck. He cranked while holding a kill switch he had rigged. Meanwhile, *Boom Boom BOOM!* The biggest ones yet!

Paco ran from the doorway to Brad's truck. He banged on the passenger door and screamed, "Gringo, I'm going to kill you!"

Boom, Boom, Boom!!! One after another…sometimes two at a time!

Dennis was outside now, standing on the walkway and he began laughing at Paco. Knee-slapping laughing. He was enjoying this show! Obviously this kid had taped a bunch of fireworks to his truck and was going to go impress his friends somewhere. Somehow, the fuse had been inadvertently lit and the result was a new radiator for Paco. Now the kid's truck wouldn't start and the arsenal continued. Fluid poured from the big New Yorker!

Paco was furious! "Get it outta here! Get it outta here!" he screamed.

"It won't start!" Brad screamed back through the rolled-up window. He turned his palms up. He was playing his part well but hadn't planned on Paco being so close. Josh, Eddie, Giselle, and Nick watched from the shadows. What they saw next terrified them. Paco reached into his jeans and pulled out his Glock. With one *whack*, he broke the side glass on Brad's truck. He shoved the gun straight into the cab with the end of the barrel at Brad's head.

"No!" Giselle screamed. Josh put his hand up to cover her mouth. It was just a reaction for her. She realized immediately she could do Brad harm by screaming.

With Paco's car completely disabled, (and not to mention the gun to his head), Brad knew it was time to go! He released the kill switch he had been holding and the truck fired to life! He yanked the gear selector down into reverse and floored it. He swung the nose of the truck around so fast, it took Paco's arm out of the window and threw him to the ground, the gun scooting away under another vehicle that was parked close by.

Brad's truck was now pointed at Dennis' Buick. Dennis immediately stopped laughing. The second round of the fireworks began to ignite, zooming just inches above Paco's head and finding their target in Dennis' grill. This was Brad's plan since discovering the second vehicle with the accomplice…as well as the second gun, which hadn't shown itself yet.

Ffftttt…Ffftttt…Ffftttt…Boom, Boom, Boom!!!

Dennis was momentarily dumbfounded. An immediate lime green trickle began to seep from under the car. Seeing the fluid, his Irish temper immediately "rang the bell" and he took off running towards Brad's truck.

This was Nigel's chance.

With Dennis running towards Brad's truck and Paco shaking the cobwebs, still lying on the ground with rockets going off just above him, Nigel dashed into the room. Brad saw Dennis coming and swung his truck around a little more to get pointed at him. Dennis reached for his gun. *On the dresser!* He angrily remembered. Now he realized what Brad had done as rockets began zipping past him like…rockets! The next one caught him square in the belt buckle and took him to the ground.

BOOM! A big one. Dennis was now hearing impaired and

shell-shocked just like Paco and with all the commotion, they had completely disregarded the intoxicated British guy at their motel door.

Nigel scanned quickly and couldn't believe his good fortune. Just across the room on the dresser was the chart and the coin! There was also a Ruger 9mm. He grabbed them all.

Out the door Nigel flew, gesturing to Brad to get out of there *now* as he made a beeline down the sidewalk to try to get behind the motel and disappear into the shadows. Brad saw the fleeing British man, pulled the truck into reverse and spun the nose around to be pointed in the same direction as Nigel. He then floored it in order to follow him around back, pick him up and get out of there.

Dennis and Paco saw the same thing and realized they had been bamboozled. That British guy was no longer staggering and slurring but was sprinting out of sight and they knew why. Paco scurried over and grabbed his pistol from underneath the car it had slid under. Quickly running to the sidewalk, he had one last chance. He took a deep breath, calmly drew his aim and squeezed. *Boom!* One shot.

Nigel's' momentum and the force of the bullet propelled him forward, down to the sidewalk at the end of the building.

Brad saw the whole thing and screamed out as he wheeled his truck around the corner. "Nooo!!!"

Josh, Eddie, Nick and Giselle all gasped in unison as they saw Nigel take the hit.

Eddie broke from the group. "I'm going to get the bus! Stay here and watch where Brad goes!"

Brad turned the corner at the end of the small parking lot and then jammed on the brakes. He would not leave Nigel behind. Paco and Dennis saw this and took off down the sidewalk towards the British guy who had just fooled them royally. Paco fired another shot and hit Brad's truck in the right front fender. Paco wanted to keep Brad in the truck and get to Nigel to retrieve the chart and the coin that he was sure he had.

This worked as Brad stayed in the cab for the moment, remembering what Nigel had told him.

Nigel had other ideas. Shaking off the hit to the back, he rolled over, sprang to his feet and in two steps was in the bed of Brad's truck.

"GO!" he screamed to a wide-eyed Brad Radcliffe.

Brad wasn't the only one impressed. The three kids in the shadows couldn't believe their eyes as Brad's truck roared away. Neither could the old Italian man with the noticeably lazy eye who was also watching the event unfold.

Tony knew patience was his virtue.

CHAPTER FIFTEEN

"Get in the car!" Dennis screamed.

Paco and Dennis ran back and jumped into the Buick, which now had a substantial puddle of anti-freeze under it. After a few seconds of key fumbling, Dennis got it started and punched the gas. He made the same right turn at the end of the parking lot that Brad had made and pulled out onto Conch Lane, heading west.

Brad had about a two-block head start and momentarily his brain had a hard time comprehending what had just gone on back there. He had seen Nigel take the hit to the back and go down. He had also seen him spring back to life and jump into the bed of his truck! Brad was alternating looking forward and then backward to check on Nigel's condition. Nigel popped his head up to tell Brad to *just drive!* He then looked behind him to see where the pursuers were. He saw the steaming, swerving old Buick swing out onto Conch Lane and ducked his head back down.

Eddie pulled up in the bus to pick up the others.

"Straight ahead!" Josh pointed as they climbed in.

Giselle was frantic. "Nigel was shot but he got in the truck! They are headed for the bridge across the Intracoastal."

Eddie pulled away hard and spun the tires of the bus a bit in doing so.

"I hope he's not hurt bad," Nick said.

Brad got lucky at the bridge and caught a green light. Either way he wasn't stopping but he was happy to do it the safe way. Brad began to notice a film on his windshield—an oily film.

"Oh man!" he said. "Not good."

He then began to smell it. *Coolant*, he thought. Glancing behind him he saw the Buick charging like a steam engine. Looking forward again, his engine compartment erupted into a plume of white smoke. It seemed that Paco's warning shot had nicked a radiator hose and now it had let loose completely.

Now there were two smokers headed west over the Intracoastal bridge, looking like a steam train competition. Eddie and his passengers were close behind. It was going to come down to whose engine could hold out the longest. And that is what would separate life and death.

Nigel sat up just enough to have a look behind him, the steam off the engine choking him a bit. He had an ace in the hole that no one knew about. He had Dennis' pistol.

The Buick had closed to within a block of Brad's truck due to Brad slowing just a bit at the intersection at the end of the bridge. Dennis was not willing to err on the side of safety and blew the light completely, gaining him the extra couple hundred feet in the pursuit. Paco cringed in the seat beside him.

What this did for Nigel, however, was bring them into range.

He could at least put a couple of holes in their windshield and force them to call off the chase. Nigel rose up, drew aim on the front of the car and began to squeeze. Instead he released the trigger and lowered the firearm. The bus—Eddie's bus was too close to chance it. It was right in the line of fire albeit a good four hundred feet behind Dennis. For a bullet, that distance was nothing and it was just too much of a chance to take at this point. Nigel would have to wait until they turned a corner. There were a couple more cars behind the VW bus in the distance but other than that, traffic was light.

The chase continued onto the mainland. Now the valves in the engine of the old Buick were beginning to chatter. The smoke from Brad's truck began to dissipate but that was not a good thing. That simply meant he had spit out all of his coolant and it was just a matter of time before his engine expired. At this point, warning lights were flashing on the dash boards of both vehicles. As they turned and headed south where Highway 1 turns into A1A, both vehicles performed beyond expectation. Still under power, they found themselves in a strangely remote area on the historic road. For a stretch of about a mile, the land was strangely undeveloped, with the exception of an old quick-stop gas station that was not a part of the property. The large parcel of sand dunes and sea oats had been bought in the late 1960's by a Canadian multi-millionaire who just wanted to sit on it for a few years and then give it to his only son to set up his own fortune. The only structure on the entire property was a very old and very large wooden boat house which was built after the Second World War and was now abandoned. The investor died soon after purchasing the land and his young son migrated to California, finding the Hippie culture more appealing than his father's cut-throat, stressed-out, business world.

Just after Brad's truck and Dennis' Buick made the left onto A1A South, Nigel had a chance to put a couple of rounds in the windshield of the clattering Buick before the Bus turned and pulled in behind them again. He rose up, aimed and fired. His shots found the center of the windshield, zinging between Paco and Dennis before burying themselves in the back seat. Nigel lay back down and curled up as small as he could in the bed of the truck. Paco, not finding this amusing, hung himself out the passenger side window and drew aim. *Boom, Boom.* Two shots to the tailgate. Nigel winced as he took another hit to the back.

Brad knew the end was near. He found himself shoving harder on the accelerator to maintain speed as the truck began to lug more and more. He prayed that the Buick had the same problem—and it did. Seeing a road up ahead that turned left, Brad knew he had to do something different than just let the truck die right there on A1A and be an easy target for the pursuers.

"Hold on!" he screamed back to Nigel.

Brad whipped a quick left onto the narrow paved road that lead straight east back to the Intracoastal Waterway. The road was covered with drifted sand, the pavement barely visible. With hardly any traction, the truck slid sideways, but Brad held on and corrected, pointing the truck straight once again. He no more than got it back on the pavement when his engine began knocking heavily. It had had enough and began to seize and Brad felt the immediate knot in his stomach. He checked his rearview mirror and it looked like the Good Lord was with him. He saw a quick orange flash from underneath the Buick, which indicated it had just thrown a rod through the engine block as oil splattered the hot exhaust—Dennis' car was cooked as well!

Brad let the truck roll as far as he could and then threw open the door to check on Nigel. To his surprise, Nigel leapt over the side of the truck, grabbed Brad by the collar and commanded, "Let's go! Run!"

Brad looked back at him with wide eyes as they ran up the dunes to get out of sight. Nigel read his mind.

"No time to explain now, mate. Just go!"

The two guys ran a diagonal course away from the sand-covered road to try to "get lost" in the dunes.

Dennis and Paco coasted to a stop about one hundred yards behind the truck, jumped out and began the foot pursuit. They, too, headed up into the small, rolling dunes as they had seen the two men in the truck do, on a similar diagonal course away from the road. By this time they had figured it out—these two guys they were chasing had to be associated with the kids who Paco had stolen the coin and the chart from. What they couldn't believe was that they actually pulled it off! These kids had orchestrated a plan with this British dude to get the coin and the map back…and it had worked!

Brad and Nigel were slicing sand as they ran up the small dunes and down the other sides, over and over again. Brad was impressed with Nigel's athleticism, considering his age. Not only did he have endurance, he didn't run like a man in his 60s. There was something about this guy.

Eddie swung the bus onto the sand-covered side road and immediately saw Dennis' Buick as well as Brad's truck one hundred yards ahead. Both vehicles were smoking and steaming in Eddie's headlights.

Josh rolled his window down. "They had to have gone across the dunes!"

Giselle jumped from her seat and onto her knees between the two front seats to get a better look. Nick also unbuckled. Giselle then pointed. "Go straight down this road!"

Eddie floored it and sped east towards the Intracoastal Waterway, just a few hundred yards ahead.

It didn't take long for Paco and Dennis to get winded. After about fifty yards of plowing through the deep sand, Paco was ready to throw up. He stood atop one of the dunes with his hands on his knees, his lungs sucking oxygen. Dennis faired somewhat better but neither man was ready for that! A few quick breaths later, Dennis saw two shadows cross another sand dune not too far ahead. It was enough to give them the burst of energy they needed and off and running they went again—this time Paco ran with his Glock drawn. He was getting tired of this game of chase.

Brad and Nigel continued their course and as they topped one dune, Nigel paused and pointed. "An old boathouse—we have to get there! We have to set up an ambush!"

He had no more than finished his sentence when he and Brad heard the unmistakable report of a gunshot. The sand kicked up beside them and they both looked towards the direction of the report. Standing on top of one of the dunes behind them were Paco and Dennis.

"Get down!" ordered Nigel.

Brad jumped down the dune as Nigel drew Dennis's own gun and returned fire. Nigel wanted them to know they weren't shooting at unarmed targets. Paco reacted as the favor was returned—the bullet zinging past him. He looked at Dennis.

"They have my gun," Dennis said.

Paco fumed. "Let's go!"

The chase continued as Brad and Nigel did their best to stay in the valleys of the small dunes. This strategy worked and soon they reached the road that ran alongside the Intracoastal Waterway. They looked left as they crossed the road and saw the headlights of a VW bus approaching. This was good and bad. There *is* strength in numbers but there are also more targets. He who travels fastest, goes alone—but that was not going to be the case tonight. Nigel suddenly felt the overwhelming burden of keeping five young people alive. He knew they must all get to the boat house. The bus pulled up and stopped beside Nigel and Brad.

"As fast as you can…get out of here!" screamed Nigel.

"No way…we're not leaving you guys here," Eddie responded.

Anticipating that response, Nigel ordered, "Get this bus to the far end of the boat house and park it out of sight! Then, get up as high as you can in the structure! Stay still and quiet! Go!"

Eddie sped off as Dennis and Paco struggled to run across the dunes. They didn't run the valleys. They climbed each dune for the vantage points—trying to spot the thieves who dared to steal back what they had stolen. This cost them time and energy and allowed Brad and Nigel the seconds they needed to get to the boat house and form a plan and for Eddie to hide the bus.

The boat house was temporal anomaly. It was a completely wooden structure, heavily built and gray due to age, the sun, and the salt air. It stood two stories tall plus a large attic area in the rafters. Built in the 1940s and abandoned in the late '70s, it had miraculously withstood hurricanes, decay, scavengers and developers. It was constructed on steel pilings in the water and had a "drive-thru" design. At one time, boat captains were able to pull in through the massive doorway openings at either end, tie up and have necessary rigging repairs, carpentry issues or any other marine revamp done to their boats for a fee. The building was easily seventy feet wide and twice as long. The waterway that flowed through it would let two forty-foot boats tie up side by side with space between them. At one point, skilled workers crawled all over this facility and kept many, many boats—especially work boats, coming in one door and going out the other in A-1 condition. Nowadays, it creaked in the wind and smelled like antique hemp and fifty-year-old grease and oil. Coils and spools of old hemp line littered the floors, completely safe from looters (because no one uses hemp line anymore) as well as fishing nets, crab traps and rusty tools that hung on the walls. In the darkness at the far end, an old trawler sat, bobbing with the tides, unclaimed by its owner after all these years.

The front side of the boat house was anchored to the land by the road and sand and sea oats piled alongside the front of the shadowed, ghostly structure. As Eddie hid the bus, Brad and Nigel dashed inside through an old door that led into the area that the front office staff once occupied. They ran through a Dutch door and then another doorway that led into the main area of the boathouse. Josh, Eddie, Giselle, and Nick met them by entering through a doorway on the south end of the building.

"We have to get to the top!" Nigel said. "All of you find your way. I'm the only one armed here."

Giselle shook her head. "Why don't we just get out of here in the bus?"

Nigel looked at her and all the rest of them with stern eyes. "Because we have to stop this. It has to end tonight and I must do it. I want you guys up high so I can do my work and then we will take the bus and get out of here."

This was a Nigel they hadn't seen. Brad lifted one eyebrow to the others. He had already made the observation. Nigel was commanding and sure, and his strong British accent seemed to give him more authoritative credibility—much different from the beach bum they had met earlier in the day.

Giselle shook her head again and spoke what the others were thinking, "Nigel, don't kill anyone—this was supposed to be a fun, relaxing vacation with some mild adventure thrown in…but not this, not killing."

Nigel looked back at her and then around at the rest. With no time to argue, he exhaled sharply and shook his head. He was obviously outnumbered. He said, "No promises but I'll try. You *are* aware that they will kill any of us without thinking twice, right?"

Nick raised his hand, "I can tell you that's true."

They all heard the front door open that Nigel and Brad had come through. It startled them all; now it was time to move. The bad guys were in the building.

"Second floor!" Nigel barked.

The five young people darted towards the old wooden stairway as Nigel pulled out a small Maglite and took a quick look around, taking inventory of what he could use. Suspended from steel beams that crossed the water were cranes for lifting boats—their electric motors long seized by corrosion. Ropes, nets and heavy, rusty tools were plentiful and could come in handy but he had no time to gather anything on the main level. He too, had to get to the next floor to see what he could use to capture these guys. Up the stairs they all flew, treading as lightly as possible.

Paco was the first one in the front door. He stopped and looked around the dark office, with only the moonlight to see by. Dennis came in soon after and they both stood momentarily still, while catching their breath. Paco, with his gun still drawn, eased through the Dutch door, taking his time and carefully checking the short hallway before moving on to the door that led to the main operations area. Their caution bought the others some time.

Safely reaching the second floor, Nigel quickly flicked his light on and off. In that brief moment he had taken a picture in his mind of the layout of the second story. Keeping the light on was not an option. The second story was like any huge hay loft one would see in a barn. It spanned the full width of the facility and much of it was open to below. There were no safety railings along the edges of the floor so one wrong step and you were on the concrete below or, if you were lucky, in the water. It had more than one block and tackle affixed to the overhead beams for lifting heavier things from the ground floor up to the second and there was a ladder that led to the rafter storage area. Again, there were old nets, ropes, and nautical hardware strewn about, the kinds of items replaced routinely back in the heyday of the boathouse.

Nigel motioned for the rest of the team, who had huddled together at the top of the stairs, to go to the far corner of the lofted second floor. The five young people quietly made their way to where he had pointed.

Nigel had noticed some old wooden barrels off to the side, along with a pile of sponges and some baitfish netting. It's all he had to work with. Getting these guys without bullets was going to be a challenge.

The door below them opened slowly as Dennis and Paco eased inside the old work area. Their eyes moved around the room slowly, looking for any movement. Only a single shaft of moonlight found its way inside to assist in the search. Taking a couple more steps, Paco led with his gun up and ready.

In the meantime, above them, Nigel had managed to roll one of the barrels over to the edge of the loft—slowly and quietly. He had it positioned at the edge of the flooring which was open to below. It wasn't an option that he felt good about but if he could catch them in just the right position below, it could work. He also managed to bring over an old casting net and some sponges. He carefully peered over the side of the loft and noticed the two guys were walking away from him towards the other end of the boathouse. He took that opportunity to go over to the corner and have a word with the kids.

"Can you guys see me in the darkness over there?" he asked.

Josh replied, whispering, "Can see your shadow real good. What's up with the barrel?"

Nigel gave them the quick version of his weak plan—everything had to go just right for it to work.

"Brad, I might need you to toss a couple of sponges for me. You're the diversion guy, right?"

Brad smiled and chuckled softly, "Yeah…that's me."

"OK. When I motion the first time, I need only Brad to come over…as quietly as possible. The second time I motion, I need two more of you boys to come as close to the edge as possible without being seen from below. One of you stay with Giselle and if all goes wrong, you are in charge of getting her out safely. Get to the attic, jump out the window to the water…I don't care. Just make sure this pretty lady does not get hurt."

Giselle put her hand on Josh's back. He had been given the job.

Nigel eased back over to the edge of the loft where he could see below. He observed the two shadowed figures walk all the way to the far end as they were carefully looking behind drums, tool benches and anywhere else these kids and the crazy British guy could be hiding. They found nothing, of course. Dennis turned slowly and looked back towards the other end of the boathouse. He then had the help of the moonlight behind him as it skipped its way through the massive doorway opening for the waterway entrance. From this position he could see pretty well where he had just come from, he could see across the water to the other side of the boathouse, and he could just make out the bow of an old vessel in the water at the far end. His eyes then drifted upward to where he noticed a second floor. It was pitch black up there and nothing was discernible in the inky darkness.

Nigel stayed behind the barrel—watching.

Paco cursed himself for not having a light. The two men turned and slowly walked the same path back towards the door they had entered from a few minutes ago. This was no good for Nigel—he needed them out in the center of the building, but that would be foolish for Paco and Dennis and they knew it. This is where Nigel needed Brad. He waved his arm.

As quietly as a cat, Brad moved over and into position by the pile of sponges.

Dennis pointed to the stairs and Paco nodded.

"I go first," Paco said quietly. "I have the gun."

This was not at all what Nigel wanted to see. As Paco put his foot on the first step, Dennis pointed to Brad. Brad took one of the sponges from the pile and fired it into the waterway below. It hit the surface with a slight splash. Dennis heard it but thought it was a small wave lapping against the side of the wall. Paco took another step with his gun up high as Dennis also began to ascend the stairs.

Nigel gasped slightly and pointed repeatedly to Brad. *Fire at will!*

Brad chucked two more sponges into the water with the same effect and reached for another. That's when his hand touched something different—a cork float for a fishing net! About five inches in diameter, this would make the splash they needed! Paco and Dennis took another step as Brad fired the float into the water like a major league fastball. *Splash!*

Dennis stopped in his tracks—*that was not a wave*. He grabbed Paco by the belt loop and motioned back down the stairs towards the waterway. "They're in the water," he whispered smiling.

Paco considered how clever these kids were to try to lure them to the upper levels and then make a run for it out the door. He also thought that maybe they were thinking of setting the place on fire once Paco and Dennis were on the upper levels. *Que bolas.* He shook his head.

As Paco and Dennis eased back down the stairs, they looked wide-eyed across the room to the waterway. They were sure the kids had to be hanging along the seawall and this would be as easy as shooting fish in a barrel. Nigel was ready. He could see them below and they were walking just where he needed them to go. But now there was a problem—he only had one barrel and Dennis had slowed down behind Paco, creating a gap between them of about six feet. Nigel could only get one of them at best with the barrel trick.

Barely able to see one another, Nigel made some hand gestures to Brad. Brad seemed to understand. They had a backup plan and they both prayed it would work. Nigel knew he had to take out the scrunched-faced guy with the barrel because he was the one with the gun. The backup plan would be used on the extremely pale, taller one.

Nigel Tompkins readied himself as they stepped closer to the point where he needed them to be. Brad did the same. Josh, Eddie, Giselle and Nick watched from the corner shadows.

Paco approached the waterway that ran through the boathouse with extreme caution. He knew the British guy also had a gun. Dennis maintained his distance a few feet behind. Paco took another step towards the area where they had heard the splash in the water, wishing again for a flashlight. He was now a bull's-eye. With a firm heave, Nigel shoved the barrel. Over the edge it went and in a split second he heard the splintering of oak followed by Paco's scream of intense pain.

As Paco hit the floor, so did his gun. It bounced its way across the old wooden floor to the edge of the seawall, teetering but not falling into the saltwater. Completely flabbergasted, Dennis's eyes were as large as saucers. Paco lay on the floor in front of him with a fractured leg and barrel pieces lying all around, growling in pain. Dennis's eyes flashed upward and when they did, a casting net hit him right in the face and covered him all the way to the floor. Brad had thrown a strike!

"Now!" Nigel yelled to the others.

Eddie and Nick came running.

"Grab the rope and pull!" Brad yelled as he had already begun to do.

The two boys did just that as the net quickly tightened around Dennis's feet. They were sure that they had him. As Dennis lost his balance and the boys continued to pull, the open end of the casting net closed tight around him.

"Pull towards the water!" Brad screamed as Dennis fought like a marlin and swore like a sailor.

From the upper level, the three boys were able to drag Dennis across the floor to the edge of the seawall. With one more hard pull, Dennis was in the water with a splash. Nigel ran over to assist them and to give further instruction.

"Tie him off back there on that beam!" he said. "I want his face just out of the water…just enough to suck a little air once in a while! Keep in mind, these guys were shooting at us!" Nigel reminded the group.

Josh and Giselle rushed over to the edge of the upper level to assist. Josh looked down at a thrashing Dennis, bagged like a codfish with his minutes numbered. His mouth would pop up for a moment to gasp for air and then back under water he would go. He appeared to be getting more and more entangled in the net and getting to the surface was becoming harder and harder to do.

"Relax my friend," Nigel said. "The tide is with you."

Dennis seemed to have heard him as the boiling of the water eased a bit. He came up and drew a long breath.

Nigel looked back at the first available—it happened to be Josh. "Josh, grab that short piece of rope there and follow me." Nigel pointed to the short length of small-diameter rope and then drew his gun. Josh grabbed it and followed Nigel down the stairs they had previously ascended. At the bottom, Nigel held his gun on Paco as he and Josh approached him.

Paco lay on the floor in great pain and his leg was bleeding as a result of the slight laceration. Nigel walked up to him and put the gun to his head—Dennis's gun.

Paco's laceration was not life-threatening, but Nigel wanted him to believe it was. He said, "Mate you have two choices and you will like neither. We can leave you here to bleed to death—or I will allow my young friend here to tie a tourniquet around your leg. We will then leave but before we do we will call an ambulance…and the police. Your friend's situation will get better as the tide is receding. Now it's up to you, mate, what'll it be?"

Paco found himself between a rock and a hard place. Neither choice would lead to a winning outcome. He had an uneasy balance of pain and anger in his eyes as he looked back and forth between Josh and Nigel. Nigel shoved the gun up against his head once more.

"And if you decide to get cute while the boy is wrapping you, mate, I won't hesitate to squeeze."

Paco exhaled, as he conceded and his eyes glanced towards the water. "OK…OK, yes please tie it."

Nigel looked over at Josh, giving him the go-ahead. He then looked back at Paco sternly, reminding him to behave as Josh got close. Dennis surfaced and gulped more air.

Josh carefully kneeled as Paco rolled to give Josh access to his injured leg. The others slowly descended the stairway and circled the tourniquet operation. Nick leered at Paco…almost wishing Nigel would just squeeze the trigger. Paco leered back. Josh took the rope under his leg and the grin was instantly replaced with a wince. Josh pulled the rope around, tightened it, and tied it off with a secure knot. The pain was evident.

Dennis was beginning to relax enough to keep his face out of the water. His defiance was unmistakable, judging by his choice of vocabulary. He calmed himself, took a deep breath, and submerged once again.

Nigel smirked but the others were still somewhat uneasy with the situation. He put the gun away and pulled out his phone. "We're going to drive out of here and in five minutes I will call 911. That's a promise. But let me tell you something right now, mates…If…you…ever come within a mile of these kids again, you will not live to tell about it. It is because of them that you are still alive. You can make up your own story for the police about your situation here, but I'm telling you…once they are done with you, you better leave town!"

The water by Dennis rolled. Paco glanced towards Dennis and his situation. He nodded and said, "Gracias…No problema. Muchas gracias for my life, amigo."

Nigel leered at Paco. He didn't like leaving them alive but that was the deal he had made with the others. "Alright guys, it's time to go…"

At that second Dennis exploded from the water in one huge thrust! Wielding the knife that had cut him free, he landed on the platform of the boathouse with a roar of anger and revenge, his blanched and waterlogged skin giving him the look of death. Giselle screamed as Josh immediately grabbed her hand to get her away.

"Get her out of here! All of you—go! Go now!" Nigel screamed, as he drew up Dennis' own gun in a two-handed grip— aiming directly at his chest. "Drop the knife…drop the knife!" Taking rapid breaths and dripping with saltwater, Dennis was still in an attack position with the knife held high and his feet positioned to charge. His eyes flashed with fury but what little common sense he had was beginning to overtake his raw anger. Paco could only watch—his injury quite possibly kept him from making a bad decision. Still breathing hard, Dennis began to lower the knife but as he did, he let Nigel know of his displeasure by throwing out a few more choice vocabulary words. Nigel remembered the Glock still lying at the edge of the floor by the water. He eased over to get it and when he did, Dennis saw what he was going to do. Dennis flinched as if he were going to make a move and then stopped. Nigel walked over and put the gun to his head. He gritted his teeth like a British Clint Eastwood. "Mate…you're making it real hard for me to keep a promise. Now get on the floor, hands behind your back and feet together!" Nigel kicked the Glock into the water.

The young people quickly made their way towards the far end of the building where Eddies VW Bus was parked. At that end there were some interior rooms that looked to be old tool rooms or parts storage areas. They had to run along the waterway inside the boathouse to access the door to exit the facility. This was an extremely dark area of the boathouse. Josh led the way with his ever-present Maglite, still holding Giselle's hand as they ran. Eddie followed and then Brad and Nick. They ran alongside the two old rooms on their right and the old forgotten boat that sat in the water to their left. The vessel still sat high in the water as the team ran past its swooping lines that came to a high point at the bow. Josh made it to the door with Giselle and had to give it a little kick to get it open. He then turned his Maglite back inside the building to light the way for the others. When he did, the beam hit the side of the boat just as Nick was running past it and what Nick saw froze him in his tracks and took his breath away.

Right there beside him on the port side of the old stripped down trawler, and still legible after all these years, was the name…*Maria.*

CHAPTER SIXTEEN

All finished with his business inside the boathouse, Nigel ran the same path towards the end of the building the kids had. In the space between the old boat and the tool rooms he came upon Nick, who had one hand on the old boat, touching the name on the boat in disbelief.

"It's her...It's got to be her," he said.

"Come on, mate. We have to get out of here. Police are on the way!" Nigel urged, nudging the young man.

Nick began to move towards the door but his eyes held the name on the boat for as long as possible.

Everyone now safe, alive and remarkably uninjured whatsoever, they all piled into Eddie's VW bus. Eddie fired it up and roared away, heading down the road along the Intracoastal. They made a right and a left and were back out onto Highway 1 where they could now catch their breath.

A black sedan sat on a concrete pad which was surrounded by sea oats just north of the boat house. Tony had followed them all night and had witnessed everything. He had seen eight people enter the boat house that evening and only six come out. Being in that line of work himself, Tony knew there was some "no-good" going on. The aging Italian with a noticeable lazy eye repositioned his car close to the door where he had seen everyone enter. Tony's dome light came on as he slowly opened his door and stepped out. Pulling a huge .357 Smith and Wesson from under his jacket, Tony entered the front door, clicked on a small flashlight and looked around. Proceeding through the Dutch doors and past the small hallway on the left, he slowly opened the door that led into the main operations part of the building.

Tony was taken aback at what he saw. Before him on the floor lay a Spanish-looking man with a badly broken and bleeding right leg. Close by was a tall, thin, pale fellow who had been bound up like a hog. Dennis looked like a rocking horse. He was on his belly with his hands behind his back. His knees were bent to where his heels touched his hind-quarters and his feet and hands tied together. Paco and Dennis looked up at Tony with a mixture or surprise and fear.

Tony calmly walked over to them, his gun still drawn and his footsteps echoing throughout the boathouse.

"Tell me about the coin," Tony said.

Paco and Dennis hesitated. Tony fired a shot into the post behind Paco. The post exploded and wood splintered all around them.

"I don't have time to mess around. Where is the coin and the chart?" he asked calmly.

Paco winced as he tried to turn towards Tony. "Señor, we had it…but as you can see, we lost our last battle. They got it from us…that British guy and those kids. Left us here to die, too."

In the far distance a siren could be heard. Tony knew these two guys would only be in his way from this point on. He lifted his gun to Paco's head as he estimated in his mind how far away the sirens were. Paco gasped as his eyes showed desperation.

"Wait!" Paco said. "Wait…we…we know where the treasure is!"

Tony's eyes widened and his mind flashed back to the early seventies when a pleading man bobbing in the water had said the same thing to him. As it turned out, Tony had missed an opportunity of a lifetime by not sparing the man's life and listening to his story. True—it's the oldest trick in the book when begging for your life but in that instance, it had been true. The man in the water, hiding behind the piling that night over four decades ago, had a secret to share and Tony had inadvertently delayed his opportunity for good fortune for over forty years.

Tony lowered the gun a bit as the sirens were getting closer. "Convince me in ten seconds," he demanded.

Paco continued, struggling with his pain but negotiating for his life, "Señor…I have the coordinates in my head where the *Patache Nuestra Señora de la Concepción* lies.

The pitch of the sirens changed—they were now on Highway 1, maybe a mile away.

Tony looked Paco dead in the eye and then over to Dennis. "I'm going to tell you what to tell the cops. I have a password that will keep you out of custody in case they want to question you, and then you…paleface, you are going to meet me tomorrow morning at that rat-hole motel you guys are staying at."

Both men nodded in agreement and Tony mumbled something to them, mentioning a particular District Attorney by name whom Tony had in his pocket. He had long ago learned how to use the corruption and greed of the political and judicial systems to his advantage.

Tony ran from the building as the sirens made the turn to where an old Buick and a pickup truck sat disabled. With his headlights off, Tony floored it and got away from the old boat house without being seen by the authorities.

A few miles down Highway 1, Eddie wheeled the bus into a twenty-four hour IHOP restaurant.

As the van emptied, everyone breathed a sigh of relief. Nigel reached into his back pocket and pulled out the folded chart and handed it to Nick Dawson. He then reached into his front pocket and retrieved the Spanish *Escudo* and flipped it into the air for Nick to catch.

"There ya go, mate. Are those what you were looking for?" he smiled.

"I can't thank you guys enough…all of you," Nick said, relieved and happy to have his treasures back. "I had no idea it was going to get so dangerous or I woulda…"

"…Don't worry about it!" Josh interrupted. "We're not happy if we're not doing something stupid!" He laughed with the others.

"We have to figure out a plan for your truck, Brad." Nick said. "The cops will run the plates and be calling you soon. They will have some questions."

Brad nodded in agreement and walked over to Nigel and stuck

his finger through a couple of holes in the back of Nigel's shirt. "Kevlar, huh?" Brad said.

"Don't leave home without it, mate." The British man smiled.

"I never saw it under that tropical shirt over the t-shirt."

"I'm just a drunk tourist," Nigel pled, grinning with his palms turned up.

Giselle walked over to him as they stood in the parking lot, shaking off the stress of the last few hours. "What else, Mr. Tompkins? You are quite obviously more than just a retired investor. You demonstrated that." She grinned.

Nigel looked at Giselle and then around at the rest of the group. He smiled, "Well…it's true that I am a lucky investor…and it's true I don't do *that* anymore." Nigel contemplated the remainder of his answer. "But yes—you are absolutely right, I am retired…British MI-6." He was pretty sure they didn't know what that was. He paused a moment and added, "That particular secret security service deploys agents such as myself all over the world to detect international intelligence threats and then to…neutralize them…before they become a problem."

Everyone looked at him.

Nick spoke up. "And by telling us that, you will have to kill us?"

Nigel laughed. "No, no, no. MI-6 is not secret in the sense that no one knows we exist. We are just secret about who we are…individually. If there were another MI-6 agent beside me, I may not know him. We wouldn't even know each other."

There was a lot of head shaking as they looked at the unlikely former special ops man who stood before them. Too many questions for Nigel would be awkward as he could not give them too much information. They would likely talk more about it someday.

"Well, that explains the special tactics," Eddie said.

Nigel nodded. "I still know some of the tricks, mate." He grinned. "But I must say I was a little nervous about you guys being so close to the action."

The group started walking towards the restaurant.

Josh grinned. "We wouldn't have it any other way…"

"…and I knew that," Nigel replied.

"Can we get some pancakes now?" Nick asked, happy to have his relics back.

As the group walked towards the door of the IHOP, a black sedan cruised by. Tony was both lucky and good.

With the morning sun finding its way between a blind opening and into his eyes, Lou Cannon couldn't believe his ears as he held the phone. "And this all happened since you guys left here the other day?"

Eddie had called Lou to fill him in on the situation and to see if he could persuade Ray the dive instructor to give them the quick version of the SNUBA course and possibly get in the water any sooner.

"Eddie, here's the thing…Even if I can get you guys in with Ray today, we still have to wait on permitting to come back…but from what it sounds like to me, your problem is behind you. Those guys are likely in jail or in a hospital up there somewhere. I don't think we have to rush unreasonably. Plus, Ray is throwing in some rip-current and tide education for you guys, too. It's very important and not worth rushing. It's also required by me."

Eddie sighed. "We are just a little more than concerned. These two guys may have friends or accomplices they can hand off the coordinates to."

"Not likely, if you ask me. They know your situation…that you will do the recovery legally, and they know they have time to get there on their own—at least one of them. Sounds like the Mexican guy may be out of service for a while, however."

"Lou, is there anything we can do to speed up the permit process?"

"Way ahead of you, man. Called a buddy in Tallahassee yesterday to flag the online app and see if he can get it in the expedite pile. He owes me one and he knows I'll flip him a coin or two in the end, you know what I mean? It's all about scratching backs in this business."

"Excellent. Well, we're gonna spend the day in vacation mode then and see Ray tomorrow. We'll wait to hear from you after that—hopefully sooner than later."

"We'll see, man. I'll call you as soon as I hear something."

Eddie ended his call and told the others what Lou had said. With a decent night of sleep behind them, the four vacationers plus Brad attacked a breakfast buffet at the Vista al Mar. About an hour later a local towing company was nice enough to call Brad to let him know they had his truck and he could pick it up for one hundred dollars anytime he liked. The police had given the tow company his contact information but had not bothered to call Brad themselves. It seems whatever "password" Tony had given Paco and Dennis had been unintentionally extended to cover Brad's troubles as well.

Brad spent the morning on the phone with a buddy he had done some boat work for who owed him a favor. The man owned a machine shop and agreed to get Brad's truck for him and do the engine rebuild for just the cost of parts. Nick offered to cover the rest of the cost after they found the *Concepcion*.

Giselle wanted to get back in the sun. The guys agreed it was a good idea, so everyone packed up and back to the beach they went. They walked across the pool deck, down the three steps to the beach and past the empanada stand.

Nick jerked his thumb towards the stand. "I promise, today I will successfully buy an empanada."

Josh laughed. "Didn't work out so well yesterday, did it?"

Nick shook his head as he grinned.

The morning was hot but peaceful. The five of them alternated between sunning themselves, throwing around the football, and bodysurfing. An occasional cloud would give some relief from the summer rays as morning progressed into afternoon. Frequent reapplications of sunscreen were necessary and Giselle repeatedly commissioned Josh for the spots she couldn't reach. By one o'clock Josh had migrated to Giselle's large beach blanket. Something was cooking there and it was unspoken but obvious to all. Eddie always knew Josh had a thing for Giselle and he hoped it would someday work out but worried that it might not. Giselle was such a good friend to them all. He hoped if they tried, they would take it slow and do it right.

"Empanadas!" Nick announced.

Nick slipped away and came back with a white sack (greasy on the bottom) full of beef, chicken and cheese empanadas.

"You are the man!" Eddie praised.

Everyone sat up on their blankets as Nick handed out the deep fried delicacies.

After a couple of minutes, Giselle mentioned, "This time tomorrow, we will be in SNUBA training."

Josh nodded before taking another bite. "I can't wait."

"I can't wait to be out there." Nick pointed towards the sea. "You guys can't imagine how excited I am. Most of my life up to this point has been spent trying to get to this moment. "I'm excited *for* you," Eddie said. "With any luck, Lou Cannon will get a quick approval letter and we can get out there."

"What if it takes longer?" Giselle asked. "We planned on being here a couple of weeks, but what if it goes beyond that?"

Josh shrugged one shoulder. "Could be profitable to stay."

"I can almost guarantee it," Nick offered.

"Providing that particular pile of coins hasn't already been found or been scattered by hurricanes," Brad said.

Nick shook his head. "If anyone found the coins at those exact coordinates, they would have also found the ribs of the ship that Grandpa found. That would be a ship discovery and not just a discovery of artifacts. There has been no documented discovery of any antique vessel in that location…ever."

"That's good news for us then," Josh finished.

Giselle's next comment added a hint of pessimism. "It's hard to believe that it hasn't been found in any dredging operations through the years."

Nick swallowed a bite of empanada. "It's too close to the reef. They don't dredge there. They only dredge shipping channels."

"Again, that's good news for us!" Josh said.

The group of five wolfed down the bag of empanadas and then everyone returned to the water to cool off. Josh brought along the football and they threw it around, enthusiastically making diving catches as the ball was tossed in each other's direction. Of course Giselle was positioned close to Josh but it was unclear whose strategy that was—his or hers. Eddie took two steps back and heaved an NFL spiral to Josh who made a leaping, fingertip catch. Giselle creamed him with a blindside tackle, taking them underwater. They both came up laughing as Eddie shook his head and once again. Things happen at the beach that don't happen anywhere else…the frolicking had begun. The game continued for a few more minutes with some more of the same until everyone had had enough sand and saltwater for the day.

Drying off and gathering their belongings, they all agreed a nap was not a bad idea. The sun had sucked the energy out of them, so they would shower and reenergize before reconvening for a fun dinner, once again, at Captain Joe's on the pier. They began their walk from the beach up to their room.

With four boys in one room that had two beds plus a couch, Brad said, "I get the floor!"

"No, no," Nick argued. "I'm good on the floor. Heck, I was planning on sleeping under trees down here. I'm just grateful to have a roof!"

Giselle shook her head, "Doesn't make any sense...I told you before. Baker, just grab your stuff and bring it to my room. I have an extra bed that's just holding my suitcase."

Josh agreed and the problem was solved. Only Giselle could have approved that.

"You just have to promise to stay on your side of the room, Baker," she joshed, with her green eyes looking over the top of her sunglasses.

He grinned, trying to hold in check anything beyond a feeling of friendship for Giselle. It was getting more difficult to do. This was either going to be awkward or a lot of fun.

"You have my word," he said, smiling.

The five friends made their way upstairs to their new room assignments and agreed to meet up at 5:30 for dinner and an evening of cheesy gift shops and cover bands. So far so good.

CHAPTER SEVENTEEN

Age and experience had made Tony a patient man. Like the alligators native to this sunny paradise of a state, he would stalk his victims for days before making his move. He had met with Dennis that morning at the Honeymooner Motel and Spa and, wisely, Dennis had provided him with the coordinates. Dennis was concerned he wouldn't live through the meeting—that Tony would get the information and then whack him. That hadn't happened. Paco was laid up on the bed with a cast and the cops had no reason to detain these two after Paco dropped the name that Tony had given him. They were simply counseled and released.

After getting the coordinates, Tony advised them he had paid for their room for the next five days. He then gave them both a stern warning not to interfere from here on out and he would cut them in on the profits at the end. Of course Paco and Dennis knew that wouldn't happen but they certainly didn't want to get on the Tony's bad side. The old Italian man wanted to keep these two guys right there where he knew where they were. He still may have a use for them. Paco and Dennis now needed a new plan.

5:30 rolled around and Eddie, Nick and Brad had made their way to Café El Bota, the predetermined meeting place before taking the walk down to Captain Joe's, on the pier. They sat at a small round table with high stools, each having their own choice of cold caffeinated drinks to help shake off the zombie effect of the nap. While Eddie looked out through the lobby area, expecting to see Josh and Giselle coming to meet them, he made eye contact with a very dark-skinned man who was watching them. The man looked away when he saw Eddie looking in his direction.

The look on Eddie's face turned curious as he tried to recall where he had seen that guy before.

"Nick, you see that guy over there in the khaki shorts and yellow t-shirt…with dreadlocks?"

Nick turned around and studied the Jamaican man for a moment. "What about him?"

"Does he look familiar to you?"

Nick studied him harder and then the man turned back around to look their way. Nick got a glimpse of his face before the man quickly turned away.

"Ah, yeah…he does look familiar but I'm not sure from where."

Brad looked as well. "Very typical Jamaican look, guys. Could be a lot of people down here."

"Could be but he keeps looking at us," Eddie continued.

Just at that moment, Josh and Giselle came into view, laughing about something. Josh leaned towards her to say something else. Giselle laughed again and then playfully punched him in the arm.

"Five minutes late…not too bad," Eddie poked.

Josh replied with that old lop-sided grin that had been his for as long as Eddie could remember, "This girl had the shower for a half hour!" Giselle punched him again.

"I'm on vacation! I'm not in a hurry for anything," she jibed back. "Plus, a girl has to look good."

The boys all nodded. Giselle did look good. The sun she had carefully absorbed that morning had given her a golden glow. She paired her new aura with light yellow dress shorts and a loose-fitting white button-up top and sandals. Josh was a tad more dressed up than the other guys, deciding on a button-up, collared shirt and dress khaki shorts. Josh's collar-length, sandy-blond hair was beginning to streak with the sun, a good look for him. Josh and Giselle looked very good together but other than the hint of playfulness, they were not giving any indication that they had made any big steps towards changing their relationship. It was easy to tell, however, that there was a mutual admiration that had probably been there for a long time. *Baby steps were good,* Eddie thought.

Brad jumped off his stool. "Well…you guys rea…"

From seemingly out of nowhere, the Jamaican man now stood by their table. No one had seen him approach. He had a look of cautious concern and it was obvious he had something to say.

"Excuse me," he began. "You tink ah may have a couple minutes? Eet important." He looked back at the lobby area and then to Eddie.

Eddie stammered but said, "Ye…yeah. What's up?"

The Jamaican nodded. "My name Buck…Buck Naked. I have to warn you of some ting.

Giselle laughed and turned away to not offend the guy.

Nick curled his upper lip in disbelief. "Your name is Buck Naked?"

"Yah mon. It was de first name dat come to me fatha when I was born."

"Really!" Josh exclaimed.

"No, jus kidding…is a nickname." He smiled for a brief moment and then resumed his look of concern.

"So what's up, Buck?" Eddie asked.

"I do de pool service here and at de resort nex door, and many utter places, but dees two ah very beeg accounts fah me. I have dem for da long time and I spend a lot of de time here."

"That's where I've seen you! At the pool deck here."

"Das right. You see, I get to see a lot of people and get to know da locals, de regulars who like to come here to prey on de tourist girl. Or de regular who jus' like to come here to drink."

"OK." Josh was following along.

"Yesterday, de Mexican guy…he watch you from de pool deck. He follow you up and dat when trouble start." He looked at Nick.

"Tell me about it," Nick said.

"Today, someone new watch you."

"You're kidding," Giselle responded.

Buck shook his head. "De guy yesterday…I not know him. Never see him before. But…today…" Buck paused and nodded his head, "Dis guy I know. He been here and nex door longer dan me all dees years, an he was watching you all."

"Who is he?" Eddie asked.

Buck took a deep breath and exhaled through his nose, looking away for a moment. "He old Italian man…wif mob ties. Florida mafia. He a big gun too, like a boss."

"What?" Eddie asked in disbelief. "Mafia?"

Buck nodded. "Oh, ya, mon. He be doin bidness here for de long time. Big spender and de hotels know it. He and his guys show up and someone at der table…hotel people come and move dem. He have many meetings here tru de years."

"What in world would a Florida mafia boss want with us?" Eddie asked what everyone was thinking.

"He bad news," Buck went on. "Wherever dis guy go…so do trouble."

"That's unthinkable. The last thing we want." Giselle said.

Josh looked at Eddie. "You think he may be connected to the two guys from last night?"

Eddie thought about it. "It has to be connected somehow. It's the only trouble we are making right now."

Buck snickered. "You don wan make trouble wit dis guy mon."

Eddie looked at Buck. Buck was not dressed to service pools. "Did you make a special trip out here to tell us this?"

With a genuine and honest look back into Eddie and Josh's eyes, he nodded. "I did mon. It dat important and it good karma. I you guardian angel, mon." Buck then relaxed into a broad, white smile that reminded Josh of his old pal back home, Tiny Brooks.

Josh glanced around at the others. "Well, Buck…can we buy our guardian angel dinner?"

Buck shook his head. "Tanks but no tanks mon. Runnin wit you guys scare me." He smiled. "Trute is, Buck have a date. Maybe anodder time doe." The serious look returned, "Mons, dat guy, his name Tony. He have a lazy eye, older Italian mon. Be looking behind you backs. Don know what you got goin on, but he play for keeps, OK?"

Josh extended his right hand, "Thank you Buck Naked. We appreciate it, and we won't ask how you got the nickname."

"Good, den I won' have to tell you de story." He smiled again.

After handshakes, Buck left the resort through the main entrance and went on with his evening with some lucky lady who was maybe intrigued with his nickname or possibly his sincerity and good nature—or possibly, all three.

"Well, I'm not sure why he went to all that trouble, but I'm glad he did," Nick said.

Eddie's sigh was nearly a grunt. "Just when we thought we could relax!" I can't imagine what the connection could be. Those two idiots from yesterday are in no way connected with the mob."

"Oh that's for sure." Giselle offered. "Do you guys remember seeing an older Italian man with a lazy eye here or anywhere yesterday? Someone like that can pick up the trail of a treasure hunt pretty quick. I mean, if it involves money…the mob wants it."

Josh looked at her. "You think he might have overheard something?"

"It's possible. It was a pretty big scene here yesterday, with the shooting. If this guy Tony was here then, he would have gotten some wind of it, don't you think?" she asked.

"Buck said this guy is a frequent flyer to these two resorts." Nick said. "I don't know any other way he could know what we are up to, other than if he somehow learned it from those two guys yesterday."

Brad added, "And why else would this guy Tony be watching us? Only for the treasure, right?"

"Like I said, it's the only trouble we're causing at the moment." Eddie grinned.

"At the moment is right," Giselle finished. "Let's go eat. We can talk more about it on the pier."

They paid their bill at Café El Bota and exited the lobby through the same doors as Buck Naked. It wasn't too far to the pier so they elected to go on foot tonight and see what they could get into after dinner.

It wasn't fifteen minutes before they were sitting at their table and ordering drinks. They had arrived just before the evening crowd and were able to slip right in. Captain Joe's really had the atmosphere you wanted when you came to the beach. The plywood tables and nautical debris hanging everywhere was just cool. They would miss this place when they went back home.

The server arrived with the drink tray and everyone, parched from the walk, grabbed their thirst-quenchers.

Brad offered his thoughts after he sat his drink on the coaster. "If this guy, Tony, got any information from the two bums from yesterday, why would he be watching us? I mean, all he needs are the coordinates, and those guys will have given him that."

Eddie replied, "You think they would have given him the coordinates?"

"Yeah…if not, Tony would have… terminated them. The mob has very persuasive methods," Brad answered.

Giselle offered, "So the fact that we saw the two guys last night…alive, means Tony got the coordinates from them yesterday and let them live?"

Brad added, "I think we have to assume that."

Josh looked concerned. "And what do we have to do now?"

Brad leaned in to the table. "We have to get in the water. We have to get down to Canaveral and get in the water. I guarantee if the mob knows the location, they will be there pronto!"

Eddie shook his head. "We can't. We have a contract with Family Jewels and, quite frankly, it's illegal. It's also not easy! There are restricted areas there."

Brad squinted one eye and looked back at Eddie. "You guys signed a contract with Family Jewels…I didn't. We can go down there and I can go out for ten minutes and see what I can find—just see if it's there."

Eddie leaned back in his chair. "Oh man…I don't know. What do you think, Nick?"

Nick struggled with it for a bit—starring off and thinking. He shook his head and said, "If we let Brad go out there for a few minutes, push some sand around and see if he sees the ribs of the ship or if he gets luckier and finds something shiny, then what? We can't recover it, legally."

Brad shrugged, "Like I said, I don't have a contract with

anyone. Who's to say I didn't drop my dive watch off the boat while fishing and I went down to get it and when I did, I found a few coins? These guys with metal detectors on the beach find things all the time."

"Lou said it's legal on the beach. But past a certain point you have to be permitted."

Brad turned his palms upward. "It's up to you guys, but this guy Tony…he's not going to wait for permits and neither will those other two guys, if they are able to get back on the trail anytime soon. I think we have to at least go see if it's there and then figure out a way to keep the mob out of it."

Josh took a drink of iced tea and then said, "That's not going to be easy…"

"…Or safe or even smart!" Giselle added.

A pretty young server walked by their table carrying an empty tray above her head. She looked at Josh and smiled. Josh grinned back at her, courteously. Giselle kicked him under the table. Josh looked at her. *What?* Their attention turned back to the conversation.

"Nick, it's kind of your call," Eddie said. "This is your gift, handed down to you from your grandfather. If we do it, we would just have to do it so as not to be in breach of contract with Lou. I don't want to double-cross him. He's a good guy."

Giselle added, "Don't forget the legal ramifications."

Josh rubbed his shin. Giselle jokingly scolded him with her eyes.

Nick thought for a moment and then nodded. "OK…first thing in the morning then? Really early though. Before the crowds are on the beach and then we have SNUBA with Ray later. So I'm thinking six o'clock."

"Brad will have to go out by himself. None of us can be with him." Giselle shook her head then added, "There is a very big safety issue there."

Brad smirked. He had an idea.

"What?" Josh asked.

"I'll call Nigel. I'll meet him at one of the marinas down there. I'm sure he knows the best place to rent a boat and maybe even has a contact."

Eddie nodded. "That's a very good idea. I'm sure he'll be ready and willing."

Their server returned and took their orders. They had a delicious dinner provided mostly by the ocean, followed by a couple of hours of simply chilling out and enjoying good conversation in the bar area. The friends managed to rehash everything that had happened the past three days, laughing at times, at things that weren't funny when they happened. They finished up their time by doing some browsing at Captain Joe's gift shop. Eddie, Brad and Nick decided it would be best to turn in early, since they had an early day tomorrow. Eddie had to drive Brad down to Canaveral since his truck was out of commission for a few days.

From the pier, Giselle heard a live cover band playing on a poolside stage that she wanted to go listen to for a while. The band was doing a mix of music from the 50s all the way through the 90s. They sounded pretty good and Josh agreed to go with her. They all parted company and decided to meet up again sometime tomorrow mid-morning after the three guys got back from their exploratory dive off Canaveral. No one wanted to admit it but they were all pretty excited to see what Brad might come up with. On the walk back to the resort the boys kept a close eye out for an aging Italian man with a lazy eye. They saw no one who matched that description, to their delight.

Josh and Giselle took the stairs from the pier down to the sand so they could walk the scenic route to the resort that hosted the band. They kicked off their shoes in order to enjoy the walk even more.

"Let's walk down to the water," Giselle suggested.

"We gonna hold hands like everyone else down there?" he joked.

She laughed flirtingly, and shrugged one shoulder—not saying yes *or* no.

The pair walked underneath the pier to the point where the warm water began lapping at their toes. There was a half moon high in the sky that painted its reflection across the sea in front of them. Standing underneath the old wooden structure, Giselle put one hand on Josh's shoulder for balance and picked up a small seashell with her toes. Without taking her left hand away from Josh, she used the other hand to rub the sand away revealing a cream and purple colored beach treasure. She looked up at him and stared into his eyes in a very new way. Giselle had a light in her eyes, a look that told Josh she was really happy to be with him— just him. They had never been alone before and with the music in the background setting a romantic mood, Giselle felt playful— adventurous. Josh could sense it and felt his heart begin to race. He hoped he was reading things right—but at the same time, he was pretty nervous.

Giselle then spoke softly, "I just love the beach, Josh. Don't you?" She held her gaze. "I mean…it makes you feel like you can put things the way you want them in your life. It's like a cleansing for the soul to come here where you can wash away all the stress, and only feel the things in your life that are good." Giselle looked out at the blackness and vastness of the ocean before them and then sighed and looked at Josh once again.

Her gorgeous green eyes were warm and soft—friendly, honest and even loving. The warm lighting off the pier gave her tanned face a beautiful and healthy glow that Josh couldn't get enough of. She wanted him to be glad *he* was there with her also… and he was. He was trying his best to remain composed and simply take one minute at a time. Josh had dreamed many times of one day having just the right moment with Giselle to tell her how he felt about her. He was never sure it would ever happen but if there was ever a time where it could, it was during this time at the beach. Things were different there.

Josh nodded then replied, "I like the beach too. I feel refreshed here. Not like physically, but mentally refreshed." Josh was struggling with what he wanted to say. "I think…I think you feel things at the beach the way you want them to be. It's the atmosphere that does it." he smiled.

Giselle's left hand slid off of Josh's shoulder as she looked back to her small seashell and then used both hands to clean away the final bits of sand. These two weren't fooling anyone, including themselves. They both knew there was something between them that was just a little more than friendship—that mutual admiration and chemistry.

She beamed up at him. "Exactly," she said. Her eyes fell away but her lips held the smile. Her ears then heard a song she liked.

"Oh...listen!" She exclaimed.

Oh when the sun's beats down, melts the tar up...on the roof...

"Oh I like this... such a good beach song," she said, as she continued with her playful mood.

And your shoes get so hot, you wish your tired feet were fire-proof...

Having fun with it, she began to sing as she swayed back and forth while walking.

"Under the boardwalk...down by the sea, on a blanket with my baby, is where I'll be..."

She smiled again, teasingly, mischievously, as she looked at Josh while she continued the little dance. The old song had helped to set a mood. She grabbed his right arm and jumped in front of him as they both came to an abrupt stop. Giselle felt fearless and confident yet playful. It was the magic of the beach with the sounds of the surf and the music and the scent of the salt air and nobody watching. The moment was just right for her as the stars aligned themselves for these two young kids who had a destiny since the day they met at the library, four years ago. Her green eyes glistened as she looked deep into his and cocked her head slightly, just inches in front of him. Time stood still for Josh as his eyes widened slightly in surprise. They stood so close, he could feel her breath on his lips.

Then just above a whisper she told him, "I like you, Josh Baker. You are fun. I feel safe around you. I feel *me* around you. I don't have to pretend and do you know how important that is?" She paused for a moment and then finished. "What do you think about that?"

Josh's heart was hammering. The beach had done its magic as his skin tingled with anticipation.

He took a quick breath and did the best he could.

"Giselle." He paused to get his words right, "Do you remember when you came to our boat dock that day when Eddie and I were fishing? You came to tell us about the wallet that had been found with Art Otis' initials in it."

Giselle slowly let her head tilt to one side, sultrily, as she listened and her eyes held his without a distraction.

"How could I forget that?" she replied softly.

"I came to the top of the riverbank to help you down to the boat dock."

"I remember," she said, dancing her eyebrows up and down once.

"I held your hand as you went down the bank to the dock. I held it so you wouldn't fall." He paused again and took another deep breath and looked straight into the green eyes that had spent many nights in his dreams.

"You held my hand longer than necessary." Her eyes sparkled. "I didn't mind."

Josh grinned, not believing what he was about to tell her.

"Giselle…that moment…that feeling of holding your hand has stayed with me all these years. I would lie in bed at night, and that would be what I thought about until I fell asleep. I locked it into my memory…my heart, along with every other time you touched my hand or my shoulder or…or like when I had to carry you from

Eddie's van the other day because your leg fell asleep. I was very happy to do that! Those moments are treasures to me and I have every one of them locked away for whenever I want to lie in bed at night when it's quiet, and think of you! I've liked you since that day on the boat dock and, let me tell you, it's been a long four years keeping it a secret." He laughed nervously and she did too. Their eyes fell away from each other's in embarrassment but quickly reconnected.

"I've always wanted to tell you and I didn't know if I would ever get the chance but...there it is. I've had a crush on you since I was fourteen years old. I've thought about you so much and...and I have always thought that we could be good together."

Giselle shook her head in disbelief even while Josh was still emptying his heart. Her warm smile and soft eyes told Josh it was completely mutual. She backed away from him a few inches, looked down at her toes in the sand and then up at his eyes once again, smiling as the moonlight highlighted her beautiful auburn hair.

"So...what do we do now Mr. Baker?"

They stood on the shore, saltwater washing over their feet as they looked at one another. Both were nervous and neither one had ever thought beyond this moment nor what would be next. Just a couple of hundred yards away, the band continued its 60s set, absolutely nailing Mel Carters *Hold me, Thrill me, Kiss me.* Josh stepped closer and took Giselle's hands in his. She looked at him— his blue eyes and long, sandy blonde hair were the epitome of a beach romance. Giselle was captured by him at that moment and now it was her turn to be short of breath.

"Josh...I have a confession," she said softly.

He looked at her—waiting but confident.

Looking right into his eyes with tears in her own, she shook her head and admitted, "My leg really wasn't asleep getting out of Eddies' van."

Josh Baker leaned towards Giselle O'Connor and tenderly kissed her on the lips. Their arms went around each other as the seashell fell to the ground…

Thrill me, thrill me
Walk me down the lane where shadows will be, will be
Hiding lovers just the same as we'll be, we'll be
When you make me tell you I love you…

CHAPTER EIGHTEEN

Josh and Giselle enjoyed each other's company until about 1:00 a.m., completely opening up to one another, laughing and dancing, both really happy and relieved to have finally admitted to themselves what everyone else had known all along. They discussed the age difference and agreed it didn't really matter to them so it shouldn't really matter to anyone else. Afterwards, Josh did the right thing and slept on the floor in his own room, although he didn't actually sleep very much at all. Giselle, too, lay down in her bed, contented, and fell asleep smiling.

The others had turned in early, as planned, and were very excited to have Brad and Nigel go do an exploratory dive.

Eddie's phone alarm sounded at 5:45 a.m. He shut it off and rolled out of bed to begin waking the others to go meet Nigel and do the free dive. He hadn't heard Josh come in last night and tripped on him in the darkness of the early morning.

"Hey!" Josh complained, waking suddenly.

"What are...I thought you were sleeping in the other room,"

Eddie said, regaining his balance.

"Nah." Josh replied.

"You guys fight or something?" Eddie asked, trying to figure things out.

"Hardly. I'll tell you about it later."

Eddie stopped and looked at his friend lying on the floor, wondering.

"Huh!" was all he said.

Within a few minute they were all up and stirring—ready to get down to Canaveral and get wet. Nick and Josh had planned to stay behind, but once they woke and felt the adrenaline and anticipation of what they could possibly uncover today, they had to join the others for the ride down the coast. They did not wake Giselle, who had said she wanted to stay behind and sun herself once again. Josh slid a note under her door as they left. Eddie stopped at the vending area on their floor and got a bag of ice for the Bus AC.

Heading down I-95, Josh's head was doing the sleepy wobble. Eddie looked over at him and laughed.

"Hey…wake up!" he joked.

"Whew." Josh shook his head. "Tough time this morning." He sat up straight.

Eddie looked towards the highway and then at his best friend. "So what went on last night? What did you guys do?"

Josh glanced at him and then did his little trademark lop-sided grin. "Well we walked on the beach," he replied, nonchalantly.

"Uh huh…What else?"

Josh smiled. "What makes you think there was anything else?"

"Well, did you go listen to the band?"

"We did…eventually," he said, smiling and looking straight ahead.

Brad and Nick were in the back but not really paying attention. They were in a conversation of their own about the dive.

Eddie pleaded and gestured with his right hand, "Dude…why do I have to pry this from you? Did you guys get kissy on the beach or something?"

Josh just bit his cheek to hide the larger smile and said nothing, still looking straight ahead.

"You did! Are you serious? You guys are a *thing?*"

Josh turned and looked over at Eddie. They didn't keep secrets from each other. He hesitated for just a moment and then simply said, "I think so."

"Whaaattt?" Eddie said. "That's crazy! How did that happen?" Eddie begged for information.

Josh shrugged and shook his head. Smiling, he said, "It just happened…I don't know—she just had this look in her eye last night and she was so sweet and beautiful—Giselle is always beautiful, but…it was just the right time for both of us…and it happened. We kissed and then we talked and really opened up to each other." Josh shook his head again, "I'm telling you, it was incredible. I didn't want it to end."

"Wow…That just blows me away. That's so cool, Josh! I'm really happy for you! I know you've always had a thing for her."

"Can't deny that."

"You guys have to take it slow, Josh. I mean really slow. You don't want to mess up a good friendship. I would hate to see that. I would hate to see it not work out and then you guys lose your friendship."

Josh nodded. "We talked about that. And it's easy to say *take it slow* but these things have their own legs. They become what they become at their own speed. It's hard to keep the reins pulled back sometimes, you know? But we are. We're going to try to take it slow."

"I just want the best for you guys. I'm really happy for you."

"I appreciate that, Eddie."

"Dream come true, right?"

Josh grinned again and a fist bump concluded the conversation.

A short time later, Eddie wheeled the bus off of Interstate 95 and onto Florida 528. After a couple of miles, he hung a right onto Highway 1 South along the Indian River, and soon came to Bud's Marina by Highway 515. Bud's wasn't the biggest or best-equipped marina in the area but Nigel knew the owner and could get a "no questions asked" boat rental for a couple hours, cheap.

Eddie parked the bus and Brad spotted Nigel in a gray SUV tucked out of the way in a shady area. Floridians know that shade always trumps proximity when it comes to parking. The four guys walked from the bus to where Nigel was parked as the British man stepped from his vehicle. He took the time to scan the parking lot to make sure no other cars pulled in. They had to be certain nobody had followed them.

A courteous exchange of handshakes started things off.

"I already set things up. We're ready to go," he said.

"Sweet," said Brad. He looked around at the many boats in their slips. "Earlier the better, right?"

Nigel nodded and took his last drink of coffee. "Let's get on out there, mate. It's early and the fewer eyes on us the better."

Eddie felt energetic, full of anticipation. Although their plan was risky and far into the gray area of legality, he was very excited to see what was under the sand at those coordinates. The four guys walked over to a short wooden walkway that led to the slips. Nigel had rented a simple little nineteen-foot Bayliner Capri. His intention was to blend in and to look like a tourist. He also rented a couple of fishing poles to complete the package. His idea was to look like a father/son team who had thrown a fishing idea together at the last minute—and he had nailed it. Of course, Nigel had on his flowered shirt, khaki shorts and Panama hat, which sold the look. He also had his tourist beach bag with him to carry a couple of items, just in case.

The guys approached their rental at slip number thirty-one. Bud had not bothered to walk out with Nigel and the boys, but he did have the Bayliner gassed up with the key in it, ready to go. Brad and his captain for the day stepped down into the boat and readied themselves for an early morning dive. Nigel pulled a handheld GPS from his beach bag as Brad began doing a series of deep-breathing exercises to stretch and fill his lungs.

Eddie looked on as the two guys prepped and familiarized themselves with the rental boat. Brad, being a Marine Mechanics Institute graduate, would do a thorough check before leaving the marina.

"Well…Josh, Nick and I will drive on over to the beach and watch you guys from there," Eddie said.

Nigel nodded. "Right by the barge channel. We are going straight through the barge channel and then northeast out to the point of the coordinates."

Nick was very excited at this point. Even though they were not supposed to be doing it this way, this is what he had been waiting for all his life. He just wished he could be on the boat! But confirmation would be great. If Brad and Nigel could go out there and fan away the sand and find the ribs his grandpa had located, it would be a great day. If they could find something shiny, it would be an indescribable day.

"You have the camera?" Nick asked.

Nigel nodded and grinned at him. "We'll go see what we can find for ya, mate. Hopefully we'll have a celebration dinner tonight."

"I'm happy to buy if we do!" Nick replied.

"Two thumbs up for that!" Josh joked.

Brad fired up the engine and let it warm for a moment. Nigel untied the lines and they were ready to go.

Brad grinned, saluted, and said, "See you guys back here." He put it in gear and began idling out of the slip.

"We'll be watching," Eddie replied.

Nick slapped Eddie on the shoulder and took off towards the bus. "Come on…let's go get into position!"

"Right behind ya man!"

Eddie started the bus and, within seconds, the three of them were back out onto Highway 1 north where they would take 528 across to Merritt Island and then on out to the little town of Cape

Canaveral, on the beach. Soon they arrived at Jetty Park Beach, right beside the barge channel where they could see Brad and Nigel motor past.

Walking out to the beach, Nick pointed. "Guys, we can go all the way out there."

Josh approved. "That will be perfect. Right out to the end of the jetties."

It was 7:50 a.m. and activities along the beach were beginning to come alive. Of course the real fishermen on charters were already out. Brad and Nigel didn't have that boat traffic to contend with but the pleasure boaters were now buzzing along through the no-wake zones of the area. They motored along, obeying every sign and marker along the way. Brad took the time to fill Nigel in on the visit from Buck Naked and what he had to say about the *Italian man with the noticeably lazy eye*. He also told him the bits and pieces he had overheard about Josh and Giselle. Nigel was happy for them and told Brad he had a feeling about them

As they exited the barge channel, staying to the right-hand side, they noticed three familiar figures at the very end of the walkway that paralleled the jetty.

As they powered past them, Josh called out, "Happy fishing!"

"Hope you catch something!" Nick finished.

Nigel and Brad grinned and waved as Brad added power to the Bayliner and headed out to sea. In just a few minutes they would know. Nigel removed his Panama hat as the boat skipped along like a stone on the river.

Nigel leaned towards Brad. "We should probably make a few runs back and forth, so it doesn't really look like we are heading out to one spot," Nigel recommended.

"Like we're just out here playing around," Brad agreed.

"Right."

Brad turned south and hummed along on a sightseeing tour of Canaveral and the upper Cocoa Beach area. Nigel stuck the poles in a couple of aftermarket rod holders that had been badly mounted on the boat. He wanted to make it look like they were doing anything besides what they were really doing out there!

After a few minutes of diversion maneuvers, Brad cut the boat around and headed towards the spot they wanted to "fish."

Nigel laid the GPS on the small area between the steering wheel and the windshield so Brad could navigate to the point with ease. Josh, Eddie and Nick watched from the end of the jetty. Nick was using binoculars Brad had given to him earlier.

The Canaveral Peninsula is the area of the outer islands that hooks its way around and points east, and by doing so, creates a pocket for catching debris along its shoreline—such as nets, cork floats, Styrofoam coolers and…possibly, treasure fleets! Nick's theory of the *Concepcion* being the ship that his grandfather located was actually quite plausible. A westward--blowing storm could easily carry a ship into this pocket and take it apart on its reef. They would know soon enough.

Most of the other boaters had vanished with the exception of one at pretty much the same longitude as Brad and Nigel, but that boat was nearly a half-mile away. Most likely fishermen on the reef.

Getting close now, Brad eased along as he watched the mark on the GPS closing in on his bow. At that moment a small U.S. Coast Guard vessel rounded the Cape. Brad and Nigel were relieved to see it continue on into the barge channel, going about its business.

Brad then said, "We're home," as he cut the engine.

Nigel scanned the horizon and then the shoreline. The only other vessel even remotely close to them was the fishing boat to the south. The situation was perfect.

"Let's drop anchor," Nigel said. "We just need a few minutes and I think we got it."

Brad cast the anchor and then tied it off to a stern cleat. They drifted for just a bit as the anchor line grew taut. They had reached their target.

From the end of the jetty, Nick watched intently. "They're on the mark. They dropped anchor." Nick was very excited but also somewhat somber as he saw where his grandfather had spent some of the last moments of his life. At that exact point Butch Dawson, back in 1973, could have made his greatest discovery. If this really was the site of the sunken *Concepcion*, Butch, along with Chuck Henderson, will have made an incredible contribution to history in the rediscovery of this ship. Nick snapped himself out of his melancholy and again became very driven with anticipation. His heart pounded like a jungle drum.

Brad took his shirt off and threw on flippers and a mask. After doing so he did a few more deep-breathing exercises to stretch his lungs as far as he could and be able to take in as much air as possible. Brad was in good physical condition and the last time he timed himself, could stay underwater for about a minute and a half. He then sat on the bow of the boat and hung his legs off the side.

"Are ya ready, mate?" Nigel asked.

"I'm ready," he replied.

"Depth sounder says it's eighteen feet. If you feel a rip current along the reef…well, be very careful. If it's bad, we can secure a line to you after the first trip down."

"Let me go down and see first. Worst case scenario, I will bob up over there somewhere. You can always come and get me."

"As long as you can tread water, mate."

"I'll be fine. Let's do this."

Nigel nodded and then Brad pulled his goggles down, took two deep breaths, held the third one and dropped over the side.

"He's in the water!" Nick shouted.

"Shhh..Nick, quiet," Eddie reminded him. They didn't want to attract any attention either.

Once in the water, Brad was amazed at how clear it was once you were away from the stirred--up murkiness of the shoreline that he was more accustomed to.

Instead of looking down right away, he took a couple of seconds and looked out to sea. He could see the gradual slope of the coastline that would eventually drop off into the abyss a few miles out. It was quite intimidating and made him feel quite small in the universe. Everything was quiet and he was now in a completely different world.

It was time to get to work and with a few kicks, Brad was quickly at the bottom. Not wasting any time, he looked up at the bow of the boat which marked their coordinate target. Making sure he was right on the spot, he started scooping sand around. He noticed that the water seemed calm at the bottom and felt no current pulling on him whatsoever. He alternated between fanning the sand and grabbing handfuls of it and moving it aside. So far, no piles of gold but plenty of seashells and many schools of beautiful fish. It was also important for him to watch for reef sharks but so far there were none in sight. He swished his hand back and forth once again and a flounder decided he didn't like Brad in his habitat and scurried off in distress.

Brad had a good look around but it was time to surface, get some air, and think about this for a second. He felt like he was searching too willy-nilly and wanted to bring some sense into the plan.

As soon as he broke the surface, Nigel fired a question at him. "Whata ya see down there?"

Brad grabbed a couple deep breaths and replied, "A whole lot of sand, and a whole lot of ocean."

Nigel nodded. "Remember mate, we are sitting dead square on the coordinates. Straight down off our bow."

"I know. It just looks so big when you are down there. It's fascinating, really."

"Oh yes...but work the area straight down very well."

Brad nodded and put his mask back on. Two deep breaths later he was on his way back down, studying his work area as he descended. He noticed that one area just a few feet north was- more elevated than some of the rest of the sea bottom. Maybe it meant something and maybe it didn't but he would work his way towards it for certain. Swishing and scooping he moved the sand around— each time praying something would jump out at him from three hundred years ago. Brad moved left just a few feet from the area he had been working and, using two hands, forced a huge hill of sand to one side. He had used up a lot of his energy and was almost out of breath when he saw it. In the stirring, swirling sand he saw something that had the appearance of tarnished silver! Tarnished but metallic. He grabbed it and ascended with great anticipation—not even looking at what was in his hand. Oxygen was the priority for now.

Breaking top water again, he immediately gasped for air and grabbed the gunwale. Nigel looked at him expectantly as Brad caught his breath. He then looked up at Nigel and opened his hand. A watch! A tarnished silver Rolex.

The British man cocked his head. "Well, it's a nice find but it's not a three-hundred-year-old Rolex." Nigel took it and flipped it around. "Maybe fifty though," he said.

"That was a needle in a haystack, right?"

"Sure was, mate. Let's hope there are more needles." Nigel grinned.

Two more deep breaths and Brad was on his way down again. Swishing and pushing sand, he worked his way to the small mound he had wanted to investigate. As he worked the mound, he soon found why it was a mound. It was simply a domed coral outcrop covered with sand that had caught his attention. He was disappointed and moved left, having about thirty seconds of air left before he had to surface once again. Scooping sand with lessening enthusiasm, he quickly worked his way through his breath cycle. With just a few seconds left his hand hit something different—something splintered! He saw just the corner of it but it appeared to be wood! Brad's eyes opened wide as he continued with his excavation and there it was! A section of very old, albeit well-preserved wood! *The ribs of a ship,* he remembered Nick reading from his grandfather's diary. Could it be? It was time to surface.

As always, Nigel was looking down as Brad come up, bursting through the surface of the water. Sucking in air, he tried to talk before he was ready and began coughing while small waves splashed off the side of the boat, hitting him in the face.

Nigel knew Brad had seen something but didn't know if it was gold or a shark.

"What is it, mate?"

"Wood...maybe the ribs. It's a real heavy beam...maybe a foot across...I'm not sure how long! I can't believe it!" Brad said, still trying to catch his breath.

"You need to take a break, Brad. Come on in the boat and rest your lungs a bit. It's not going anywhere."

Brad reluctantly agreed. "OK," he said, drying his face with a towel.

Nick watched intently with the binoculars from the jetty. "He's getting back on the boat now!" He continued to study the scene. "Brad is very animated...doing a swishing motion with his hands and now he has his hands wide apart like he's describing something!" Nick yearned to hear what Brad was telling Nigel on the boat and then handed off the binoculars to Josh who was tapping him on the shoulder, wanting a turn.

After helping Brad climb back onto the boat, Nigel did another scan of their surroundings. Not much had changed in the past ten minutes. The activity along the shoreline was picking up as he noticed more and more walkers out doing their thing. Far out to sea, he could now see a freighter making its way toward the coast. To their south, the small fishing boat was still where it was a few minutes ago. Nigel picked up the recovered Rolex from the seat where he had laid it and gave it another look. The lens was scratched and foggy after untold years of rolling around in the ocean but the watch was intact. It was also very heavy and may have lain in this area for quite some time. Most likely, it was an unfortunate and overly exuberant fisherman's loss. Turning it over, he noticed some script on the back. A name, possibly. Rubbing the back cover a bit, Nigel hoped for better contrast, and he got it. On the back of the watch he could then read the name *Rocco Palombo*.

"It's amazing down there!" Brad exclaimed. "I may have found a new hobby."

"Catch your breath, young man. Maybe you can go down one or two more times but we don't want to be seen here for too long." Nigel looked around again, his eyes fixed on the other fishing boat which now seemed to be moving around. There was something peculiar about that boat but he couldn't put his finger on what it was.

Brad's cell phone rang. He pulled it from Nigel's beach bag where he had placed it before the dive. Caller ID read *Josh Baker*.

"Hey man," Brad answered.

"Whata ya see down there?"

"Well, I found an old Rolex."

"Really? Anything else?"

"Josh, I may have found the ribs...of the ship." Brad smiled, waiting for Josh's response.

"No way!"

"Maybe. I'm giving my lungs a little break, but I'm going back down to see."

Josh turned to Eddie and Nick. "He may have found the ribs."

Brad could hear Nick's excitement in the background.

Josh continued, "OK, man...let us know!"

The two clicked off and Brad put the phone back in the beach bag.

Nigel's look was distant as he looked towards the other boat. Brad took notice.

"Something bother you out there?" Brad asked.

"What's peculiar about that boat out there? That fishing boat." He handed Brad the binoculars.

After a brief moment, Brad replied, "It's a fishing boat with no lines in the water. No rods even."

"Right. So why would they be on the reef with a fishing boat and not even have rods in the holders?"

Brad looked again through the binoculars, "Is that the sort of thing they train you to pay attention to?"

Nigel shrugged. "With no training at all, you spotted that!"

Brad gasped, "Nigel...Nigel a diver just surfaced! Two divers! Another one!"

"Let me see." Nigel took the binoculars.

He watched for a moment as the two divers had a conversation with the older man driving the boat. The high-powered binoculars let Nigel see an intense discussion. The older olive-skinned man pointed towards the water with great authority and the divers disappeared beneath the surface. The aging man put his hands on his hips as he watched them go down. Nigel was still watching as the man lifted his head and looked straight at the Bayliner carrying

Brad and Nigel. Without binoculars, the man could not see Nigel looking at him but Nigel could certainly see *him*! Those men were not fishing...for fish.

CHAPTER NINETEEN

Back on the jetty, Eddie was now taking a turn with the binoculars.

"What are they doing?" Josh asked, looking towards the boat.

Eddie studied the scene for a moment, moving the binoculars right and then left. "Nigel...Nigel is watching another boat that is way, way down the reef."

Nick nodded, "He is very cautious. Probably just keeping an eye on his position."

"Hmm," Eddie thought. "That boat is about the same distance out on the reef but a half mile or so south."

Nick tapped Eddie out. His turn again.

After a moment, Nick said, "Looks like Brad is going back in now."

As Brad hung his legs over the side of the boat, he did his ritual of deep breathing to stretch his lungs and then relaxed a moment.

"When you find that wood again, start looking for a parallel rib about three feet away. If you find another one that looks the same, we may have a ship. If you find anything shiny, we may have a *treasure* ship."

Brad nodded quickly, anxious to get back in the water.

"Good luck, mate." Nigel grinned.

Two seconds later Brad took a deep breath and hit the water. Nigel looked back over his shoulder at the other boat. He was pretty sure the man was still standing in the same position but this time his hands were up. Nigel didn't want to confirm it but he was certain he was now being watched with binoculars. Time to play it cool. Nigel grabbed one of the rods they had brought along for props and cast it in the opposite direction that Brad was diving. No hook...just a big sinker.

Brad descended quickly once again and swam straight to the spot he had found the wood just a few minutes ago. The sand had found its way back to the wood beam but was still visible and Brad, with fresh lungs-full of air, swished and dug around it. It was remarkably intact and he uncovered about eighteen inches of the beam. Now it was time to look for the next one. Brad kicked his flippers to reposition himself just beyond the first beam. *Nigel said about three feet,* Brad thought.

Again, he started swishing and digging, about halfway through his breath cycle. He moved around and positioned himself to start digging like a dog. He was now more productive and was moving the sand between his legs and behind him, taking the murky cloud along with it. He was about ready to surface for a fresh supply of oxygen when his left hand hit something and stopped abruptly. It felt right. Having about ten seconds left, he frantically pulled the sand out of the area and, sure enough, the same dark color and texture as the first! *Just as Nigel said, about three feet away, and perfectly parallel to the first rib.* Going just a few seconds beyond his limit he pulled the sand to expose the second beam. From the corner of his eye he thought he saw something green in the removed sand pile. Too late...it was time for air! Pushing off the bottom he went straight up, fast.

Busting the surface and gasping for air in true "Brad fashion," he exclaimed, "I found it! I found the second one!"

"Amazing!" Nigel said with a grin. He helped Brad up to the side of the boat for a break.

Nigel continued, "So we have a *ship*! Anything shiny?"

Still breathing heavy, "Gold, no. But I saw something green as I pushed off the bottom. I want to see what that was."

"Green is emeralds, mate. Unless it's copper."

"Didn't get a good look. Maybe nothing, too," Brad said, now breathing easier.

Nigel looked back over his shoulder. The other boat was still there. He pulled up the binoculars and observed the divers now climbing into the boat. They were done with that spot.

"One more time, mate. Whenever you're ready. Last dive though."

Brad took a deep breath. He was ready. "OK."

Brad then took his deepest breath yet and dropped off the side of the boat. Kicking straight down once again, he went directly to the two ribs. Brad had made a small "debris field" with the excavation of the ribs and wanted to see what he thought he saw a minute ago that was green. He quickly started moving the sand pile around and in just a flash, there it was! A quarter-sized emerald popped right out of the sand! Brad's eyes went wide as he grabbed it right away. He knew there was no time to celebrate so he repositioned and immediately began scooping the sand between the ribs. He knew that's where the good stuff would lie. He also knew that if he found something, he couldn't take much, legally...just a sample. That would be a real test of restraint.

Nearly frantic, he pulled the sand away but wasn't having any luck. Disappointment began to set in as he raked and raked, all the while running lower and lower on air. Brad then thought to move to the other side of one of the ribs. *There should be more ribs and many places for the good stuff to be hiding.* Pulling, and pulling the sand, he again hit something familiar a few feet away! *Another rib!* he thought. With just a few seconds left, he dug around the heavy beam, looking, feeling and praying in his last seconds of his last dive. Almost ready to kick off the bottom, his hand hit something close to and maybe even underneath the third beam. It felt like a cable and his first thought was that maybe it was some old fishing rigging...until the sand drifted away and the sun above reflected the gold color!

Brad's eyes again flew open as he held in his hand a length of gold chain! He was ecstatic! The chain that he could see was about two feet in length and stuck underneath the rib. Now a few seconds beyond his breath cycle, his lungs began to ache as he pulled to try to free it. He was not leaving bottom without it. He pulled and dug, trying his best to dislodge it but was beginning to realize he may not be able to take this one home. With one final pull, he yanked and broke the splinter of wood that had it snagged and the chain was free! Brad immediately pushed off the bottom with the chain and the emerald in his left hand. His lungs were now screaming for air as his peripheral vision began to go dark.

Hitting the surface, Nigel grabbed him, knowing he was down for too long. He hauled him up into the boat as Brad lay there face down, gasping desperately. Nigel shook his head.

"I was about to dive in. That was too much, my friend. You stayed down too long."

Brad had started to compose himself and was drawing good deep breaths while still on all fours in the boat. Finally regaining some energy, he rolled his head right to see Nigel and smiled wryly. He lifted his left hand and it was then that Nigel could see what was hanging from his fingers. On the seat beside him, Brad dropped twenty-four inches of gold chain and a large, beautiful emerald.

The two guys looked at each other and smiled, and then laughed excitedly. Nigel thumped Brad on the back.

"Well mate," he began. "I think that makes it a *treasure* ship!

Brad's phone rang again. He got up into a seat and then pulled the phone from the bag.

"Hey," he answered.

"Well?" Nick waited anxiously with the phone in speaker mode.

Brad played with him. "I'm sorry Nick," he said solemnly. Brad heard the disappointment in the silence on the other end, knowing Josh and Eddie were looking at each other.

Brad continued, "I'm really sorry, buddy...but I only had enough air to bring up one gold chain and one emerald." He grinned, waiting for the response and when he got it, he had to pull the phone away from his ear.

Back at the jetty, Nick whooped, hollered and high-fived Josh and Eddie and then did a happy-dance. Josh and Eddie laughed at him and had a hard time settling him down to attention. The truth was, they were nearly as excited as Nick!

Brad continued, "We bingo'd it guys...It was right where Butch Dawson said it was! He and Captain Henderson absolutely nailed the coordinates that night."

"I can't wait to see what you got," Nick said, calming himself just a bit.

"This treasure is beautiful, guys. Absolutely pristine," Brad finished.

Nigel nudged him and nodded towards the other boat which was now coming their way fast.

"Gotta go guys. Gotta get out of here."

Brad put the phone back in the beach bag along with the chain and emerald and covered them with the towel. He developed a slight knot in his stomach as the other boat drew nearer to them. Nigel started the engine on the Bayliner and moved it away from the point of the coordinates. As he began to head for shore, the aging olive-skinned man waved to them using both arms. His divers were seated.

"I don't like this, mate. I don't like it at all."

"Should we run?" Brad recommended.

Nigel considered it but didn't want to draw their fire if this turned into a can of worms and those guys had a faster boat. He knew Josh, Eddie and Nick were watching and could possibly bail them out, eventually anyway, if there was trouble. He was now about three hundred feet away from the coordinates point and decided to play the tourist card.

Nigel waved back with all the naiveté of a British tourist.

As the other boat was throttled down and drifted towards the Bayliner he said, "Hello, mates! What be ya catchin' today?"

Brad looked at him. "Are you a pirate?"

"Play the role, Brad." Nigel smiled while waving.

As the boat got closer, Brad gasped as he noticed the lazy eye. *De olt Italian mon wit de lazy eye,* Buck Naked had said.

"Nigel, trouble. Big trouble," Brad whispered while smiling at the guys drifting close.

"Stay cool, mate. I see it."

"They don't know *us*," Brad said.

"Stay cool."

Onboard the fishing vessel were two guys outfitted with diving tanks and one aging Italian man with a noticeably lazy eye who was doing the driving. The older man was dressed in trousers and a white pullover shirt and did not look like a fisherman.

Nigel spoke up. "You gentlemen catching fish? What do you do? Spearfish?"

Tony looked back at the two divers and grinned malevolently. "Haven't caught a thing all morning and it's got me pretty upset,"

Tony replied.

Nigel nodded, "Ah...well...I guess that's why they call it fishing and not catching, right?" Nigel faked a laugh.

Tony nodded, looking straight at him. "We couldn't help notice... the boy was over the side. Anything in particular you're looking for?"

Nigel paused while thinking but still held his smile—playing the stupid tourist all the way.

"Ah...yeah," Nigel replied. "The boy here dropped his fishing knife overboard. Old family relic, so he went down to find it."

"Mm hmm." Tony wondered if there were more to his story. "And while you were down there, did ya find anything else?" Tony probed.

Needing desperately to get these guys off their backs and gone, Nigel decided to throw them a bone.

"As a matter of fact we did," Nigel said. "Just plain old dumb luck but while my boy here was down he also found this." Nigel reached for the driver's seat and Tony flinched, his hand going for what was tucked in the back of his waistband.

"Easy, mate," Nigel said as he froze momentarily, and then bent on down to retrieve the watch. "We found this."

He held up the Rolex.

Tony's eyes opened up a bit, even the lazy one, as Nigel was now talking his language.

"I guess you can have these things restored from any condition. We're not going to do anything with it. You guys want it?" Nigel smiled again...tourist-like.

Tony was interested. "I would love to see that watch," he said.

Nigel tossed it across the water and Tony grabbed it midair. "It's yours, mate!" His best friendly smile.

Tony held the watch at arm's length and looked it over. He then flipped it over to inspect the back. His eyes squinted in an effort to see the writing on the back. From his pocket he pulled out a pair of reading glasses. Taking a second look at the writing, Tony's expression went from curious to shock. His mouth dropped open and he looked over his glasses without lifting his head. *Rocco!* he thought. *It couldn't be.*

Tony's eyes drifted back up to Nigel, "I need to know exactly where you found this watch." Tony said calmly but firmly.

Nigel was sure that trick would work and couldn't imagine why the name on the back of the watch mattered to this man.

There was an uneasy silence. Tony stared at them, his lazy eye drooping now. The two men in the wet suits stood up. Tony looked over his shoulder at one of them. He held up the watch to show them. "Rocco Palombo...1973, traitor, backstabber, snitch."

Tony was putting the puzzle together now. In early December of 1973 the two men, Butch Dawson and Chuck Henderson, had come back from dumping the body of Rocco Palombo, with a story of treasure. Tony didn't believe them and had killed them both. Now, with the grandest of grand miracles, Rocco's watch had been found and where lies the watch, so must lie the treasure. And if the treasure lay where the watch had lain, that means that Paco and Dennis had given Tony coordinates which were about a half mile off. They would pay for that with their lives very soon. The good news for Nigel and Brad was that Tony didn't know they were associated with the rest of the young group at all. Nigel did look somewhat familiar but Tony couldn't place him. *These tourists all look alike.*

"I'm going to ask you again, gentlemen...Where exactly did you find this watch?"

There was a pause and then Brad swallowed hard and spoke up. "It was just down there...where my knife was."

"We didn't mark it on GPS, mates. Is it important?" Nigel held his palms up, looking confused as he played the role well.

"Tony sneered, "The guy who owned this watch was an old friend, you might say."

"Ah, OK" Nigel replied. "Did he drown?" Nigel knew better but played it like a fiddle.

Tony nodded and half-grinned. "Yeah...you might say that. The area's kind of sacred ground to us and we...we just want to know where it is."

Nigel worked hard to keep calm, his years of service serving him well once again. So far, no guns had been drawn and that was a plus. There was still a chance of getting out of this without trouble, but he had to play it just right.

"Well mates, I can point you in the right direction...I can get you close." Nigel had no intention of taking them to the point of the coordinates. He would try to keep them as far away as possible. "I'll get ya' close and who knows, maybe there's something else to find."

Brad knew it was important to keep them away from the real coordinates as well because the ribs were now exposed. Maybe through twenty-four hours of tidal changes, they would cover themselves up again, but for now, they were easy to see and that concerned him.

From the jetties, Nick had the binoculars and looked concerned.

Josh was shading the sun with his hands and trying to see over the long distance out to the boat. "What's going on out there, Nick? Who is that?"

"I don't know...it's a fishing boat...with three guys on it. Two are in wet suits it looks like." He paused for a moment as he studied the scene. "They came up really fast...I don't like this, guys!"

Eddie tapped him on the shoulder. "Lemmee see!"

Eddie took his turn and could see Nigel clearly toss something to the other boat.

"It's a fishing boat. Maybe they are just comparing notes on the morning catch."

Josh shook his head. "Not likely."

Nigel stepped behind the wheel, started his Bayliner and called out to the three men in the other boat. "Follow me, mates, I'll get ya close."

Nigel had the handheld GPS lying on the flat area beside the wheel and was watching where he had tracked and where he wanted to put these three guys—at least two-_hundred feet away from the ribs. Nigel knew he had to be close but not too close. If he took them to a point that was too far away, Tony would know it and there would be trouble. At this point Tony still did not know why Nigel looked a bit familiar and wrote it off, again, to "tourist look-alikes."

The British man motored over to an area he was comfortable leaving Tony and swung the bow around to point towards the other boat. The position was within the same longitude but a couple hundred feet north of where they had just found the ribs of the old wreck.

Nigel looked at Brad and then to the shoreline exaggeratingly, as if to get his bearings. "I'd say about right here, wouldn't you, son?"

Brad nodded, playing along. "Yeah…I think this is it," he said enthusiastically, looking over the side of the boat to the bottom of the seafloor.

Tony looked at the water and then back to Nigel. "You're pretty sure?"

"Sure as shootin', mate. I remember being straight out from that t-shirt store." Nigel pointed.

Tony nodded. He knew he had to take what he could get from these guys. They were just fair-weather fishermen, after all, and luckily knew nothing of the treasure. Tony figured he was fortunate they didn't stumble upon any treasure while looking for the knife and finding the watch that belonged to Rocco Palombo. It was now Tony's turn to put on a show. He needed Nigel and Brad gone.

He spread his arms wide and spoke somberly. "Well…we are going to pay some respects to an old friend…if you don't mind," insinuating they would like privacy.

Nigel played along, "Oh for sure, mates. We were leaving anyhow," he said. "Time to go get back to being a tourist," he finished.

Nigel had played it well. He was going to be able to motor away from this guy who was obviously *the aging Italian man with the noticeably lazy eye*.

It still baffled Tony why Nigel looked so familiar.

Tony looked at him one last time, his lazy eye almost closed. He had to ask. "Hey pal." He paused. "Are you on vacation?"

Nigel grinned and then nodded, spreading his arms in freedom. "Permanent. Permanent vacation for me."

Tony's left eyebrow went up. *That's where I know him from!* He thought. His hand immediately went for his back as he unholstered his gun and aimed it straight towards Nigel! *Why didn't I recognize him sooner?* He scolded himself.

"Hands up," he said firmly.

CHAPTER TWENTY

Nigel's stomach knotted—he had thought they were away free. "Easy mate, easy. Let's talk about this."

That jolt of terror zapped Brad's body like a bolt of lightning. There was nowhere to run or hide this time.

Tony looked at him down the barrel of his .357. "You," he growled. "You are the Brit who was talking to those kids at the Vista al Mar," he said. "Permanent vacation...your favorite line." Tony grinned wryly.

Nigel was smart enough not to deny it.

Tony continued, "So you were the one who orchestrated the plan to get the boy's coin back. You busted those two bums up pretty good. I like your style." Tony sneered as he touched his ear, "Technology let me eavesdrop on you. I heard the whole thing. Then I watched it go down from outside the boathouse. That's why I'm here...I got the numbers from those two bums and, too bad for them, they gave me the wrong spot. They're gonna be joining my friend Rocco later tonight."

The Italian man then nodded to his divers to board Nigel and Brad's boat. Using a gaff hook, one diver pulled the two boats together and the other man boarded the Bayliner.

"Search them and then the boat," he ordered. Tony looked at Nigel. "Keep your hands high…mate," he mocked.

The diver onboard did as told and, after searching the two men, he looked around the Bayliner. He checked all the compartments and then went to Nigel's bag. The diver hesitated and then stood slowly. When his hand came up, he held high a twenty-four-inch length of solid gold chain.

Tony's eyebrows rose. "That's very interesting." He slowly nodded. "So it's true…and you found it."

Nigel knew he had to bargain. Most likely, there was nothing to find where they were now positioned. They were at least two hundred feet from the true location of the *Concepcion*. If Tony's divers went down and found nothing, Nigel and Brad could be in line for the same fate that Tony had in mind for Paco and Dennis. He had to try something.

While keeping his eyes locked on Nigel and Brad, Tony told his divers to tie their hands and collect their phones. He then instructed them to prepare to dive.

Nigel had to buy some time and, in the end, try not to give away the store. The men began to bind the hands of Nigel and Brad.

Nigel confessed, "Mate, there's nothing down here. It's not the right location. Let's make a deal here," he paused for a moment, "you let me drop the boy on the shore and I'll take you right to it."

"Nigel, no," Brad said. He then winced as the man pulled tight on the ropes that bound his hands.

"We are low on options right now, Brad."

Tony shook his head and laughed at Nigel's desperate plea, "And you know as well as I do, *that's* not an option either, right? Nobody's going ashore…nobody's going anywhere." The Italian man pulled his gun up high again. "Now you're going to take me to the spot or you are both going to die right here, just like Rocco Palombo."

Nigel pleaded, "He's a young boy…"

"Shut up, Brit!" Tony commanded without raising his voice. "I've killed younger." He sneered again.

Nigel knew what he was dealing with. In his career, he had crossed paths with many organizations and he could see Tony was not a wannabe. He was for real, had moved up through the ranks of his organization and had most likely, personally terminated many people who had been in the way of his objective. That's how he had gotten to this position. He was cold, heartless, and motivated by greed and power. This could all be seen in his actions as well as the iciness of his eyes. The lazy eye just seemed to accentuate his evil—at least physically.

There were no options for Nigel and Brad. Their only aces-in-the-hole were the other three boys at the jetties, whom he was certain were watching.

And they were…

The boys had been watching the whole scene from their vantage point just eighteen hundred feet away. They had seen Nigel motor away from the wreck-site only to be intercepted by the fishing boat. They had seen the discussion and watched Nigel toss something to the other boat. Everything seemed OK until the gesturing between the two boats began to change and then suddenly, the olive-skinned man drew a gun! They had seen one of the men board the Bayliner and search it. And to their dismay, they saw the glimmer of gold in the hot morning sun, as the one diver pulled the chain from the bag and held it high for the olive-skinned man to see. Now Brad and Nigel were bound with ropes and at the mercy of the men in this mystery-boat.

"The guy with the gun has got to be the guy Buck Naked was talking about. It's too much coincidence," Nick said.

Eddie took a deep breath as he looked through the binoculars at the scene which was still unfolding.

"I can't tell if he has a lazy eye but you could be right. We have to stay calm," he said. "We have Nigel out there, who is highly, highly trained for these situations."

Josh shook his head, "He has nowhere to run. He is going to have to do whatever they tell him to do."

"Just to stay alive," Nick finished.

"Right, just to stay alive," Josh agreed.

"I promise you, those guys are going to take them somewhere," Eddie said.

"Maybe they will just let them drift...take the key to the Bayliner and leave," Nick said.

Eddie was still watching them, "We are going to have to be ready to follow them."

Josh shrugged, "Here's the problem...we don't know if they came out of this channel...the barge channel or some other channel."

"I know," Eddie agreed. "Let's hope they came out of this one. If so, we can follow them up the channel, get the bus and watch, from the road, which marina they go back into."

"Then follow them," Josh finished.

"Right."

Nigel's chin fell in despair. He had to do what he had to do but he didn't like it. He wasn't proud for letting himself get into this situation. His skills and his intuition were rusty and he hoped it wouldn't cost them their lives. He felt especially bad for Brad. But he had to do what he had to do.

"Beside the wheel over here," Nigel began, "Underneath the t-shirt is a handheld GPS…"

"Nigel no!" Brad interrupted.

Nigel looked at him sternly, "Trying to keep you alive, mate. Keep your mouth shut."

"That's good advice, boy," Tony said. He pointed the gun at Brad and continued, "Keep your mouth shut and let the man talk." He looked back at the British man and nodded once.

Nigel wet his sun-dried lips. "Power it on…and you will see a locator pin. Where that pin is, is where we found the chain. Those are the coordinates that we theorize mark the wreck of the *Nuestra Senora de la Concepcion,* a treasure ship from the 1715 fleet. I'm not saying there are chests of gold down there. I'm only saying that is the location where we found a watch and a gold chain. Truth is, maybe that chain belonged to your buddy Rocco as well."

Tony shook his head, and then grinned wide, showing his old

and stained teeth for the first time. Through a stroke of luck at being at the right place at the right time a few days ago, Tony, with all of his patience, had persevered. Tony swung the gun back to Nigel.

"Which one of the boys had the grandfather who found it? Back in the '70s. Was it you, boy?"

Brad shook his head as he looked off into the distance. "Wasn't me."

Nigel squinted and looked at Tony. Tony took notice.

"I heard it all. It's a very interesting story. There's even more to the story that you don't know about—but it's not important right now."

Of course, Tony was referring to himself being the last one to see Nick's grandfather alive as well as Captain Chuck Henderson.

Nigel and Brad just looked at him—not yet knowing.

"OK boys, it's time to get in the water."

After getting the GPS unit, Tony did just as Nigel had told him and in a couple of minutes they had both boats sitting over the area where the pin indicated. Because the two men in the Bayliner were bound, Tony had re-holstered his gun. They were not going anywhere and were instructed to sit on the bench seat across the back of their boat. The two boats were tied together and Tony remained in his own vessel, which, cleverly, was an old fishing boat that blended well in the marina and on the sea. Then, with a splash, the two divers were over the side and on their way to the bottom. Tony watched them go in.

Brad looked at Nigel in disbelief. Nigel read his face and gave him a reassuring wink. *Trust me.*

The divers did pretty much just the same as Brad had, except they did it without holding their breath. They were able to spend minutes at the bottom, swishing and moving sand around with their hands, looking for any sign at all of a ship or its contents. After a few minutes, Tony opened and downed a bottle of water—not offering any to Nigel and Brad. He looked up at the ever-intensifying morning sun and wiped his brow. It got hot early this time of year in Florida. After a few more minutes, the divers surfaced and hung on the side of the boat only to report they had found nothing.

Tony looked disappointed as well as perturbed.

"Tony, there was no sign of anything! It's just reef and sand."

Tony gave Nigel a quick glance and then looked back at his men. "Look some more. Dig deeper or whatever you have to do but find me something." He looked back at Nigel. "What are the landmarks? Where did you find the chain?"

Brad's mind raced. He now knew that Nigel had snookered them but he didn't know how. He couldn't believe they hadn't found the ribs. Brad looked towards shore and figured it out. They were nowhere near the correct point of the coordinates. Nigel had moved the indicator pin on the GPS at some point to show a false location. This guy really was a professional in this business. Brad could now play along.

Brad replied to him, "When I was down there, I found the chain just by digging around an outcrop of corral…right around the base. But, it's true…just like your guys said, there is no sign of anything that looks like a wreck."

Nigel was extremely relieved and proud of Brad, at the same time. This young man had picked up on his queue and had run with it.

Tony looked back at his men, "Look some more…where there's smoke, there's fire. There has to be more down there." Tony's eyes drifted back to Nigel.

"In 1973 two guys found a couple of coins just by free-diving. This morning your boy, here, found a chain just by free diving. My guys have tanks and gear and can't find anything. Is there something you're not telling me?

Nigel nodded and shrugged. "You see the pin on the GPS, mate. This is the right spot—I promise you that. But the boy gave me the same report. He told me it just looked like the sand around a reef. It could be we just got lucky."

Tony snorted, "I don't believe in luck and I don't believe in coincidence." He looked at his men. "Go back down, spread out and try new areas."

The two men both grabbed small underwater metal detectors from the boat storage, cleared their masks and dropped beneath the surface once again. Now armed with better tools, time would tell if they were in the right spot.

Nigel had noticed that Tony seemed to know some details about the original discovery by the two gentlemen in 1973—more than what he had overheard from Nick and friends at the Vista al Mar. It made the former British Intel man consider the astronomical odds of Tony either being the man who killed Dawson and Henderson, or the man who ordered the hit. Considering the Italian man's age, it would seem more likely that he would have been a young goon doing the hit that many years ago. He would have been of the age to have been paying his dues, showing his worth and proving himself loyal to the big guy at the time. If this were true, Nick would have a serious bone to pick with Tony. Nigel didn't have enough information, at this point, to prove it and also figured it better not to suggest it to Nick anytime in the near future.

After a few more minutes, the divers surfaced, pulled their masks off and climbed onto the boat. Each diver had a net-bag and neither one was eager to look their boss in the eye.

The first diver shook his head. "Found some hardware and what looks like a railroad spike but that's it."

Nigel interjected as he looked towards the other boat, "That's a decking spike…it was used on the old ships to secure the planking topside. That's actually a good find, mate."

Tony looked at him and then back to the other diver.

"I did a little better. I also found some hardware like this old pulley but I also found this." The diver pulled from the bag, a small gold cross. He handed it to Tony.

Nigel and Brad were both beginning to feel better about their chances. This random find would serve them well in their bid to go home today! Apparently, this wreck was pretty scattered, as wrecks often are, and they were now positioned in the debris field of a ship that was falling apart three-_hundred years ago. From the short distance from one boat to the other, Nigel thought the cross looked a little modern but wasn't about to suggest it.

Tony took the relic and inspected it. He nodded, liking what he saw. "OK…Looks like we're are on the spot." He looked towards the shore. Business was picking up on the beach and he didn't want to be noticed as being in one place for too long.

"Boys, we did what we came to do. We are done for the day." He looked at Nigel and Brad. They looked back, wondering what their fate was going to be, knowing the ball was in his court. Tony was biting his cheek—thinking.

He then said, "Well fellas, I know it might be somewhat inconvenient for you, but you're going to have to take a ride with us."

"Why?' Nigel asked. "You have what you need, mate...you don't need us anymore."

Tony grinned sarcastically and then stepped from his boat to the Bayliner. He stood in front of Nigel, bent down and looked him in the eye. "I'm getting sick of you calling me *mate*, Brit." He then backhanded Nigel's face.

Nigel took the blow and looked Tony in the eye but said nothing.

Tony continued, "Now we are going to take a ride and then we are going to pick up some friends of yours. I would suggest you keep quiet on the ride in to the marina."

Brad and Nigel were both sure he meant they were going to pick up Dennis and Paco and not *their* friends. That, in itself, was not a good sign because Tony had already told them what he was going to do with those two later that night.

Tony stepped back onto his own vessel and gave instructions to the divers to untie and follow him in the Bayliner. In just a couple of minutes they were moving away from the site and motoring their way towards the barge channel...to Nigel and Brad's delight.

"They're coming! They're coming this way!" Josh exclaimed.

"Josh, if that happens to be the guy that Buck Naked was talking about, he is going to know who we are. We have to hide until they go by," Eddie said.

"Right back over there," Josh pointed. "We have to go now."

The manmade rock jetties extended beyond the beach about fifty yards. Back on land there were some dunes that were loaded with sea oats—perfect for hiding behind as they watched the boats go by. Hurriedly, the three friends made their way down the jetty, past the beach and into the dunes. They moved as quickly as they could without being too conspicuous.

The two boats were moving quickly until they entered the slower speed zone of the channel. Brad and Nigel both looked towards the jetty to see if their partners were still in view or, hopefully, somewhere out of sight. They were nowhere to be seen.

The two boats made their way past the end of the rock jetty, into the channel, and then finally, past the dune area. Nigel knew that would be where they would be hiding.

Josh Baker always carried two things with him—always. A pocket knife and his mini Maglite. Josh pulled the light from his carrying case and aimed it towards the boats. He waited until he was sure the olive-skinned man and both his henchmen were looking away. Nigel and Brad were looking constantly but without being too obvious. Josh flashed his light three times from the obscurity of the sea oat patch. Nigel caught it right away and nodded, letting Josh know he had received his message.

Nick lifted the binoculars and was trying to get a good look at the man in charge. He wanted to see if he had a lazy eye. He couldn't tell because what the man *did* have in the morning sun, were sunglasses. As the boat neared them, the timing couldn't have been better. The Italian man removed his glasses and used a handkerchief to wipe his brow. Pausing before putting his glasses back on, he looked towards the beach and Nick had him square in his sights. Bingo—the man appeared to be Italian, with a noticeably lazy eye.

CHAPTER TWENTY-ONE

Giselle had finally rolled out of bed, showered and was making her way downstairs for a light fruit breakfast before going to the beach for her morning sun therapy. Later in the day, they were supposed to meet up with Ray, the dive instructor, for the SNUBA orientation. On the elevator she tapped out a short text message for Josh, just to check in and see how things were going with the search at the coordinate site. She gasped when she received his response. Her morning plans had just changed. She had to rent a car and be ready.

Giselle exited the elevator and instead of going for breakfast, she made a beeline for the concierge desk. The concierge quickly took her information and advised her that her rental would be waiting at the Hertz lot just one block away.

"Would you like the car brought here or would you like a shuttle?" the gentleman asked.

"I'll walk it," Giselle replied, and she took her contract and made for the doors.

To her surprise but good fortune, on her way out of the

building she passed Buck.

"Hey!" she said. "Come here." She took him aside.

It took him a second to realize who she was and then Buck's eyes widened .Giselle quickly told him what she knew and showed him the text.

"Oh…dat not good. I hab to clean dees pool first," he said. "Den I be ready! I go wit you when it time. I be quick," he said.

Giselle thanked him and told him she would go get the car and have it ready, too. She would wait to hear from Josh as to where Nigel and Brad were being taken before they left. Buck offered to take his car but Giselle wanted to drive. Of course, Eddie, Josh and Nick would be following Tony at a distance when the time came.

Josh pocketed his phone after answering Giselle's text. They waited until the two boats got far enough past them before they reemerged from the sea oats.

"Let's get to the bus," Eddie said.

Leaving Jetty Park, they took A1A back across the waterway, across Merritt Island and then to the mainland where they made a left onto Indian River Drive. From there they could see the river and the two boats, and monitor which marina Tony operated out of. This worked out perfectly and only a couple times did they lose sight of the boats. Eddie had to cruise along slowly to avoid getting too close to them and the down side was, he was holding up traffic. More than once someone passed him blowing their horn and giving him hand signals.

It wasn't long before Tony turned in to a small marina which had no name—at least it had no sign. Eddie parked about a block away where he could see the small parking lot and its exit. From their vantage point, they couldn't see the slips but they weren't too worried about that. As long as they could see the vehicle that Brad and Nigel were loaded into, they were good.

It wouldn't take long. Their two friends appeared first, followed by Tony and his divers. Tony had a towel draped over his arm which, most likely, concealed the gun in his hand. They walked towards a white cargo van parked in a corner spot under a tree. On the side of the van it read: *Fresh Seafood*. Some things never change.

After loading Nigel and Brad into the van, Tony took a quick look around and climbed into the passenger seat up front. Eddie and his friends watched as the white van turned right out of the parking lot and onto Indian River Drive. Eddie hadn't considered it, but the white van was now coming in their direction.

"Get down!" he said.

All three boys ducked down as the white van passed. Eddie fired the bus, let them get a few hundred yards ahead and then pulled out onto the palm-tree-lined road. There were three vehicles between them, which was good for avoiding detection. The *Seafood* van wiggled its way across a couple of cross streets to find A1A and then to Highway 528 West to I-95 North. Tony intermittently checked his mirror and his passengers.

Heading up the interstate, Josh called Giselle to fill her in. She told him that she had run into Buck and he had offered to ride along to help out. Josh told her they were heading in her direction and to just hang loose until they could figure out where, exactly, they were going. She agreed, they exchanged some nice words between them and then they clicked off.

Nigel had a bad feeling as they rolled north up I-95. He was pretty sure he knew where they were going and it wasn't good. It was too isolated and Tony could hold them there nearly indefinitely. The boathouse—he was sure of it. Time would tell.

Eddie maintained his distance while he followed the white van. Soon they exited the interstate and began to see some familiar landmarks. Highway 421 took them all the way to A1A and before they knew it, Tony's driver had wheeled into the parking lot of the Honeymooner Motel and Spa. Eddie made a right hand turn to run the block without being seen by anyone in the white van. He parked the bus in the same spot he had parked for Brad's fireworks display a couple nights ago but was unsuccessful at not being spotted by someone in the van. Fortunately, it was Nigel. From the rear cargo area, the ever-observant British man could see through the front windshield and he noticed the nose of the bus visible in the shadows of the building across the street. He winked at Brad and by then, Brad knew the winks were good news.

Tony spun around in his seat to keep an eye on his two captives while his two men went to the room to retrieve Dennis and Paco. As they approached the door, they could see it was ajar. Peering through the opening, the men saw the room was empty. The only issue was the bathroom—that door *was* closed, which seemed peculiar.

One man motioned to the other to cover him as he slipped into the motel room to check the bathroom. Of course, guns were drawn. The first man glanced at the other and then lifted one leg and kicked the bathroom door in. There was Paco—in all his glory, sitting there with a horse--racing program. He nearly jumped off the toilet.

"Where's your buddy?!" the man demanded.

Paco's eyes were wide as he sat there in shock and

embarrassment. "He...He's not here. He went out."

"You were told not to go anywhere!" The man held the gun on Paco.

"Señor, he had to get food...we are hungry," Paco pleaded.

"Hurry up! Finish and get out of there...And for god's sake, turn the fan on!"

"Si Señor! I...I have this broken leg..."

The man slammed the door. "Hurry up!"

In a couple of minutes, Paco came hobbling out of the bathroom, not knowing what his fate would be that afternoon.

One of the divers stayed behind to wait for Dennis as Tony and the other man took Paco, Nigel and Brad and drove away.

Once again Eddie followed at a safe distance and, as they made their way across the Intracoastal and made the left turn onto Highway 1, he knew where they were going. Josh made the call to Giselle to let her and Buck know where they would be.

Tony was sitting tall on the passenger side, occasionally turning to check on his passengers, who were bound in the back. His eyes then darted to his side mirror, out of old habit, and something caught his attention. He studied the vehicle closer. About a quarter mile back was a VW bus. He had noticed a similar, if not the same, vehicle as they were driving up I-95.

He turned to his passengers, "Does a Volkswagen Bus mean anything to you?" he starred at Brad and Nigel. Paco knew it did, but said nothing.

All three remained quiet as Brad glanced at Nigel.

"Thank you," Tony smiled, "You have answered my question with your silence." He leaned towards his driver and gave him some instructions for when they arrived at the boat house.

Nigel's heart sank. They were their hope. Now he knew, in order to survive, the team would once again have to overtake an opponent within the confines of the boat house. This time they would have to do it with their hands tied, up against a professional crime organization.

As the white van made its turn from Highway 1 to pull onto the sand-covered road that led back to the old boat house, Tony motioned with a nod where to drop him off. A couple hundred yards later, the van stopped, Tony hopped out and moved quickly into the tall patch of sea oats. The white van drove on to the boat house and the man took the three bound captives inside. Tony waited patiently. In just a few seconds, the bus turned off of Highway 1 as Eddie killed the headlights and drove slowly down the sand-covered road. At the end of the road he made a right and pulled onto a concrete pad with sea oats surrounding it—ironically the same place Tony had parked a couple of nights ago. Eddie's bus now sat about one hundred yards from the boat house.

Eddie pulled his parking brake. "Now what?" he asked. "Anyone have a gun?"

They all knew they didn't.

Josh said, "We are going to have to walk up there and see if we can see where they are inside."

"What about the police?" Nick suggested.

"Let's see what's going on first. Maybe we can spring them," Eddie suggested. "If we involve the police..."

"...I could lose my relics again?" Nick finished.

"I don't know...maybe. If we have to give them the whole story again...I just don't know," Eddie finished.

"I'm not going to take that chance if I don't have to," Nick said. "But if we don't see a safe way of getting them out, then yes, we call the police right away."

Josh shrugged one shoulder. "And that's no guarantee they will come out safe."

Tap, Tap, Tap!

Eddie about jumped out of his seat. Having sprang out of the sea oats and now positioned outside his driver-side window was an aging olive-skinned man with a noticeably lazy eye. He held his .357 tight on the glass at the level of Eddie's head. That he had approached them in the middle of the day without them seeing him was part of their shock.

"Get out...all of you," the man commanded calmly.

Terrified, Nick and Josh instinctively brought their hands up to where the man could see them. Eddie opened his door, keeping the other hand up as well, for the same good reason. Nick and Josh exited from the sliding side door and Tony moved everyone to the center of the unused road. The midday heat had caused sweat to form on Tony's brow.

Tony calmly instructed, "With two fingers of your left hand, I want you all to remove your communication devices from your pockets...slowly."

Eddie spoke respectfully, "Mine is in my holder in the bus."

"And there it will stay," Tony replied, holding the gun stiff-armed.

Josh and Nick obeyed orders and placed their phones on the ground.

Tony nodded towards the boat house and the boys started walking. Falling in line behind them, he kicked their phones over to the side of the road by the bus. "You won't need those anymore...I'll cancel your service for you," he grinned and lowered the gun to waist level.

The grimness of that comment made Josh shiver and made Eddie wish they had called the police.

CHAPTER TWENTY-TWO

A few minutes later Giselle and Buck parked on the sand-covered road, right about where Dennis' old Buick and Brad's truck had conked out a couple days before. At the end of that road Giselle could make out the back end of Eddie's bus cleverly concealed in a thick patch of sea oats.

"They're up there," she told Buck.

"No too fas," Buck told her. He had never been in this location and wanted to survey the area. "I go to da dune." He pointed. Giselle waited beside her rental car.

Buck ran to the top of the first sand dune and looked around. He then pulled his phone from his pocket and tapped the app he used to see local satellite images. He noted the roads and saw the boathouse. He wanted to know the ins and outs of this location in case they had to get out in a hurry. Buck scurried down the sand dune and nodded towards the VW Bus.

"Dat our firs stop," he said.

Giselle agreed and tapped Josh a message on her phone. As she and Buck carefully proceeded towards the bus, she thought it a bit strange that Josh didn't reply but figured he was doing his own scouting and couldn't reply at the moment. The heat was getting to the point of being sweltering as the sun rolled higher and higher in the sky.

Ray, the dive instructor, looked at his watch and shook his head. He worked out of a small hut by Ponce de Leon Inlet at New Smyrna Beach. Picking up his phone, he scrolled his recent calls and tapped the one he was looking for. Lou Cannon picked up.

"Louis Cannon."

"You sure are, dude," Ray said.

Lou laughed, "Hey what's up Ray."

"It's all cool, man...except I'm still waiting on your SNUBA crew."

"They're not there?"

"Supposed to be here a couple hours ago, man. They don't show up soon, I'm going out to Cocoa Beach seashore. I got something I want to check out."

"OK...umm, let me call them and I'll call you right back."

"That's cool, brother. Buzz me back."

Lou Cannon pulled up his contract with the boys on his computer. He scrolled down to the contacts and called Josh, Eddie, and Nick. No answer. *Weird* he thought. He then called Giselle.

Giselle and Buck were almost to Eddie's bus which was parked in the sea oats when her phone vibrated in her rear pants pocket. Caller ID read Family Jewels.

"Hi, Mr. Cannon."

"Giselle, where are you guys? Ray just called me and he's looking for you. It's SNUBA time."

"Lou, I'm very sorry. You wouldn't believe the stuff that's going on up here. Nigel, the new guy that's with us, and Brad are being held by some Italian guy...pretty sure he's mafia."

"Mafia?! How did they get involved with this?"

"God only knows," she replied, "but they are in an old boat house on the Intracoastal...at the end of Riverside Drive, I think. Meanwhile, Josh, Eddie and Nick followed them and I just got here too. We are going to see what we can do."

"No!" Lou said. "Do not approach that boat house! They will kill you in a minute and drop you on the reef!" Denise looked at Lou. "Giselle, the Florida mafia is low key but deadly. They have so many politicians and FDLE in their pockets, you wouldn't believe. They write their own rules and as long as they keep their guys greased with pocket money, no one is ever convicted. No one!"

Giselle was getting closer to Eddie's bus and there was a strange quietness around it.

"Lou, we have to do *something*."

"Police...call the police. They will come and get them out of there. Like I say, no one will be convicted but that's the smart money. Call 911."

Giselle and Buck carefully approached Eddie's bus. She could now see that the side door was open and the driver's door as well. Immediately she knew that was not right.

"Lou, hang on."

"Some-ting no look right here," Buck said. "Dey would close de door, right?"

Giselle nodded, getting nervous. "They would. Eddie demands it."

Stepping around the other side, Giselle cried out, "Oh no!"

Two phones lay in the sand by the road. One she recognized as Josh's. She picked it up and pressed the home button. She saw her text and a missed call from Lou.

She lifted her phone back to her ear. "Lou, they got Josh, Eddie and Nick now, it looks like. I just found their phones by Eddie's bus and the doors were left open. Eddie would never do that."

"You gotta call the police," Lou said.

"What if there's a shootout?"

"Giselle, they're not getting out of there without a shootout."

"Oh my god!" She began to cry. "Lou I have to go." She clicked off.

"Giselle!" he shouted. The line went silent. "Dang it!"

Buck walked over to her. "Look, we hab to keep our heads." Eb'ryting OK right now. We hab to not mess eet up. We hab to wait and see eef day stay or eef day leeb again. We hab to make sure tings stay OK. And we will."

Giselle took some deep breaths and calmed herself. "You're right. You're right, they are OK right now. And they are smart...they have Nigel, too, who will do the negotiating. Josh and Eddie have been in bad situations before and have found a way out. They will do it again."

Giselle was mostly talking to herself—convincing herself that they would be OK and she would, once again, be able to hug that guy that she had always liked so much...since that day on the boat dock.

Lou called Ray back and explained what was going on and what had gone on the past few days since these guys rolled into town with a gold coin and a nautical chart.

Ray listened carefully and asked, "Do you know what boat house it is? Is it the one along Riverside, up there below Daytona Beach Shores? That old wooden place that went out in the late '70s, I believe?"

"She *did* say they were at the end of Riverside Drive."

"Yeah, man. That's the one. Great big wooden place. Retro...super cool joint. Been shut down for years. Went into foreclosure a long time ago and just sat there."

"It would be a perfect place to imprison someone," Lou followed up.

"True, man. It's gotta be the place. What should we do?" Ray asked. "We gonna help 'em?"

"Not sure if we should get involved or not, Ray. Let me do some thinking and I'll call you back."

"Cool, OK man. If ya need me for anything, I'm there."

Thanks, Ray." And they clicked off.

Lou Cannon had a lot to consider. He was a local businessman in good standing with everyone—local law, state law and Federal as well. He did not want to overstep his bounds and lose his privilege to get contracts to search for the Treasure Fleet of 1715. That was his lifelong dream and he couldn't let his fondness for these young adventurers, who reminded him so much of himself back in the day, cloud his judgment. Yes, he would have to think about it.

Tony looked at the guys who were lined up along the old wooden wall in front of him.

He sneered, "Pitiful...just pitiful. You guys would make terrible criminals." They remained silent. Everyone knew anything they said could only make the situation worse. Their hands were tied behind their backs and then, with the same rope, they were tied to a rail that ran along the bottom of the wall. Their feet were not bound but they could not stand up anyway, due to the way they were tied.

Tony stepped over to his man and told him how things were going to go down. The other diver was back at the Honeymooner Motel and Spa waiting for Dennis to arrive. When Tony got the call that Dennis was captured, Tony would go pick them up and the one remaining diver would stand guard on the five men before them. Once Dennis was back and tied up, and nightfall came, the three of them would go back out to the site and do some "night fishing." They would use an underwater light and a portable underwater blower to move the sand away and see what else they could find. If they found something big, these guys had a chance. If they found nothing, then six guys were going to die that same night because they were all lying to him about the location. At least that would be Tony's threat when the time was right.

Nigel's experience told him no one would die until the wreck was located—then they would *all* die because they could identify Tony.

The diver nodded in agreement and they all settled in for the duration. Tony's van was well hidden at the south end of the building, ironically where Eddie had hidden the bus a couple of nights ago, so he wasn't too concerned about a passerby getting curious.

Nick's thoughts wandered to *Maria* behind him just a few yards. This was the boat his grandfather had last sailed on before losing his life back in the '70s. How ironic it was to be tied up so close to her and with possibly the same fate to look forward to.

Tony wanted to explore the building so he left his one man there to watch over them as he walked towards the waterway that ran the full length of the former facility. As he checked things out, he began to pick up the scents of the place. The old hemp rope and the fishing nets, the mustiness of the constant presence of very slow moving water, and whatever was contained in the old steel drums along the wall—probably old motor oil. He could still smell heavy gear oil from many years ago and decaying seaweed from today's tides. Tony walked the length of the waterway, past the old parts rooms where he saw the trawler which was still firmly tied and proudly floating. He strode past it, snorting at the useless old vessel with its faded paint and rusty winch. He finally made his way to the door where he could see where his *Fresh Seafood* van was parked. Everything looked good outside and he hadn't heard a car go by the entire time they had been there.

With Tony out of sight, Josh's mind flashed back to just a little over a year ago, when he was tied up by Russians and placed in an old closet at a closed-down lumber yard. He recalls how he was able to find a sharp edge on something within the closet and rubbed and rubbed until he cut the rope. Now, with his hands bound again, he had about a foot of slack in the rope that held him to the rail. His fingers began their search behind him. Nigel, who was seated beside Josh, figured out what he was doing and he, too, began looking for something sharp. The diver, in the meantime, found an old grease can to sit on and became occupied with his phone for the time being and Josh was careful to make very slow movements with his hands. The steel rail was secured to the wall with heavy brackets, also made of metal. Josh felt one bracket and it was smooth. He then began feeling for the next one but couldn't quite reach it. He was hoping to find a casting seam that had some texture to it so he could grind the rope long enough to cut it. No such luck. His heart sank at the thought of there being no way to escape. He only hoped one of the other guys could find something.

Josh took a deep breath in despair and sat up straight to at least get comfortable. Tony's guy looked over at him and then back to his phone. After Josh sat up, his hands could reach the old wooden wall the rail was mounted to behind him. The wall was rough lumber and he could feel the boards were pulling away from where they were originally intended to be secured. There was also some rot at the bottom and, feeling around, he found something! A nail. A very old and rusty nail stuck out from the wall about two inches. It was in an area of the rot at the bottom of one of the boards and was accessible but his wrists would have to be bent at a very uncomfortable angle in order to grind back and forth for quite some time. At this point, comfort was not a concern—staying alive was, and Josh knew he must do everything in his power to give him and his friends every chance. He looked at Nigel and winked.

Tony walked back to the "main operations" area of the old facility where the group was tied up. No one made eye contact with him and he said nothing as he walked by them. He looked at the stairs and then to the open upper level. Curiosity got the better of him and he ascended the stairs. At the top he looked around at a useless mess of old junk. Old barrels and nets—ropes and various mechanical pieces lay here and there—nothing at all useful to him. He noticed a ladder that led to a small third-level loft but was not at all interested in what was up there. The old boathouse did intrigue him however, and he was very satisfied at what a great place it was to hold someone captive.

Tony looked around one more time, wrinkled his nose and then descended the stairs. He walked the lower level some more with all the cockiness he could muster. Josh halted his rope grinding for the moment. He could feel he was making progress, however small it was. The diver was still looking at his phone.

Tony sneered as he looked towards the group tied to the rail. "So, whose big adventure is it? Who had the coin and the coordinates?" he asked as he slowly walked towards them, studying each face.

Nick shivered with anger. *How dare this man ask!* No one said anything.

Tony grinned. "Ah, come on fellas...I'm just trying to make conversation," he said sarcastically, "lighten the mood a little."

Josh couldn't take it. "Make conversation with your little boy over there!"

Eddie elbowed him and Paco, who was tied up nearby, cringed.

Tony looked at his man and waved him off with a slight head shake. He would not get a piece of Josh just yet.

Tony walked towards Josh. "That's disrespectful. That's not a very nice way to talk about my man Marco." Tony walked slowly in a big circle with his hands now behind his back. "Marco is a professional. He started out just like me back in the day. And speaking of back in the day, since we have some time, I can tell you a story about that nice coin that you own."

Nick's brow furrowed. What would *he* know about his grandfather's coin?

"You see, back in the early seventies, I was new to the...club, you might say."

Marco snickered as Tony spewed sarcasm. Josh resumed rope grinding as Tony walked around and gave his story. Nigel knew where this tale was going already and hoped Nick could take it well. It wasn't going to be good.

"Our club is a tight-lipped organization, and we had a guy...Rocco was his name... and Rocco couldn't stop talking, it seemed. Bad thing about Rocco was he talked for money." Tony looked back at the bound group with his palms turned up. "Rocco was a snitch."

Josh continued grinding the rope on the rusty nail when Tony looked away. Marco paid no attention.

"So one night Rocco dropped some dimes on us to an old DA and got one of our guys whacked. A good man, too. They took him down right in front of his family. He just got back from his kid's graduation and the cops were waiting for him at his house. Bad timing...bad judgment if you ask me. I mean, we make a lot of wrongs right but never in front of the kids, never." Tony shrugged. "So we had to take care of Rocco and make sure he never was seen or heard from again." Tony looked at Nigel. "You remember that name, right? Rocco Palombo?" He sneered again, his lazy eye drooping.

Nigel nodded to pacify Tony.

"So Rocco was taken care of, not by me, but he was taken care of. I had the job of delivering Rocco to the docks...this was down at Vero, the old fishing docks down there. That was my job at the time...making deliveries and making sure things were carried out. Today I got Marco and a few others to do that stuff for me. But back then, that was my job and so me and another man took Roc to the Vero docks to a hired captain."

By now, Nick was leering at Tony—wondering. He knew his grandfather worked out of Vero with Captain Henderson. He knew that from the letters he had read that were sent to his grandmother in the early 70s. Josh, Eddie, and Brad were starting to put the puzzle together as well. Someone else was also listening in disbelief. Giselle and Buck had their ears to some openings in the outside walls at the north end of the boat house and could make out what was being said.

"So we dropped off the...seafood box...to the captain of an old junk trawler and told him to take it north, far away and on the reef. Shark bait...Rocco became shark bait."

Nick began to breathe harder as Tony's story was beginning to mesh with his own. Josh looked over at Nick and saw the anger building. Nigel noticed too and desperately needed Tony to stop talking before he got too far and Nick exploded on him verbally.

Paco was soaking up the details—amazed at the coincidence of it all.

Doing his best to stifle Tony, Nigel spoke up. "Why did you tell us that story, mate? It's not important to us. We don't care."

Tony sauntered around casually, shrugged again and nonchalantly turned one palm upwards. "You guys...you guys know so much already. What's it gonna hurt for you to know the whole story? And besides...in case you haven't guessed, we are just waiting to get the Mexican and the albino here and that's going to be it for all of you." He shrugged again. "I'm sorry but you know too much—you are going to be in the way from this point on. You guys understand, right? It's business...it's nothing personal."

Nigel knew better but played Tony's game and shook his head. "Are you out of your mind, mate?" You are going to execute seven people for a couple gold coins?"

Tony looked down the whole row of captives. He nodded and looked at Nigel solemnly. "Yes...yes I am. And you're going to be first Brit. I'm sick of you calling me *mate*!"

Nigel released a deep breath and shook his head. His only solace was knowing that Josh had found something to grind his ropes on and was doing so feverishly when Tony wasn't looking.

Tony continued, "We know...we all know... that it's about more than a couple coins. I heard your story at the Vista al Mar. I know that story to be true and I know there are at least four of those ships that have not been located yet. I know there were at least two coins, maybe more, pulled from those coordinates just from free divers and I have in my pocket, a gold chain that was pulled from those waters just this morning. The only thing, and I mean the *only* thing that might save one of you is the true coordinates. Me and Marco, here, are not so sure that any of you guys have been telling us the truth. I personally think a couple divers with tanks and masks should have come up with more than a gold cross that may or may not be old...if we were on the wreck site, that is."

"It's a big ocean, mate. That stuff is going to wash around..."

Tony drew his .357 and jammed it to Nigel's forehead. "That'll be the last time you call me *mate*!"

Tony pulled the hammer back.

Josh screamed, "Nooooo!"

Tony's phone rang in his pocket. He was the one who was now breathing hard. He didn't like Nigel at all. His phone continued to ring and he slowly dropped the barrel while starring straight into Nigel's eyes. He released the hammer and tucked the gun away as his eyes held Nigel's. He yanked the phone out of his pocket.

"Yeah?" He continued watching Nigel. "OK." He clicked off.

"Your brothers are ready to join us," he said with a vile grin. He looked at Nigel. "It's good that you are lucky instead of smart, Brit."

He walked over to Marco. "Watch them, I'll be back."

"Finish your story, tough guy!"

Tony turned around to see Nick, red in the face, eyes flaming. He paused for a moment and then stepped over to Nick.

He stared at him for a moment and then said, "So it's you. You are the one who was given the coordinates...and the coin...the coin that looks like mine." Tony pulled out his necklace and showed them. "They are sisters...our coins came from the same pile."

"You killed my grandfather didn't you? You shot him after he did what you needed him to do that night, didn't you?"

Tony took a deep breath and released it slowly. He looked at Nick with artificial remorse in his eyes. "I'm sorry, son, but it looks to be true. And, like I say, it's just business. He knew too much!" he said shrugging.

Nick repeated himself, screaming now, "You killed my grandfather... you murdering scum!"

"Well, you deserve to know the truth. And do you know what? I think you may look like your grandfather, even. I remember the face of every man that I ever put a bullet in...it's a disturbing thing to have to live with. But you know, it's the price I pay for all this power. And you know what else? I think I saw the same desperation in his eyes as he bobbed there in the water, pleading for his life. It was...the eyes. I think you have your grandfather's eyes. The eyes... of a desperate coward."

Nick just sneered at him. He shook his head slowly. "It's amazing how having someone tied up makes you so brave, isn't it," Nick said. "I wonder if *you* were tied up if you would tell me the same story with so much bravado. Or would *you* be the coward that I know you are?"

Tony stepped towards Nick and backhanded him with all that he had. Nick fell over to his left, blood trickling from the corner of his mouth. Outside, Giselle gasped and covered her mouth.

Undeterred, Nick stared into Tony's eyes and said, "You better pray with every amount of sincerity you have in your hell-bound soul that I never get free from these ropes. Even if it costs me my own life, I will take yours!"

Tony laughed at Nick and looked over at Marco who was grinning as well. "Oh, you will be free from those ropes soon enough. Don't worry about that, young man."

Tony then looked towards Marco. "Marco, I'll be back in a few minutes and we will get this show on the road. We have treasure to find."

He then walked past the captives, along the waterway that ran through the facility, past the old junk trawler and out the door on the south end of the boathouse. In just a few minutes he would be back with Paco and Dennis.

CHAPTER TWENTY-THREE

It was now past 2:30 pm. Giselle and Buck were still outside the opposite end of the boathouse from where Tony exited and where his car was parked. Through a knothole, she could see him leave.

"Buck, we have to pray that when he pulls onto the highway, he leaves in that direction." She pointed south. "If he comes back this way he will, for sure, see the rental car."

"Dat true. But he don know dat car. Could be anyone to him. But you right...better eef he go dat way."

To their relief, Tony did just that. He turned south to go to the next cross street to get back over to Highway 1. With the man they now knew as Marco standing guard over the guys inside, the task of them getting freed was simpler but still difficult. Giselle had no idea Josh was grinding away on his ropes inside.

Lou Cannon sat at his desk tapping his pencil and contemplating what to do and how to do it. He decided to text Giselle and see what the situation was. After a minute, he received a message back:

All five guys are tied up, Lou! Inside the boathouse. The old guy left but he'll be back soon. One guy left guarding them. I'm with the local guy who tipped us off about the Italian man. We need a plan. "My gosh," Lou said to himself. Denise walked over to him. He showed her the text.

She grimaced. "What should we do?"

Lou shook his head. "They are in a bad situation and don't want the help of law enforcement because they don't want to have the coin and the coordinates go into an evidence file and eventually be made public record."

"Lou, the first thing they have to do is get out of that place alive. With only one guy watching them the cops could roll up and..."

"...And maybe go right into a hostage situation," Lou finished. "I don't like any options here...including doing nothing."

"So what do we do?" Denise asked.

"I'm going to call Ray. Talk it over with him. He's so crazy, he makes the most sense sometimes."

"OK. Did you check emails?"

"Not after lunch. Why?"

"Your buddy, Terry in Tallahassee, sent the approval for those coordinates. He actually got us approved for ten target dives there."

"Sweet! We have to get those kids out of that boathouse. I'm very excited about this one."

Denise smiled and walked back to her desk. "Thought you might like that."

Josh rolled his wrists back and forth across the rusty nail until they ached. He could feel that the rust has been completely cleaned off of the nail and the only thing giving him a cutting edge now were the pits in the nail the oxidation had created. It was slow going but Josh was about halfway through the rope. Nigel slowly and carefully turned towards Josh and bounced his eyebrows. Josh returned a wink. They both understood the silent conversation. Through a series of head and eye signals, Brad, Eddie, and Nick could tell what was going on. Of course, they didn't know how Josh was managing an escape, but they knew he was in the middle of something.

Marco was getting bored and Nigel could see it. He was beginning to sigh and fidget. He had done all he could do to entertain himself on his phone and began to look around the facility more while sitting on his grease bucket. That was a good sign because when people get bored, they get tired and when they get tired, they get sloppy—make mistakes, lose concentration. Nigel was beginning to feel better about their chances but they would need a plan, providing Josh could get loose. Of course, not being able to communicate with each other made that difficult.

Nigel had an idea. All five of the guys were sitting against the wall with the rail behind them. Their legs were extended straight which put their feet in the same general area of the floor in front of them. Nigel looked towards Marco. He was looking at the second story balcony, not paying attention to the captive men. Nigel's foot began to move—not spasmodic but somewhat rhythmic-like. The guys didn't pay too much attention at first but as he continued, one by one, they each looked at him a bit confused. After a few seconds, it was Josh who picked up on it. *Morse code!* It looked as if Nigel's foot was tapping out a message.

When Josh was just fourteen years old he bought an early 1960s Hallicrafters short-wave radio receiver at a flea market close to his house. He paid a whopping two dollars for it and it had given him a million dollars' worth of entertainment over the past four years. At night, he could listen to faraway places, many different languages and yes, on certain bands, even Morse code. This was all thanks to a copper wire antennae strung between two trees in his yard. Hearing the beeps of the dot and dash communication code always intrigued him— enough to learn it for himself. He was no professional but he still knew most of the letters. And he knew something else…Nigel was trying to talk to him or anyone else who knew the code.

Josh thought for a moment and then moved his own foot back and forth—much slower, concentrating. *R-E-P-E-A-T,* Josh tapped out.

Nigel repeated his message while looking around the room nonchalantly. *Ropes cut?*

Josh replied, *Halfway. Using nail.*

Good. Keep working, Nigel tapped.

Eddie saw what was going on, but the extent of his Morse code experience was done on his walkie-talkies as a young kid. He remembered SOS and that was about it. Same for Nick and Brad— they could see what was going on but had no idea what was being said. The plan had to be formulated between Nigel and Josh and the others would have to figure it out as they proceeded.

Josh was grinding harder and harder on the nail behind him— his wrists aching badly but he powered on through it, knowing this was life or death. A few more minutes went by and Josh could feel he was almost there. Suddenly, Marco looked over at Josh and he froze instantly. Marco stood up and walked towards the group. He looked at them all, one at a time, and then did a large circle around the shop. His legs had apparently fallen asleep from sitting on the bucket because he began to shake them as he was walking. When he turned away from them, Josh took the opportunity and began sawing on the ropes as hard as he could. Back and forth using not just his wrists but his arms to move back and forth—rubbing, rubbing, rubbing and then *POP!*, he was through! Josh had done it!

With Marco's back still turned, Josh reached over to Nigel with one hand and started untying his binds. They were tied tight and it took a couple of minutes to make any initial progress but he was doing it. Once he got the first knot untied the second was easier. Josh then put his right hand back in position to look as if it were still tied, and just in time. Marco had walked off his leg-sleep and went back towards his grease can. He sat down, the boredom overwhelming him, and he pulled out his phone again.

"You guys are no entertainment at all, you know that?" he remarked.

"We're not in a playful mood, man," Brad replied. "Sorry."

Marco snorted a laugh and went back to his phone.

With their captor's eyes and attention back to his phone, Josh reached his left hand to Eddie's ropes and began the same process as with Nigel. Josh had learned a trick in undoing Nigel's knots and applied that experience to Eddie's binds—albeit left-handed. Nigel did the same thing with his right hand, reaching over to Brad's ropes and working them free. Brad then took care of Nick and in short time, they were all free. The guys all kept their hands in position until the time was right. About thirty minutes had gone by since Tony left and they knew he would return soon. They also knew this plan had to be perfect because Marco had a gun.

Outside, sweltering in the midday sun, Giselle knew something was going on. Watching though the small hole, she saw Josh moving his hands and she also noticed the footwork of Nigel being answered by the guy she adored so much. She and Buck quietly discussed it.

"They have something going on," she said. "We have to wait and see what it is."

Buck turned to look at the road behind him. He and Giselle were partially obscured by weeds beside the boathouse but were not totally hidden if Tony returned from behind them.

"Dat mon be bock soon," Buck said. "Dey betta hurry der plan."

Giselle watched as Josh's foot began its code work again and then noted Nigel's return message. "They're working on it, I can see that."

"You friends ah cleva," Buck said, as he watched the conversation.

Giselle nodded. "You wouldn't believe the trouble they've gotten out of."

Buck grinned. "Seem like fun people to be 'round."

"They are" She smiled. The sandy-blonde-headed one is mine," she claimed.

Buck nodded and smiled. "I knew dat."

Back inside, Marco's boredom sighs were getting closer together and he began to yawn. He glanced at the five guys tied up on the floor over by the wall near the waterway and then let his head fall back, looking at the ceiling thirty feet up.

Nigel now liked their chances. He and Josh had cleverly and carefully used Morse code with their feet to formulate a plan of escape. The only trouble was, the other three had no idea what was about to go down. He was confident they would figure it out after it started.

Tony turned south onto Highway 1. Paco and Dennis were bloodied and tied up in the back of the *Fresh Seafood* van and knew they were headed to their doom. Tony had had his second diver and hit man Leo work them both over pretty well for lying to him about the location of the coordinates. Leo was seated beside Tony up front and they were now just about five minutes from the boathouse that Tony had grown very fond of. It was out of the way, out of sight and out of mind—perfect for a mob house.

It was silent inside the boathouse and all the "footwork" was done. It was now go time. They just had to wait for the perfect opportunity and Marco would soon give it to them. He stood again and walked around, inhaling deeply and exhaling. A man with attention deficit was a bad man to leave behind to watch captives and Tony would regret it. Marco's mistake was getting too confident that nothing could happen. He stepped towards the offices and opened the door to the hallway to satisfy his curiosity. As he looked at the dustiness and disarray of an area that hadn't been used in years, Josh made his move.

Springing like the cougar that once nearly killed him, Josh jumped up and, in two strides, launched himself from the main floor of the boathouse straight into the waterway that ran through the facility. *Katoosh!* He landed with a splash and then hid himself along the concrete wall of the waterway so Marco couldn't see him.

Outside, Giselle gasped and Buck's head jerked, amazed at Josh's daring move. Eddie, Nick and Brad were equally shocked but remained seated, anxiously awaiting instructions. Hearing the splash, Marco turned around, drew his gun and ran towards the waterway. He was performing perfectly for what Nigel needed. As Marco ran by the group, Nigel sprang to his knees with reflexes quicker than a much younger man. Mustering all of his energy he leg-whipped Marco in the right shin. This hurt Nigel nearly as much as it did Marco but what it did was bring Marco to a halt, causing him to bend forward. This gave the British man time to get to his feet and recoil his leg for a second kick. It also gave Marco time to bring his gun up. Just as he got his arm level, Nigel released his right leg again and high-kicked him to the face. With that, Marco's head snapped back and the gun left his hand and the rest of the guys jumped up to detain him. Brad hit Marco low in a textbook tackle as Eddie and Nick followed up by grabbing his arms and turning him to his stomach. Josh then crawled from the waterway.

Paco observed the scene with wide eyes, wondering if he would be invited to the "rope release" party. He would not.

The gun had flown about twenty feet across the platform. From the south entrance, Giselle and Buck ran in through the huge opening meant for boats and Buck grabbed the handgun which was lying near the doorway. With Marco pinned down, Eddie recovered some of the lengths of rope that were used to tie them up and brought them over to Nigel. Once again, they would use the hog-tie system like they had used on Dennis. He wouldn't move.

Giselle's eyes caught Josh's and once the scene was secure she went to him and hugged him tightly, soaking wet and all. "I was scared for you, Josh."

Of course, Josh returned the embrace. That little sideways grin of his made its way across his wet face as he looked at his friends.

Buck flashed a big smile and said, "She said dat one hers."

They all laughed as tension was relieved for the moment.

Nigel then interrupted the feel-good moment. "We have to go! And we have to go fast."

"Let's get out of here," Eddie agreed. "Keys are in the bus."

"Come with me in the rental, Josh." Giselle said.

"I'm driving," Josh replied.

Before leaving, Josh ran over to a workbench and retrieved his Mini Maglite and knife which had been confiscated earlier.

CHAPTER TWENTY-FOUR

Tony turned left off of Highway 1 onto the street that would put him just south of the boathouse—his preferred route for the hidden parking spot he was using. He parked the *Fresh Seafood* van and then met Leo at the rear doors to escort Dennis into the boathouse. Dennis followed him, but slowly because of the beating Leo had inflicted for giving the wrong coordinates. Tony brought up the rear. The old trawler sat there as it had for many years, nice and level and apparently not yet beginning to take on water. They walked on past it, and then Tony turned around and looked at it as if a forgotten memory had been awoken. He looked at the aft deck of the boat as his mind chased the memory. He shook his head a bit and walked on and then heard Leo cry out.

"Tony! Tony they're gone!!!"

Tony snapped out of his memory-fog and stepped quickly towards the main room of the old repair facility. Hog-tied and laying on his side was his man, Marco. Marco's nose was busted and still bleeding and when he spoke, a front tooth wiggled—barely hanging on.

"Untie me!" he demanded. "They just left!"

Leo pulled a knife from his belt sheath and cut Marco loose.

"What the…what happened Marco?" Tony asked in disgust. "Shoulda left you here, Leo."

Leo's stock just went up.

Marco was breathing hard. "I don't know how they got untied. I was right here…all the time, I was watching them."

"The situation says otherwise, Marco. I may add you to my list tonight!" he scolded.

Dennis did not know what to think but was not too surprised considering he and Paco were bamboozled by the young team themselves. *Those guys must have nine lives,* Dennis thought.

"Boss, we have to go. We have to get them," Leo urged.

Tony shook his head. "Patience, Leo. We know where to find them. They are predictable, and it will cost them. We are not going to look like fools running blindly in search of them."

"I'm sorry, Tony. I don't know how they did it…" Marco pleaded.

"Shut up, Marco."

Dennis was securely tied once again, near Paco. Tony looked at them as if they were swine and then walked away.

Paco glanced at Dennis. *Maybe we live a few more hours, gringo,* he thought.

He was right…for now.

A safe distance away from the boathouse and with no *Fresh*

Seafood van tailing them, Eddie's bus, followed by Giselle's rental car, turned off Highway 1 onto a cross street which put them onto a service road behind a strip mall. In an earlier phone conversation they had agreed to pull in there to discuss what to do next. They exited their vehicles as Nigel carefully checked their surroundings. Everything looked safe enough for a few minutes. The late-afternoon heat was stifling and at this point they just wanted a pool, some food, and a safe environment—something they hadn't had in a while.

Nigel put his hand on Eddie's bus, leaning against it. "Well…we can't go back to the resort. You guys know that, right?" He looked at them.

They all nodded.

"It's the first place they will look. He's going to post men at the resort, at the beach near the coordinates, and probably at some random points on A1A and Highway 1. He will add men and step up his game. He knows your bus, Eddie, so you are going to have to park it."

"Could I park it at the self-park at the resort…and leave it?"

"How bad do you want it vandalized? No, mate. We will put it at my place and then you guys must use the rental."

"May have to upgrade," Giselle said, counting heads.

"I can offa my cah," Buck said.

Eddie put his hand on Buck's shoulder. "Thank you Buddy, thank you for everything. If you hadn't tipped us off about this guy, it could have been…different."

"Was dee right ting to do mon." He smiled. "You steel manage to get eento trouble."

Nigel said, "I need to get back down to Bud's Marina and get my car. I will also have to settle up with Bud about his missing boat. I'll call him and explain."

Brad continued, "There's something else…in that boat is your bag and in that bag, is an overlooked emerald."

Nigel nodded. "I hadn't forgotten."

Giselle stepped forward. "I am going to call Lou Cannon. I talked to him earlier and I'm sure he is curious, if not concerned. I'll fill him in on everything."

Josh was biting his cheek, thinking. "We have to find a place to stay."

"With me," Nigel offered. "I got plenty of room and a garage for the bus."

"Are you sure?" Giselle asked. "You want this circus at your place?"

Nigel smiled. "Well, desperate times call for desperate measures, you know?"

Giselle smiled and clutched Josh's arm. "Any port in a storm, right?"

"That's right." Nigel smiled.

The afternoon faded into evening as all the catch-up errands were being completed. Buck Naked ended up taking Nigel from Daytona down to Canaveral to get his car. Brad rode along and, after retrieving the car from Bud's, and settling with the marina owner, they located Tony's *no-questions-asked* marina and grabbed their remaining possessions from the Bayliner, including a spectacular emerald that Marco had overlooked earlier. Bud told Nigel not to worry, he would send a man to get the Bayliner back in the morning. Nigel hid the key by the bilge pump in the engine compartment with a one-hundred-dollar bill for the guy who had to go get it.

Giselle called Lou Cannon and he told her he had his buddy Ray on alert, and knew the locations of the boathouse where they had been. Lou also told Giselle that he had gotten the OK from the State to search the site for the wreck. Giselle was thrilled but Nick felt like he could do back flips. Josh and Eddie were anxious to get started but they had a problem…they had Tony looking for them and he knew the general location of the wreck site and it was certain he would be watching.

Nigel had given Josh and Eddie the gate code to his place. The former British Special Ops agent lived a little better than he had let on. His community was secure and his lifestyle was slightly more than comfortable. It seems that his investments had done pretty well in that little Apple company.

Eddie, Josh, Giselle and Nick went on to Nigel's to hide the bus while Buck took Nigel to Canaveral to get his car. They arrived at the guard shack and keyed in the numbers to open the gate. The gates swung open to a community of manicured lawns, multiple swimming pools, two golf courses with club houses, and its own marina on the Intracoastal. The entrance boulevard wound its way back and after a couple of left turns, they were at Nigel's house on Nautilus Lane. He lived about ten miles north of the boathouse.

Josh looked out the bus window. "This might be better than the Vista al Mar."

Eddie laughed. "Makes you wonder why he hangs out at the

resorts."

"For the social life," Giselle said. "He likes to be around people. Could be because he had to be so secretive about himself for so long…he just enjoys that freedom now."

They stepped from the van and were greeted by a beautiful three-tier fountain in the middle of his driveway that led to a four-car garage. Nigel's house was a large Spanish two-story stucco complete with arches and a half pipe terracotta tile roof. He had told them to go on in and make themselves at home. His last words to them had been, "the key's in the conch shell."

The four young people stood looking at Nigel's landscaping. It was a freeform design that extended out from the house anywhere from six to twelve feet, depending on the curves of the design. Inside the curvy, freeform layout were, possibly, two hundred…conch shells.

The kids stood staring.

"Cruel joke," Nick said. "Cruel, cruel joke."

Josh shook his head "Well I guess this will kill some time."

He and the other boys began picking up shells one by one and shaking them, listening for contents. Giselle wasn't so sure and looked around for something different. It didn't take long.

"Oh, good lord," Giselle said. "It's over there. It has to be."

Paying closer attention to the fountain they had just parked beside, Giselle noticed there was mermaid holding a conch shell. Water flowed out from the top of it and down over the beauty and then into a holding pool.

She stepped over to the fountain and put her hand in an

oversized cement conch shell. Her expression turned to bewilderment as she pulled out a small metal plate with four numbers engraved on it. She looked at the numbers and then looked at the boys. Josh thought for a moment and then looked at the door.

"Electronic lock. That's the code," he said smiling.

Eddie nodded. "He's testing our savvy."

"I bet he's expecting a phone call asking where the key is," Giselle continued.

Josh shook his head and walked over to enter the code. The door unlocked right away.

"I'm going to call him to tell him I'm sitting in his chair," Josh laughed.

The four entered and were met by a blast of cold air—a great relief from the sweltering 90s outside.

Later that evening they all sat around Nigel's dinner table, Eddie's bus safely stored in the garage and all of them out of harm's way for the time being. Of course, Nigel had invited Buck Naked to dinner providing he did not demonstrate how he got his nickname. Buck agreed and was happy to spend the evening with this adventurous bunch. He was also curious to hear the rest of the story—the details of what exactly was going on here…if they offered it to him.

Nick was fascinated with Jamaica and its culture and history so he and Buck bonded quickly as Buck presented the quick version of his background and culture. Brad found himself listening intently as Buck described his island and its history of pirates and decadence. He also told them of his long road to citizenship in the U.S.

As they all finished a delicious seafood paella dish prepared by a pretty Spanish lady Nigel would not call a house-lady nor a girlfriend, they began to discuss what was next.

Nigel started with Buck. "Well, I have to say, Mr. Naked, you have proven yourself a trusted soul, and we appreciate, wholeheartedly, your giving us a heads-up about the man with the lazy eye. So therefore I believe you deserve an explanation of what has been happening and why."

Everyone nodded. Buck smiled and said, "Buck can hodly wait! Moos be good."

Giselle chuckled, wiped her mouth with her cloth napkin and said, "It's just the normal, crazy, adventure life that seems to follow us. We have some stories!"

"I'm all 'eers," he responded.

Nigel gestured towards Nick. It had all started with him.

Nick began, "Well, it seems that back in 1973, after a divorce, my grandfather moved down here and, after a while, was hired on as a first mate on an old trawler, the very trawler I believe that sits in that boathouse down the Intracoastal."

Nigel interrupted, "Mate, you know how many boats there could be with the name *Maria*?"

"I have a feeling, Nigel. I want to get on that boat and look around."

Nigel nodded. "Maybe not the best idea right now. I think our buddy with the lazy eye kind of likes the boathouse too."

Nick shrugged and continued, "So, according to a diary that we have from grandpa, his name was Butch...Butch Dawson. They were hired by a man to make a run to the reef. They were to drop something and return to the docks. As it turns out, sometime during the drop they found a couple of these." When Nick pulled the *Escudo* from his pocket, Buck's eyes widened. "This was given to me when I was very young and I was told the story about what it was and where it came from. Of course, at eight years old, I had no idea what the 1715 Treasure Fleet was but it didn't take me long to start learning about it."

Buck interrupted, "Dat coin from da Treasa Fleet?"

Nick nodded. "Sure is. And we are very sure there are many more. You see…my grandfather logged the coordinates in his diary where he found these, with the intention of returning with Captain Henderson a day or so later to investigate further. Well…I have… I have learned a lot since I have been down here," Nick went on somberly, "and one of the things I have learned is when Butch Dawson and Captain Henderson returned to the docks after dumping Rocco Palombo on the reef, this guy who we now know as Tony, shot and killed them both."

Buck leaned back in his seat in disbelief. "Ah mon…no way. You found de mon who keel you grandfatha' after all dees yeahs?"

Nick nodded and looked around at everyone…letting that sink in.

"Mon…day is no statute ob de limitations law fah murder…dot mon con steel go to de preeson."

"I know…I know and I intend to see to that."

Nigel was finishing an espresso, up to now just listening to the recap of the adventure. Now he spoke up. "It will be a long road, Nick. It's a very cold case and what evidence do you have other than a confession that won't matter?"

"I know. I know it will be a long road but I intend to see him go down it," Nick said.

Nigel nodded, "I'm with you on that, Nick."

Nick continued telling Buck about Paco and Dennis and how they had stolen the coin and chart initially, and the lengths they all had to go to, to get it back. Buck was very amused with the tale of Brad's fireworks diversion and told them he only hoped to be lucky enough to witness one someday. They all laughed about it…because it was over.

Josh added, "We will have to have a late-night story-time and tell you some of the things we have been into the last few years. You won't believe it."

Each one of them added a few details of the past few days and Buck had a really good idea of what was happening by the end of dessert, which was a fabulous *Tres Leche* cake.

"Eet sound like a grand adventure, mon," Buck said, shaking his head.

"I just want to get these guys out of our way so we can get in the water. We have the OK from the State of Florida to proceed and I can't wait. It's my fault though—if I hadn't been waving that coin around up at the rest stop, we would not have all this trouble now." Nick took the blame.

Josh waved him off. "It wouldn't be any fun if we didn't have a bad guy or two after us. That's *our* history."

Nick grinned. "I want to hear those stories too!" he said.

Giselle moved her dessert plate away and shook her head as she looked at Nick and then Buck. "You won't believe these stories. They have had so many people with guns chasing them just in the last few years. Most people don't experience that in an entire lifetime!"

The group laughed and then Nigel brought up the next subject. "Well friends, we have to decide what's next and how to approach it. Do we bring in law enforcement?"

Nick stiffened and Nigel took notice.

"I know…I know, Nick, and I understand. But at some point, we must decide when too much is too much. I know that the coin and the chart are sentimental to you…and I can't promise that they won't go into an evidence locker for a while as the story about the first two idiots and Tony and his bunch are revealed."

Nick nodded, knowingly. "We also have to get with Lou Cannon and see what he is comfortable with."

Eddie agreed. "I'm sure he doesn't want to treasure hunt when Tony's men have him in their sights."

Brad said, "I guess Tony has the first two guys at the boathouse. I wonder how long he will keep them alive."

"Until he has no more use for them," Nigel replied. "He won't keep them just for pets but I do think he will keep them as expendables…to do things he wouldn't have his own men do, if needed. Also, you can be sure by now, that Tony has the correct coordinates—he will have beat them out of his two captives. My gut feeling is he will not be out there tonight but maybe in the morning."

Nick followed up, "So we can count on them being at the boat house and maybe Tony too. Maybe we can use that to our advantage."

Nigel looked at Nick. "What do you mean?"

"You won't like what I suggest."

"Try me."

Everyone was looking back and forth between Nick and Nigel.

"They say the best offense is a good defense…but in this case, I think the best defense is a good offense. I'm tired of reacting."

"You think we should turn the tables," Nigel confirmed.

"I do."

"With the Florida Mafia?"

"Yes sir."

Nigel looked hard at Nick. "You know…you have to have an objective. You have to have a reason. What will it benefit you to go on the offensive? Do you have a plan?"

"Somewhat, yes. I mean, you say the mafia but so far we have only dealt with three of them," Nick observed. "It's not like we are up against an army."

Nigel sat up straight, assuming an attitude of authority. His next words were a testament to his training and knowledge. "The reason his manpower has been minimal is because this is a personal project of this guy, Tony. Something from his younger days that he missed…he screwed it up and now he is trying to make it right…make up for lost years. If he would have let your grandfather live back in '73, Nick, he would have been a very rich and powerful man all these years. Do you think that doesn't bother a guy like Tony? By not listening to Butch Dawson, and therefore not knowing about the 1715 treasure, he had to do it the hard way. He had to beat his way to the top of the food chain in his…organization. I'm sure Tony is not hurting for money, but he's nowhere near where he wants to be." Nigel paused for a moment. "You see, guys, that's the thing with people who want lots of money and power…enough is never enough. Always one more step, always the next level, one more rung on the ladder, until it begins to make you crazy—takes over your mind. It's an infinite obsession of greed. I've seen it a lot in my career."

Nick nodded along with the others.

"Guys, I'm sure Tony has already stepped up the numbers. Now, he will keep his circle as small as he can because, even in organized crime, the fewer who know, the better, but like I told you, he will have men positioned at the boathouse, men watching A1A for your bus, Eddie, and men at Canaveral watching for any activity at the site of the coordinates."

Nick was listening intently. "So, maybe he won't have bunches of men in one spot but, rather, he will have them spread out."

Nigel replied, "I can't promise that. That's what I say, Nick. Maybe enough is enough because we just don't know. Any of those three places I just mentioned could have double or triple the manpower."

Nick looked straight at Nigel. "Do you really believe that?"

Nigel held Nick's gaze. He drew a deep breath and relaxed in his chair and thought for a moment. He then answered him. "Nick…I believe it enough to refuse to let any of you take a bullet from this man and his organization. I will not have your blood on my hands. It's not worth it and I couldn't live with that."

Nick nodded while biting his lower lip. "What if we had a really good plan and we all agreed to it?" Nick grinned. His wheels were turning.

Nigel thought for a moment. There was total silence in the

dining room. After a moment he said, "Then I would say we would have to use a minimum crew and I would pick who goes, and I would hand out the assignments."

"You'll listen to my idea?"

"Only if I can add to it, or take away from it. And…those over 21 will be armed. That would be Buck and you, Nick.

Nick glanced over at Buck Naked to see if he was onboard or wanted to bail at this point. Buck grinned ever so slightly and nodded once.

"Deal," Nick responded. He pointed at Brad. "Brad…we may need a diversion!"

"And some firearms training," Nigel said.

"Ooo yeah!" cried Buck. "Dat deedn't take too long!"

CHAPTER TWENTY-FIVE

A ray of morning sunlight found its way through the vertical blinds and square into Josh Baker's eye, waking him and causing him to blink and squint. He, Eddie and Brad had piled into one bedroom which had two beds and a couch. Nick and Buck slept in the TV room on two other couches, and Giselle drew the long straw for the bedroom with the private bath. The night had gone long as they sat up telling and listening to each other's stories. Possibly the most fascinating were Buck's tales of the numerous caves and tunnels of Jamaica that can go on for miles and connect different parts of the island nation to each other underground. There are many tales of treasure still unfound in the caverns of his island, and this only fueled the interest of the rest of the guys to want to go there!

Josh squirmed and rolled over to escape the sun's awakening rays, but felt like he had slept very well. He and Giselle had stayed up later than the rest—slipping outside to talk privately before turning in for the night. Josh heard a phone ringing in the TV room next to them. It was Nick's ringtone. Nick slowly came to life as his phone continued. He reached for it on the table beside him and, with very foggy eyesight, could read Family Jewels. Nick took the call and put the phone to his ear—barely awake.

"Good morning." Nick shook his head, wondering why he had said *good morning* instead of *hello*. Morning cobwebs.

Lou laughed lightly, knowing he had awoken him. "Good morning, Nick. How are you?"

Nick sat up and rubbed his eyes while yawning. "Late-nighter, man. Too much story-telling last night."

"Well, I don't know what your plans are for today, but if you are counting on treasure hunting, we are going to have to wait."

These words pressed the adrenalin button in Nick's brain as he shook out a few more cobwebs.

"Why? What's wrong? I thought we had the go-ahead."

"Yeah, we do but there is a launch today…A SpaceX unmanned something-or-other going up in the afternoon."

Nick thought about that for a moment. "So that area will be…"

"…Restricted. Those coordinates lie in the *Keep Out* zone. They will not clear that zone until four hours post-launch."

"And how long before?" Nick wondered.

"They start clearing twelve hours prior to launch time."

"Hmmm, this is actually good news."

"Why do you say that?"

"Well, because the bad guys have the true coordinates and we don't want them in there."

"You won't have to worry about that. The coast guard will be on them like stink on a monkey if they go out there."

"What time is launch?"

"2:05 this afternoon."

"OK, so roughly six o'clock before it's clear."

"Right. Unless something drops into the zone." Lou cannon paused for a moment. "Hey Nick, what is the story with these guys? Are you ever going to call the authorities or…what are we going to do? I'm not willing to go out there with a threat of someone running up on me in a threatening way like I'm some fly-by-night organization. I mean…I'm a licensed treasure hunter…not so much a pirate."

Denise looked at Lou. He actually *did* like to go rogue every now and then. There's a little bit of pirate in *all* who go to sea.

"We are working up a plan, Lou, and before we all go out there we will make sure they are bagged one way or another."

"OK," Lou responded. "Today is shot but you guys keep me up to date on what's going on and let me know when we are good to go."

"Sure will, Lou. Thanks for the info. I'll let the rest of them sleep."

"Lou laughed. "OK, buddy. Take care."

Later that morning, after a good breakfast, a plan was formulated and finalized. Nigel listened to Nick's idea and then, after considering it and polishing it somewhat, they had a plan that offered a bailout option if all went bad…that would be where Brad came in. Everyone loved the fact that the SpaceX launch would give them time to breathe, but they knew Tony would be watching and he would be moving, but not before that evening, and maybe even nightfall. They had called Lou to discuss the matter with him via speakerphone and, after stirring up that pirate blood that lain deep within him, he agreed to have a boat in position close by the coordinate site, just in case any support was needed. Lou didn't want the bad guys in there either. They discussed the possibility of Coast Guard protection while they searched, but Lou explained the Coast Guard was not obligated, nor funded, to offer private protection. They would only come out to escort a boat that was "treasure-heavy," but it would cost a pretty penny. He would, however, call Ray for another set of eyes and expertise on the water.

Afterwards, Nigel took the group into the living room and did a firearms presentation with a couple of empty Glock 17 9mm handguns. They spent about an hour getting Nick and Buck up to speed on the safety features and getting the gun to feel comfortable in their hands. The guns were then passed around for all to handle. The goal was, to never have to fire one shot, but the motto was: *prepare for the worst and hope for the best*. Not only *hope* for the best but do everything in their power to make things go the right way. The first thing they had going for them was that Tony was not expecting an offensive maneuver from these guys. Never in a million years would a group of young people make a move on the mob. He would be very surprised.

Paco and Dennis were leaning up against the very same wall with the railing that Josh and the guys had been tied to yesterday. They had neither the advantage of the rusty nail close by, nor the cleverness to use it.

Tony had gotten the word on the SpaceX launch. One of his men had called him from the Cape Canaveral area and told him they were clearing boats all morning and it would be evening before any vessels were allowed into the "keep-out" zone. Tony had to make a new plan for himself and his team. He would keep Paco and Dennis through the day, and then they would join Rocco Palombo on the reef tonight. These two bums had lied to him twice and Tony simply didn't tolerate liars. Tony had given Paco and Dennis the bad news to think about all day. They pleaded with him, saying he now had the exact site and they could be of service to him but they knew they were dead men—there was no one to save them. It was now only a matter of hours for this not-so-good crime team.

After making a couple of calls, Tony thought of something interesting and sauntered past the bound men, past the tool and parts rooms and back to the old trawler that sat bobbing in the water. He looked at her and he wondered. An old, thick rope was looped over a short post and separated Tony from the vessel. He lifted the rope from the post and stepped aboard *Maria*. The planking seemed firm and solid for the age of the boat as he walked across the foredeck. Making his way toward the pilothouse, something haunted him. He wasn't sure what it was, but there was something quite cold about this boat—he just couldn't put his finger on it.

The pilothouse was bare-bones basic and towards the aft of it were steps that led down. Tony looked through the window to see Leo step onboard. He followed Tony into the pilothouse.

"Thinking of buying it?" Leo asked wryly, looking around at the cobwebs and mouse droppings.

Tony grinned just a bit and shook his head as he looked down the steps into the darkness. "I just had an idea. You think this old tub would run, Leo?"

Leo winced. "This old diesel has been sitting for years, Tony. The fuel alone would be bad not to mention the filter and any gook in the lines. Even with new fuel it would be doubtful." He looked at the aging Italian man. "What do you have in mind?"

Tony was biting his lower lip in thought "It would be good to use. If it would run, we could take it out to the reef tonight, dump these two guys and move on to the shipwreck. I can order a bogus license and numbers to throw on her, and we're in business."

Leo looked down the hole. He was very handy with boats but he was no master mechanic. He also knew that if Tony wanted to try, it would be in his best interests to accept the challenge.

Tony said, "This would be a good working boat for the next couple days for us. It would keep us off our own boats and it would keep us off rented ones. We can relocate it down the coast later tonight."

Leo nodded. "*If*…we can make it run. Let me go down and take a look. Make sure it even has an engine."

Tony grinned as Leo pulled his flashlight from his belt and went below to check things out. At the bottom of the creaking steps, on both sides, were crew compartments and straight ahead was the engine room. Leo opened the small door that led into the engine "room." The room was more of a compartment—about the size of a standard walk-in closet in a new home. On the left side was a battery box with the lid missing and in the box sat two very old and corroded twelve-volt batteries. Without a doubt, they were dead as door nails. Tony could hear Leo banging around as he worked to diagnose the engine issue. He looked around the pilothouse. Making his way to the helm, he rolled the wheel back and forth and then moved the throttle control forward and back. He was happy to see they were still free as he got a complaint from

Leo below to stop moving things around while he had his fingers in the works.

Leo spent a few minutes checking things out and then climbed back up to report to Tony.

Wiping his hands on a thirty-year-old towel, he began, "Well...everything is there—the starter, alternator, everything. It hasn't been stripped. It has a belt on it that is actually in good condition...it's just old and dry."

"You give me the engine size and I'll have them bring a belt."

"OK. The fuel tank is dry, which is good. Maybe it was drained and, with any luck, maybe they drained the lines too. But here's what we are going to need: two strong batteries, a drum of fuel, two fuel filters and an air filter as well as the new belt. Also an air tank to blow out these fuel lines, if it hasn't been done, and a case of motor oil." Leo looked over at Tony, "Is it worth it?"

Tony nodded confidently. "I can make that happen. We're gonna give it a shot, Leo. I'll have some tools sent over, too, and you can get to work on it. Marco can help you if you need him. We need a boat that we can use and then ditch with no ties back to us and if we have this one sitting here, and the time to do it, then that's what we're gonna do."

Leo nodded once, "I'll do my best, boss."

"I know you will, Leo."

Tony made the call to get the parts and tools for Leo to do his magic...on *Maria*. A couple of hours later, an unmarked white van showed up with everything Leo said he would need, minus the fuel. That would come later. He would spend the next few hours trying to work a miracle.

Afternoon rolled into evening as The SpaceX launch went off without a hitch and, to the amazement of Nigel's company, they saw it clearly from his home forty-five minutes north of the Cape. It was nearly 7:30 pm, however, before they started letting vessels back into the "keep-out" zone, without an explanation. That happened sometimes.

Nigel had made a sketch of the boathouse and had sat down with everyone a few times during the day and gone over different scenarios of "what-ifs." They were all confident they had all of the bases covered. Maybe Tony would have more men than expected or maybe he would have fewer. Nigel had made it clear that they would know how many before going in. Surveillance and recon would be a mandatory precursor to any action they would take. And if it were too risky, they would bail out and they had plans for that as well—meeting points if they had to run, and ways to cover each other.

For now, they needed to know if the Italian man was there and that's where Buck came in. Tony didn't know Buck or his SUV. Buck would go first and do a drive-by. He needed to see if there were any vehicles parked amongst the sea oats or in the parking spot at the far end of the building where Eddie had once parked his bus. That spot had good cover and was nearly undetectable unless you were looking for it. Early evening gave way to nightfall and it was now time to roll.

They left Nigel's house at around 10:00 pm with two vehicles. Nick and Nigel rode with Buck Naked in his old black Suburban that he used for pool service. Josh, Eddie, Giselle and Brad would take Giselle's rental car with Josh at the wheel. Their job for the night was to hide the car and then set up a perimeter. The old road was nearly unused because there was nothing south beyond the boathouse *on* that road except one street that would take you back out to the main highway. They would have to watch that street as well as the sand-covered side street to make sure no one sneaked in on Nigel and the boys while they were in "operation" mode. If that happened, they would need to bail out.

Buck Naked turned off of Highway 1 onto the sand-covered cross street that led over to the boathouse.

Nigel nodded to Nick. "This is where we go to the back."

Nick and Nigel climbed into the back of Buck's Suburban. The dark-tinted windows allowed them to scout the area without being seen from outside the vehicle. The Jamaican resumed driving slowly down the sand-covered road and made a right at the end of the street. There was a vehicle parked on the cement slab surrounded by tall sea oats.

"Don't slow down, mate. Just keep on driving right on by the boathouse like normal."

Buck did as ordered and, as they passed the boathouse, Nigel and Nick could see a faint light through the cracks of the old facility. At the north end of the building, nearly obscured by some scrub oaks and undergrowth, was the white *Fresh Seafood* van.

Nigel and Nick tried to take in every detail as they passed by.

Nigel said, "No way of knowing how many are in there yet, but we do know they are there." Nigel paused. "OK Mr. Naked, make a right on that cross street and let's go hide this beast."

Buck grinned and shook his head.

Tony's head spun around as he heard a vehicle drive by. From the engine room of *Maria,* he ascended the steps so he could hear better. The vehicle drove on by and didn't sound like it slowed at all, but Tony still didn't like it. There was nothing at the end of this street and no reason for anyone to be down in this area. Tony scoffed at the thought of being surveilled. Someone was just looking for a place to party. *Had to be!*, he thought.

Leo had done all he could do and now they were just waiting for the fuel truck. He had replaced the filters and the belt. He had blown out every fuel line to the best of his ability and had cleaned the rat's nests from the radiator shroud as well as checked hoses and topped off fluid levels. New batteries were installed and the starter was removed, sprayed with electrical cleaner and reinstalled. It spun free so they hoped for the best on that. Leo had time, so he drained the old, sludgy, oil and replaced it. The longer this engine lasted, the better.

"Fuel should be here in a few minutes," Tony said calmly.

Leo nodded, "I feel pretty good about this."

Tony sneered and nodded as well.

CHAPTER TWENTY-SIX

At his house, Nigel had a safe-room with an impressive collection of toys, including two-way micro-radio communication devices—his own being water-proof. The plan was for Nigel to enter via the waterway and Nick and Buck to enter through different points. Buck was given the assignment of entering through the north end opening on a narrow walkway beside where the boats entered. From there, on Nigel's command, he could rush in, gun drawn, creating a huge element of surprise. Nick had to be very careful—he had to enter right through the front door that led into the offices. As long as no one was in those offices at the time, he was going to be OK. At the synchronized time, his assignment was to kick through the door that led into the main facility, gun drawn on the closest occupant. They had to detain Tony and his men at the boathouse for the time needed to safely begin the search for the *Concepcion*—a day or so. Once, and if, they could confirm the old ship was discovered, the official announcement was to be made and then the wreck site could only be excavated by Family Jewels.

At that point they could send the police to the boathouse where they would find Tony, and, *with any luck,* Lou's treasure-laden boats could be protected by the Coast Guard for the duration of the excavation. They had practiced their maneuvers many times, using different rooms and the garage. Nigel taught them all he could in a short amount of time and felt pretty confident with the mission. These guys were fast learners and understood the seriousness of the situation. He knew, too, that he was in charge and must do all he could to cover these guys in the event of a surprise.

Buck Naked parked his black SUV beside Giselle's rental car out on Highway 1 at the lonely gas station. From there, and under the cover of darkness, they walked across the dunes and positioned themselves around the boathouse in the predetermined positions. Returning to the boathouse armed, wired and on the offensive to detain Tony and his men, the playing field was now leveled, if not in Nigel's favor.

Giselle stayed with Josh. Nigel wanted her to remain back at his house but she would have none of that. They were on a perimeter post, just like Eddie and Brad, making sure no vehicles rolled in unannounced. With the perimeter in place, it gave them an outer layer of security, thus giving Nigel, Nick and Buck time to bail out if Tony's reinforcements arrived. Josh and Giselle hid amongst the sea oats on the left side of the sand-covered cross street where they could still smell the antifreeze from Brad's truck and Dennis' Buick a couple of days before. Eddie took the other cross street on the south end and Brad positioned himself very near the cement pad where Tony already had a car parked. Brad's job was to watch the road that ran along the Intracoastal Waterway, where the boathouse sat. None of the four on the perimeter were armed, other than with radios.

Nigel, Nick and Buck began to move into position. Splitting up, Nigel went to the south end of the boathouse to enter the waterway. He needed to ease past the old trawler, and create his surprise from just about the same spot inside where Josh had taken his plunge earlier.

Nigel's instincts told him, at the maximum, there were five guys inside and, with the element of surprise, they could take them, but he still wanted to confirm that before they went in. Nigel had Nick hold back from going inside the offices until he and Buck were into position.

Nick hunkered down in the tall weeds across the street for the time being. He had just gotten into position when Josh blasted in his earpiece, "Truck! Truck turning onto my street!"

Nigel responded, "What kind of truck?"

After a moment, Josh replied, "It's a truck with a tank on the back…like a fuel truck." Josh paused for a second. "Yeah it's a diesel fuel truck."

"Let me know where he turns, Josh," Nigel said.

Brad jumped in. "He's turning right. Nick, you're gonna see him."

"Yep…I got him. He's passing by me and slowing down. He's at the south end of the building. He stopped!" Nick said, somewhat frantic but just above a whisper

Nigel took over. "OK…I'm in the water outside the boathouse. I've got him. He's pulling in beside the white van. Everyone just hold fast. Don't move…we may have to bail." Nigel would take no unplanned chances.

Nick asked, "What are they doing with a diesel truck? They gonna torch the building with those two guys inside…and the boat?" It was clear which one Nick was more concerned with.

"No, mate. I don't think so. Torching this building would only take a match. Just sit tight."

Nigel had a good idea of what the fuel was for but didn't want to tell Nick, just in case this turned out to be the old boat his grandfather worked on years ago. That would crush Nick, if not infuriate him and Nigel needed cool, clear-thinking heads tonight. It was also possible there was another boat now inside that needed to be fueled discreetly. Nigel had to take that into account as well.

Eddie came on. "All clear over here."

"Copy," Nigel replied.

Nigel could see the activity well from his vantage point in the water outlet about twenty yards outside the building. A man exited the fuel truck and went inside the building. A couple of minutes later he came out with Leo, both of them talking low and nodding. The driver began pulling a long hose from a reel on the truck and took it well inside the building.

"We're gonna fill it up," Leo told him, inside. Also, I need to prime this filter, so when you're done with the tank, we can shoot some fuel in here."

"Got it," the driver responded.

He commenced filling the large tank, knowing well not to make small talk…knowing well who his clients were. Outside, the truck engine revved as it operated the fuel pump. About ten minutes went by before the engine idled down and the fueling was over. Two hundred gallons of fresh diesel now sloshed in Maria's tank for the first time in over thirty years.

Nick could hear the truck as well and he had figured out what was going on. "Nigel, is there a second boat in there?" he asked.

Nigel's head dropped. "I don't know. But stay where you're at. I have to get inside to see."

The truck engine revved up and down one more time as the driver squirted a shot of fuel into the new fuel filter for Leo. He was finished. Stepping outside and pressing a button on the side of his truck, he recoiled the fuel hose and collected his money from Leo. Climbing back into his truck, the driver backed out onto the road and drove off—this time going towards Eddie to make his way back to Highway 1.

Nigel popped his head above the wall of the waterway, still outside the building. "I need 'all-clears' from the perimeter."

Josh, Brad and Eddie responded with *all clear* and now it was go time. It wasn't a kick-down-the-door-with-guns-blazing plan…not yet anyway, but more of a finesse plan. And Nigel would go first. Again…the idea was to not have to fire a shot, but time would tell.

Inside, Leo screwed the new filter onto the engine and now he was ready to crank it over. Hopefully, the fuel pump would do its thing and start sucking the diesel from the tank and the old beast would fire to life. With everything ready, Leo went up the short set of steps into the pilothouse to the helm and flipped on the battery switch. An old green light glowed on the dash panel indicating battery power for the starter. Tony walked back to the old trawler after hearing the fuel truck leave while Leo was making his last preparations for the engine start-up attempt. Paco and Dennis still sat in the same spot, secured to the rail and now quite certain they were down to minutes to live.

"I should have known better than to hook up with you again," Dennis said. "Every time before, I ended up in jail. This time, I'm going swimming…with my hands tied."

"Shut up, gringo…I should have done this by myself. I would be alive and rich by now."

Tony paid no attention to their conversation as he walked past. His focus was on Leo.

Leo wiggled his fingers as he hoped for the best. An old rubber-covered button was the start switch and Leo, twirled his finger dramatically and confidently pushed the button. The fresh batteries did their thing as the starter engaged and *Maria's* old diesel engine began to crank. Over and over the engine spun, getting faster as the new oil made its way to the bearings after all these years. Leo held the button as the beast spun and spun but, so far, did not fire up.

Outside, Nigel was now quietly using a hand-over-hand technique along the seawall to enter the boathouse, being careful not to splash. He suddenly heard the old trawler's engine trying to crank up. This answered his question about the second boat inside—there was none. He was now just outside the boathouse and no more than twenty feet from the stern of *Maria*. He heard it crank and crank and wondered what work they had done to prepare this boat to run again.

With the night being quiet in the vicinity of the boathouse, Nick could faintly hear a grinding sound coming from within the boathouse.

Nick keyed his mic. "What is that Nigel? What's going on inside there?"

"Sit tight, Nick. I'm going to work my way inside and see what's going on. Buck, are you in position?"

"Buck een position, suh,"

"Nick, you stay right where you are, outside. Do not go in the office yet."

"Are they trying to start that boat? Are they taking *Maria*?" Nick asked, even more frantic now.

"Nick! Stay put! Don't go in there!" Nigel ordered.

Josh looked at Giselle and shook his head. "It's gonna fall apart if Nick runs in there before Nigel is ready. He'll get somebody killed...maybe himself."

Leo released the start button to give the batteries and the old starter a break. Tony stepped onto the boat. He was now smoking a cigar. "Try it again," he ordered Leo.

"I need to let the starter cool. If we burn it out, it will never start," Leo answered.

"It's gonna start, right Leo? You did your job well, right?"

A small amount of optimism had left Leo's eyes. After giving the starter a few seconds to cool, he hit the button again. The engine spun more freely from the beginning this time as it wound its way through compression cycles. The old engine sounded like it was capable of starting, but, once again, didn't fire after about fifteen seconds of trying. Tony scowled at Leo.

"Tony…there has to be fuel pressure. These fuel lines have to get full before this engine is going to go. Give me a little time."

Tony blew a smoke ring at him. "We don't have much time, Leo. Get it running and don't burn up the starter."

Tony stepped off of the boat and casually walked back out to where Paco and Dennis were seated. He walked past them and went over and sat on the old grease can beside Marco. He could hear Leo cranking the engine and letting it rest over and over.

Marco looked at Tony, "What do we do if it doesn't start? What's the plan?"

Tony put his arm around Marco's shoulder and squeezed his trapezius muscle as Marco winced. He paused for a moment as he removed his cigar and said, "Then we go back to the original plan, Marco. There's a big ocean out there…ya never know, a boat could float in here from anywhere." He laughed. "I always have a back-up plan, Marco. Remember that."

Back outside, Nigel stayed put just beyond the stern of *Maria* and tight up against the wall. The engine rolled over and over and then would rest and then it would do it all over again. In communication with the team members on the perimeter, Nigel knew that all was still clear, but he had to wait to see what was going to happen with this boat before making a move.

Nick's heart raced as he listened to the starter roll the engine time after time. It was killing him. All Nick wanted since he had seen the name on her bow was to get onboard and look around. If this was the same vessel, he wanted to see where his grandfather had spent his last hours. Nick even had thoughts of trying to obtain the boat, and restoring her. If the *Concepcion* lay where they thought it did, then surely it could be possible. But for now, he had to endure the agony of helplessness as Tony's men tried to take her from him. Nick's fear was that Tony would sink her offshore with Dennis and Paco onboard. He could not let that happen.

After a couple of minutes, Nigel keyed his mic and spoke softly. "Brad, you're a marine mechanic—they filled this girl with fresh diesel. I'm sure they spent the day readying her to start, but she's not firing. You got any ideas why?"

Everyone listening wondered why Nigel asked. What did it

matter? Josh looked at Giselle, puzzled, as she put her arm around his shoulder.

Brad thought for a moment. "A diesel engine is a simple machine. They always told us if it won't start, it's one of three things: Fuel, fuel or fuel. There is no electricity involved in a diesel. It's all about compression. The fuel burns simply at high compression."

"OK."

"You need me over there?"

"No. Not yet, Brad, but be ready."

"OK. We worked on some old boats and I may have an idea, assuming they changed oil, filters and primed her. With strong batteries, it should go."

"OK. Sit tight."

Brad Radcliffe was getting eaten alive by fire ants. He moved out of the sand and over to the cement pad where Tony had a car parked. Brushing the little monsters from his legs, he was now positioned closer to the road but could also see the Intracoastal better. Doing his job at keeping an eye on the road that ran by the boathouse, he couldn't help but also look towards the water. When you grow up on the water, it's in your veins. Brad noticed a boat, probably a half mile away, make a turn towards them and then kill its lights—not only its spotlights but also all its running lights. This boat wanted to be invisible.

He keyed his mic. "Nigel, we may have a problem."

"Talk to me."

"A boat in the waterway…about a half mile north, sitting in the channel. He just killed all lights."

"Can you still see him?"

"I can see its silhouette against some light behind it."

"OK. Keep an eye on it. Let me know if it moves."

"Copy that."

The boat engine continued cranking, to no avail. Nick stood, his hands trembling as he looked back and forth across the street. He quickly trotted over to the front office door. He couldn't take it anymore. He had to get inside. It was like they were trying to take a family member away from him and he had lost too many of those already.

"Nigel, we can't let them take that boat," Nick said.

Nigel could hear the desperation in his voice. "Nick…don't do it. Stay in the weeds for now. I have to see how many are inside!"

"I'm by the front door. I need to go in. I'll be careful."

Tony and Leo had pressed a button. Nick was simply fed up with things being taken away from him. Nick carefully opened the front door that led into the dark and musty offices…and in he went.

CHAPTER TWENTY-SEVEN

Tony could have sworn he heard a click behind him. He turned his head to hear better but heard nothing more. This old building popped and cracked constantly when the wind blew, so it didn't concern him. He pulled his phone from his pocket and, stepping away to talk privately. It was a need-to-know call and right now, Marco didn't need to know. Tony's biggest mistake was not setting up his own perimeter that night and this was due to greed. Tony still wanted to keep his circle as small as possible for this operation so he wouldn't have to "cut-in" as many people. If he had a three-man perimeter, just three men, Nigel and his team would not have had a chance.

Nick had forced Nigel's hand. Nigel had to get inside the boathouse to see how many guys Tony had in there, as well as to cover Nick in the event he did something stupid—which seemed likely.

"Buck, you stay right where you are at the north end. Wait for my mark," Nigel said.

"Buck not moovin."

Nigel worked his way along the cement wall of the waterway. Making his way inside, he was now even with the stern of the boat. Leo continued to crank the engine and then let it rest, but it was beginning to look bad for using the boat as Tony wanted to do. Nigel continued his way alongside *Maria* and paused to listen when he got about halfway down her waterline. He wanted to hear how many voices there were. He heard the guy trying to start the engine but heard no conversation inside the boat. So he figured *one* in the boat. He would have to wait to hear anyone else. They weren't a talkative group, but he also didn't hear a lot of footsteps, so he was encouraged, thinking this may be a minimum-manpower situation. A small group just waiting to go dump Dennis and Paco out to sea for lying to the mob. It made sense to be slim on men because a run to the reef didn't take a lot of manpower.

"How's everybody doing?" Nigel whispered.

"Still clear." Eddie sounded bored.

Josh also reported clear and they were waiting for Brad's response.

Brad's eyes were to the south, on the Intracoastal. He spotted another boat on the opposite end of the boathouse, this one about a quarter-mile away.

Brad said, "I got another boat, guys. This one to the south and he did the same thing. Cut all lights. Eddie, can you see it?"

Eddie turned and looked behind him towards the south. Sure enough, in the water sat a boat with its lights off. Eddie responded, "Yeah, I do see it. It's not too far away."

Nigel was in a bad spot to respond but keyed his mic. "Copy. Watch them."

Nick stepped quietly into the front office area. He was in total darkness but could smell old wood and something sour—maybe a dead animal. He felt his way along, being careful not to kick anything or make any noise. Nick wanted to find a crack in the wall large enough to see through. He wanted to know where Tony and his men were before he went in. Nigel's idea of kicking through the door suddenly didn't sound like a good one to him. The problem was, the wall to the main operations area of the facility was pretty tight. There were no cracks or holes to peer through. With that in mind, Nick pulled out his Mini MagLite and shot a quick beam around the room to get his bearings. He captured the image with his mind and quickly turned his light off. What he saw was a reception desk beside him, and at the end of it a short hallway to the left probably to a restroom or maybe a private office, the door in front of him that he was to kick down, and, to his right, a mystery door. He had no idea where it led or what it held.

He knew he couldn't open the main door to the facility. If there were guys on the other side, they would have him dead to rights. He thought for a moment and then pulled his light out again. Pointing it to the right he turned it on and saw the door to the unknown. Curiosity got the better of him. He slowly turned the old metal doorknob, doing his best to not make a sound. He opened the door very slowly, stopping when it began to creak. He then tried an old trick that worked when he snuck out of the house a time or two and that was to lift up on the door as he was opening it. Doing that, the door never made a sound and he swung it open wide.

Taking a deep breath, he pointed his flashlight into the darkness and clicked it on. He was amazed to see…a stairway!

"Oh my gosh," he said quietly. He had found a way to the second level that they had not known about. "This is perfect."

Nigel's plan was going out the proverbial window but he was going to have to get to where he could see the operations area, to know what he was dealing with. He made his way along the waterline of the trawler as slowly and quietly as possible. As he approached the bow, he felt something brush his leg in the water—something substantial in size. It was extremely unnerving but Nigel remained composed and positioned himself to peek around the bow of the boat. The waterway lay in shadows so he knew he could not be seen.

As he looked towards the work platform he could see Paco and Dennis tied to the same rail he had been tied to yesterday. He could also see one of the divers sitting over by the office door and then he heard the hard-sole footsteps just on the other side of the boat. That was most likely Tony. The boat engine cranked again and turned over and over for a few seconds but, just like the other attempts, it didn't start. Nigel was encouraged that maybe there were only three of them, including Tony.

He then heard Tony's belligerent voice as the Italian stepped onto the boat. "You're doing something wrong, Leo! If it turns over, and it has fresh fuel, it should start!"

Leo shook his head as he let off on the start button. The batteries were beginning to give up some of *their* enthusiasm as well. Something wasn't right and Leo had no idea why this old engine wouldn't start. He came out of the pilothouse shaking his head.

"I don't know, Tony. It's got me stumped."

Tony blew one more cloud of blue smoke into the air and then tossed his cigar into the waterway between the cement wall and the trawler. Something in the water came up and bumped it and then swam off.

He wasn't happy but he did have a backup plan.

"It's OK, Marco. I know you tried. Don't waste any more time on it."

Tony then pulled his phone from his pocket and selected his contact. After a moment he said, "Yeah…let's go. Give me five minutes," and he ended the call.

Outside, Eddie heard the second boat's engine start. He turned to watch it. While it still hadn't moved, it sounded like someone was preparing to get underway. Eddie wouldn't say anything until it was in motion. Brad also heard the boat start up and glanced behind him to check the first vessel that had pulled in. So far it remained silent. Brad could also see Buck over by the north end of the building as Buck's silhouette moved just a little.

Tony walked back into the main work area. He looked at Dennis and Paco.

"Time's up boys. We're going to take a boat ride."

Paco's head dropped and Dennis sighed. They knew the end was now minutes away.

Nigel backed into the shadows behind the boat. He let Tony get farther away and then keyed his mic. "They are getting ready to go. We have to make a move, quickly. Nick, are you in?"

"I'm in."

"OK. Hold your position. Buck, you ready?"

"Ready mon," Buck replied. "I can see dem troo de cracks."

"OK. When I say go, go hard and fast with lots of noise."

Buck and Nick acknowledged.

Giselle hugged Josh quickly. "Here we go. Oh my gosh."

Eddie readied himself to make a move if needed.

Brad checked the boat to the north once again—still no movement. He then looked towards the other vessel with its engine running. It was now motoring towards the boathouse at idle speed. Brad was ready to key his mic when he heard Eddie chime in.

"Guys, the second boat is moving! He's coming towards the boathouse really slow." Eddie said.

Tony walked over to Dennis and Paco and pulled a knife from his pocket. Paco's eyes widened.

Tony noticed his reaction. "Don't worry my Mexican friend. I don't want your blood on my hands. The sharks will commit that crime for me. It's a shame you lied to me…we could have been partners." He shrugged.

Neither looked up.

Nigel moved back to the bow of the boat hidden along the inner wall of the waterway. He then worked his way towards the area even with Paco and Dennis, where Josh had taken his plunge yesterday. He was now next to a ladder built into the cement wall. He could see no one from this spot so he had to "give the go" by just listening to their voices to determine where they were. He needed them grouped together. Hearing Leo walk from the trawler, he buried himself tight against the wall.

Back outside, Brad was watching the building when he heard the second boat start its engine. His heart raced.

"Guys, the second boat! The second boat just started up."

Nigel keyed his mic to acknowledge but could say nothing. He was uncomfortable with the situation, not for himself but for the sake of the young people with him. Nigel had an idea that Tony might have some support from the water but he didn't build that into the plan. Now they must improvise. Business was picking up.

Nick was ready. Buck was ready. Both had guns drawn, ready to take aim on a man for the first time in their lives. They just hoped they didn't have to fire but would do so if necessary. Nigel was ready and pulled his Glock from an underarm holster. It was go time.

Nigel took a deep breath and put one foot on a rung of the ladder. He grasped his mic button with a couple of the fingers of his gun hand, and was ready to spring from the water while "giving the go."

Just before he pushed from the water, he was suddenly and viciously freight-trained in the legs by something large and strong. The impact knocked Nigel away from the ladder and he landed with a splash. Tony spun around in shock, his eyes wide in disbelief as the tail of a huge black grouper flipped by the seawall.

Quickly resurfacing, Nigel keyed his mic. "GO!"

Buck immediately ran in.

"Honds op!!! Honds op!!! he boomed. Two-handed and stiff-armed, he aimed his gun at Tony.

Tony danced around, his feet not knowing what to do, as he raised both hands. Leo and Marco, equally shocked, were looking at Tony, waiting for orders or some cue as to what to do.

A half-second later, Nigel sprang from the water like a leopard and landed on the platform with his gun drawn on the two divers, his aim going back and forth between the two.

"HANDS IN THE AIR! HANDS IN THE AIR!" he bellowed.

Nigel didn't know where Nick was. He was supposed to kick through the door on command. Tony saw that he had them outnumbered and decided to make a move. In a split second he jumped backwards to get out of Buck's sites and drew his .357 Smith and Wesson from behind his back. Nigel had never seen a quicker move from an older man. Wasting no time, Tony fired, grazing Nigel in the left shoulder. A second shot rang out. Nigel waited for the pain. It was Buck who had fired, just missing Tony, an inch to the left.

A third shot rang out and Nigel saw the flash that came from the second level of the boathouse. Tony fell to the floor. Buck ran forward and held the gun on Leo as Leo was going for his own weapon.

"Don't do it mon!" Buck ordered. "I won't miss again!" Buck's fiercely hard eyes darted to the second floor as he saw Nick emerge from the shadows, his gun still pointed at Tony. Marco, too, decided not to make a move as their boss lay on the floor.

Nigel swooped in and pulled guns away from the trio as Tony lay bleeding—his wound to the abdomen serious but not yet fatal.

"On the floor…all of you!" Nigel commanded, his shoulder stained with blood.

Giselle screamed at the sound of gunshots and she and Josh jumped instinctively to run towards the boat house. Brad and Eddie did the same as Eddie keyed his mic.

"You guys OK? Talk to me!"

There was no time for talking on radios yet as Nigel, Buck and Nick were still neutralizing the situation. Nick had his gun drawn on Tony, the look of four decades of vengeance in his eyes. Leo and Marco were on the floor with hands behind their heads as Nigel and Buck patted them down and prepared to tie them up.

Still on the upper level, Nick was breathing hard as he began to walk towards the open stairway. Nick held Tony in his sites as he descended—his eyes hard and cold. He wanted the final shot.

Nigel saw Nick approach Tony and calmly begged him, "No…no Nick, don't do it."

Nick looked at Tony with a killer's eyes and Tony recognized it. He had seen it many times. Nick's mind flashed back to the stories that had been told to him about his grandfather. A good man. A hard-working man. An honest man.

With clenched teeth, Nick shook his head slowly and scolded Tony. "You scum. You murdering, low-life. You killed my defenseless grandfather like the coward that you are."

Tony looked up as Nick walked closer to him—gun pointed at his head. Tony's eyes were begging but he said nothing.

"Nick, Nick…please, don't do it," Nigel again said, calmly. "He will go away. They will lock him up, I promise. I know people too!"

Josh, Giselle, Eddie and Brad all made their way inside after making sure it was safe to do so. They had watched the tense scene unfold.

Nick was not letting up. He was determined to finish Tony off. "Now, my friend, the karma-train has come back to take you on your final ride."6

Giselle decided to intervene. "Nick," she begged with a sweet voice. She walked towards him. "Nick, please…it's not what your grandfather would want you to do. Think about it—you could go away for a long time for taking the law into your own hands. That's not what Butch Dawson would want for his grandson! He would have loved you, Nick. He would want you to go on and find the treasure. He would want you to walk out of here and finish what he started, and carry on his good name. You didn't spend all that time as a kid, researching and learning and planning, just to come down here and go to jail for taking the law into your own hands." Giselle paused and stepped closer to Nick. "Nick, it's *really* what he would want. Please... let's go find the treasure…we have the boat!" She pointed towards *Maria*.

It worked. When Nick heard his grandfather's name and Giselle's honest words, his eyes changed. They lost some of their fire, though he continued to aim the gun at Tony.

With his breathing relaxing, he looked over at Giselle. He nodded, ever so slightly, and his aim relaxed.

Nigel nodded at Giselle and then gave an order to the rest. "Tie these guys up fast!"

He had no more than gotten those words out of his mouth when they heard a vehicle screech to a halt out front… and then another.

Nigel looked towards the front office, his eyes worried. "Really fast…really fast!" he said urgently.

Brad, Josh and Eddie did the tying and Brad and Nigel held the guns on Tony and his guys.

Nick instinctively ran to the front door that led into the office and locked it. It would buy them only seconds but maybe that would be enough. He then pushed an old metal desk in front of the door—maybe a couple more seconds.

If all of that wasn't bad enough, they now heard another

engine. The second boat was approaching the boathouse from the south and they had no idea who that could be, but good sense told them it was a bad guy. Nigel looked at Tony.

Tony still had enough sass in him to sneer and say, "You think I don't have a backup plan you stupid Brit?"

Paco and Dennis were watching all of the activity worriedly— not knowing what their fate would now be.

Nigel looked over at Tony once more as he quickly gathered their guns. "You have a single 9mm wound. You probably won't die from it but the world won't miss you if you do. Nick's right…you are scum…*mate!*"

Nigel gestured to the rest of them. "We have to go! No way to get out the front…we have to go by sea! Brad…get the trawler started!"

"What about the cars?" Giselle asked frantically. They were all now running toward the boat.

"We won't make it to the cars! Go to the boat!!!" Nigel ordered.

The group dashed past Dennis and Paco. Nick looked down at them as he was running.

"Amigo?" Paco's eyes pleaded…

Nick stopped and leered at the two filthy criminals before him. He started to move away and then stopped again. Death was certain for them. He quickly pulled his knife from his pocket and, with two swift swipes, cut the ropes that held them.

"Run!" he commanded. "Don't ever let me see you again!"

"Si! Gracia! Gracia!"

And with that, Dennis ran past Maria with Paco hobbling behind him, out the south end of the building and into the darkness of the dunes and sea oats, before Tony's men could see them.

Everyone was now onboard the boat and Nigel ordered them down below—except for Brad and himself. Brad Radcliffe ran straight to the helm—his eyes showed great stress. This was Brad's most important marine test ever.

CHAPTER TWENTY-EIGHT

Once on the boat, Brad quickly found the battery switch and flipped it on. The green light on the panel lit up and he then pushed the start switch. Just as with Leo, the engine turned over with great enthusiasm but did not fire. Brad tried it again as he looked aft. He was looking for the exhaust outlet.

"It's not getting fuel! It should at least be putting out white smoke, even if it doesn't start!" Time was running out and Brad was getting anxious.

He thought for a split second and then dropped to his knees—searching under the dash panel. Frantically, his hands moved around in the darkness, searching for something that shouldn't be there—something out of place. There was nothing. He stopped and thought some more—his mind racing as he recalled his days of training at MMI. Where could it be? "Nigel…step out," he said.

The crash of a broken down door could be heard. Whoever they were, they were in the facility! Brad had to hurry.

Nigel stepped out of the pilothouse as Brad moved around on his knees, still searching with his hands. Nigel watched as Brad rubbed his hands across the boards, going from one to the next, and then he found something! A loose decking plank about three feet long and six inches wide. Brad dug his fingernails into the crack and pulled. The board popped up and, sure enough, right there in the floor was a fuel cutoff valve. Before the days of secured marinas with gates and passwords, boat theft was rampant. Captains would install fuel cutoff valves in their own selected locations to help prevent having their vessels commandeered. Luckily, this one didn't take long to find and luckily, Brad had had a module at MMI that covered old boats and how to fix them!

Nigel stood right beside him and could now hear the banging as Tony's men were shoving the old metal desk out of the way. *Maybe those seconds would be the difference*, Nigel thought.

Brad turned the valve to the flow position, replaced the floor board and immediately stood and pushed the start button once again.

They could now hear shouting and chaos in the work area. In seconds Tony, Leo and Marco would be cut loose and Tony's goons would be coming towards the boat…guns afire. One just doesn't shoot a mob boss and negotiate his way out.

The engine spun, just as before, and within a few revolutions the white smoke began to pour out of the exhaust at the transom. It cranked and cranked for what seemed like forever with the crew below cheering it on, knowing their lives depended on it. Nick was encouraged as the old diesel began to spin faster! It liked the fuel it was consuming! A couple more revolutions and the engine seemed to outrun the starter motor! The old beast was coming to life and then, with what sounded like every rod in the engine coming out of it, as diesels do, it fired to life! Black smoke replaced the white as Nick buried the throttle to the bulkhead and wound the engine up to maximum RPM. This absolutely went against everything he was taught about starting an old engine for the first time in years, but this was for their lives. The engine revved beautifully and the black smoke poured out of her, filling the waterway portion of the building with a cloud of soot. A beautiful cloud of soot!

Tony had been cut loose but was still lying on the floor, bleeding. His eyes widened as he heard the engine fire to life. He looked at Leo in anger, "You're a dead man, Leo. My blood is on your hands!"

Tony's men now ran towards the boat with guns drawn.

Brad quickly pulled the throttle down to idle and engaged the forward drive. Brad felt it kick then buried the throttle to the bulkhead. This time the boat lurched forward and took off. As the engine spooled up, the acceleration could be felt and in just a few feet, *Maria*, the 1946 Cherokee Trawler, was churning up a wake.

Below, Josh knew what was coming so he pushed Giselle to the floor and shielded her body with his own. Eddie, Nick, and Buck also found the lowest point they could. They would be safe where they were. It was Brad and Nigel who they were really worried about. They were in the pilothouse, sitting ducks.

Tony and his boys watched in disbelief as the old junk trawler accelerated in the waterway like a ghost ship. Black smoke belched out of her and now began to fill the main room of the facility. Many, many years of gunk and sludge burning its way out of the cylinders helped to provide a distraction, at the very least.

With the pilothouse now coming into view of Tony's guys, Nigel tapped Brad on the shoulder and yelled, "Get down! Get down!"

Brad pushed forward on the throttle, making sure it was at full, and then looked straight ahead to make sure they would make it through the door opening without busting out the wall. He held the helm straight and then hit the floor, joining Nigel.

The scene was surreal and if lives were not at stake, could have even been comical. The trawler was churning water, blowing smoke and powering past the platform where Josh, Eddie and his friends had once been tied up. Five of Tony's men opened fire on the vessel as she passed—splintering wood and shattering glass in the pilothouse, the debris falling on Brad and Nigel. Nigel then took Tony's own .357 and reached up into the now broken out window and returned fire. The gun sounded like a cannon and because of the way Nigel was positioned, recoiled dramatically—throwing his arm back as he fired over and over.

The men jumped for cover on the work platform as flashes of fire blasted from the black smoke in front of them. Bullets glanced off the floor and skipped around the room—burying themselves into the old wooden walls. This was just enough cover to get them out the door with everyone onboard safe and sound—for the time being.

The engine provided a ton of torque and the boat threw a large wake as it exited the building, nearly swamping the platform. As Tony's goons watched *Maria* power away, they ran out the south end of the building to get off several more shots. By then, *Maria* was hitting her stride.

Brad had *never* piloted anything so powerful or large in his life and his mind, for whatever reason, flashed back to his old milk-jug raft on the quiet little Elk River back home in West Virginia. Drifting quietly and dragging a fishing line behind him. In those days, he was just a modern-day Huck Finn. Boy… how things changed.

Snapping out of his flashback and now clear of the doorway,

Brad raised his head just enough to see out of the broken window as he looked back at the boathouse. A couple more flashes of gunfire erupted from the darkness with the bullets hitting the framework above his head. The gunfire stopped for the moment as Brad and Nigel stood up—now about fifty yards from the boathouse. Brad looked forward, got his bearings and turned the trawler hard right to prevent running aground straight ahead. He still had the throttle buried as the engine continued to clean itself out and gain RPMs. The old trawler leaned over and powered on.

It was then that they saw the boat off the starboard rail—Tony's cover from the water!

"Ah man!" Brad exclaimed. "Can we not catch a break?!"

With its lights still out, the boat sped towards them and was only about a hundred yards off their beam when orange flashes began to spurt from the bow.

"Brad…turn and run straight at them! It's their worst firing angle on us."

"Nigel, go below!"

"Are you out of your mind, mate? I haven't had this much fun in years!"

"You're crazy!" Brad laughed.

"Straight at them, mate! Just like a flyby in an airplane! Make 'em think you are crazy! Make 'em think you're going to bury your bow into theirs!"

Brad made another hard turn to starboard and lined himself up for the "flyby" down the port side of the attacking vessel.

Below decks, the other five were now curious. They were

getting up from their protected positions and stretching their necks to see what the situation was after blasting out of the boathouse.

"Are we good?" Josh asked.

"No, no! Stay down! We got a boat after us now! Tony's guys, no doubt!" Nigel replied.

The trawler was now coming up on plane as the diesel continued to spool up more and more. Brad loved the feel of it but feared for all of their lives at the same time. Just as before, when they came out of the boathouse, he lined himself up with the other boat, now just off his bow. The attacking boat swerved left and right somewhat nervously, but held its course coming right at the trawler. At that moment Brad and Nigel ducked down again and the automatic gunfire resumed from the bow. They got the windshield this time and more glass fell on Brad and Nigel as the two boats rocketed past one another.

"What in the world?!" Nick shouted as some of the glass and splinters fell down the stairs.

"Eddie, remember back when we threw gas on that wasp nest?" Josh asked his friend.

"Yeah."

"Kinda feels the same way, doesn't it?"

"Kinda does," he replied.

Buck laughed at them.

The attacking boat made a hard U-turn to come back after them. Rather than being chased, Brad decided to do the fly-by again as he, too, turned the big trawler one hundred eighty degrees. They lined up again like jousters in an arena and blew by one another, this time with Nigel returning fire with his Glock.

"We can't keep doing this, mate…and we can't outrun them." Nigel went to the stairway and called down to the ones below. "See if you can find something, anything to use as distraction or a surprise!"

Brad, being the diversion expert, had an idea. "Look for a distress box!" he called out.

Nigel nodded. It was a great idea but a long shot for this old boat.

Brad made a sweeping U-turn, this time with the throttles still full ahead. He used a much larger area of the Intracoastal but kept the engine revved and the boat up on plane, the wake now a huge plume. To starboard, he saw the lights of Tony's *other* boat illuminate and heard it power up and leave its moored position to the north.

"Fantastic!" Brad said, shaking his head, "Now the other boat is after us!"

Below, the group began to search for something—anything at all that could help improve their situation.

At the bottom of the stairs were two opposing doors—each one opened into a cabin for crewmembers. No one had been inside these cabins for many years. Josh and Giselle entered one and Nick, Buck and Eddie took the other. They were desperately searching for anything that could help save their lives. Brad said to look for a distress box but Josh couldn't imagine why. The two rooms were identically built and outfitted. Straight ahead, the bunk was laid lengthwise with the boat. At the head of the bed was a small locker for personal items. At the foot was a hanging locker for foul weather gear, extra clothes or any larger personal things that may have been brought aboard. There were also many smaller compartments in every little nook and corner of the cabin. They would check them all.

At the helm, Brad continued to make sweeping evasive maneuvers, buying as much time as possible and never backing off the throttle. The old diesel seemed to be getting stronger by the minute but even at its best, would never be a match for Tony's smaller, faster vessels. The second boat captain now began to make cut-off moves, playing chicken with Brad as he sliced across his bow time after time, firing repeatedly. Nigel and Brad returned fire, preventing the attack boat from stopping or slowing down beside them. They did a good job of not getting shot in the process.

Down below, Giselle and Josh began to rummage through the first cabin while Eddie, Buck and Nick ripped apart the second. They pulled out the very old and quite moth-eaten mattresses, they checked the lockers and every little drawer and cabinet they could find.

As Nick opened all the little doors and drawers, he noticed there was still a good bit of junk left behind. Shining his light around, he looked for any compartment or drawer he might have missed. He aimed his light across the bed, and then lifted it high and pointed it downward to get the beam into the area where the bunk attached to the wall. Something reflected and caught his eye—something shiny. Nick crawled onto the bunk and reached into the area where he had seen the reflection. His hand grabbed a small rectangular object and pulled it out. A lighter! This was a mediocre find for Nick until he saw the engraving. Nick had found a lighter with the words:

Presented to Butch Dawson for Twenty Years of Service— South Bend Steel Corp.

Nick's eyes lit up as he tucked it into his pocket but said nothing about it to Eddie. They were still in a dire situation and needed to find something to save themselves from certain death.

In the opposite cabin, Josh shook his head. "There's nothing here! Let's check the hallway."

Josh and Giselle ran to the short companionway. There was a narrow locker on the left side, just before entering the engine room. Josh pulled the door open, finding some very old rain gear as well as a couple of three-piece fishing rods in the back. He looked up to a shelf to see a container about twice the size of a shoe box. Pulling it from the shelf, dust fell upon him as took it to the floor and gave Giselle his flashlight to hold. Josh quickly popped off the top of the old wooden box and inside was two 12-gauge flare guns and about eight cartridges in questionable condition. The old flares were made of paper and were a bit deteriorated.

Josh's eyes lit up as he thought these might be a good enough diversion to keep Tony's men at bay until they could get to safety—if they fired.

Josh ran up the stairs to the pilothouse, dropping to his knees as another round of automatic-weapons fire ripped through the section above them.

"Giselle…stay below," he called out. She had no trouble with that.

"You be careful, Josh!" she responded.

Eddie and Nick were encouraged with the find as well and positioned themselves at the bottom of the steps. Buck was about half-way up. They were not going to stay there for long as their instincts told them they could be of better use above decks.

The three boats were now running large crisscross patterns. It was still the only option for the trawler since they could never outrun the little boats. Brad would have to keep doing this until another option presented itself—which was unlikely. As Brad made a large sweep on the east side of the Intracoastal, he saw the lights of yet *another* boat get turned on. Up to this point they had not seen this vessel sitting in the darkness. *Lovely* he thought.

"Nigel, there's another boat now…three in all."

Nick and Eddie rushed to the top of the steps with heads down as Nick and Nigel began loading the cartridges into the flare guns. In the distance the first two boats were turned in unison and appeared to be lined up for a double pass down the sides of *Maria*—most certainly their crews would be firing with everything they had onboard. Tony's guys were getting tired of playing games.

The third boat was off to Brad's left about a quarter mile and was now under way.

"We are dead in the water!" Brad said.

"Don't give up, boy!" Nigel commanded. "Drive the boat from your knees and keep your head down! Guys…when I say now, I want you to fire these two flare guns right at the helms of those two boats. Put them right through the windshields! You hear me?!"

"Got it!" they both replied.

Brad kept the trawler under full power, the old diesel never missing a beat as the three vessels lined up to joust once again. They roared towards each other, firearms blazing and at just the right time Nigel said, "NOW!" Nick and Brad jumped up and fired straight toward the drivers of the two attacking boats. Nick's shot sailed high and right while Eddie's went low and left. The attacking boats once again splintered the woodwork of Maria as they roared past, just missing Nick to the right. That was too close and Nigel had a different idea for the next run.

"Guys," Nigel said, "They are firing only at our pilothouse. This time, let's all three of us go to the bow and hunker down! Brad…you line up the boat then lie flat on your belly. They are getting too close with their shots and they know we are low behind the helm." He looked at Nick and Eddie. "You know how the flare guns fire now…make your shots count."

"Yes sir." The boys spoke in unison.

Josh ran up beside them. "Give me a gun."

Nigel looked into Josh's eyes. He nodded, knowing more fire was better and then quickly explained the plan to him. Buck was next as Nigel handed him a 9mm and gave him instructions.

One last time, Brad whirled the trawler around and lined up. Each time they had made a pass, Tony's shooters had managed to get closer and closer to their targets. Nigel's idea to vacate the pilothouse was a good one and a risky one at the same time. He would be exposing three young men, barely out of high school, to the unbridled viciousness of organized crime. It was this or die, certainly, as their options were running out.

Nick took a deep breath as he pondered the irony of dying at the same hands as his grandfather. Knowing this pass could be life or death made him focus. He blocked out every other thought but putting a flare into the helm of the boat coming down the starboard side.

Josh looked down the steps at Giselle. "Get down, flat on the floor, and no matter what happens, don't come up!"

Her green eyes welled as she bit her lower lip to hide her

emotions. She so loved the caring and protective nature of Josh Baker. She would do as he had said.

Eddie looked at Josh and Brad with a nervous smile. "Well guys…this may be the worst situation we have ever been in…" Eddie stopped talking. Nothing more needed to be said. They all knew what they were about to try was a long shot and their luck-meter was running low. They put hands on each other's shoulders—friends since kids. They said goodbye to one another without a further word.

Nigel nodded. "Let's do this…we can do it," he said with reassuring confidence, as he looked into each boy's eyes.

Brad nodded towards the third boat. "What do we do about that guy out there, Nigel? He looks like he's going to run us from the port side…coming in from the nine o'clock position." He spoke quickly, urgently.

"The plan is to take out these two boats. We have to deal with that one afterwards." Nigel didn't like it, but it was all they could do.

The boats roared toward each other again as Nigel, Nick, Eddie, Buck and Josh ran to the bow and hunkered down behind the three-foot tall wooden rail. Josh and Buck, under Nigel's guidance, were ready to empty their Glock 17s on the attacking shooters, thus giving cover to Eddie and Brad with the flare guns. The trawler skimmed along, its bow dancing up and down as the gap continued to narrow.

Brad glanced to his left as the third boat was now full throttle and timed to intersect the other three boats in what seemed like one massive collision. Brad's eyes widened in fear, he didn't know what to do—back off or charge ahead. He was relieved to see the third boat maneuver to pass *behind* the trawler instead of in front.

It was almost time to hit the deck as he lined up and yelled out, "Here we go!"

When the approaching boats were no more than one hundred feet away, Nigel screamed, "NOW!"

Gunfire erupted from the attacking boats. More glass exploded in the pilothouse. Brad lay flat on his stomach, his hands covering his head to protect him from the shards falling all around him.

Nigel, Buck and Josh stood, aimed at the point where the gun flashes were coming from and fired repeatedly. Nick and Eddie carefully aimed at their respective targets and…fired. Nothing happened! These two cartridges were duds… dead with age and deterioration. Their plan had failed. The other boats were now nearly broadside *Maria* and the shooters quickly opened fire on their new targets. All four on the trawler hit the deck and covered their heads. Wood splintered all around them but no one was hit.

The third boat, whose intentions were still unknown, began to slow as it neared the stern of the trawler. With everyone onboard *Maria* as flat as they could be, the two boats roared past. BOOM! A huge explosion had come from the third boat and startled everyone onboard. They all rose to see a plume of blue smoke rise from the bow of the mystery boat. A split second later, the boat that had run down the port side of *Maria*, its helm suddenly in pieces, veered left and hit the other boat broadside, splitting her nearly in half. Lou Cannon had fired a bull's-eye into their helm!

The two boats rolled and then lay tangled in the water as fuel began to spill from their tanks. Brad throttled down and u-turned the trawler to go have a look at the carnage. As they pulled up, Nigel could smell the fuel and gave the command for Brad to stop as he grabbed the flare gun from Nick, as well as another cartridge. Nigel Thompkins was furious.

"They can't all be duds, mate," he said to no one in particular.

Nigel reloaded, walked to the bow and fired at the mangled remains before them. The flare went off and landed in the middle of the mess of fiberglass and fuel. Instantly, what was left of the two boats was engulfed in flames. Lou Cannon and Ray, the dive instructor, looked on from the bow of Ray's boat, *Grim Reefer, and smiled.*

CHAPTER TWENTY-NINE

Giselle emerged from down below, meeting Josh at the pilothouse door. She hugged him and wiped her eyes. "So glad you're OK," she whispered, looking now at the destruction all around the deck and in the water..

Josh squeezed her tight. "I've *never* seen bullets flying like that… and you know the messes we've been in."

She nodded with her face on his shoulder, composing herself.

"I didn't give us much of a chance. You see the guys over there who saved our lives?" he asked her, nodding towards Lou and Ray. The two walked to the bow.

Nick put his hands on the rail, shook his head and shrugged. He didn't know what to say. It was a very surreal moment.

The two boats drifted closer together as Lou patted Ray's bow-mounted signal cannon. "It's a crazy thing…but apparently, a signal cannon is only a signal cannon if there is nothing in it. If you load a projectile…it becomes a real cannon!" He grinned.

Josh Baker observed the mess before him in awe. "The question is; what did you load it *with*?"

Lou just shrugged.

"You *are* a pirate!" Josh finished, smiling.

"Thank you, Lou," Nick said, still catching his breath as the remains of the two boats began to disappear beneath the surface of the Intracoastal Waterway. "How did you know?"

"Well, we knew where that old boathouse was and we knew that you were in over your head…even with a trained professional leading the way, so we decided to stand by just in case. Plus, I mean…we have an interest in you guys staying alive for a while, ya know?"

Nigel was standing with his hands on his hips. He nodded to Lou Cannon. "Appreciate the backup, mate. It wasn't going to turn out well for us."

Quick introductions were made and then they began to hear sirens coming from the direction of the boathouse. They all looked in that direction as lights began to strobe the scene a quarter-mile away.

"We called…since you were too stubborn to do it, Nick," Lou snickered. "Whoever's in the boathouse will be in the paddy-wagon soon. I filled them in on what was going on and they were very happy to come and get Tony Maniglia. You guys have no idea who you were messing with," he said, shaking his head.

Nick Dawson reached into his pocket and pulled out the lighter. He walked over to where Josh, Giselle, Eddie and Brad were standing at the bow.

"I found this down below." Nick passed around the small silver object. "I knew this was Captain Henderson's old boat…the last boat my grandfather ever worked on. After they dumped Rocco Palombo that night, they found the shipwreck…the one I believe to be *Concepcion,* using this very boat!"

Lou added, "The shipwreck that we can now go look for…safely!"

Giselle read the inscription on the Zippo. "That's an amazing find, Nick."

Eddie flipped it around in his hand and shook his head. "Ya know Nick, whatever happens from here on is just gravy on the biscuits. You've already hit treasure down here. The man who shot your grandfather is going to jail after all these years, if he lives, and you have found this little relic along with the boat that he sailed on."

Nick nodded. "I was just planning on coming down here, jumping in the water and swishing away some sand. I never could have imagined all of this happening. Putting Tony away will be better than the treasure, and I mean that!"

Ray stepped to the bow of *Grim Reefer.* He was a very thin middle-aged hippie throwback who wore cut-off jeans, a very old and faded Cheech and Chong t-shirt and leather sandals. He spoke for the first time. "Uh...dudes? If it's cool with you all, we may want to take this feel-good party somewhere else. I got a real good hunch that we may have attracted some attention out here and patrol boats will be here soon. Is that cool?"

Lou added, "He's right…we better scoot. Let's go down to Ponce Inlet. Ray's shop is there and he has some slips we can use."

Nigel nodded and looked around. "That sounds good, mate. Can we grab some coffee there?"

Ray nodded. "I got some great Columbian there. You'll love it."

Nigel grinned. He wasn't sure Ray was talking about coffee but a good safe-house was what they needed.

"Is that old boat up to the journey?" Lou asked, looking at Nick.

"Try not to get in our way, Lou!" Nick replied, smiling.

They all enjoyed a laugh and they prepared to pull away from the scene. All except for Ray and Brad were still on deck looking at the somber sight before them—hot-spots on the water with floating cushions, all sorts of shredded boat parts, and empty lifejackets. This was the lifestyle these men had chosen and living by the sword almost certainly ensures you will die by the sword. Some said little prayers for the men and their families, but at the same time, it could have just as easily been the other way around. It was a battle and, once again, Josh Baker, Eddie Debord, Giselle O'Conner, and Brad Radcliffe had beaten the odds—three of their nine lives used up, most likely. Their new friends, Nick Dawson, Nigel Tompkins and Buck Naked had also come through unscathed with the exception of the grazing Nigel took earlier and a few minor cuts to Brad's back from the falling shards of glass in the pilothouse.

Brad was in the pilot house removing some triangles of loose glass from the window sills. He cleaned off the dash and controls carefully so no one would get hurt by any small slivers. He then used a thirty-year-old broom from a closet below to move the debris from the floor. It was now time to perform a changing of the guard.

"Hey Nick!" he called out.

Nick looked back from the bow.

"Come here a minute," Brad said, beckoning.

Nick Dawson stepped into the pilothouse of the Cherokee Trawler. "What's up?"

Brad stepped away from the helm and, with an open palm, offered the position to Nick.

"The way I see it…this is your job. I'm sure your grandfather did some time at this wheel and that alone makes you more qualified than me to pilot this old gem."

Nick looked at Brad as the others began to gather for this solemn ceremony. It really began to sink in with Nick. He was standing on the very deck of the boat that his grandfather had made his living on. Butch Dawson had, no doubt, stood at the helm and *held* that wheel, and looked across the water and dreamed—especially on that last night he dreamed of a treasure and adventure! These were the same things Nick had dreamed about since he was told the story when he was just eight years old! Nick had never considered finding the boat—only the treasure and oh, what a cherry on the sundae this was! Eddie was right in saying he had already found treasure.

Nick looked at Brad one more time and then put his hands on the wheel.

"It's all yours, man." Brad then backed away.

Nick looked at the simple panel with a couple of engine gauges, a throttle, a wheel, a battery switch and a start button and nodded while smiling, "I can do this!" he said, his smile growing.

Nigel looked nervously up and down the Intracoastal. He was certain business was about to pick up and he looked in at Nick. "Uh, mate? I know it's a real tender moment and all but maybe it's time to bury the throttle and go!"

Boat lights began to flick on in the distance up and down the waterway. Nick nodded to Nigel and engaged the forward drive. Giving it some throttle, he spun the 46-footer around to head her south to follow Ray and Lou. Ray knew a creek between some land formations that would offer them some quick cover and also take them over to the main flow of the Halifax River and on down to Ponce Inlet.

Nick's face beamed as he got more accustomed to steering the old Cherokee. He marveled at how responsive a rudder she had considering how heavy she was. This was too much fun!

Brad offered some advice. "Go easy on the steering mechanism right now…it's old and I don't know if I damaged her any doing those full-power U-turns. We could have weak linkage anywhere after all these years. Run the engine steady but not hard…it's still cleaning itself out and circulating oil. Also, keep an eye on the cooling system. I'd like to see that engine temperature at about one hundred eighty-five degrees, max."

Nick, and everyone onboard, greatly appreciated Brad Radcliffe's marine knowledge. It had saved their lives that night. They had all the confidence in the world in him and knew his skills were credible—after all…he had built the finest milk jug raft on the Elk River just a few short years ago and, ironically, it had saved their lives, too, while evading an angry Russian!

Back on land, police activity grew around the old boathouse. Upwards of twelve cars were now on the scene and nobody was getting away—with the exception of two shadows who made their way across the sand dunes towards Highway 1. The short one couldn't keep up too well and the gringo would not wait for him.

CHAPTER THIRTY

7:30 am, two days later

The ocean floor was not what Nick had expected. It wasn't a smooth sand bottom that gently sloped its way into the abyss, but a terrain much like land itself, with shelves of coral...low points, high points, rocky points, plant life and *then* sand—plenty of sand that lay on everything.

The group had all completed Ray's SNUBA course the day before and had agreed to swim and search within their ability and comfort level. They were reassured they had no competition and the search area was all theirs, so rushing anything and compromising safety was not necessary.

That morning was not unlike any other in Florida in June. As soon as the sun showed its face on the horizon, it made you look for relief. That came easy for all these treasure hunters who just wanted to be in the water. When they arrived at the coordinates site that morning, excitement levels were high and the group was giddy with anticipation—and that included Lou, Denise and a couple of Lou Cannon's divers, whom he had invited along. Lou also invited

Ray to be there in case any of the new divers had a problem or needed further training. Ray was his buddy, after all.

Lou took charge from the beginning and ordered all the new divers into the water but not to touch anything—even if they saw something. They had approval to search ten sites and do an archeological recovery from those points. Anything that they touched became a "point" and Lou didn't want them to determine those points just yet. The first swim was a "get to know the environment" swim. Afterwards, Lou would go down and survey the area, mark his first site, and then, after laying out a metal grid, the sand removal could begin.

Lou had two boats on scene, both equipped with prop-suction equipment to vacuum sand away and discharge it somewhere else via tubes or large hoses. The suction was gentle and would leave heavier materials behind…such as gold, and move away the lighter material that was covering it. The trick was not to dump your old sand on a future spot you wanted to excavate. That's where Lou's experience and professionalism came in. That's why *he* would determine the points of excavation and that's why he had been hired.

Giselle and Josh stayed close together as they got accustomed to the new world they were discovering. They had never before experienced such tranquility and peace. It was like a different world where all was calm and any worldly stress was simply left on the surface. Eddie marveled at all the new fish he would need to learn about—solid black fish everywhere and blue tangs, which he had seen before but only in an aquarium. Parrotfish, angelfish and then a nice grouper scooted away along with a flounder.

Buck Naked had been underwater many times around his Jamaican island but never with SNUBA gear and was enjoying the freedom immensely. He was excited to get started and truly appreciative of being invited to do so.

Brad and Nick loved the fish and the tranquility as well as anyone else, but their eyes were more interested in the landscape of the seabed. Brad had recalled the general location of the ribs from a few days earlier but they were covered once again by the moving tides. As much as he wanted to, Brad would refrain from swishing any sand until he and Lou had consulted on the approximate location back on the surface. After a few minutes, everyone was pretty comfortable with the SNUBA experience at the coordinate site. They all surfaced and climbed back on the boat.

As they sat on the stern benches for a short briefing, Lou said, "What I want you guys to remember when we go down to start working is you are dragging a hose. Make sure you are mindful of where the hose is trailing behind you so you don't entangle one of your partners. There are crevices in the coral where it can get snagged so before you move, make sure your hose is free."

"Safety is everything, dudes. Everyone cool with that?" Ray added.

Everyone nodded and agreed.

Lou continued. "OK Brad, I am going to lean on you pretty hard for the first location. You free dove and brought up a chain and a really nice emerald."

Nigel held the uncut green gem up to the sun to marvel at its beauty. "We were dead, spot-on the coordinate numbers when Brad found the ribs. It's got to be right under us Lou," he said, smiling. Nigel was happy to stay topside with Ray and keep an eye on the air supplies for the ones below. He was now back to his usual khaki shorts, flowered shirt and Panama hat.

"I remember it was just left of a small mound of coral. I think I saw that mound again, just now, and I can't wait to get started!" Brad's tone echoed the excitement level of all on board.

Lou nodded. "You and I will go down first and set the first location. We will move some sand and try to locate the ribs. If we find the ribs, then we officially have an archeological discovery for the history books." He looked around at all of the wide eyes. "Yeah, guys…it's that big! If this is the *Patache Concepcion*, we are all famous…not to mention wealthy," he grinned.

Lou's words did nothing to calm the excitement. Everyone onboard *knew* they would locate the ribs, determine the fore and aft of the ship and make many exciting discoveries. Lou's diligence to details was killing them however as he was a stickler for logging positions and cataloging everything found. They would get used to it.

Lou looked at Brad. "So, you ready?"

Lou had no more than finished his sentence before Brad had his legs over the side of the boat and was pulling on his mask and clearing his regulator.

Lou smiled. "Let's go. Come on, Nick. I think you deserve to go with us… as an observer."

Josh smiled and slapped him on the back. Nick couldn't get his mask on fast enough.

The three dropped into the water, took a couple of breaths and then kicked the eighteen feet to the bottom. Brad re-familiarized himself with the location and pretty much swam right to the mound of coral where he had been just a few days before. He pointed to it and Lou nodded. Lou fanned his hand to indicate what they would do together. Moving just to the left of the coral mound, they all began to pull sand away from the area. This time only a couple of inches of sand obscured the ribs and almost instantly, Brad found one. He pointed enthusiastically as Lou's eyes now widened with excitement and he moved over to investigate. Through his mask, one could see that Nick was beside himself with excitement. Lou and Brad moved more and more sand out of the way, and exposed about four feet of the rib for the first time in three hundred years. Brad pointed to an area about four feet away from the first rib and began moving sand from that location. Lou joined him and in seconds they had located another—just as Brad had done and just as Captain Henderson had done in 1973. Lou got close to take a good look at the preserved wood. Inspecting it, he reached for something and gave it a pull. After removing it from the wood, he brought it up to Nick's mask to show him a hand-forged, square-head nail. With that, Lou knew the age was right and he gave Brad and Nick two very confident thumbs up. It *was* a ship and it *was* from the right era. Lou put the nail in a net bag tied to his SNUBA harness.

The two guys continued to pull sand away for the next couple of minutes as Nick observed, exposing the tops of four symmetrical sixteenth-century hull ribs. By then, Lou was just as excited as Nick and Brad—fist pumping and smiling as best he could with the regulator in his mouth. Lou knew what was next—they needed to get between the ribs and find something—just one little thing to take to the surface. He motioned to Brad to signal what they would do and Brad immediately resumed his "dog-style" sand removal technique, shoveling large amounts of sand between his legs and behind him. Lou used a different technique to remove large amounts of sand by curving his arm like a comma and pulling the material. With just a few swipes, Lou's hand hit something other than sand. At first it looked like a rock or a chunk of coral rolling along in the cloud of sand but when the sunlight hit it just right, it showed all of its beauty and instantly infatuating charm. It was a coral-encrusted clump of gold coins.

Lou grabbed it, studied it for a brief moment and then nodded and yelled through his regulator, "Escudos! Escudos!" Nick and Brad had no idea...but would learn.

Lou then motioned for Nick to come and see what he could do. Nick wasted no time swimming to one of the areas between the ribs. He looked at Lou to make sure it was OK and Lou motioned for him to dig. Nick began pulling the sand away, getting caught up in the surreal dreaminess of the moment. There he was in an underwater world completely new to him, pulling sand and searching for what his grandfather had left him. Nick swished away handful after handful until his fingers became entangled in something he first thought was plant life—until he saw the color! Chain...heavy link gold chain! When he pulled it from the sand he saw the crucifix at the end. It was alternately laden with emeralds and rubies, the cross itself being nearly four inches in length! Nicks eyes nearly filled his mask as did Lou and Brad's!

The team of three was ecstatic and did an underwater group hug and lots of handshaking. Lou pointed to the surface, Brad and Nick nodded, and up they went. They couldn't wait to share the good news! Lou placed a small flag with a metal rod in the sand between the ribs. This was certainly location number one.

Brad and Nick no more than burst the surface when they began yelling, whooping and hollering.

"That fast!? Josh Baker exclaimed, helping Brad to the swim platform and then Nick."

Everyone onboard moved aft to see what all the excitement was about. Lou surfaced and swam to the stern platform, holding between his thumb and index finger the stack of Escudos that his two divers, Jimbo and Big Mike, instantly recognized.

"That's a good find," Jimbo said.

Lou nodded. "Not as good as what the boy found."

They all looked over at Brad and then Nick. Nick's smile was spread across his entire face as he lifted up the large-link, gold chain with the beautiful, beautiful emerald- and ruby-inlaid gold cross. This piece could have been destined for the Vatican, it was so nice and so well preserved. There were gasps all around as the reality set in that they were on top of one of the ships that had carried a king's treasure. This very treasure was intended to help rebuild Spain and its economy from its post-war state. King Phillip V also had a substantial dowry onboard one of the ships for his bride-to-be that never made it to Seville. She forgave him and married him anyway.

After the back-slapping was done, the excitement level hit a new high. Lou cleared all divers to prepare to salvage. He went to the bottom with Big Mike and Jimbo and set up a metal grid. This *was* an archeological excavation and Lou would stick to his guns about going slow and being methodical. He wanted everyone to go below to experience what was going to happen but they would follow a correct procedure, catalogue everything, and do all they could not to disturb the reef any more than was necessary.

The suction system was rigged to vacuum the sand out of the grid-work and by 8:30 am they were doing it.

Patache Nuestra Senora de la Concepcion had only seven survivors on that fateful day in 1715, all of whom reached shore only after a great struggle in the storm. With the small number of survivors and no witnesses to its grounding, she sat down, dismasted and broken, completely under water off the reef at Canaveral and lay undiscovered after only being partially salvaged by its survivors sometime later. This meant there was still a fortune to be recovered and as the morning went on, this theory was confirmed! As they suctioned, stacks of silver and gold coins appeared right before their eyes as well as rubies and emeralds the size of one's fist—all stacked as if the wooden chests were still around them.

Hundreds, probably thousands, of chests filled the armada's hulls and *many* must have been on the *Concepcion* as they cleared away what the sand had concealed for so many years. Lou found a few dead spots as well, which made sense because the *Concepcion's* manifest had her hauling cacao, tanned hides and Brazil-wood along with the silver, gold, emeralds and rubies from Mexico and Central America. Some of those items had long ago decomposed.

"Treasure Fever" struck both of Lou's boats and it got so good that Lou went ahead and called for Coast Guard protection. He had a king's ransom onboard his two vessels and would take no chance. Nigel Tompkins went back on his word and jumped into the water to witness this once in a lifetime sight firsthand. Ray did the same, at one time free diving when all the equipment was being used by the others. Ray could hold his breath for nearly three minutes anyway. Denise stayed topside, tagging and bagging as the items came to the surface. She could hardly keep up! Giselle offered to help her and the two young ladies put together a system that Lou was not only appreciative of, but impressed with. Giselle and Denise joked, had fun and got to know each other. The mood was pure happiness onboard.

The initial salvage went on for many days as the recovery produced some amazing and beautiful artifacts. On the third day they found the ship's bell and confirmed what they all believed— this old vessel was the *Patache Nuestra Senora de la Concepcion!*

They also found items which were not even manifested, not uncommon for the armada, as there was often nearly as much non-manifested cargo as there was manifested. Every corner of these ships in the Treasure Fleet was loaded with gold, silver and jewels and it was said that even the cabin boys were exercising entrepreneurship. With the summer off, the boys found it necessary to extend their vacations in order to continue to be a part of the recovery effort.

Josh and Eddie were, once again, having an adventure of a lifetime and could not believe what the good man above had sent them and their friends into, *and* protected them from. They were destined for this lifestyle of search and recovery of historic items, it seemed. Money, at this point in their lives, was already not an issue, but they put no more importance on it than a bag of rocks. A bunch of money was never what they wanted out of life! Adventure—that's what these two friends yearned for. Happiness with what they did on a daily basis was imperative to them, and figuring that out at such a young age was a treasure all its own. It was also contagious, as Brad and Nick were also starting to understand that possibly one could enjoy this thing called "work." Lou Cannon had the coolest job in the world and made them wonder why their high-school counselors never told them they could be treasure hunters for a living! It wasn't on the list!

Josh Baker had also found a different treasure along the way on this road trip—he had found Giselle and she had found him. Everyone knew these two crazy kids had liked each other from an early age but it was never the time. The time—the moment when these two revealed their feelings to each other had to be one devoid of distraction, and that moment had been given to them on the sands of Daytona Beach Shores on that beautiful moonlit night. It had been a magic moment delivered to them at just the right time and place. Josh and Giselle were perfect for one another. The age difference was not an issue for either one.

The sun set on another Florida evening, that day in June, and also set on another grand adventure for Josh, Eddie, Giselle, Brad and their new Florida friends Nick, Nigel and Buck Naked. All necessary royalty arrangements were made between Family Jewels and the young treasure hunters and payments would most likely continue for many months and possibly years as new items were occasionally recovered.

Of course, the state of Florida benefited greatly from the discovery, both from their cut of the treasure and with the increased interest and tourism along Florida's Treasure Coast. Metal detector sales spiked and many a new treasure hunter could be seen sweeping the beaches of Canaveral.

Nick Dawson did a round of media events up and down the peninsula, telling his story over and over until he was sure he had told it enough. He had some other plans he wanted to get started on and he would have Brad and Buck to partner with him in that venture.

....

The three West Virginia-bound travelers stood by Eddie's bus as he warmed the engine for the trip up the road. He added a bag of ice to his AC cooler-contraption and then walked to where Nick, Nigel, Brad and Buck were standing.

Josh stuck out his hand. Nick looked at him for a moment and shook his head. Nick took a deep breath, stepped forward and grabbed Josh in a bear hug. These guys meant something to him and the feeling was mutual. He hugged each one and his emotion was hard to hold back.

He did his best to speak, choking up just a little. "You guys have shared a part of my life that I have dreamed about for many years…since I was a kid. You brought your experience, your talent and your skills…but what meant the most was, along with all of that, you offered your friendship" He choked again while trying to speak. "I…I appreciate that the most," he finished.

Nick had all of them trying to hold back what they felt but many in the group had leaking eyes, including Nigel, who had said many goodbyes over the years.

"Darn Florida eye allergies," Giselle joked, wiping her eyes. They all laughed.

Eddie spoke for them all. "It's just the beginning, Nick. You think you are going to keep us away from these beaches, you are crazy!"

Nick shook his head. "You guys better come back. We're a heckuva team. That was an amazing adventure."

Josh and Eddie nodded as they shook hands to say goodbye. They exchanged a few more words and then took their seats, as the engine was warm and ready to go.

With all of their luggage loaded and everyone strapped in, the beautiful little red and white VW bus rolled out of the driveway of the Vista al Mar Resort and pointed north, back to the beautiful hills of West Virginia.

THE END

EPILOGUE

Nick Dawson had fulfilled his dream—his destiny as the only grandchild of Butch Dawson. Together, and without even meeting one another, they had crossed the boundaries of time and rediscovered the *Concepcion*.

After a few months of haggling with the state and many trips to the courthouse to pay a long list of back taxes, Nick was the proud owner of a very old, but very retro-cool boathouse. The laws state that everything found within the boathouse would also become the property of Nick Dawson, and that would include...*Maria*!

He planned to partner with Brad Radcliffe and Buck Naked on the venture. Nigel didn't have an interest other than suggesting the boys may want to add a deck overlooking the Intracoastal with a well-stocked bar. Nigel took some time off and got back to his relaxing retirement routine. The boys did add the deck on the front of the facility but held off on the bar for the time being.

After a six-month renovation, the boathouse once again served as a full service boat repair and outfitting facility. It was no longer faded gray but now painted in bright colors, modern looking and inviting to all who passed by her on the waterway. The interior used up most of the renovation budget and was newly wired, sheet-rocked, and incredibly lit with state of the art LED lighting. Of course, the front offices were refurbished with modern equipment and a super WIFI system for guests as well as employees.

The upper level became three apartments where, once inside, you would not think you were on top of a boat house. They installed spiral staircases and very modern, contemporary furniture sitting on tile floors. Each owner got one!

Brad was the master mechanic and hired a couple of good friends he had made at MMI to work under him. Nick took care of the business end of things, paying the bills, paying the employees and making sure the supply rooms were stocked, and that's where Buck came in. He was no longer cleaning pools but was now the parts manager as well as a darn good installer of aftermarket parts and accessories.

Louis Cannon continued to work the wreck site often with Denise, Jimbo and Big Mike. The artifacts became sparse as time went on but each time they went out, they would still find little things. Maybe the coolest artifacts were the cannons which had been found further out from the initial site and were loaded with gold and silver coins. The captain had wasted no space onboard *Concepcion* for that voyage.

Paco's leg healed just fine and in a few weeks he was back to his old ways of trying to make a dishonest living. He vowed never to work with Dennis again until Dennis showed up at Paco's grungy apartment with a case of stolen wristbands for a very popular theme park just up the road. For three weeks they dressed the part and sold them on the street corners of Daytona Beach to extremely naïve foreign tourists for fifty dollars each until they ran out. Having succeeded at crime for the first time, Paco and Dennis wasted no time in planning their next scam.

Not far away, an aging Italian man with a noticeably lazy eye and a new white beard sat on a bench at Jetty Park watching a salvage boat continue to do its thing about eighteen hundred feet offshore. "Teflon Tony," they called him...because nothing ever stuck.

The End

If you like the work of an author, the best way to say so is to go back to Amazon.com and leave a review! I read every review and love to hear the feedback from you, the readers!

Join my reader Email list by emailing me at steve.kittner@yahoo.com.

You will be the first to know about new releases, book signings, giveaways, contests and more! You will get the first look at new release book covers and sometimes have the opportunity to be an "early reader" of my newest novels. Read them before they publish!

Books by Steve Kittner

Josh Baker and Eddie Debord Series

River Rocks; A West Virginia Adventure Novel (#1 in the Series)

What Lies in the Hills; A West Virginia Adventure Novel (#2 in the Series)

What Lies in the Sea; A Josh Baker and Eddie Debord Road Trip Adventure (#3 in the Series)

More coming soon!

Follow Steve on Facebook at : Steve Kittner Books

Twitter: @SteveKittner

Instagram: Steve Kittner

Made in the USA
Columbia, SC
03 July 2017